MACULAN'S DAUGHTER

MACULAN'S DAUGHTER

Sarah Gainham

G. P. Putnam's Sons

New York

PART ONE

CHAPTER I

THE DEEPEST wounds of war are invisible. They may be almost mortal injuries and still remain unconscious in a whole people. Only the few charged with the management of the nation's affairs know or even feel them, or those with special talents in the recognition of reality. Such deep and unrecognized wounds were sustained by the British in the war of 1939 to 1945, and the real condition of the nation for years after that war was nearer that of the overtly defeated enemies than anything that could be named victory. The terrible truism that there are no victors in modern wars was demonstrated past all doubt in that country and at that time; the atmosphere of ruin and a disillusion close to despair was palpable everywhere, especially in the capital where most of those who knew the true state of affairs were gathered and where the universal self-deception had worn most threadbare. The almost impossible task of maintaining a fiction of triumph was put in London under such a strain that large sections of the people suffered from a mass psychosis which spread its stealthy poison through the whole vast city and was instantly to be felt by any stranger who went there or by any Londoner returning after an absence. Since the truth about the outcome of the war was never mentioned, it became for those aware of it a secret closely akin to guilt, as if everyone who knew it or apprehended it were to blame for it. It was a burden they carried and that was made more burdensome by the need to deny its presence.

Towards the end of 1947, at the time when the moral and physical misery of London was at its worst, two men were travelling across the immense surface of the town to talk to each other. They had never met, but the elder of the two knew a good deal about the man he was to meet and on several occasions had been given the opportunity to watch him. They were very different men in every important characteristic but, apart from their nationality, which was English, they had one thing in common. They were both aware of the real postwar position of Britain in relation to the world as well as domestically, and they both belonged to the small group of those who had taken their own measures to deal with it.

The night was very dark, although it was not much past six in the evening, and the weight of a Dickensian fog, such as has not been seen for many years now, threatened just above the level of the weak street lighting and could already be felt with its acid sting and sulphurous stink. It was cold and raw, with a windless damp-soaked chill so that the heavy, much-worn outer clothing of the passengers in busses and underground trains smelled sour and sordid. The features of those still struggling towards their homes from work were almost all strained, weary, pallid from poor food and irritable with years of near exhaustion. From the mainline station the bus was overfull and Vincent Cheyney was obliged to force his way onto the platform amidst the grumbles of those already standing there.

"Too many standing," growled the conductor, fighting his way through the lower deck. "I've got eight inside already."

In the meantime the top-heavy vehicle started with a lurch and moved diagonally into the traffic so that although the conductor rang his bell furiously the driver was unable to stop and ignored the signal. All round could be heard the hooting of horns from drivers enraged by the blocking of the roadway caused by the bus moving out so suddenly.

"You'll get down at the next stop," he threatened the smallest of the three passengers hanging on for dear life to various grips and railings as the monster jounced and shuddered with increasing speed.

"You're not putting me off," said Vincent Cheyney decisively.

"Nor me," agreed the small, elderly man to whom the threat was made. "You'll have to put me off by force. And then I'll have the law on you."

"I'll decide that," shouted the conductor furiously over the

4

general din of traffic. "I say how many stand, and nobody else."

"Lay a finger on me," replied the small man, "and I'll have the law on you." He repeated this magic rune with angry triumph.

"You want a strike on your hands?" demanded the busman. "I'll clear the whole bus if you'd rather."

"Couldn't care less about your bloody strikes," cried the third standing passenger, a woman with her head covered by a scarf tied under her chin and with a heavy and shapeless shopping bag in one hand. She pushed the palm of a worn black glove under the man's nose, with four pennies in the hollow of the palm. "Here's my fare and if you don't want to take it, you know what you can do."

The matter was resolved by a ring at the bell, while a tall sergeant in battledress pushed his way out from a seat, followed by a young woman whose head scarf was wrapped up like a turban, carrying a small child fast asleep. She reeled, and trod heavily on the conductor's foot as the bus swayed ponderously, slowed and then quickened speed again.

"You've gone past our stop," she shrieked. "And me with the kid to carry!"

The weary little boy awoke and gave a wail at his mother's tone so that the beginning of the man's reply could not be heard. His eyes narrowed to bitter slits of hatred and he was drawing breath to shout when the soldier tapped him on the shoulder.

"Shove it," advised the sergeant from his great height. "And stop the bleeding bus, mate." He stretched over the heads of the others and gave the conductor's own signal to stop, which was obeyed a moment later as they reached the next stop.

"All full up," yelled the conductor at the line of waiting people on the pavement. The sergeant helped his wife down and the busman spread his arms across the entry platform while the three illicit passengers hurried into the interior of the transport.

Vincent stood, hanging on to the overhead rail for forty minutes until a number of people got down at Swiss Cottage, when the conductor shouted from above that there were three upstairs. A front seat was vacant on the upper deck and

Vincent was flung into it as they swung wildly round a corner of the crowded roundabout, jolting with one wheel over the edge of the kerb, and with a roar from the engine pulled into Finchley Road.

"That was my foot," said the woman against whom he fell. "I believe the drivers do it on purpose."

"Sorry," said Vincent breathlessly. "God, this town is hell. I will be glad to get out of it again."

"Well, we've had a war on, dear," said the woman, sarcastically using the constant phrase of the time. Her heavily made-up mouth stretched in a grin and, glancing sideways, Vincent saw that her lipstick looked almost black in the livid yellow street lighting. She, too, wore a coloured scarf over her head and tied under the chin. The people opposite rose to descend and Vincent slid across to the corner seat where, the load having now thinned out, he could sit alone and stretch his legs. Why on earth didn't I stay with the Control Commission, he thought angrily. At least one had a car in Berlin. In the six months since his return home the need to use public transport had hardly arisen, for his lodging was quite near the office of his new civilian job.

So lost was Vincent in nostalgic memories of the pleasures available to the occupying forces in Germany that he almost missed his stop in the darkness and his own unfamiliarity with the district. Fortunately a voice behind him said wearily to someone else that the next stop was Golders Green; he heard the shuffle of two pairs of feet moving and followed their example. The murk was now so thick in the parking yard that Vincent felt a nervousness near to fear at its strangeness, the feeling of many unseen people moving about where the inadequate lights reflected rather than penetrated the mass of blackness.

"It's coming down thick now," said a deep voice almost at his elbow. "Hold my arm, Mildred, do."

"I don't know how we're ever going to get home again," complained the woman, and they disappeared with startling suddenness before Vincent could formulate his feeling of intense irritation with them and everybody else struggling about on this horrible evening and seeming to know, as if

6

pointing out his own ignorance, where they were going. He should cross the road here, here were the traffic lights, glaring red. On the other side he turned back the way he had come and there, a few yards along, was a dim sign that announced Benno's Restaurant. He was relieved now at the minute directions given to him for finding this rendezvous; when making the appointment they annoyed him by their exactness. He was humiliated by not knowing such details; London always made him feel inadequate because he was not a citizen of the great town. The dirty baize curtain, hung in 1939 over the door as a blackout precaution and retained to catch the draught, fell against his face and he pushed it away with disgust at the reek of frying fat. The peculiar smell of this fat was the accompaniment to entry in all but the most expensive places at that time; it was generally believed to be rendered down from aged horses, and from its odour may have been something worse than that. The steamy warmth of the room was heavy with it and with other unidentifiable substances supposed to be edible. A hand waved to Vincent and he made his way to the back of the room where an unknown man sat alone. That Vincent was evidently not unknown to him was one of several things that occurred to Vincent only later.

"Well, hallo Powell," he spoke the formula. "I didn't expect to see you here."

"How nice to see you," replied the man in a precise, educated voice. "I hate eating alone."

Vincent was unbuttoning his coat. Most of the eaters in the crowded room were sitting in their overcoats, but Vincent had learned better than that in the army. "Do you come here often?" he asked.

"Quite often," said the man, "when I'm in London. I live out here, you know."

This completed the prescribed greetings and Vincent hung up his coat and sat down.

"It's a foul night," he said resentfully. "I'm glad I don't have to live in London. Over an hour on busses."

"You were lucky, in fact. Sometimes takes much longer than that. Of course, you couldn't take a taxi."

Vincent had been told not to use taxis this evening, but he

7

could not have afforded one in any case and the thought of the official transport he commanded a few months before angered him again.

"What is the town like where you work?" asked Powell. "I've never been there."

"Compared with London it's splendidly clean and fresh. Small, you know. I don't see much of the town except for the cinemas and one or two pubs. I suppose, you know, the Company is outside? It's provincial, I suppose, but I like it." He added this preference defensively. He already felt that Powell spent his life in universities or in clubs in St. James's and in this he was right. He was still too inexperienced even to suspect that Powell was not this man's name and he failed, too, to comprehend that everything said by his companion was said to gain a reaction from him, to supply evidence of his character, his attitudes, his proficiency.

"You were in Berlin for a year or so, I hear?"

"Yes. Do you know Berlin?"

"Before the war. Not since. What is it like now?"

Vincent glanced up in surprise at this; he thought everybody knew what Berlin was like now.

"It's completely ruined. I was never there before, but men who were told me they couldn't find their way about any more. It's just a vast heap of ruins."

"Yes. The Russians made a job of it, didn't they? It was quite a town once." He broke off his tone of reminiscence to confer with the waiter, who recommended sausages or cottage pie with chips. There was no meat tonight, he said. It was one of those places licenced, not to serve drinks for customers' meals, but to fetch them from outside—one of the curious aberrations of the drinking laws. The off-licence of the public house on the corner had some Algerian red wine, the waiter said. The kitchen boy would get Powell a bottle if he wished. This was clearly a sign of particular favour, and Powell did wish. It was better than nothing.

"Pinot noir," said Powell, smiling scornfully across at Vincent. "But there's nothing else out here and we're lucky to get that. Mixed with a little warm water it's just drinkable. Yes, Berlin. I had a boyfriend there, years ago. He went to Moscow in 1935."

"Do you ever hear from him?" asked Vincent, determined not to be shocked at the implication.

"Oh, no," said Powell, as if that was to be taken for granted. "I expect he's dead years ago. The Russians are a tough lot, not like us."

In spite of his determination not to show a provincial narrowness of mind, Vincent frowned nervously at the tone of praise.

"My dear boy, all London talks like that," murmured Powell. "It would be noticeable, rather, if one didn't. Makes life a lot easier than it might be, as you can imagine."

"It wouldn't go down very well in the Maculan Company," said Vincent, pretending to laugh. "I don't think I'd better get into the habit."

"Ah yes, I expect your bosses are all high Tory, aren't they?" The voice and smile were patronizing, inviting Vincent's agreement.

"Well, the old boy never mentions politics, as a matter of fact. Of course, he's a foreigner, as you know. But the others, the directors, are practically fascists."

"Yes, you must tell me all about them. But later. We'll go back to my place. D'you find your job interesting? In itself, I mean?"

"As far as I've got, yes. They don't let me do much yet. The former sales director is coming back from the RAF soon. They kept him on for some Boffin job and the Company is waiting for his return before they get any export plans going. So I'm really learning at the moment, that side of it."

"The business side, you mean? Not all those fascinating electronics—you know all about that?"

"I know enough to cope with the job," said Vincent cautiously. He laughed. "At least the bloody army was good for that. I put in for all the training courses there were. Matter of fact, I spent most of the war training. I didn't mean to go back to the sort of thing I was stuck with before. I always kept that in mind, long before I got this chance."

"We must see that you make the most of your chance," said Powell smoothly. "About this man who is coming back from the RAF. What is his name?"

"That's the man who introduced me for the job. He was in

9

Berlin a few months, but he's at Netherdown now, the experimental station, you know? His name is Jackson, Clement Roy Jackson, he's a Wing Commander now."

"Clement Roy Jackson, Wing Commander," repeated Powell, fixing the name in his retentive mind. "He introduced you, did he?" He raised an eyebrow and Vincent shook his head.

"Pure chance," he said round a mouthful of cottage pie.

"I see. So much the better. I'll have a word with a friend of mine who knows someone on the Air Council. Perhaps this Jackson would like to stay on in the Service? Who knows!"

"Could you—can you really fix that?"

"*I* can't, no. But *we* can, perhaps. This is a fairly important matter, you know, for *us.*"

"If he were out of the way that would mean I'd get a chance at the big job. There isn't anybody else in the running, unless a new man was brought in, and they mean to go in for exporting in a big way. They know they have to do that."

"How do you mean, nobody else in the running? Surely there must be a whole staff on the sales side, in a company that size?"

"Not for years now, not since '39. If you think of it, their customers were all lined up, eager and waiting. The problem was to fill the orders, not to get them."

"Very true. And very interesting," said Powell with approval. "Ah, here comes a delicious bit of mousetrap."

They had eaten what was put before them with speed but without appetite, knowing they were lucky to get anything to eat at all, for by eight o'clock evening places like this were closed because there was simply nothing left to offer latecomers.

"Incredible that people will put up with this sort of thing, nearly three years after the end of the war," said Vincent, looking with disgust at his greasy plate which, now that it was empty, could be seen to have a crack right across it.

"They have got used to it," said Powell, shrugging. "We put up with it, too, after all."

"But not without protest," pointed out Vincent. He pushed the plate to one side and moved a smaller one with a little square of cheese reposing in the middle flanked by a round bisquit on each side. There was a grey fingerprint on the edge of the plate; with a slight shudder Vincent pushed it away again.

"Reverse side of the good fortune of being an island, I suppose. The sea saved us from invasion, but it also means that most of our food has to come from overseas, since we can't grow it ourselves."

"Other countries manage better than this," objected Vincent. "I came through Brussels a few months ago. You should see the food there! And they were occupied for years."

"Yes, but they get the stuff overland. Britain has no ships and no money, remember. The black market in foodstuffs —free enterprise, as they say—can't operate in a small, over-populated country where the import of food is so easily controlled."

"I suppose we could be starved out in a few weeks by anyone who had the naval force to do it," said Vincent, looking round the crowded room with a curious mixture in his regard of scorn for the ignorance and docility of these representatives of the masses and a kind of angry, puzzled pity. This look, like every other detail of the occasion, was not lost on Powell.

"A point that has not been ignored for the future, you may be sure," he said, with a smile of quiet triumph.

"And in the past. Fortunately unsuccessfully."

"In that case it was fortunate, yes. I believe the situation was quite serious in the winter of 1942 to '43. But they never gained control of the coastal skies. One of the important little ideas of your present employer had a good deal to do with that, I daresay you know."

"Yes, so I hear. But those things are still very much on the secret list for new boys like me." Vincent sounded both nervous and resentful at this reference. He expected to be tackled on that subject later in the interview and was keenly aware of having nothing to tell. "They like to make mysteries, it's a sort of unofficial slogan of the company that Maculan won the war and it's quite a ritual even to mention his inventions. Supposed to make me feel that I may be let into the holy of holies if I'm a good boy, in about ten years' time."

"They won't be secret from you much longer, if we can arrange dear Jackson's future," Powell comforted him.

11

"You'll be right in the centre of things fairly soon, I rather think. Don't look round in that scary fashion, dear boy. I know exactly how far my voice carries. And, you know, we *are* sitting in the corner *and* facing the room. Nobody can come near us without our seeing him." Powell's drawl took on a teasing note that made Vincent uncomfortable.

"This sort of thing is quite easy, once the principles of it are grasped. You'll get them very quickly, you're so intelligent. Then you'll find you enjoy it. I wish my wretched under-graduates picked things up with half your speed, my dear. And don't mind my being so cosy with you. That, too, is calculated to deceive. It's all in the cause, you know. You're quite safe from me. Nothing could be less intriguing in that way than a chap whose only thoughts are for girls. Oh, yes, I see how you inspect every piece of female flesh that comes within sight. And you're a handsome fellow, too. But one can't have everything, I always say."

The affectation of a working-class idiom was a psychological mistake, and Powell noticed at once the sharp inward flinch with which Vincent took in what was to him not a joke but a hint at his origins. The error was immediately grasped as an advantage. Powell attacked this weakness in Vincent with an openness that was a form of enjoyable cruelty but was also a relief to Vincent; it was just what he needed.

"Don't you like me quoting my charwoman? You will learn not to feel that way, except that you should be proud. Yes, proud to have taken a chance when you got it, in spite of the filthy class structure of this country, proud to have educated yourself at the army's expense, and proud that you're going to *be* somebody by your own efforts. D'you imagine I don't know what effort it costs a poor boy to get anywhere in this social-fascist world we live in? I admire you, I envy you, for your brains and character. You've understood in time what is going to happen and put yourself on the winning side, where you can help the cause and yourself as well. Yes, and you'll live to see it. It can't happen during my active career, but you will have the satisfaction of helping to bring it about *and* you'll live to revenge yourself for every humiliation you ever suffered."

Vincent stared fixedly away from Powell, narrowing his bright blue eyes as if trying to espy something almost out of

12

sight. The shock of having his secret inadequacy dragged out into the open so bluntly turned in an instant into a swelling pride, satisfaction, determination. He was aware for the first time in his life of being understood; every stage of his education, whether social, moral, hygienic or professional, from the first smacking in childhood and even before that, was instantaneously now presented as he had always privately taken it, as imposed humiliation. Now, not only was his own inward posture understood, it was accepted as being right and natural. From his mother and schoolteachers to the hard conventions of the first Army Mess as a junior lieutenant, from the fifteen-year-old girl who refused to go to the cinema with him "because you sniff all the time—it's disgusting," to the Major who stared contemptuously on the first occasion he entered a regimental anteroom, they were all now, in the twinkling of an eye, respectably hated instead of hated with guilt. The "inferiority complex" of popular psychology that may be, and in this case was, rooted in unjustified conceit, was in that moment confirmed for Vincent and justified.

Especially the shaming waste of effort and time that he already refused to admit even to himself, of the carefully adopted customs of his early days as a commissioned officer, now known to be not well-bred but hopelessly lower-middle class, was to be seen as a deliberate class deception intended to keep him in his place. The hasty relearning of voice and manner that cost so much anguish and shame in the last year or so was now, he was told it on the best authority, a personal triumph and a necessity, a reputable achievement of his own innate superiority. At the same time Vincent could hate the middle-class attitudes that once despised him and reject them for what they were, the shibboleths of a class outworn by inexorable historical forces. That he abandoned these ideas for equally unreal and unimportant notions remained unknown to Vincent as well as the powerfully class-conscious nature of his own outlook; he instantly adopted Powell's proposed view because Powell's manner and voice, his whole bearing, were those of the few men Vincent had met whom he still thought of in military terms as being from really good regiments. He would not have accepted these liberating explanations unless they came from someone who was not only socially his superior but who was also stamped by the mysterious aristocracy of power. Only one other man Vincent knew carried that invisible authority without requiring any badges or titles to indicate it and he was intimidatingly strange, reserved, and conveyed an unnerving, threatening quality of penetration. This was Vincent's employer Maculan.

Vincent did not know that his expression changed when he thought of Maculan, or that what his look showed was an unwilling and uncomprehending respect. But Powell could follow the process in Vincent's mind as if his skull were of glass and without being told the objects of his thoughts, for a thousand students had passed before Powell's discerning and cynical eye.

Powell knew deeply and used subtly the unbalance of a system of upbringing excellently suited to an imperial nation in which all talent and ambition turn towards a very real source of power as daisies turn towards the sun, but which is useless and dangerous in a drained and exhausted society. The pressures of overt and implicit bullying, which will be gladly accepted by those who look to a future as representatives of a glittering crown, go sour in anger and rejection in the presence of power lost.

"You wonder how it is I know what you feel?" asked Powell, his bantering, intimate tone returning in contrast to the simulated but convincing passion of his foregoing remarks. "I'll tell you if you wish and even if you don't. Generations of students have passed through the needle's eye of my perception during my career—both of my careers. So, partly experience. Then, I am talented in a rather rare way. I am what in today's jargon might be called a natural psychologist. I can feel and decipher what people are, especially men. I suppose it's what used to be called second sight."

"One does feel with you that you understand," agreed Vincent, wishing to flatter Powell in return for the seductive compliment of being taken seriously. It was unusual for Vincent to feel liking and still less admiration for a man who showed sympathy for him and took him at his own valuation. Like most people with the distrust of themselves that comes not from true modesty but from secret overestimation, he felt scorn as a rule for anyone who was taken in by him. It was

Powell's gift to convey approbation without arousing its attendant contempt. "Did you study medicine? I mean, you have to, don't you, to specialize in psychology?"

"I believe so. But no, I'm an historian. And don't be too much impressed with medical degrees, my dear boy. Consider: any student of average intelligence can become a doctor of medicine and therefore of psychiatry, sometimes less than average if he works hard. He learns what the books teach in that school of the psyche his teachers happen to be trained in; then he learns in hospitals what senior staff point out to him in the patients. He rarely sees anything that is not pointed out; there is too much to be memorised for examinations for him to disperse his energies on observation. All this he takes as gospel and, what is more, as the only gospel. By the time he begins on his specialised field of psychiatry he has already put so big an investment into his career that he *must* pass, or ten years and God knows how much money is wasted, though usually it isn't his money. He *must* conform, he must take in what he knows his examiners will ask for and what his consultants and professors have spent a lifetime committing themselves to in public because they are the ones who will give him his little chances once he is qualified. Later he may—I say he may—really learn something about human beings and their souls, but hardly before he is in his middle forties. What is never asked is whether he has any insight into human nature, whether he even knows that other people are as real and woundable and complex as he is himself; all his training has made him into a mental tram and, if he's clever, into a powerful train, a mainline locomotive. On lines. He is analysed himself, but on the lines of the school he learned in, almost certainly. Other schools are rivals, opponents; his interest in his own school is inevitably by then a life-and-death matter to him. And who knows, least of all himself, by what instinctive or conditioned standards, what conventions, what beliefs, or lack of them, he forms his judgements?"

"It's a ghastly thought," agreed Vincent, attempting a flippant air because he did not understand what Powell meant.

"Consider. The son of a puritan pastor and his narrow wife in a small Swiss town, educated in the stifling provinciality of Bâle, who never even sees a major city until he is over thirty.

15

Can he know what is 'natural' to a person of another faith brought up in a huge urban clutch of entrails like London? And to put it at its simplest, doctors learn about sick people. Faced by a genius, for instance, he must assume some pathological distortion of personality brought to him by a possessive, ignorant mother because he bites his nails. He adjusts the boy's nervous condition and cures the genius out of him with it. No, don't trust your mind or your body to doctors without reservations. They are technicians and neither morally nor intellectually competent to leave their tram lines."

"You know, I never thought of all that. You obviously speak from a lot of experience."

"Oh, with despair I've watched it happen to talented homosexual boys. Their idiot parents think they are ill. Being queer *is* an illness, but an illness of our bourgeois, guilt-ridden, class-ridden society, not of the individual. Stupid philistines are panicked by terror of the neighbours, by the state of our savage laws, by what they call morality. They persuade themselves they care about their boy's happiness, but all they care about is to force him into a pattern. When I hear some moron prating of happiness, I retch; happiness! What an ambition, to be happy!"

"It's true, the very word morality practically means sex," Vincent picked on a word he thought he understood, but Powell was hardly listening. He was talking as much for the pleasure of talking as to further his evening's purpose, knowing that this was working itself out just under the surface of the conversation that stimulated him by its byplay inspired obliquely by his pleasurable absorption of Vincent's powerful sexuality. He drank into his own veins Vincent's emphatically physical presence, feeling in imagination the body inside the conventional clothing, as Vincent himself would do with a woman, and enjoying his own sensations.

"Sex and the bourgeoisie!" he cried softly, delighted by his own malice. "Sick-making sentimentality about happiness —eyewash, purest hypocrisy. Power is what they *mean*. And in nothing does one see it in all its Georg Grosz obscenity as in the joyous self-righteousness about homosexuality, the lecherous beasts. But their hold on power is what it is really all about.

16

Consider, dear boy, why must all ruling classes forbid homosexuality? The training of the rulers must continue the élite and its traditions as a more or less closed circle. The majority of future rulers must come from the ruling families because they need less training and because too many new recruits at any time will thin out the pure wine of confidence in power. But while future rulers must marry for sons, they must at the same time be taught to reject the instinctual, gentle, female inner world. The Anima, if you've read your Jung, about whom I was being so naughty just now. The ambition to power won't operate in that inner world. Therefore the laws against homosexuality have to be fierce—listen, now! The most talented trainees will naturally be the most instinctual and perceptive. This means that the best future rulers are also those most in danger of slipping into love or art rather than ambition and will. Where instincts and perceptions are strong they must have some outlet and the danger is always present that, prevented by training from loving or poetic activities, the drives will recoil onto the permitted friends, onto those of their own sex, their fellow-trainees.

"This is why so many queers are revolutionaries. Partly no doubt out of a justified hatred of the system that has robbed us of a whole world of experience and *being* by its education for power, partly for a pragmatic reason. As long as the dangers of friendships within one's own class are so great, nearly all homosexuals are bound to have relationships with boys from the so-called lower classes. Occasionally one finds a friend within the permitted circle who combines desire with discretion. More often a working-class boy is easier to control and to keep out of sight. D'you see? Like all distortions of nature, the ferocious punishment of homosexual love, which is itself caused by the crippling of natural forces in the service of class power, results in further aberration: in our seeking our emotional life outside the class barriers. This leads quite naturally to revolutionary ideas, for the love drives turn the brotherhood of sex into the brotherhood of man. To love a poor boy fills one with anger at his condemnation to a lesser life and with the desire that he should have a fuller one, a chance to be himself, to grow into a larger world. Rejection of the power world and the bourgeois class comes of itself out of this situation, and from then on the rejection becomes conspiratorial. We are forced into conspiracy in sex if we don't want to lose our position and our power to help our poorer friends, so we turn our political ideas—which our need for love and friendship have taught us—towards the conspiratorial forms of socialism and revolution."

"But not everybody becomes queer," urged Vincent, nervous in the knowledge of his own obsession with female sexuality and feeling himself obscurely excluded.

"Of course not. But the less accessible peaks of our universities and the civil and armed forces tend to segregate young men in a pervasively masculine atmosphere that encourages a homosexual feeling in everything but the physical activity of sex, so that sex is not eliminated physically, only its *real* power, its loving and intuitive or artistic power. As many women as you want or can get, but they must not matter to you, they mustn't open to you the world of feeling. If you want power in the bourgeois world you must fear the reality of love and therefore the reality of women. I use the term women as shorthand, you understand?"

"Shorthand? Oh, yes, I see," lied Vincent quickly.

"Look, we've finished the wine, shall we go on now?"

"D'you think that's why ambitious men marry such dreary women? I've often wondered about that."

"Women who won't hamper them emotionally, you mean? I daresay it is." They were struggling into their coats now. "Of course, when I say don't trust doctors, I don't mean that conventional psychology should be ignored, or anything like that. Rather not, I find its jargon very useful. Controlling ignorant and stupid people is much easier with technical terms used with the air of unarguable confidence. That goes for economic or sociological clichés as well as psychiatric ones. But I wouldn't use them with anyone like you, so quick to learn, so intelligent. Let me see, I have paid, haven't I? Come along, then."

Powell gave Vincent a quick, searching smile, but was relieved although unsurprised to find that no puzzlement or doubt showed in the regular, open features. He's swallowed it all, he thought, and was suddenly depressed.

Vincent, for his part, was thinking that Powell was bound to arrange some justification of his deviation from normality, some virtuous explanation. This thought gave him a sensation of kindly understanding and got rid of his own defensiveness, a pleasant feeling of Powell's weakness that combined with an almost frightened admiration of the older man's "cleverness," the ease and speed with which he expressed himself. The combination distilled a stimulant much more heady than the wretched wine, and Vincent was now as easily elated as he had been irritable and nervous at the start of the evening. He did not examine, still less analyse, the content of what Powell so eloquently said.

"This way," said Powell as they emerged into the chilling dark, so heavy now with the damp that it was almost rain. The weak lights glimmered on pavement and roadway covered by a thin film of greasy mud, and this sheen, together with a yellowish tinge reflected off lights into the solid blackness, reminded Vincent of a northern mining town near which his first military training had been carried out. He shuddered with disgust as well as cold and his enjoyment sank into the thought that this whole vast city was sliding downwards into an industrial slum.

They turned a corner by a dairy where crates of empty milk bottles piled for collection made an additional hazard in the murk, and walked up a slight rise to the next street. All the houses and street turnings were like each other, with low wicket gates into little front gardens of barren bushes behind which the uniform couples of semidetached houses vaguely copied "Tudor" and "Georgian" styles in pathetic imitation. In his childhood, Golders Green represented to Vincent the idea of a prosperous, even a rich, suburb. But in this first view of it, it was as sordid as he imagined a dockland area, perhaps Bethnal Green, to be.

"Do people have to live like this?" he muttered, half audibly, most of his attention being on the next step.

"The filthy climate, partly," answered Powell and pushed open a metal-framed glass door into the hallway of a small block of flats. The door caught on the footmat and stuck with a creak. They stepped round it and along a narrow passage, tiled in dark grey, past a closed lift door.

"Lift doesn't work, of course," explained Powell and led the

19

way up cement stairs patched with what was once paintwork and with more recent mud from the streets. On the third floor he opened one of the three identical doors on the landing with a single key that he drew from his waistcoat pocket.

A detail that Vincent did notice was that Powell looked neither at the row of postboxes in the entrance hall nor at the letter box outside the apartment door; he made no attempt at all to keep up the fiction that he lived here. And Vincent received an impression that this omission was not intended to show Vincent with what complete trust he was being treated, but was simply carelessness or lack of any rudimentary training in "security." Such practical matters seemed, and continued to seem, very important to Vincent in his exposed situation, and from the careful carrying out of routine precautions he gained comfort and safety, the assurance of order. That Powell obviously felt no need of any such assurance was another sign of his superiority.

In the small square room the curtains of old-fashioned cretonne were drawn so that the pattern of formalised flowers could be seen in shades of beige and faded orange. The thin carpet resounded to every step on the varnished boards of the floor; its design, called modernistic in the thirties, was carried out in beige and dark-brown angularities. The furniture of fumed oak tried flimsily to be an Elizabethan table and sideboard, and the upholstered chairs and sofa were draped in crumpled and soiled loose covers of a dim green.

"Quite a place, isn't it?" Powell smiled round the room. He bent down to switch on both bars of the electric fire in the tiled fireplace and then crossed back to the door to turn off the hard light of the ceiling lamp. There were two table lamps, so much better in design and quality than the rest of the room's furnishings that they had clearly been added by a different hand.

"The last chap who actually lived here," said Powell, "comitted suicide. D'you want to wash your hands? Bathroom is off the hall, though hall is a bit large for the entry." It was clear he found the place funny and expected Vincent to do so too, and Vincent played up to this view, while in fact the skimpy, faded dreariness of it was too near to his own boyhood in memory

20

for him to react with anything but the hatred he felt for his own past.

The narrow bathroom was even worse. It was so dirty that Vincent felt physically sick with disgust, and the smell of the very cheapest scented soap brought back a vision of his mother's untidy mop of permed hair and the clutter of sixpenny-store rubbish she spent her meagre week's money on and which lay about half-used, chipped, with broken handles and bent hair clips over every flat surface of bathroom and bedroom. Nobody had cleaned or used this bath for years, from the look of it, and the hand bowl was slimed with old soap rings and black hairs. A scatter of soot and paint chips flew out of the gas geyser when Vincent turned the water on; he was surprised to find that the flame lit and produced hot water. He dried his hands—after holding them under the stream of water well away from the edges of the bowl—on his own handkerchief.

"I hope they don't ask important people to use this place," he said sarcastically on his return to the sitting room, which now looked much more pleasant in the discreet pools of light thrown by the two lamps. Powell gave him a sharp look. Himself, he was indifferent to his surroundings.

"Yes, it really must be cleaned, at least," he agreed sympathetically. "Is the loo very bad?"

"Sick-making. Whoever lived here must have been—" He stopped, thinking that the unknown could have been a friend of Powell's.

"I'm so sorry, dear boy, I shall report it. But come now, have some whisky to kill the germs. It's warming up a little in here."

Vincent went across to the glowing heat bars to dry his still-damp hands. By contrast with the bathroom, it was not too bad in here. On the narrow shelf over the fire a book was propped; glancing at it Vincent was surprised to see that it was a German novel. When he picked up his glass Powell noticed that he looked carefully to see that it was clean.

"Cheers," he said and then frowned at his lapse in using this despised toast.

"*Salud,*" said Powell. "This is all right, anyway. I brought this myself." It was indeed excellent whisky. "Cigarette?"

"Thanks." Vincent sat down and lit a cigarette from the box open by the bottle. Powell saw that he looked before he touched the arms of the chair and did not lean his head against the back, but after making a move to do so, changed his mind and sat forward with his elbows on his knees.

"I've got a bit of a thing about dirt," he explained defensively. "My mother was a perfect slut. Lived in a dressing gown and never washed up."

"How foul for you, poor boy. Home life *is* rather hell. I've reacted quite the other way, I fear. My father is a doctor, or rather he was, he retired years ago. And *my* childhood was made miserable by hygiene. The old devil made a fortune out of silly women." He chuckled to himself, for the first time sounding effeminate. "But I've told you a lot about myself, talked altogether too much. Now you tell me about yourself. Tell me how you came to us. It always interests me to know why people do."

"How I came?" Vincent was startled and then saw what Powell meant by "us." "I'm not sure I know why," he said hesitantly, untruthfully.

"Not remember such a momentous decision?" teased Powell. "But surely you do? Left Book Club, was it? Ah, Zimmerwald, 1863, Martov, Luxembourg, the July Days. The very words conjure up charming memories of boys discovering 'the other history.'"

Vincent, he could see, was not listening, the words meant nothing. He waited, watching lovingly, his grey eyes sharp behind the round smeared lenses of tortoise shell framed glasses, one side bar of which was broken and bound with sticking plaster. He made a constant little gesture, pushing this side bar up with one fingertip, but there was no sign that this nervous trick irritated or was even noticed by his companion. Vincent was thinking with a sensation of excitement almost like sexual lust: I could tell him the truth, just how it happened. He's the only man I could tell it to.

"I've thought about it a lot," he said, trying not to sound too eager and leaning forward with his glass in his two hands so that he had something to focus his eyes on. "It began with something I hardly noticed at the time. I only sorted it out afterwards. I was with this specialist outfit of REME—that's

22

the electric and mechanical engineers, you know. We were at Herford in the Zone and there was a Russian liaison team visiting, all very chummy and allied. We did a lot of drinking in the Mess, it was their Day of something, and there were speeches, you know, Nazi beasts and all that. They were inviting us to come over and visit them. My CO saw one of them talking to me and called me over. He told me to make a speech in return, just did it to embarrass me, of course; he was always getting at me. I hated him and he knew it. Well, I'd taken the first course in Russian with an educational group, just to pass the time more than anything. You know all those Army Education chaps were as red as hell and dead keen on Russian courses. I couldn't speak it or anything, just enough to understand some of what they said in their speeches. So too bad for the bloody CO, I could make quite a nice little speech just turning some of what the others said into English, real rousing slogans about the glorious Red Army. I said that bit in Russian and they cheered like mad. The CO was mad in the other way. I got a fierce rocket afterwards and of course I said I'd just done it for a joke and pretended I hated them as much as he did, only wanted to keep the party going and have a laugh, you know the sort of thing. Then this fellow came over to me again later, after the senior officers had cleared off to bed, and said again what a smashing speech and all that. He talked about the marvellous life engineers and scientists had in the Soviet Union in his crazy English and how they were honoured and respected. And I told him what I did. He asked if I had a job lined up when I was demobbed and I explained it wasn't that easy for us. Well, we just nattered on, and before they went he said once more that it would be nice to meet and have a drink. I did meet him, too, by chance in the street, and he took me to a German pub for a beer, but I didn't think much about it, one way or the other, at the time.

"Well, that was all, then. The reason I didn't think about it was that a fellow I'd met some time before on a course was posted to Herford with his mob. He was in the Welsh Guards, a posh chap, his father had a title but he was all right, we had a good time before, that was on this course in Scotland. He knew a lot of people and got about a good deal, had a big car of his own and all that. He even knew Germans. Up there, you know, there are some big estates, horses, sort of county people, I suppose you'd call them. He took me with him a few times, we kept quiet about it because of non-fraternisation and I felt a bit queer at first going into German houses, but they were as friendly as could be, not snooty like the same lot in the UK. Then this chap said if I could get a weekend pass we could go and see some other people he knew, farther south in the US Zone near Hamburg. He laid on the passes and petrol vouchers and everything."

Vincent stopped, drank whisky and took another cigarette.

"Well, Christ, it was a bloody great château, a real castle and nobody there less than a Graf or a Graefin. And the weird thing was, the place just had a small garden and orchard inside its wall. It stopped at the walls, there was no estate. The Nazis took all their land off them after one of the sons got into trouble—he was shot—and shared it out among evacuated peasants they'd brought back from some place in the Balkans, Volksdeutsche, they call them. So there were all these Counts and Countesses penniless and starving in the castle, with most of the shutters closed. I soon found out what the idea was. They were selling off their pictures by a painter called Riemenschneider—I expect you've heard of him, I hadn't then. The place was like a museum. This little picture was worth a fortune, but of course it was going for a song, practically. Well, I'd nothing against that although I knew it was dead illegal. He was going to pay them the money in England —they had British relations like all those big families and were expecting to get asked over. I've often wondered if they ever got here.

"So Nigel said to me—Nigel was the man who took me there—he said why didn't I buy something and sell it again at one of the big auctions in London. He had a funny sort of manner about it, as if he was ashamed, and when I asked him, he said these people were related to the girl he was going to marry and how awful it was to see them in this state, having to humble themselves to get food to eat. He didn't *mean* it like that, but I knew he meant how awful for them to have to sell their things to scum like me; it was all right to sell things to him, you see. All in the family, as it were. I had a bit of money, the usual profits, and I thought I might make a bid if only to annoy them all. They kept showing me some silver and they were so keen I knew it couldn't be any good, so I picked on a statue. Not a real statue, Nigel called it a high relief, in stone of a man at arms with his head bent and hands crossed on his sword hilt, the point down. The old boy said it was not for sale, it was some ancestral thing. I said I was not interested in anything else and he asked me why I wanted it. Just to get his goat I said to remind me of the valour of German arms. He gave me a very funny look so I knew I'd made my point.

" 'It is not for sale,' he said again. He spoke perfect English, I need hardly say. 'But in any case, that was an Irish knight and not German.'

"He had me there and I knew it, but I wasn't going to be done, and after a moment I thought of something.

" 'Somebody like Sir Roger Casement, you mean?' I said.

"He stared straight at me for a bit, very calmly. Then he turned to Nigel and spoke sort of clipped and quiet, almost through his teeth.

" 'Perhaps you see now, my dear Nigel, what I meant when I advised you to choose your company with care?'

"I will never forget the insulting old bastard, never.

"So then I really let them have it. I told them what I thought of them all, their bleeding family pride, their Germany, their war. I said it was a good thing they'd lost their land, that was what should happen to all their kind and under socialism that was what would happen and a pity they weren't in the Russian Zone where they would really get the treatment. I said they'd lost the war like all their wars and now they came crawling to the victors for help. And d'you know what he said?

"He said, 'We lost the war, yes, but you are not the victors. You, too, are the losers. Only the Americans and the Russians have won and that you will find out, soon enough.'

"Then Nigel took hold of my arm and said he thought I'd better go. I said I wouldn't stay if they begged me to. He followed me to the great doors and asked would I be all right for transport. I said I would go to the American post in Bamberg and get a rail voucher. They looked worried at that and I heard something said behind me as I went out and slammed the door. It made a boom like a gun almost. Nigel came after me at a run and called me.

" 'You won't report this to the Yanks, will you?' he said and didn't look at me. I didn't answer. Let them sweat a little. But of course, I could have been in trouble, too, if I said anything.

"All the way back in the military train, two changes, I thought about it. I knew then it was no good just to be angry, I had to learn from it. The next Monday I went and registered for a transfer to Berlin with the CCG, the Civil Control Commission."

"And did you look up your Russian friend, then?" asked Powell.

"No, not then. I didn't even think of it. That wasn't what I learned."

"What was it, then?"

"I knew that if I ever wanted to get anywhere I must learn to mix with people like that. Talk like them, never show what I felt, never lose my temper. Learn their ways and never say what I meant. But it burned inside me. Like the Americans say, it burned me up. That's just how it felt. I thought of nothing else for weeks. And from that moment on, I watched myself. I made myself talk properly, didn't use slang, didn't drink too much. I knew I had to be so that a man like that would never insult me again. When I saw Nigel I pretended I didn't see him before he could cut me. I cut out all the fellows I'd gone around with before, as well. Talked to the ones who were properly educated, and every book they mentioned I got hold of and read. I went to the museum and the local sights, I even went to church and I got myself asked to other units to watch how things were done by men in decent regiments. About a month later the transfer came through and I was demobilized and drove up to Berlin.

"I'd worked it all out in my mind, quite calmly. Being a civilian and moving out of the Zone gave me the chance to be a new man. And I think I may say," added Vincent, now visibly and audibly the new man, "that I took the chance with both hands."

"Go on," urged Powell, "I'm breathless."

"I still didn't know how to solve my biggest problem, the future. The job I meant to get had to be one that offered a future. You see? That old boy in the castle didn't know what a favour he was doing me. Well, there were jobs going from time

26

to time; I could have transferred to the real Foreign Office, but I knew I'd stay a technician, a low-ranking job, in the FO: no university, poor languages, then. I've been working at them since. Once a big American combine was around recruiting people for training as future executive material and I could have gone to them. But I didn't altogether care for the idea. There's something flimsy about the Great American Bombast.

"Well, then I met Jackson, the Wingco I told you about before. He was staying on a bit in the service. He suggested his company. I'd heard of them. So he wrote me a letter, straight to the old boy himself. I still wasn't quite sure, I was considering cutting out of England altogether and going to Australia or somewhere. Jackson invited me to the opera in East Berlin, I knew they were supposed to be the best though they played in a makeshift theatre, the real Opera was a ruin. Jackson wanted to hear an old singer in *Rosenkavalier* by Richard Strauss, and I wanted to learn the difference between the Strausses. I even remember the soprano's name, it was Tania Lemnitz. Jackson knew about music and he said she was wonderful. Well, I don't think opera is ever going to be a passion of mine, but it was something I had to know about so of course I went. It went on for hours and one feels a bit trapped there in the middle of a crowd in a narrow seat.

"And who do you think we met in the interval? The Russian! It's a long interval, he took us into a special private bar where we could get a drink without struggling in the mob. I expect you're wondering how that happened, just like that. Whether the Russian knew I was in Berlin and arranged to be where I'd be, that I don't know. But I'm pretty sure Jackson knew nothing. He seemed quite impressed at me knowing a Russian, and made this other man laugh by telling him he'd never met a real Russian before. Well, I watched Jackson, and he behaved quietly and formally, pleasant you know, but not too eager, not trying to flatter. So I did the same. The Russian was very friendly, asked if I would be staying long in Berlin, and Jackson interrupted and said he hoped I should be leaving shortly to join the company he worked for in civvie, in civilian life. He was nice about it, said they could use ambitious young men in the future and we chatted about what the company did and so on. Then the bell rang and we went back to our seats.

"Next day I got a telephone call at my billet; I shared a flat with two other men, requisitioned. It wasn't my Russian, it was a German woman speaking for him in perfect English. She suggested I might like to go to the opera again. She said she was sure I'd love *The Magic Flute* and she would send me tickets for the following night. As it turned out, Jackson couldn't go that night, so I went alone. And, you know, we got so many things free and all laid on at that time that I didn't really think anything of it.

"The official car put me down at the theatre, a different theatre by the way, and straightaway I saw my Russian waiting for someone, but he didn't speak then. The same thing happened in the interval, only this time a woman came up and talked about the music like a real expert. I just let her talk along because I didn't understand much of what it was all about, Mozart I mean, the opera is quite confusing. While she talked she was taking me along towards a side door and into a special bar, just as happened in the other theatre. There was the Russian waiting and he bought me a drink and asked me to supper after the show. We went to a private restaurant; it looked just like an unlighted shopfront from the outside and he had to show a pass to take me in. Well, that was it, the rest you know."

"No, I don't know. You mean, he urged you to accept the Maculan job and promised you support? Did he suggest then, that night, that you should work with us, come to us, or was that later?"

"Oh, no, that night. It was all arranged. He explained everything, but he didn't need to. I'd been several months in Berlin by then and I knew already that what the old Graf had said was true. I knew *they* were going to win."

"That rather puts it in a nutshell, doesn't it?" said Powell admiringly. "They are going to win. And you with them."

They sat in satisfied silence for a minute or so while Powell took Vincent's glass to refill it with whisky and water. He pushed forward the box of cigarettes and Vincent took another. The bad impression made by the dirt in the bathroom was forgotten. In the diffused warm light the young

28

man's face and his strikingly brilliant blue eyes were dreamy like a boy's who is wrapped in a fantasy of heroic future adventure. His features were neat, the hair grew well from his forehead. Over the cheekbones the light caught a faint blond fuzz that made the face seem younger than it was, and its expression, not frowning but stern with resolve, was very young, too, so that Powell's heart moved within him with sympathy and understanding.

"You're twenty-six, aren't you, Vincent?" he said, so quietly that his voice came softly with an androgynous warmth.

"Nearly twenty-seven," Vincent nodded, almost lost in his dream.

"It is time for you to begin your real career." Powell's voice was now distinct, and as Vincent looked up at the challenging tone, he took into himself a charge of vitality that Powell suddenly gave off as if he were a different man. "We didn't bring you all this way from the west country to this museum piece of petty bourgeois taste *just* to chat, fascinating though that is."

"I didn't suppose you did," replied Vincent, alert and wide awake from his reverie.

"You have to move now, and move fast. It is great good luck that we have a man just where you are. Although it is not luck at all, of course, but good organisation. Where you are is of great importance. The international situation is rapidly getting more and more threatening and we need all the skills and knowledge we can get from Maculan. This you know already, but the matter is now of great urgency. We can't wait for things to develop of themselves in your job as was originally intended. We have to make them develop, to get you at once into a position where you can act. And by 'we' I mean you, you with us, you part of us. Everything will be put in motion within a few days, you can have complete confidence in that, and when the breach opens, you jump straight in and *act*. Now that I know about Jackson—I can't imagine how that factor was missed—I see what to do. Now, let us get down to details. There is one important area in which your progress in the company is disappointing. You don't appear to have penetrated the personal confidence of the chief. Maculan *is* the company, we know that; the chairman, Lord Tantham, is a cipher. As an inventor Maculan is probably finished; I have that from people who know about such things; in his late fifties, as he now is, nothing really new is to be expected from him. But what he has already done, that is vital. And we know that even if leases of the dozens of patents involved were possible legally, Maculan never would cooperate with us. I recall myself, on one of the committees he was on, he was implacably opposed to any of his inventions going to the Russians, even in the middle of the war. Equipment with his inventions could only be operated by British or American officers. Naturally, in the atmosphere of comradeship during the war, that was easily got round, but the results were scrappy and unsatisfactory. We have to have complete specifications, models, machine-tool designs, samples in working order, everything. I won't try to put it into correct terminology, I should get it all wrong. Someone else will brief you on the technical side. What I am concerned with is the human side. Now, think before you answer. Can you rapidly make Maculan a friend of yours, win his trust and work your way into his inner circle?"

There was silence for some minutes before Vincent answered, quite naturally and seriously, without any trace of his former defensiveness.

"Rapidly? I take it that is the operative word? I don't think it could be done quickly, certainly not at once. The old man doesn't care about the business side enough for me to be able to get close through the new export plans, which are anyway waiting for Jackson, as I told you. Even if—when, I mean —Jackson is out of the way, Maculan is not likely to interest himself personally in the trading details. And there's something else, much more difficult to put into words. They are a tight little group down there, the old members of the company who were there in the war. A real little band of brothers, the engineers and boffins and Folliot, the administration man. Take Tantham's daughter, she married the son of one of the old directors and *he* went straight back into the slot the day after he came out of the army. You see? They are a proper clan. The sales side has never been considered part of that inside group—yet. On the other hand, that disadvantage is also a plus for us. If they looked upon exports and sales generally as crucial, I wouldn't have a chance at the job as a newcomer. They know it is *going* to be vital, but things have not yet reached that stage, and that is how I shall eventually make it to the inside group."

He stopped to think out what more he wanted to say and then went on, speaking more slowly.

"Then, too, there is the old man himself. To anyone outside his circle, there is a strong barrier there. He keeps a ring of reserve around himself somehow. You understand, Maculan is a strange, powerful man. He's not the type you could jolly along, still less deceive. I mean, he's not the sort of bluffing CO type who can be baffled by science, if you know what I mean."

"Do you suppose he feels something in you that makes him not quite trust you? You, I mean, not this general atmosphere?"

Vincent looked up, interested and startled by this suggestion.

"I hadn't thought of that. It could just be. He's a foreigner, of course, and sharp as needles. He has none of that taking people for granted that the British have, even the other members of his group of friends. He is quite different from them. He watches and *knows,* you feel it all the time. So you could be right there. Although, as you know, the waiting for Jackson could play a part there. He may change a bit if I move up into Jackson's place."

"Yes," said Powell, thinking. "Don't worry about Jackson, though. Maculan himself. Can you get past that barrier? I know just what you mean, by the way. I've sat on committees and attended Intelligence meetings with him in the war; one has the feeling he looks into one's very soul and *knows,* just as you say. He's a dangerous man."

"Do you think it's possible?" asked Vincent hesitantly. "Quickly, I mean?"

"I rather think probably not—rapidly," agreed Powell slowly. "We may have to go another way round. But I shall have to consult on that."

Vincent took this to mean that someone else would be chosen to attempt the task, and this threat stimulated his wits. He narrowed his eyes in concentration and bit his underlip.

The expression totally changed his face; Powell was looking now not at a dreaming boy but at a sharp and determined manipulator, quick-witted, hard and concentrating on his own concerns with an exclusiveness that was forbidding.

"There is one factor I have not yet mentioned," said Vincent at last. "Maculan has a daughter. I met her in the summer holidays and we got on quite well. She's seventeen, leaving school at the end of this year."

"A daughter," breathed Powell on an outgoing sigh. "I'd forgotten he has a child. A daughter." He laughed suddenly. "A daughter."

He stared into Vincent's face.

"Could you make it with the girl?"

"I shouldn't be surprised," said Vincent, smiling. "In fact, I'm pretty sure."

"You understand, of course, it would have to be marriage?"

"Well, naturally. Anyway, they are Catholics. She's at a convent."

"There are no impediments?"

"Nothing that can't be dropped without fuss." Vincent was confident. "If you mean legal ones, no. I've never even been engaged."

"Excellent. My dear boy, that alters the whole picture if you can carry the girl off. You're a genius, it solves the whole problem. You will have to reduce her to helpless submission, total love, so that she would defy even her father if necessary. I don't mean that you should allow that possibility to arise, but to make sure of his consent if he is jealous or reluctant. Seventeen is young, after all. Do you really think you can pull it off?"

"I rather think," said Vincent, smiling to himself, "it can be done. Turn the tap full on, you know. The secret always is to convince them that you adore them. Prick with devotion, that's what does it, everytime."

"You little swine," said Powell affectionately. "Maculan's son-in-law!"

"I should think I'll be able to give you news within, let's say, six weeks. I shall know fairly quickly whether I can pull it off, and then it's just a matter of time."

"Less, my dear, less if you can. Force the issue, as one might say."

"It'll be a pleasure," Vincent assured him, grinning happily.

"I shall think of you," said Powell in a tone that left no doubt what he meant by this conventional phrase.

"Yes," continued Vincent, after a pause for consideration, "but there are other problems. Outlets. Cover outlets, I mean."

"That can be arranged. I believe it is already on the stocks. There is a firm in Zurich and another in Lebanon, Beirut. Your other adviser will tell you all about that, he will be getting in touch with you soon, perhaps tomorrow. You'll know the whole process, all its stages, before you ever make your first trip abroad." He watched Vincent's eyes as he said this, but there was nothing in the younger man's face to give him pause. "This really calls for another drink, to celebrate."

"Well, don't count the chickens too soon," cautioned Vincent. "The time to celebrate will be in about a month's time."

This was prophetic, if a trifle too optimistic as to time.

"It will work," said Powell with confidence. "I feel it, the feel of success. One can never mistake that. And any celebration *we* have has to be done now. You won't, I much regret for my own sake, see me again for some time, perhaps not ever. And if you do ever see me, by chance, you don't know me from Adam. That's my name, by the way, Adam."

"Well, Adam, here's to success!" A slight condescension had crept already into Vincent's tone; he was now the man of decision, the dynamic and magnetic doer. "I'll get moving as soon as I get back and you set up the detailed information side of the operation. I leave all that to you. Yes, and in a few weeks it will be Christmas, with all the parties and so on. And immediately after that Maculan goes to the States for several weeks. I shall have a clear field."

"He's going to America? I wasn't told that."

"I don't think anybody knows yet. Consultations with the Department of Defence. Top level stuff. He has an aeroplane practically to himself, from RAF Transport Command's V.I.P. Flight, the sort of treatment Prime Ministers get."

"Oh, my paws and whiskers," crowed Powell, "this, my dear

Vincent, is it. Mistletoe and Maculan's private plane!"
"Mistletoe and the V.I.P. Flight. We'll drink to that."

Powell, or Polter to call him by his real name, remained behind when Vincent left to take the underground train to his railway station in time to get the night express back to the west country. He pulled a portable typewriter out of the sideboard cupboard and a packet of copy paper. His typing was awk- ward and inaccurate, but with the aid of many cigarettes and more of the whisky, he drafted his notes on the evening's work.

"Gyves, and I suggest altering his cover name to Jive since the present version is too likely a play on his real name, is a handsome young man of the stocky, fair-coloured type usu- ally thought of as Saxon. A broad forehead with unusually level brows gives him a reliable, open look, his eyes are of a strikingly light and vivid blue, but this feature is not impres- sive enough at a glance to make him overly noticeable. Overall physical impression is of a solid, vigorous, decent boy, not particularly clever but sensible, competent, somewhat power- fully concerned with his own sex satisfactions but not enough to inspire distrust in older men. He is a good example of the danger of judging by looks, since in reality he shows every sign of a coarse-fibred and opaquely egotistic insensitiveness. So- cial background: semiskilled artisan with petty bourgeois as- pirations, the signs of which are the object of his constant attention and I should judge are quite rapidly disappearing. Change of voice pitch, accent and mannerisms very noticeable when recounting his recent past, which he did with accuracy, everything checked. Shows distinct talent (unconscious) for acting; dramatised narrative of his experiences since the end of the war with natural artistry, even the timbre of voice changed with his gradual assumption of a veneer of upper- class mannerisms. These still quite faulty, but, considering the short time, creditable, and will clearly improve rapidly.

"Ideology: none. Showed no reaction but slight disguised puzzlement to standard stimuli of revolutionary conscious- ness, was not aware that I produced them in wrong chronolog- ical order. Clearly has not read even most obvious basic works. Therefore no danger of traces of ideology appearing.

"Drive is certainly not ideological but little danger of directional change, since drive is of powerful ambition and vanity, strong traces of hostility to established authority overlaid with desire for conventions. Personality structure simple: in essence, Jive is a class war in one man. Extreme and touchy vanity, dominated by animosity, hatred not too strong a word, dispersed but aroused by any sign of superiority including real achievement. In handling Jive, therefore, a positive, friendly and confiding manner is essential. Personality quite unintegrated, no understanding at all of his own motives, while possessing a certain surface practical intelligence and quick wits that enable him to plan and execute his ambitions. Susceptible to flattery, of course, criticism accepted easily if presented as his own idea but should never be directly reproved or given orders. Extremely suggestible to indirect leading, picks up thread at once when offered."

Powell, or Polter, read through these points of reminder, decided that they were sufficient to his purpose of writing a detailed report and proceeded to outline the plan produced by the consultation with "Jive." Here he went into exact detail. Finally he added a note. "Important to note that the idea was Jive's, probably been in his mind for some time as a vague possibility or fairly concrete fantasy. Major drawback, character of his employer and projected father-in-law. This barrier to success may be insuperable, but in view of the crucial nature of project and its great urgency, Jive should be tried. I was obliged to make a decision about this on the spot, since Jive must be back in his office tomorrow and I took the responsibility of encouraging him to proceed. If no success after two months (I gave him a time limit of six weeks), then alternative suggestion of this operative's removal will have to be put into effect. This course should be viewed as last resort owing to difficulty of replacing Jive with suitable substitute. Would almost certainly result in return of former sales director Jackson to the company, which would ruin all prospect of success, Jackson being completely unapproachable and well trained in security procedures.

"I shall present further suggestions when we meet on Thursday."

"That will suffice for the moment," said Powell aloud to

himself. "Not well phrased, but it will do as a memorandum. And one must never forget that one is dealing with fifth-raters. They are reassured by jargon. Now for the silly little apparatus."

This was a miniature camera with which the typed sheets were photographed. The roll of film was sealed and slipped into the hollow, vaselike base of the lamp on the table and left there. The papers Powell took into the bathroom with him.

"It really is a bit mucky," he muttered in the same half-tone as he burned the papers with his cigarette lighter over the lavatory and dropped the ashes into the water. "I must comment on the place when chance offers." He pulled the chain and the ashes disappeared.

Powell then returned to the living room and rolled a fresh sheet of paper into the typewriter. He began a letter with "Darling Theo" and filled half the sheet with mild obscenities before leaving it in the machine and putting it back into the cupboard in case the sound of typing had been heard in a neighbouring apartment so late in the evening.

"One can never be too careful, or rather one can never be too careful to give our friends the impression that one is careful. And it amuses the boys when they come."

Unlike those he thought of as his friends, Powell was little impressed by routines of secrecy. Many years of having his occasional oddities written off tolerantly as part of his personal idiosyncrasy gave him complete confidence; he knew how little notice Londoners take of each other's lives, even where there is no ready-made explanation.

However, conforming to the conspiratorial habits of others, he made sure everything was in order before he left the house. He took the underground to Piccadilly Circus from Golders Green, picked up a cab and returned to his usual life. Nothing, as he might have said, could be more simple.

Vincent Cheyney waited for an hour in the buffet at the station for his train. Why it should be forty minutes late when this was its starting point he did not even try to find out; no one would have told him. At any other time this slackness would have enraged Vincent, but that evening an elation that even London in its stagnant cold misery could no longer depress filled him with euphoric dreams. He no longer

36

noticed his surroundings except as a contrast to the future. This he felt to be already his with an unquestioning confidence. The expedition to London had, after all, been the start of good fortune; the uneasy expectation of trouble with which he arrived had proved unreal. Powell did not even challenge Vincent on the subject of his meagre reports, of which Vincent himself had been very much aware. In fact the possibility of his being relieved of his task had been real at the start of his evening, and his awareness of the threat proved just how well suited Vincent was to his double-dealing. But every circumstance of time and people was falling into place as if drilled into obedience by the brilliance and simplicity of his, Vincent's idea. Even the momentary regret that his present mistress would have to be dropped could not spoil Vincent's satisfaction with himself.

He would hint to Eileen that suspicious looks were worrying him. The wife of a "rising young director" had enough to lose by scandal, even though she was herself an heiress, for her to decide herself that a quick ending to a pleasant affair was preferable to risking her position or her marriage. If I let her put an end to it, Vincent thought, she will be sorry for me instead of angry, and she will still be on my side. With a bit of sentimental weepiness I can convince her that only because she can never be mine am I thinking of—whatever is her name? Everyone calls her Jenny but it isn't Jennifer. Oh, well, she isn't too bad and I shall have her eating out of my hand in a few weeks from now. That was clear from the couple of times we played tennis, in her summer holidays. God, she still wears her school uniform, I must get her to wear it one night. The house is said to be smashing. Eileen talks about it as if it were unique. Grove House on Grove Hill, certainly sounds marvellous. I wonder what it's like. I shall invite Colonel White for a weekend, that will finish him off once and for all. Pity I can't invite Nigel too, but, who knows, perhaps some time I will. I shall live at Grove House and be the son-in-law of a genius, a famous man who could have a peerage if he wanted it. Eileen said he declined to let his name be put forward, queer that. Imagine not wanting to be Lord Maculan. Pity it isn't summer, with swimming and that. But Christmas isn't bad, either. What did Powell say? Mistletoe and the V.I.P. Flight? Wonder what he meant by that, or did he mean anything? Just *sounds* amusing, I expect. Pity about Eileen, nice popsy, always ready for it. But there are plenty of women about and I don't have to stick to marital joys for more than a few months. Well, I'll have to watch the old boy. But I shall be travelling a lot.

He picked up his empty glass and, stepping over two ditty bags belonging to two sailors who, like himself, were waiting for the Bristol-Plymouth night train, Vincent pushed it along the counter and asked for another. As he sorted coins from his pocket to pay for the beer, he thought with a thrill like an electric shock that he would soon be rich.

CHAPTER II

THE MEANS by which these wide plans were to be put into effect were for the planners the least of the factors to be weighed. She was, indeed, a not very weighty factor for anyone else either, except for her father, still half-absent in the limbo of school days as she was.

Jenny herself was eager to leave school, not in order to be grown up but to be able to go every day instead of only during holidays to her teacher Connors. His little house, really hardly more than a shack attached to the converted barn of his studio, was conveniently near and it was agreed between Connors, Maculan and Jenny herself that she should in effect be his apprentice during the coming year. This was an achievement, for the famous sculptor disliked the idea of teaching and Jenny knew that his agreement to "put up with the kid about the place" was in fact strong evidence of her talent. There was no childish conceit about this knowledge. In almost everything else childish or childlike, the profession of her future was taken as it had been since her first year in England, with the seriousness of the professional. The fantasy that is adolescent speculation about the world and living was as strong in Jenny as in any other girl, but it did not touch work. She took her calling for granted, and with the knowledge that it must be laboured for with devotion, used and not dispersed in frivolous disregard of the laws of its nature that began with the artisan's training.

Neither her father nor her teacher were men who made compromises; if they accepted her as an equal she could be sure of herself provided she worked. And after inspecting the figure of a singing bird in its third form—having told her twice to go back and do it again—Connors committed himself

39

to Maculan in one of his rare statements that Jenny was born with the skills of their trade already in her hands; she needed only experience. It might be a good idea for her to get a few months' formal anatomy, he added vaguely. He dared say that a teacher would insist on that and it could do the girl no harm. Otherwise, she would do.

For Connors, this was a speech.

A few weeks after that Jenny, still not quite sure he would accept her as a pupil, or, as he called it, an apprentice, met Connors by chance in the town. He did not notice her; she touched him on the arm and he turned to look who was near him, eyeing her cautiously from under the brim of his slouch hat as if seeing her for the first time. Then his bloodshot eyes focused.

"Oh, it's you. I knew there was something." He withdrew into himself again and Jenny waited patiently until he remembered. "I was going to ring up. You're coming in the new year, then?"

One always needed to lean towards his burly, unkempt head to hear what he mumbled.

"Oh, Connors, may I? That's . . ."

Warned by his scowl she said no more, but nodded in imitation of his own taciturnity. He was ten paces away when he recalled something else. He pushed his way back through the market crowd, indistinguishable from the farmers in his heavy tweed coat.

"Tell your father. I've finished the figure for Mainter. I want to get his head done before he clears off." Without waiting for a reply he slouched off once more, shambling along with his head bent almost to his chest and brushing against people at every steps, while he muttered to himself.

"You'd never think he'd done the old King, would you?" said Mrs. Blane, with whom Jenny had come into the market, "he's worn that overcoat to my certain knowledge since 1919."

"Now how can you be sure of that?" challenged Mrs. Limmert, primly pedantic.

"Of course I know. Wearing a uniform still he was when he first came. Just out of the army. I remember him giving his greatcoat, khaki army coat, to our old Jonas and that was just about lambing time, the war was only over a month or so. He

40

didn't look much different then to what he does now, looked old then. Well, Blane looked old too, three years in the trenches. That war was worse than the second one, you can say what you like."

"When we leave here we must go and collect your dress for the dance at Mainters'," said Mrs. Limmert, getting the name wrong as she always did. They went into the shop next on her list. "Now you will help us choose, Mrs. Blane, won't you?"

The search was for a china vase much desired as a Christmas present by the cleaning woman, who did most of what was ever done in the way of cleaning Grove House.

"I hope it's ready." Jenny was suddenly anxious and excited, the serious business of life slid into a make-believe where it was possible to combine two conflicting futures, one in which she continued to live with her father in their home while at the same time she was beautiful and happy as well as famous with a figure who remained unclear, although for the first time having the features of a real man. This recurring fantasy provided Jenny with a family of young geniuses for the eminent sculptress whose fame influenced the whole of Europe and yet was as young as Jenny was then.

"It will be," Mrs. Blane assured her, and pointed at a large imitation Toby jug. "I saw Elsie and she said so."

"You think that one?" Mrs. Limmert was justifiably dubious.

"It's too big for the front room," objected Jenny tactfully. "I know she wants it for the sideboard there. Mrs. Folliot says that color is too old for me."

"But that was what you wanted, Jenny, to look older. I expect it will be very pretty. How about this one, Mrs. Blane?"

"I like the swan one."

"So do I," agreed Jenny. "Let's have that one."

"Won't the beak get broken?"

"Oh, she won't *use* it," said Jenny.

"Yes, you'll have all the young men after you." Mrs. Blane smiled at her while the shop man took away the vase to pack it. "How's it feel to be a grown-up lady, eh, Jenny?"

"I don't know yet," answered Jenny seriously. "But I hope the pink isn't too daring. It's called shocking pink. Isn't it funny?"

"All your poor father's coupons!" Mrs. Blane pretended to be scandalised. "But there, you're only young once."

"Oh, Father doesn't need new clothes. He doesn't mind."

"When does he go?"

"Straightaway after Christmas, the twenty-eighth."

"It's a long way, America. I'm glad it's not me."

"He is going to take me with him next time. He promised."

"Well, if you do, go, don't you go bringing an American husband back with you. There were a lot of Americans over at Wythen in '43. Black as your hat, Blane said. I never saw any that I remember, but that's what Blane said."

Mrs. Limmert was just about to explain the ethnic composition of the United States population, but they were perhaps fortunately interrupted by the arrival of their parcel.

"It is now time to meet Mrs. Folliot for tea," pronounced Mrs. Limmert as they all three emerged from the only possible dress shop with the first long dress Jenny had ever owned, the hemline duly shortened to fit her small stature. They would part company here and the Blanes' car would meet them later outside the public library, so they stood on the corner making fairly elaborate arrangements for what was a rendezvous that recurred about once a week but was just the same the subject of discussion. Both Mrs. Blane and Mrs. Limmert, who was really Dr. Limmert, were careful to amplify the details of transport to and from the town with a precision sufficient for a journey into the next county. This was because Jenny was absent-minded and had once forgotten to agree exactly where and when the little party would meet again, with the result that she was obliged to walk the three miles home alone in the dark rather than wait for the eight o'clock bus for Gullion. Jenny tended to be vague, that was agreed, but in any case she enjoyed the walk and would gladly have repeated it in the dim and misty light of a waxing moon. However, for different reasons, which Jenny neither shared nor understood, both Mrs. Blane and Dr. Limmert disapproved of evening walks alone; Mrs. Blane because in her youth young ladies did not stroll about by themselves in the daytime, let alone at night; and Mrs. Limmert, because she came originally from a society where laissez faire was neither customary nor approved.

Sometimes Jenny teased the farmer's wife for being so old-fashioned in this and other matters—she never teased Dr. Limmert—but she got no further with her old friend than a smiling shake of the head and the information that she, Mrs. Blane, knew what was what and Jenny would understand when she was older.

"Don't go leaving your dress behind in the tea shop, now will you, Jenny?" admonished Mrs. Blane as she turned to go. The dress was packed in a stout cardboard box with much tissue paper, all of which would be returned to the shop for reuse, for it was nowadays impossible to obtain. Indeed, the dress itself, with its brilliant colour, thought unsuitable by the unassuming taste of local ladies and their narrow views, was in the nature of a treasure trove, being the only garment of its kind available in the shop.

Outside the tea shop Jenny stopped for an instant, as she saw the sports car standing at the kerb; a sharp jolt of pleasure and anticipation made her eyes widen and her colour rise. But since Mrs. Limmert made no comment, Jenny was silent, too, and followed her companion through the door into the untidy little café, already decked out with holly for the festival. It seemed perfectly natural that Vincent should be sitting there with Mrs. Folliot and Brenda, as if it was inevitable, as if she knew in advance. And yet there was the blissful shock that made the whole busy little scene focus with a rush on that one face lifted quickly towards their arrival with visibly drawn breath and eager smile.

Excitement blurred both sight and hearing, confused and shy, Jenny could hardly speak for the delight that was at once so hypertensed and so dreamlike. She must gasp and stammer, she feared even to glance at the others who talked, as if nothing were happening, about the Christmas party of the evening before, when Vincent was invited for the first time to Grove House and where this intensity of excitement first overcame Jenny. She did not hear Brenda's question about the new dress.

"Manage?" she asked faintly.

"For the coupons, silly," repeated Brenda with a meaning smile.

"I could have managed some clothing coupons for you," said Vincent, and Jenny could hear him clearly. "You should have told me you didn't have enough."

"Oh, Father gave me his," said Jenny laughing because Brenda said at the same moment, "I used poor Mummy's."

"Well, I can always lay on a few extra if you need them," he said and Jenny did not notice that everyone was for a second silent. But Vincent noticed it and knew that to claim a source of what must be illicit textile permits was disapproved of; indeed, it was almost unheard of.

"My landlady doesn't use hers, she told me so," he explained, in a slightly too definite tone. A sensation of disbelief made itself felt about the crowded tea table, of which Jenny was the only person there to remain unconscious.

"Will your motor car be large enough for you and the two girls?" Mrs. Limmert changed the subject. "It is very kind of Mr. Folliot to come all the way to pick up Jenny and take her back."

"Oh, there'll be plenty of room." Mrs. Folliot was about to say something more but Vincent spoke, his eyes on Jenny.

"But aren't you coming with *me*, Jenny?"

"I think . . ."

"Oh, Jen, what fun!" cried Brenda.

"It will be better if Jenny comes with us," said Mrs. Folliot calmly. "Especially the return journey."

For a woman of Mrs. Folliot's conventions, this was almost insulting, and Vincent took it as that.

"But we'd already arranged," he began hotly.

"Mr. Maculan himself made the arrangements with Mr. Folliot," said Mrs. Folliot.

"We shall expect you all, then, for the evening meal, at seven," said Mrs. Limmert quickly. "You will come too, will you not, Mr. Cheyney." It was a statement, not a question. For a moment it looked as if Vincent's hard-won urbanity would not rise to this tactful way out; his brows came down and he moved impatiently, making the ramshackle wicker chair creak. But Jenny's eyes glowed into his with such an anxious, eager, shining look that he remembered his manners just in time and smiled back at her with assumed ruefulness, a smile that confided a secret.

44

"Lady Mainter has made great efforts with supper. Thanks to the Blanes and half a dozen other good people, she says she will produce an almost prewar *souper*." Mrs. Limmert pronounced the last word in a way that Vincent thought very affected, suspecting an intention that was not in the speaker's mind, to condescend to him by using foreign words.

"It's splendid that the Blanes will be there," Jenny sighed with pleasure. "Even Connors is coming. He's actually had his dinner jacket cleaned! All my friends will be there! I feel as if next week will never come."

The idea of the sculptor even possessing anything so unlikely as an evening suit made them all laugh, so that Vincent felt he could now not ask who Connors was. He supposed it must be one of the farmers of the district, since evidently the dance was to include people like the Blanes, whose inclusion seemed to Vincent strange. Like many people who make great efforts for success, Vincent was apt to make social distinctions much more sharply than did ancient local families such as the Mainters. He felt somewhat offended now at the possibility that the evening at the great house of the neighbourhood was really to be a modern form of a tenants' ball and not a gathering of the élite and noble. There was no way by which Vincent could understand the very old ties between the yeomen like the Blanes and the Mainters, who were the heads of the Blanes' extended clan rather than remote aristocrats; neither did it occur to anyone to try to explain this subtle relationship to him. He was, potentially at least, so completely accepted in advance that instruction would have appeared absurd to anyone able to give it to him. The only person nearby who could see these matters from the outside and who was, from her foreign standpoint, capable of understanding them, was Dr. Limmert and she was, in a not quite formulated way, hostile to Vincent. He felt that she watched him warily, and he was right. Dr. Limmert measured other human beings by the experiences she suffered just before she came to England and which she knew—also by experience—were incommunicable to British people. To those like Maculan, who themselves knew, she did not need to explain anything; those who did not know lacked a dimension of the mind needed to understand her insights.

Having established the point that Jenny was not to go to Mainter or return, alone, Mrs. Folliot was now much concerned to make friends with Vincent. She liked him and was touched by his ardent pursuit of Jenny, taking for granted that his ardour must be restrained without in the least condemning it. He did, indeed, as Brenda had already told her, never take his eyes off Jenny.

"I must get back to the testing shop," he said after half an hour, and he glanced at his wristwatch. "I ought not to have gone out, really."

"We shan't tell," Mrs. Folliot assured him indulgently.

"Don't forget, I'm to have at least every other dance," he said to Jenny. He smiled into her adoring eyes, and touched her hand surreptitiously.

"Don't I get any dances?" protested Brenda, almost as much enraptured by the amorous atmosphere as the other two young people.

"Of course! That's why I said every other dance!" He winked openly, drawing her into a happy little conspiracy.

"Isn't he bliss?" cried Brenda as the door closed with a clinging sound of its bell. She leaned close to Jenny and whispered, ignoring her mother's frown at this rudeness. Jenny laughed and blushed even more and shook her head.

"But why not? I bet he will," urged Brenda. "Mummy was only nineteen, weren't you, Mum?"

"Please don't call me Mum, Brenda. That was different, your father and I had known each other all our lives. And Vincent would certainly not speak while Jenny's father is away. I'm sure he wouldn't do that."

"I hope you are right," said Mrs. Limmert, and somehow her doubt dispersed the gaiety. She looked through the bow window of the tea shop and watched the low sports car swing away from the kerb with its exaggerated roar. "It is too sudden to be serious."

"Both you and Vincent will be in love half a dozen times before both of you marry two entirely different people," Mrs. Folliot assured Jenny.

"It's not sudden, though," Brenda rebelled at this middle-aged and dull idea. "He was in love last summer in the holi-

46

days. He told me so yesterday. And anyway, there's such a thing as love at first sight."

"Silly child," sighed her mother, gathering up her gloves and handbag. "Heavens, my gloves are shabby."

"I do hope you will not allow Brenda's romantic notions to influence you, Jenny dear," said Mrs. Limmert as they walked through the spangled dark street to the library. "What Mrs. Folliot said is quite true. You mustn't take it all seriously. Enjoy it, rather, as a little adventure."

"Of course," agreed Jenny docilely, hardly taking in what was said. "Aren't the shops pretty, all decorated for Christmas!"

Her companion was reassured and decided not to speak to Julius and perhaps worry him unnecessarily before his departure.

"Now, have we done all our shopping, before the Blanes arrive? I must count. Where is my list? Oh, here, in my pocket."

"I hope we haven't forgotten anyone?"

"Here is the car."

"Mr. Paynter says we're getting traffic lights at the crossing here," Blane informed them as they stopped for a farm lorry near the Catholic church.

"High time, too. It's a wicked corner."

"Paynter's not best pleased, though. He'll lose a constable, transferred to the other station."

"Which one? Elsie's boy?"

"Didn't say."

"Ah, there's a lot of chance in life," sighed Mrs. Blane as the old farm carrier ground ponderously into the Gullion road. She was thinking of the young policeman, Elsie's boy, who would be almost next door to his sweetheart if he were chosen for the move to the second police station by the railway on the far side of the little town; that would pretty well clinch the still unsettled question of whether the young pair would marry. Mrs. Limmert, beside her on the lumpy and slippery back seat that shifted uneasily on the curves of the road, agreed with a murmur to this expression of what she herself was considering as a comforting postscript to the half-hour in the tea shop.

It was very lucky that a great talent like Connors should have chosen all those years ago to settle just where a generation later he could help form a new artist and carry on in this way the mysterious continuity of life. It was a chance in a thousand that Jenny could learn from someone worthy of her gift, here in so remote a place, unconnected except by Maculan himself with the stimulations and rivalry of that dispersed company of the excellent, without which no artist can develop fully. That young man who had conveyed an impression of a somehow obsessive concentration on Jenny would not be able to maintain any fascination for the child against the influence of Connors and the reality of creation.

If Jenny had been twenty-seven instead of seventeen, Mrs. Limmert would still have thought it a waste for her to marry, to become a mere wife and mother and disperse her vitality in babies and the dominance of a man. When the festivities of Christmas and the New Year were over, when Julius was back from Washington, young Cheyney would quite naturally merge into the background, not one focused figure but one of a number of peripheral companions touching but not reaching into the inner circle of Jenny's consciousness.

CHAPTER III

"Ah, THERE you are," said Sandford in a tone of anxiety and indecision that seemed to Vincent to imply that he was late. Only a month or so before, Vincent might have flared up at this implication, which existed only in his own mind. But his new consciousness of a purpose, of an advantage he possessed over everyone about him in the knowledge of things they did not dream of, this gave him confidence and kept him silent. Sandford was a fool, with his sandy hair and round, short body. Already an aura of pomp moved with him. He was the future boss, and the only reason for not saying so openly was that everybody knew it. He had a degree, a good war record, his father had been an engineer and he was an engineer; his wife was the only surviving child of the Chairman of the company. He belonged. The only thing Vincent envied him for was that he understood, or to be precise, he did once on leaving the university understand, the theories behind the processes and products that were their business. Sandford learned nothing by rule of thumb, he never needed to pick things up as he went along. This advantage Vincent held against him but nothing else; all the other things were collected under the cover of Vincent's secret joke, including Eileen Sandford.

"Come in," invited Teddy morosely, and Vincent followed him into his office, where old Folliot sat in an armchair by the window. Folliot was not really old but his character was; he must have looked the staid lawyer before he ever left school. Folliot did not turn to greet Vincent but stared fixedly out towards the green lawn ringed by neat garden beds raised in symmetrical humps of well-turned earth ready for planting. Why doesn't the old fool say good morning, Vincent wondered. He's usually punctilious enough. There is something wrong.

"This frightful news, it is so terrible that I still haven't taken it in," said Sandford and stood by his wide desk, touching papers as if they gave him reassurance by their familiarity. "There's no longer any chance. You know that?"

"Chance? Frightful news?" Vincent stammered. He could feel the blood rushing away from his head, his face paled and a sensation of dizzy dismay spread a chill so that his hands were suddenly cold. "Wha—what d'you mean?" He must gain time, if only a moment.

"What? Didn't you get my message last night? Don't you know?"

"Message? My landlady must have forgotten it. I've had no message."

That will be the last time you stay out all night, my boy, if there is going to be any more time.

"Maculan's plane is lost over the Atlantic."

Vincent felt for the chairback with a swaying movement of shock that was perfectly real.

"It can't be true."

"It is true," said Folliot's voice, flat and expressionless. But he did not turn from the window.

Vincent closed his eyes in an effort almost greater than he was capable of, to control a wave of horror mixed with relief that weakened his knees to the shaking point. It isn't me. They've found nothing. Maculan. The plane. He's dead.

"You mean the Chief is . . . ?" The sound of his voice was faint but it echoed as if in a vault inside his own ears. "Just a minute. I—" He sat down with a stumbling movement. Then in blind haste he rose again.

"Jenny! Does she know? I must get over there!"

"They sent her a telegram when we got ours. Eileen is just going over. Do you want to go with her?"

"My God, I . . . Yes, of course. But I don't think I could drive."

"It's all right. The driver is taking Eileen in the Daimler."

"Are you sure she will want to see you? Anyone?" Folliot's voice was only a whisper. The two younger men stared at the back of his rigidly held head, and in the same instant realized that he did not know and glanced back at each other. It was the kind of thing Folliot would not notice for himself.

"Oh, I think so, sir," said Sandford. "She will need all the help we can all give her and, you know, they've been seeing a lot of each other."

Thanks for the explanation, thought Vincent, very kind of you. He was beginning to recover.

"Of course I must go," he said with force. "And at once."

"Here's the car now, driving up. It went to get Eileen from home. Come on, Vin. Let's go."

They left Folliot, still staring out. At the sound of the door closing the older man pushed himself up a little with one hand and swung his head round, his narrow mouth slightly open, his eyes blank.

"What was all that?" he muttered. "You must excuse me. Oh—they've gone." He sank back again into the chair. This was worse than when George was killed at Alamein, he thought, and a name recurred over and over again in his empty mind. Julius, old friend, he was more than anyone to me. The deaths, the deaths. It is as if the war went on in secret, disaster without end. We are decimated by the deaths and it is the same all over the country, not only here with us. Since my George went, Tantham's boy at sea, and now Julius. Although Julius was not shot down. This was a peacetime disaster. Peace, what a name to give this state of affairs. It brings back the war atmosphere so that I feel I am back in that time, that's what it is. One lonely aircraft over the north Atlantic in January, cold, bitter seas and winds. But it *was* the war, the last one or the future one. For years everything we did has been for killing, and the wages of death is death. Old Tantham in an air raid, his son at sea, my boy brewed up in a tank in the desert. Now Julius. How shall we carry on? The best are gone and we are left with underlings like Tantham's brother and this new pushing young fellow here. I suppose Sandford will develop, acquire solidity, but they are juniors, no weight to them, no experience, no talent. Brewed up, my poor boy. What strange slang they use in this war.

A mutter of sound made him look again out of the window. There was a group of the men, their heads together, over by the main gate. One of them gestured with an arm, a curiously

51

lonely, wild movement in the sullen winter half-light. They were moving, crossing the grass, which was not allowed, and the trivial misdemeanour revived Folliot's sense of order and decorum. Then he saw what they were concerned with. The company flag, limply clinging to its staff in the still cold, was falling downwards. They slid it too far and jerked it up again. For a second it billowed out and fell back listlessly. Folliot pushed himself stiffly to his feet and stood there by the blank sheen of the window.

Sandford's wife and Vincent sat in the corner seats of the big limousine, which proceeded with unobtrusive speed towards the west. The barrier of convention that divided them was so strong that when Eileen, in glancing sideways at the moving landscape, saw her companion and the unbidden thought entered her mind that if he were driving they could stop on the way and make love, she went rigid as if the idea were audible and the chauffeur could hear it. No transference took place, the square shoulders of the driver remained unmoved and Vincent continued to sit with his hands gripped together and his face shut in, absent with shock and concentration on the moment to come. This is it, he kept thinking, grasp the moment as it flies. When the breach opens, jump straight in and act. That's like a play. He did not recall where the phrase came from. So completely was all that Powell put into his mind adopted that no connection was present there between himself and any other influence. He did not even, for the moment, find it strange or gratifying that distant events should work together so neatly for his advancement; he was now the man he was acting, and for that man success was assured.

The illegitimate child whose father cleared off before he could be remembered no longer existed; he was dead and buried. The schoolboy, wretched even by the standards of the suburb of a provincial industrial town, snivelling and unmannered, was not as much as a goad to action. The avidly film-going apprentice whose only aspirations were the riches of the cinema dream world, to be attained in a moral vacuum by any trick that worked, as the stories made repetitively clear; he, too, was gone. His buried, never-lived youth was a gap in memory and nothing more. The man who sat in the big motor car became fully grown when the society that produced such rootless beings from its bankruptcy by the thousand found itself obliged by its own terrible miscalculations to employ and further anyone who could manage machines. No choice was possible in a crisis recognised only after it was already a conflict to the death, not a war but a catastrophe that could end only in the complete destruction of the loser. This man was born afresh when those who had ruined his world needed him enough to ask no questions as to his character, enough to grant him a patent as its own admired prototype in a modern form—the "officer and gentleman" who could handle technology. The only heritage of his upbringing that survived the change was the sole root of his consciousness: the confrontation of himself by "them" who were at once enemies and the envied holders of privilege, suddenly seen to be obsequious instead of insolent. What more satisfying than to transfer his allegiance from a grudging recognition to the rising power that intended the end of "their" world? It never even entered his mind to pay gratitude for the training and advancement he had received; it obliged him to nothing, for he knew it was granted only for as long as "they" needed him. That this view was false and that its falsity was proved by his present employment was, or would have been if anyone thought of pointing it out, meaningless. Reciprocity was never taught him; it was an opaque blank. What was given was his alone. His only experience of a community in his growing years was his mother's querulous complaints against the exiguous doles that never satisfied her demands. The demands were unformulated and therefore boundless, and although his own demands had grown long since past anything his parent ever envisioned, they remained boundless; he was incurably fixed in the posture of demanding without ever specifying his terms. The attitude of contempt stabbed into him by a thousand pinpricks had been reversed by the discovery of his own importance to "them," from himself onto society.

The first time Vincent Cheyney was presented with a clearly stated framework of a definite task to be paid for with a definite reward was by his secret employers. The payment was entry into a world of security, reputation and prosperity. The commitment was clear and the reward too; for the first time in his life he knew just where he was. If it occurred to Vincent that his reward was to be paid by the loot he was to plunder from those who trusted him, that was only an added inducement. As for the penalty of failure, that quite simply did not exist for him; he knew he was going to succeed.

It was neither time nor distance as they were driven the twenty-five miles; it was a transfer, a blank passage between waiting and action. Only as the big black car swung up and round the hill lane did an impatient murmur from his unwitting companion arouse Vincent from his formless thoughts. A prickling awareness woke him up. Here was the imminent challenge and here, too, the sight of his reward. He did not really see the ring of beech trees, the grove that gave the place its ancient name, for the car slid too quickly by as he was only just taking it all in. But there, with the reality of his dream, was the house. This he felt himself entering; this, he knew, was to be his.

Visited only once and then after dark, he had never seen the outward appearance of the house. It was not a great house, not even large, but Vincent had picked up enough by now to recognize it as infinitely desirable, of an absolute worth. It existed in its own right, owed nothing to chance, could never be diminished from its quiet, grey stone reality. A king might well envy it and yet it was modest enough to have been built by a queen's servant, a coachman retired from the service of the first Elizabeth with a staid competence to bequeath his heirs forever. A yeoman's house built when England was itself and untouched either by the inclusion of Celtic imagination or by the seduction of strange glamour from the far shores of exotic seas then only just being searched. Empire was undreamed of by its creators. Their sons might be marauders in distant lands, or, more likely, distant oceans, but they never thought of settlement. They thought of returning home with booty, to this granite, quiet house enclosed by its immemorial beeches.

The sight, if decision still needed confirmation, was enough. Impelled by a force that might have seemed sincere to much more discerning eyes than were on Vincent Cheyney, he left the car and was inside the door of the house almost as it stopped. There was no moment of question, no hesitation.

The vacuum of an immense loss was enfolded in his arms and he, who knew no foundations, assured a lonely and frightened child that he could and would replace her safety with his own solidity, that he would continue the broken certainty lost with her father, that in him she would recover love and loyalty to replace the past by the promise of the future.

There was never an instant of question. The little girl clung to him, her whole being dissolving in weeping grief, disbelief, terror. Kisses had been exchanged on several occasions before, light, flirtatious kisses suitable for a girl still in the schoolroom and rarely left alone. Kisses that could be explained with respectful smiles if interrupted. Jenny's embrace now was no more sensual than those little hints of Vincent's; it was a clutching prayer for rescue.

Her hands were tiny, her head narrow, her body lean and taut with the sports of school, yet she felt fragile in his arms, and the sensation that Jenny was breakable threatened Vincent's self-confidence with a fear of pitying her. This, combined with the physical impression of tempered delicacy, for her bones were fine-drawn, gave him a sharp desire for brutality that surprised him, for he had felt it before only when erotically challenged by an open, undisguised demand. He felt a warning in himself not to show this desire, for this untried virgin was not indicating her own desire to him as was usual when he felt that impulse to hard physical combat. She was clinging to him for support, not knowing that her need was for physical comfort. The knowledge of her ignorance filled Vincent with scorn because she betrayed herself to his experience without intending to, without knowing what she was saying to his body. And the instinctive scorn was mingled with a fear that he never felt before, fear that she might claim something from him that he did not have to give. He promised himself quite clearly that she should pay for this weakness discovered in himself as soon as the formalities were over and no going back was possible. For the moment he must restrain himself, and this unusual self-denial was added to the scores he would repay as soon as his will should be paramount. The need for control in a moment of desire aroused his quick resentment; he was unused to it for, like most vain men, he normally chose women who wanted him before he wanted

55

them. And they were not few. But he held Jenny in his arms now with an almost fierce passion which to Jenny was the promise of love and comfort and even seemed sincere to Eileen looking on, who felt a sharp, desirous envy.

The sight of them at this moment made a deep impression on Eileen Sandford that Vincent was really in love with Jenny and touched by her sorrow; that but for her bereavement and her youth he would have wasted no time in seducing her almost on the spot. She did not lose this impression and expressed it to her husband and their friends and colleagues, and this contributed greatly to the subsequent attitude of almost everyone who knew Vincent and Jenny.

There were the many wearisome tasks to be carried out that accompany sudden death, and the two of them did as much as they could. The house was in an extraordinary state of muddle, being in effect a bachelor establishment run by a housekeeper who was no professional but a woman doctor with neither training nor interest in her temporary occupation. Eileen and Vincent were both somewhat shocked at the confusion everywhere that bordered on the sordid. They were surprised, too, that Jenny seemed not to notice it and their surprise reached the point at which Eileen, at any rate, who did not share Vincent's need to be overly discreet, expressed it when they found the main drawing room with its furniture pushed to one end and in use as a studio for Jenny's first attempts at sculpture.

"Really, this woman should have cared a bit more for the place!" she expostulated to Jenny. "I know nothing much could be done about decorations in the last few years, but the place didn't have to be let go to this extent. Don't you realize, Jenny, how valuable this place is?"

"We had to stop restoring in about 1941, I think it was. Father meant to begin again, but then you couldn't get permission and of course, he would never do anything 'black.'"

This explanation was one often used to strangers admiring the house and was always accepted, but Eileen frowned and shook her head as if at an empty excuse. The idea of not using one's influence to its limit was not one that appealed to her feminine competence and decisiveness.

"He was longing to get on with restoring it," began Jenny

shakily, intimidated by Eileen's criticism, which she took to herself. But the thought of her father's love for the house brought back her loss in all its frightening pain and she began to weep again helplessly.

"It's all right, darling," Vincent hastily reassured her. "We'll take care of everything. Don't worry about anything, try not to think of it all."

He looked for aid over Jenny's head at Eileen.

"I shouldn't have said anything. There, Jen, don't cry darling." Eileen obligingly took the blame. "Come along, let's have some tea. Where's that weird housekeeper of yours?"

"Doctor Limmert isn't very good at tea," sobbed Jenny. "I'll get it, shall I?"

"Doctor!" cried Vincent. "A woman doctor! That explains everything." His contempt for emancipated women was audible in his voice, a mistake he took care not to make again aloud, for he knew what the dead Maculan would have thought of it. And there would be plenty of time to change all that. He was already planning his changes, and every fresh aspect of his future home stimulated his fancy anew. It was even more impressive, more full of dignity, than he had dreamed. It would reflect a prestige on him that would make him untouchable. The first thing was to get rid of this woman doctor, whom he recalled with dislike, back to her own country where she could not interfere, and he already felt the stir of a plan as to how she should be replaced by more controllable servants who would owe their security and prosperity entirely to himself.

Eileen herself went to make tea, leaving Vincent to cuddle Jenny and promise her every ease that devotion could provide.

"My little girl, you're still a child. Don't even try to cope with anything. Leave everything to me, that's all I want, to do everything for you." This and much more he said and was trustfully believed. The child's whole life had been passed with people whose concept of personal relationships was of a most delicate scrupulousness, her father out of the integrity of his nature and the nuns at school out of the restraints of religion. They may have been puritanical, her father may have been too intensely serious, but nobody had ever treated

57

her with anything but candour and affection; she accepted everyone with the trust of one who has never been lied to. To her father domestic concerns were secondary compared with the important considerations of the mind and the sensibilities.

There was no need for Vincent to suggest any urgency about their marriage. It was at once taken for granted, and an end to Jenny's solitude was so ardently desired by herself and so clearly indicated by her youth and defencelessness that any delay would have appeared cruel. And Maculan, incredibly, died intestate so that Jenny was not provided even with a guardian who might have intervened with talk of settlements, supervision, possible further education and the like. The only people who might have protested to some purpose were the two doctors, the Limmerts, but they were as stunned as Jenny by the loss of their friend. Moreover, their influence, for outsiders, was reduced to nothing by their apparently menial status in the household. They were, in fact, not even consulted.

The memorial services for Maculan were hardly over before a private wedding was agreed upon. Sandford and Folliot showed the benign and relieved assent of those who might otherwise have been saddled with responsibility for the orphan, though to do them justice neither of them thought of it consciously. It was the best solution and a great good fortune for Jenny in her misfortune that she had someone to turn to. The great good fortune of her future husband somehow diminished to vanishing point in the general approbation of Vincent's loving wish to protect and pamper her.

It was Eileen who arranged that clothing rationing should not prevent Jenny from having a new dress and coat for the occasion, of pale grey since they were all in mourning. It was Eileen, too, who arranged for the Limmerts to leave during the week the young couple would be away, and her choice was relied upon for the large hotel at Torquay, which was the most luxurious offered by the stringent times.

On a bitter cold morning a small group stood speaking quietly together in the silent and to them strange church, waiting for Mr. Folliot to arrive with Jenny. Vincent looked about him and shivered.

"You really need that coat in this barn," he said, indicating

Eileen's sumptuous summer ermines. "I'm freezing. What a place. We shall have to get her out of this habit."

Mrs. Folliot looked surprised and disapproving at this, and having once looked, frowned as if she considered something for the first time; she was, in fact, thinking of her own daughter, who was just Jenny's age. But whatever she thought, it passed.

"My dear boy, remember where you are," she reproved for form's sake, and strolled rather markedly away from the little group to inspect the Stations of the Cross. She felt for a moment an unease, but pushed it out of mind with the thought that the boy was young, he did not mean that rather coarse way of speaking.

"This sculptor Connors is very good," she remarked on her return from the carvings, which were recent works. "Poor Julius admired him a great deal. Jenny is fortunate to have so eminent a teacher."

Vincent heard of Jenny's having a teacher of sculpture for the first time, and he was not sure either what the Stations of the Cross were, so he made no reply. The sound of an arriving car was heard, interrupting their silence, the priest appeared and without preparation, it seemed, without ceremony, the service began. They all waited afterwards while Jenny took Communion; she was the only Catholic among them.

Jenny looked up into the priest's face and found no comfort there at being left alone for the sacrament; he disapproved of the mixed marriage. He was a fairly new priest here, the old man of her childhood was retired and she felt strange and abandoned when he admonished her not to allow her faith to be changed in the future.

The small party of witnesses and guests grumbled discreetly at being kept waiting in this frigid place; they were embarrassed by Jenny's belonging to the old confession although none of them except Mrs. Folliot felt much devotion to the rites of the Established Church. If they had known more they would have known how little difference there was; as it was they felt uncomfortable in more than one sense. The Limmerts embraced Jenny in silence and left in the small rattling car used for shopping to finish their packing and lock up the house. The rest of the group drove into town for luncheon.

The priest did not accompany them. The resemblance to the Memorial Mass held here as well as in London for Jenny's father was depressing, and all of them were silent and constrained. It was not a happy occasion and the weather made it less so. Everyone was glad when the execrable food and the excellent champagne were decently consumed so that the young people could be seen off in Vincent's car.

"I do believe she would have been married in that frightful macclesfield silk dress she had for school, if I hadn't got her something," said Eileen as they turned back into the hall of the country hotel.

"She does still seem such a child," agreed Mr. Folliot. He sounded worried as well as sad.

"I don't know," said Eileen, "I feel simply terrible." They could see that there were tears in her eyes.

"I feel a bit sorry for Vincent," said her husband slowly. "It's not a situation I would care to have to cope with. D'you think they'll be all right?"

"They are young," sighed Folliot. "The young forget quickly. They'll be as merry as grigs by tomorrow, I shouldn't wonder."

"Of course you're right," said Teddy Sandford. "I told the hotel people to put flowers and wine in their room, and there is dancing every evening too."

"Bridal suite," said Vincent proudly. "It's smashing, isn't it, Jenny?"

Jenny looked about her, surprised; she thought the extravagant and slightly worn finery of the rooms very ugly.

"It's a bit tarty," she agreed, borrowing a word from a girl thought of at the convent as "fast." She was pleased with the grown-up sound of this and giggled. They had been rather silent in the car and Jenny was so nervous that every time she stopped to think she felt a little sick. Vincent's face told her now that her reply was not the correct one and she stopped laughing. The worries of the journey returned; she knew what marriage was all about, on the one hand from the manner of the nuns when they spoke of certain aspects of "duty," and on the other hand from the girls. But she felt far from sure that she would know what to do or how to do it.

"Don't you like it?" asked Vincent, astonished.

"It's only that it's a tiny bit old-fashioned," she suggested, not knowing what he wanted her to say and perceiving that the view of it taught her by her father and Connors did not please him.

"Well, I hope you're not going to have arty modern notions," he said, laughing indulgently. And then with dismay, "Christ, darling, don't pull that face. You're supposed to be happy, remember?"

"But I am happy," she protested and began to cry.

He stared at her and for the first time the thought struck him that he was quite inexperienced with inexperienced girls. He always took a good deal of cooperation for granted, but he saw suddenly that he was in sole charge here and for a second felt panic which the lack of any desire for marriage turned into something like anger. Poor Vincent, he stared at the blindly weeping girl and then round the ridiculous white and gold room with its artificial silk draperies. His eye was arrested, fortunately for both of them, by a small black leather document case from a famous Jermyn Street shop that was one of the various gifts from his secret friends. It reminded him that his personal relationship with this girl was only a small part of the reasons for his presence here, and enabled him to put the difficulties of her youth and grief into a wider perspective, a more manageable structure of mental priorities. His view, both physical and emotional, of Jenny became sane and objective. He ceased to be intimidated by an aesthetic sense schooled by her eminent father, which for that reason was not easily to be opposed at the moment. And he recognised that her moods were part of a larger task and to be taken with the same neutral study as any other problem, such as gaining the trust of his colleagues or maintaining his unknown communications without causing remark.

"Come, sweetheart," he said, "go and powder your little nose and put on some perfume and we'll go and explore the bar. That will cheer you up."

He led her, still crying, but now as much with gratitude as with grief or nervousness, to the bathroom and shut the door firmly upon her.

It was a mistake to hold the wedding in that damned

61

church, he thought, the same place as the Memorial Service only a week or so ago. He did not know that any other would have been impossible, but the thought put the blame for Jenny's misery somewhere else and removed any suspicion that his own affection might be lacking and that Jenny might unknowingly feel this.

A quick drink from the tray standing there also helped, and in a few minutes Jenny reappeared with only slightly red eyes and a smooth, scented face. As they walked into the large and well-furnished bar he felt for the first time that Jenny added to his presence. She was not, he thought, pretty but she was clearly a little lady with beautiful manners. The prestige of Maculan was already noticeable in the demeanour of the manager, who met them in the hall and took them into the room to find them a table in spite of the overcrowding of every place of entertainment that was a symptom of the time.

Champagne was brought for dinner when they transferred to the dining room, and it followed champagne at luncheon and two champagne cocktails in the bar. The value of this wine, like the money unfortunately necessary to obtain it, would be hard to exaggerate. It lifts the spirits and imparts a deceptive lucidity to the wits as flattering as the sparkle it brings to the eyes. Above all it acts as a sly aphrodisiac, putting charm into the drinker's view and softness into his heart; not even desire eases defloration better than champagne with its happy dishonesty and its double effect of stimulus and relaxation. Jenny drank more in that day than in her whole life before and for some years after, and to good effect. She was too tipsy to take in anything that happened after that with more than a blurred and acquiescent lack of immediacy, which was just as well. For the wine that relaxed feminine nerves and muscles produced quite a different result in a man ten years her senior and a lifetime older in experience of a kind, on the whole, ill suited to the initiation of innocents.

Vincent was intoxicated by more than the wine. He was too much dominated by his own interests to let himself go completely in circumstances in which anything could afterwards be held against him, but he had occasionally experimented with a mild sadism. He found himself now in a situation in which nothing could be held against him, or even known except by one who lacked all means of comparison; whatever pleased him, she would not only accept because she knew nothing, but because she had been made pliantly trustful and dutiful by the dual influences of her upbringing. He discovered a lust that was not the excitement of one who pays a high fee in a brothel for the extra pleasure of spoiling a virgin, but was more like the incidental reward of female plunder given to a soldier who does his dangerous and difficult duty and earns the sack of a conquered fortress. The knowledge of having entered a lifelong relationship with a woman for whom he felt not the slightest kindness gave an edge of resentment to his sensations. The only thing Jenny offered him physically was something he did not know: an untouched body. And his continuing duty required that he should completely dominate this child given with all due form of law and custom into his grasp. He entered into this perfectly conscious undertaking with all the brutality of a strong young male who has been kept waiting, with the added pleasure of a covert dislike of the human being inside the flesh. Moreover, Jenny was for Vincent a symbol of the whole aim of his life, wealth and power that were not granted but needed to be taken and possessed; through her he could insult her father and assume his power, property and privileges.

The hotel, built in the last century, did not stint space and the suite booked for them was two large rooms, the bedroom being reached only through the sitting room; it was also a corner and faced outwards onto rocks and sea. These were the kind of details Vincent noticed; it was one of the talents needed for his career. He hung out the instructions to the staff not to disturb them and locked the outer door. The rattle of metal on the glass top of the table as he dropped the key startled Jenny and she looked back from the bathroom door. Something in his set face, perhaps the look in his brilliant blue eyes, frightened her, but she expected to be scared and the wine dimmed a perception that was soon quite drowned.

He used her with considerable violence and she was already unconscious before he fell into an exhausted sleep that lasted well into the following day.

The pattern of that night was repeated with slackening urgency throughout the days and nights of their absence from home, and by the time Vincent took up his life in Maculan's house with Jenny he was already bored with her and was concerned mainly to impress on her yielding mind the conviction that his steady loss of interest was caused by her own inadequacy. Which to some extent it was, for she did not discover any joy in physical lovemaking, nor did she learn to simulate a response to his masculinity. She was, unfortunately for both of them, the sort of woman who experiences desire only through love.

CHAPTER IV

THE DEATH of Julius Maculan not only removed a possible obstacle to Vincent's marriage to his daughter. It produced effects in the outside world. The company of Tantham and Maculan lost an asset which previously ensured them an advantage over all their rivals, for Maculan was not only an inventor of genius but also a counsellor to Ministers and administrators in many matters only indirectly concerned with his own business, and his membership on various reviewing boards, supply committees and the like reflected his personal prestige onto his colleagues. At his death he was, and he knew it if his associates did not yet, probably past his most fruitful years as an innovator, but this circumstance would not diminish the quality of his judgement or his immense experience, which could only grow with time. All his influence was now lost to his company, as well the products of his inventive genius as a possibly continuing series; his inventions were now a completed treasury. The accumulated riches of Maculan's own career became greater in value as they lost any hope of being added to. The absolute necessity of increasing their sales in the competitive markets of international business became in a moment the paramount concern of Tantham and Maculan if they were to maintain their position.

Within a year Vincent Cheyney was the centre of this urgent enterprise. He worked extremely hard, often at the utmost stretch of his vitality for months on end. And he was successful. He was pushed outward to new countries, new experience by virtue of being first in the field, while domestic sales, which were more assured, were left to new and junior employees. His enthusiasm and ambition, it was said of him with admiration and envy, were boundless. Maculan's company became a foremost earner of income for the country and for itself, and if specialists in the use of electronic engineering noticed from time to time that devices very like Maculan's work were being produced and used in countries which could not have obtained them legitimately, that was assumed to be part of that insecurity of secrets that stamped the 1950's as an era. There were many ways of perforating trade secrets, even those with high military potential, and Vincent was never even thought of as being one them. He himself, in fact, occasionally complained of leakages through the civil service and the military and this blame stuck the more easily because the number of espionage scandals in Western countries was a recurring event of the time.

There was only one occasion on which Vincent felt any conscious fear after the day of Maculan's death. This was some years later when he returned from a journey abroad to find a police detective in his office questioning a tearful and defensive typist. There was, naturally, nothing at all of a compromising nature in Vincent's office, nor did he normally undertake the work connected with his second career in England and never in his office at all. Still, it was a vertiginous moment, not only because the story as it came out was such a perfect example of just how matters could go wrong.

The typist was a girl with whom Vincent was planning an unserious affair and whom he had taken out already once or twice. He learned now that she was in fact engaged in an affair, a new and on her side highly emotional one, with the representative of a rival firm. This in itself was annoying but not more, for Vincent who was by then too grown into his acquired position to be much put out by a lapse of taste by a girl who could be replaced in either sense of her usefulness without difficulty.

However, on a visit to her lover she saw a snapshot of a woman prettier than herself propped against his shaving mirror, and the photograph was marked on the back with the legend, "Irene Tr. at the Wawel, *that day.*" The emphasis was clear enough, the girl was blind with jealousy and sent the photograph with an anonymous note, not to Scotland Yard where it might have done no harm, but to the State Buying Agency in Warsaw. Her friend was arrested on his next appearance for a further round of negotiations. A man foolish enough to keep the picture of one mistress exposed in his bedroom when another is expected is capable of any folly and this poor wretch had left his pocket diary about as well. Among addresses listed was that of the girl in Vincent's office. And there in Vincent's office was an officer of the County C.I.D., delegated by the Special Branch in London to deal with this local side of the story.

"Do you know how she met him, this Watson?" asked the policeman who seemed somewhat dubious about his brief. "I mean, it seems odd that she works for you and has an affair with another man in the same line of business."

"It isn't odd at all," said Vincent gloomily, grasping the nettle. "That's the idiotic thing about it. I took the stupid bitch with me to a party at the Polish Trade Mission in London. She was going to London and I gave her a lift and you know how these things happen, I suggested she should come along to this dreary bash, since I didn't have anybody to go with. My wife doesn't care for London. In other words, I introduced her to Watson. The things one does!"

"Hmm. And have you heard of this Irene Tr.?"

"Sure, she's an interpreter, at least it must be Irene Trilonska. At the Foreign Trade Ministry in Warsaw, not in London, I mean. She travels with trade representatives, or did. She must have gone with this chap Watson to Krakov, it's the usual outing there to go up to the old fortress. And there is an electronics factory being built outside Krakov and he may well have been having talks with the designers. I've been there myself twice. We all have. I suppose you know what I mean by 'we'? Unwise way of putting, I see that, in the present circumstances. But I only mean the foreign reps who go all the time to these ghastly countries and try to do business with the goons. We can't help having a fellow feeling, since we all suffer in the cause of exports. Even though we belong to different firms. I'm bosom friends with textile engineers, building materials specialists, paper processing technicians, and all sorts of others, not to mention chemical fertiliser men."

"You knew Watson well?"

"No. He's a new boy. I think I've met him twice including the cocktail."

"Do you think he was up to anything when he was arrested?"

"Of course not. It could happen to anyone. Any denunciation is acted on in these countries. There are thousands of people in prison in Poland alone who are no more guilty than you or me."

"Then you could be arrested any time on just such flimsy evidence?"

"Certainly, any time I expose myself. And who says evidence? From what you say there is no evidence. Simply denunciation by anonymous letter."

"Would you think this Irene Trilonska has been arrested too?"

"Shouldn't think so. I shall probably see her on my next visit. She reports to the police on all of us, that is taken for granted. Only this poor fool got involved with her and. . . . Oh, Lord, do you want me to tell you how these things are done in eastern Europe?"

"I suppose you would know," sighed the policeman.

"If I didn't have a pretty shrewd idea I shouldn't still be around."

"Well, tell me what you are guessing."

"Sure. But just a moment, if you don't mind." Vincent pressed the button to the outer office and a moment later a young woman entered, a bushy, dark girl in her late twenties, well grown and assured in manner. Vincent stared at her.

"Who are you?" he asked.

"I've been told to fill in for Miss Smith," she said smiling with no sign of nerves at his blunt tone. "She's gone home."

"And well she might," said Vincent. "Tell the Personnel Department that Smith is on no account to come into this part of the offices again, not on any pretext. And ask them to send over your papers. I'll check them myself, this time. Are the files locked in the outside office?"

"Yes, Mr. Cheyney," she said, still smiling as if humouring him.

"This is not a joke," he said angrily. "Bring me the keys and if I find anything unlocked when I come out you're fired without notice. Clear?"

The girl raised her eyebrows, unimpressed, and disappeared. Vincent also raised his eyebrows, drawing in a deep breath and looking meaningly at the policeman.

"Security," he pointed out. "They never learn."

The policeman hardly had time to shake his head sympathetically before the door opened again.

"Oh, Teddy, it's you. I just stopped myself in time from shouting at one more interruption. This is Mr.—"

"We've met," said Teddy Sandford, nodding. "Haven't seen you on the greens lately. This is a fine state of affairs, isn't it. You're looking into this end for London, I gather? Look, why don't we go along to the bar? You probably haven't seen our directors' room since we had it all done up? Oh, come on, of course you can, man. You're not that much on duty here, after all!"

The directors' room was bright and long, designed by a well-known interior decorator who specialised in expressing the go-ahead atmosphere of modern captains of industry. It looked out of wide windows over well-laid-out gardens and car parks with the nearest workshops in the middle distance. There was a long bar and a number of tables, all gleaming with scarlet and white paint, polished steel and glass, brightly coloured linen cloths. The works canteens were decorated in precisely the same fashion.

Sandford led the way and heaved himself awkwardly onto one of the high stools, his short, sturdy body, sandy head and round jaw making him look almost as if he wanted to appear clownish.

"What'll you have? This poor sod Watson rather seems to have had it, eh? Pink gin for me, Fred."

"Did you know him, then?"

"No. Vin did, didn't you, Vin?"

"A bit, yes. Look here." Vincent turned to the police officer. "I've been thinking. I'm sure Watson was not up to anything. His firm is very sound, you know. I know they stick strictly to civil uses of their stuff, not to mention the Strategic Embargo List."

"But if Watson was up to anything for us, you would know, wouldn't you?" asked Sandford, taking a first swallow of his drink. "And if he's working for the Poles they wouldn't have arrested him."

"There's nothing as definite as that, Mr. Sandford. This is just a routine enquiry, you know, because of the Smith girl."

"Oh, yes. I want to talk to you about that, Teddy, afterwards. The way we take on staff is horribly slack, when you think of all the stuff there is lying about in my office, for instance. But, excuse me, I'm interrupting."

"Not at all," said the visitor. "You are quite right about the need to inspect staff. But what I was going to say . . . There is nothing at all definite. We just have to know what happened, you know. You see, how shall I put it? The things you sell have their military side, as I don't have to tell you. And it's an odd thing, but when something like this happens, it is sometimes because there is some little complication, something not known by everybody concerned, so there is just that extra little chance of a balls-up, if you see what I mean."

"You mean, the Poles were interested in Watson's stuff to use for some purpose other than the—er, licit one?"

"Or somebody else?"

"You mean, somebody else *through* the Poles?"

"Well, something of that sort. Some cross-up the Polish police might not have known about, so that this anonymous letter was just the tip-off, and they got hold of the end of a stick that really was a stick and not—what would you say. . . ?"

"Not a swizzle stick, eh?" said Sandford and they all laughed.

"I got through that drink a bit fast," commented Vincent, looking at his empty glass. "Set them up again, Fred, will you."

He watched the barman's competent movements, pushing his lips out and then pulling his mouth down, considering.

"Oh, no. Too elaborate. What happened is this chap was just hopelessly simple. Didn't know what he was doing. Probably changed money in the street or some such lark. Probably nothing more than that. Or he talked to this Irene about freedom, Polish tradition, love and glory sort of stuff. People do when they're new to the game, and I've noticed often that for some reason everyone who doesn't know one end from the other has a romantic feeling for the Poles."

"But not you, Vin, eh?"

"Well, that's no secret. I've said it before and I've no doubt I shall say it again. I'm not sure, however much we need the export trade, that we ought to deal with these Eastern countries at all. Yes, I know, Teddy, I know. But I'm not sure sometimes that things don't land in places quite different from the ones we think we send them to. But anyway, poor

Watson has tipped us off to be a bit more careful here. It's a lesson I shan't forget."

"I think I'd better have a look round your staff office, if I may?"

"Of course. Anything you want," agreed Sandford. "Well, Fred, was there any news on the noon broadcast? Did you listen?" Teddy turned to the policeman. "Fred's our main source of news here, you know."

"Yes, there was, Mr. Sandford, sir. That Stalin's dead, so they say."

"Stalin?" said Vincent, thunderstruck. "Good God!"

"Don't know that it's much to do with God, Mr. Cheyney. They are all atheists, that lot, aren't they?"

"I must go and check," said Vincent.

"Oh, no hurry, Vin. It's not that important."

His two companions looked at Vincent, surprised at his interest. The barman was moving away. For a dizzy moment the bar seemed to shift and sway under Vincent's eyes and then he managed to shake his head.

"Of course, you don't know what the name of Stalin means in East Europe," he said.

"You know these places, Mr. Cheyney. What do you think will happen to Watson?"

"Watson. Oh, they'll hang him or he'll get life, I should think. I take it the charge is espionage?"

"Oh, yes. Our consul reports that the trial is scheduled in four weeks. Apparently that means they have any evidence they want."

"Then he hasn't got a hope. Not the slightest chance."

"Poor devil," said Teddy Sandford.

"Yes," agreed Vincent, ruefully, as if he were thinking of his own chances. "What those beginners never understand is that these boys are playing for *keeps*, as the Yanks say."

"Ah," said the policeman, "and that's a fact. Well, thank you both, gentlemen, I must be on my way. If I hear anything, I'll let you know."

"Yes, do that, won't you," they said.

"I won't lunch properly. I'll have a sandwich here and get back to the office," said Vincent. He was beginning to feel that if he could not be alone for a few minutes his nerve would go.

When he reached his own room, his wish was granted, the

new typist was at lunch. Her papers lay on his tray. She had arrived in the office two months ago, from a Naval Department at Bath, which meant she had at some time been through the machinery of "security." Her name was Laver. When he heard her moving about in the next room, Vincent called her in.

"Your qualifications seem to be quite good, Miss Laver."

"Oh, please," she said, "Mona."

"Not too fast. Why did you come to us?"

"I wanted a job where I could get on." She looked straight at him, her eyes well open, smiling very slightly. "And I like to have one boss. Something I can take an interest in."

"Did somebody recommend you to us?"

"No, you were advertising for a typist. I was sure I should get a chance once I was in the firm. You will find my work in order." She was still looking directly at Vincent, perfectly sure of herself.

"Have you made friends among the other girls?"

"Not really. I don't go much for girls. They talk too much."

"Then it's no use asking them for an opinion?" Vincent smiled too now, struck by her almost impudent assurance.

"You seem to me the sort of man who makes up his own mind." She leaned over the desk a little, to pick up her file. "Can I return this now? If you are wondering, I heard this morning in the staff office that Smith was going to be sacked. It was just what I was waiting for, and I made sure I got it."

"I wonder how you did that?" He knew perfectly well that she was saying she wanted to come into his office and no other; he even knew why she wanted that.

"I'll tell you when I know you better."

She did not sound coy, but was quite serious.

"Well, let us see what you can do," he said. "Draft a memorandum to answer this one from Personnel. To go to Mr. Folliot and Mr. Sandford. Say, in my name, that with the greatest respect I can't agree to the proposition of our using one of these private enquiry firms that screen staff. It would mean our affairs would be footballed around a large organisation—a small firm would be useless—full of half-wits and unstable temporary staff like the unlamented Miss Smith. I suggest a better system would be for us to just be a hell of a lot

72

more choosy in future when taking people on. I shall be clearing off soon, for today. Let me have a draft in the morning. Are there many letters?"

"No, Mr. Cheyney," she said softly, her eyes straight on his. "Nothing that won't wait until tomorrow. I'll have today's work completely cleared before the post comes in tomorrow."

"Good," he said coolly. "I'll see you then."

Miss Laver had made Vincent feel a good deal better, but he was still shaken. He drove home very slowly, going over and over the conversation of that morning and trying to gauge the effect of his words and manner on a complete stranger. The effect was, in fact, just what he wished it to be: somewhat detached, vague, regretful but scornful. The report from the county police to London was only one of a considerable dossier; it disposed of one angle of the matter in question and that was all. Miss Smith was required to go to London and the officer in charge of the enquiry interrogated her himself, but the incidental details and persons appeared to have been dealt with sufficiently by the local police. There was one further small result, but Vincent heard nothing of that. When the consular report of Watson's trial reached London it was noticed with slight puzzlement that among all the phantasmagoria of "evidence" against poor Watson, which included almost every person he spoke to during his visits to Warsaw, one name was missing and that was his colleague from Tantham and Maculan. But on further enquiry the local man pointed out that the company for which Miss Smith formerly worked was itself engaged in commercial negotiations in Warsaw and it was unlikely that the Ministry of Foreign Trade would want to jeopardise those discussions by dragging their representative into an espionage affair. This was sensible, and moreover Sandford let the authorities know a little later that his firm was dropping the Polish project, since they did not wish to profit from the misfortune of their rival, who received a life sentence on evidence that was hardly sound enough to be called a frame-up, let alone a case.

A few weeks later Vincent was made a Director of his company and by that time Miss Laver was indispensable to him.

CHAPTER V

"As a matter of fact," Vincent said, conceding a point no longer to be denied. "Jenny can be very devious, you know."

The person referred to was at this moment entering the room, but neither her husband nor the woman he spoke to seemed to find his overheard comment remarkable. They both turned their heads a little and nodded at Jenny as they might have done if a child or a pet was there while they were speaking of adult affairs, and not a woman only a few years their junior. The lesser status was, as it were, agreed and permanent for all three of them.

"I should pay the bill, then?" asked Mona and made a shorthand sign on the "account rendered" they had now reached in their routine scrutiny of household bills. "If you'll sign another cheque?"

"Well, of course it has to be paid. It's already a second reminder." Vincent paused and then said with care to Jenny, "I suppose it isn't much good saying this again, darling, but I do wish you'd tell me when you run up bills."

"I think, I think I probably forgot, I'm afraid," said Jenny trying to see the bill in question. But being a reminder, the goods she must have ordered were not stated on the bill, and Mona's hand was resting on the supplier's name on the paper heading.

"I expect you did," he said patiently. He wrote his signature on a cheque in his book, keeping his middle finger in the stubs side to mark those already dealt with.

"Here's the garage bill. There seem to be rather a lot of repairs to the Rover." Mona was now looking at the next sheet in her bundle and adding the items in her head while her pen travelled down the list.

74

"That goes to the company account," said Vincent. "Have we finished with the household bills?"

Mona turned over papers and as she did so the heading of Jenny's bill was exposed to view.

"Oh, that bill," said Jenny. "I remember that. It was for sculpture supplies, you know. I think I did say at the time. I mean, I needed some more . . . one can't order less . . . they won't send less." She leaned over and read the total. "I suppose it does rather add up. But it's for several months."

"So I should hope. That's a pretty expensive little hobby of yours."

"Well, Vincent, everyone agrees that Jenny needs something to do and that's what she likes to do." Mona was briskly helpful.

"It's only eight pounds odd," said Jenny miserably. "The cocktail party last month must have cost a lot more than that."

"Cocktails are business," he explained. "I've told you that a hundred times if I've said it once. If only you could understand how much this place costs to run." He considered again what he was saying and this was evidently a settled habit of their conversations. "Of course you must have what you need for your sculpting. That's not the point. The point is, you don't tell me things. You just order up this stuff without consulting anybody so that we don't know what we're spending, don't you see?"

"Is that what you meant by being devious just now?" Jenny asked. "But I'm afraid I just forgot it. I mean, I thought I had mentioned it."

"You thought, you thought," he smiled indulgently. "I believe you think money grows on trees. It's your upbringing, I suppose."

"Lucky Jenny," said Mona. "She's never had to worry about money."

As if to demonstrate that she could be devious as Vincent said, Jenny changed the subject, looking at Mona's hand holding the papers.

"I wish I had fingernails like yours, always so beautifully long and shaped." She did not mean the compliment, but said it to please the secretary. She disliked the long, curved nails and still more their red enamel, but envied them because they seemed worldly. "Don't you ever break one?"

"Hardly ever," said Mona, glancing complacently at her hand as she turned it to display the nails. "I have to do something pretty clumsy to do that, they are hard." She flicked her thumbnail against that of her middle finger with a sharp little sound that made Jenny grit her teeth.

"And you don't do clumsy things ever. You're so competent." Jenny sighed.

Vincent looked up quickly, although his wife's face showed no sign of having meant any more than she said, but there was something shameful about the way she tried to placate Mona by flattery. He laughed slightly, angrily, in spite of his self-control, at her cowardice, or childishness. He hardly knew which it was.

"Let's get this finished," he interrupted.

Rebuked, Jenny left the room, and seeing Mrs. Foster through the half-open door at the far side of the hall that led to the kitchen, she slipped quickly into the hall cloakroom. It was cold in there, the window was always slightly open. With a familiar sensation of ridiculous nervousness, Jenny saw that she had once more put herself into a corner, literally this time. So she pulled an old tweed coat off its peg and hastily bundled herself into it, pulling the hood up over her head. Just in time she saw that her shoes were wrong and pushed her feet into a pair of walking shoes, worn into shapeless comfort by being put on with the laces tied. The mud from days past was still clinging to the heels. As always when she fled, her nervousness took on the nature of panic without cause. It was all quite unnecessary, because Mrs. Foster was not visible as Jenny slipped out to the massive old door and carefully opened it so as to make no telltale creak. Outside she walked quickly away towards the grove in the direction that would avoid her passing in front of the window behind which her husband sat at his monthly task. For a few moments the presence of the tall trees of the grove made itself comfortingly felt. Then Jenny relived with dreadful clearness the exact tone of her voice speaking to Mona: "devious," dishonest, pretending to admire her. A shock of disgust and shame went over her and she shuddered at her own obviousness. How they must laugh at me, she thought, and walked even faster. She knew from reading that it was part of her own neurosis, the disgust with which everything about Mona's person filled her. Mona was a normal woman and she, Jenny, was not, so her dislike of Mona was the measure of her own inadequacy.

But in the absolute privacy of her own thoughts she allowed herself to indulge her real feeling, that Mona gave off an almost palpable sensuality like an odour, she exuded a libidinous effluent, as animals are said to do for each other. Jenny knew perfectly well with her reason that her apprehension of Mona as blatantly and lustfully sordid was simply a reversal of her own envy; she secretly wished she were like Mona, and her conscious disgust was the disguise. Jenny knew this from a book given her by Vincent that explained about psychology in a way that untrained people could understand. It was a useful book, and gave answers to all kinds of puzzles. That was some years ago, before Vincent stopped trying to get Jenny to grow up and shake off the baleful influence of her Catholic childhood. It was not Vincent's fault that Jenny did not grow up; it was Jenny's, and that was proved by the time when she was "ill." The thought of that time, only a year back or a little more, made Jenny switch her thoughts. It was unwise to allow herself to think about those things, even to indulge her dislike of Mona because of the danger of inviting a return of that time. The passive calm of the late winter landscape, now that she was through the grove and out on the open hill, offered an alternative and painless reality.

Jenny stopped by an isolated row of old hawthorn trees that once must have marked some now forgotten boundary. The spiny limbs of the bare trees were bent forever towards where she stood, grown over in a repeating sweep by the wind from the sea that cut over here through a gap in the hills. On the bare twigs she could see the tight, shiny promise of a future in the dark leaf rolls, a reddish darkness very secretive. On a low tangle of blackthorn half-covered with sere grasses there were tiny white stars of blossoms just coming out where the tussocky grass sheltered the black pins. The grass piped thinly with a dry whistle if Jenny leaned close enough, and the marbled leaves of a celandine showed a tiny strip of yellow bud. She stood quite still, staring at the hawthorns for a long time and feeling their patient shaping from the wind, the creaking stiffness when they moved in the weather. Perhaps one could catch that patient, still livingness, communicate it in stone, or wood? Wood, perhaps. . . . It was there, of course, in its reality, so why recapitulate it in another form? To communicate it to others, but what others, even if she could make a coherent statement of form. Once she had known with an absolute inner certainty that she could. But that was the sureness of unknowing, of inexperience. And known, too, that she could create forms with their own validity, a different reality from usefulness. That was a saying of her father's, whose creativeness was attuned to usefulness, that not everything must be of use. Indeed, many of his own inventions were used for death, a fact obscured during her childhood by contingencies of war and threat, but later admitted by him with his characteristic frankness. The kind of reality her father and Connors talked of and understood was clouded over lately, and Jenny was not sure any more if it existed; or, rather, whether it existed as a possible achievement of her own. In recent years utility was the only criterion admitted, and art—a word neither of her mentors had ever used—was a matter of decoration or prestige. Her father and the great sculptor understood each other and included her in their community; it occurred to Jenny fleetingly that cutting off her apprenticeship to Connors might have added to her instability; certainly, Vincent's later acquiesence in her sculpture as a hobby perhaps meant that he, too, recognized it was a kind of therapy. Useful, in fact. That was rather funny. It brought the idea of utility into a circle through what was not of any use.

Jenny cut off the thought that this was funny rather abruptly. It was a sign of her own immaturity of mind. Disloyal, too. She was always having to reject such disloyal thoughts, which came into her mind in spite of her true knowledge of Vincent's kindness to her, his patience. He would be hurt if he knew; sometimes she feared that this stranger in her nature which doubted and questioned might appear like a face at a window in her eyes so that he would know there was still a part of her that was not quite cured. That was why she did not look at people directly. It might be dangerous.

Without thinking, she was now back in the tall grove of

beeches and in their wintry dignity of nakedness, visible from the windows of the side room, as the living room was called.

And naturally her figure was not only visible but seen.

"She's a poor little soul, really," said Mona inside the room. "She ought to have more to do. Always mooching about like that with her hands in her pockets."

Her companion glanced sharply at her, with an almost flinching look of distress, which became in a second a kind of anger.

"We're lucky it's no worse," he said, offering Mona a sense of resignation that needed comforting. She turned her well-tended head and smiled.

"We'll get off tomorrow for a day or so and you can relax. It was a good idea to take a little roundabout instead of going straight to London. I'll be ready if you can get over about nine to pick me up."

"You have all the papers?" He was always careful about preparations, and the projected meeting with a customer from abroad was important.

"Of course," she reassured him. "You know I don't forget things like that." Vincent was generous and thoughtful and if the strain of the situation was often as much as Mona could carry, it was worth it and she had long ceased to want the impossible. For him it was a great deal worse; he had to live with it all the time and that accounted for his fitful irritability. She knew that the state of his wife's health—that was the agreed euphemism—was a constant weight. Sometimes she felt that it was on his conscience, as well as a worry to him, and although he did not need to feel guilt, Mona knew too much about human nature to expect Vincent to be rational about his marriage. That would be asking too much; the only way to cope with it and him was to ignore both the actual situation and his obscure feelings about it, as far as possible. Things were much better than they used to be, she reminded herself, in more ways than one.

The household affairs were finished and Mona looked at her watch. Four. She must leave.

"I won't wait for tea," she said, meaning a reminder of their system by which formality ruled inside the house. That rule was the reason for Mona trying to arrange her monthly visit to check the bills when Vincent was not there; it removed both a temptation and any danger of the Fosters noticing anything.

Mrs. Foster came in at that moment with the tea tray so that Mona was obliged to repeat the remark about tea.

"So kind of you, dear Mrs. F.," she said cheerfully. "But I really must get off in my little bug or I shall never get home."

Mrs. Foster rattled the cups, placing them neatly. "Just one cup, Miss Laver. That won't take a moment now, will it!"

Even the way they didn't look at each other gives them away, she thought privately to herself. Who do they think they're fooling. Mrs. Foster knew the answer to her own silent question very well, but she felt annoyance just the same.

"What a set," she said to Foster in the security of their own room. "One half barmy and the other a sight too clever."

Foster looked up from the evening paper.

"Not clever enough to get what she wants though, is she," he remarked with satisfaction. They neither of them liked Miss Laver, which gave them an unadmitted sympathy with Mrs. Cheyney, daft though she might be. At least she never went round looking at the henhouse or in the store cupboards.

Since she could not leave the tea in her cup to affront the housekeeper, Mona drank it, standing, at one draught. She consulted her watch again and put out a hand to the thin leather case where Vincent kept business papers for journeys.

"You checked that you've got everything?" she asked. "Shall I make sure?"

"I have checked," he answered sharply, watching her hand as she removed it. Mona picked up her bulging handbag, taking no notice of his irritable tone.

"I'll be off then. See you in the morning." At the door she turned and smiled. "Take it easy," she said and disappeared.

He stared moodily after her until the house door closed and then went to the side window to watch her get into her little car, or rather his little car, he reminded himself, and manoeuvre it in the round gravelled space in front of the entrance. Not until the car disappeared down the yellow drive, making the familiar rushing sound, almost like water, over the stones, did Vincent turn away from the window. Then he straightened his shoulders with a movement like a shrug and picked up his document case, his thumb automatically making its habitual movement against the hasp of the lock to be sure it was fastened. He wasa very meticulous and methodical man. He looked round the familiar room once; everything had been properly put away. Holding the case, Vincent went out and upstairs to his dressing room, where he locked the case as always into the old cupboard in the panelling. Apart from the blue enamelled cash box at the back of the shelf, the space was empty. The lock of the cash box did not need to be tested, for only Vincent knew the numerical opening device. The key to the old cupboard, a safety key he had ordered himself, was on his key ring. Considerable experience had made Vincent careful of such things. There had been times in the not too distant past and there could well be again in the future, when it was impossible to be sure of anything. Better safe than sorry, even if one was bound to be sorry, too. It was a sad business, but it could not be helped. There were moments that would never leave his memory and those could not, dare not, ever be repeated. He had come this far on an unavoidable course, for which so much had been sacrificed that it was now infinitely precious, and he would continue on it. Although the very possibility of changing course never entered Vincent's mind, he was still conscious of the purpose and of his holding to it. What started in ambition, determination to have everything that his origins and childhood seemed to deny him and after all had been won by him, was long since an obsession. Not only prosperity, stability and dignity but a kind of power too, the satisfaction of an innermost longing buried in his very nature that was worth anything he or anyone could possibly pay. And the higher the price the greater was the value of what it bought.

Vincent did not think of these things, they were there without thought in his mind. He pressed the ball of his hand against the now locked cupboard door, just at the height of his shoulder, and it replied with the quiet creak that was always so reassuring from the indestructible oak of the panel.

The room was small so that he could see out of the window from where he stood. The foreshortened small figure of his wife in the coat much too big for her moved across his vision as she went towards the wide door of the unused stable, in the loft where her studio had been established for years now. The slight figure was unwelcome in spite of his wanting, needing, to see it. There was a loneliness there that he could never approach, that would and must remain inviolate; but through his acceptance of a total commitment, Vincent sensed the broken glass of suffering that grated its sharp edges in the very centre of being, never admitted but never absent when the price was demanded. Always before a journey, that moment and its perception were present. In the past, journeys had proved the springs of crisis, and who knew whether that spring was really now broken.

He would be glad to go away again tomorrow, to wallow for a night or two in the uncomplicated sensuality of Mona's coarseness. The relief of her really rather gutter nature was essential to him. Lucky that he could get away this week, with that sickening anniversary party threatened for only a few days ahead. What possessed the Sandfords to suggest it, he wondered, but they were always celebrating their own birthdays, anniversaries, so it would be impossible not to agree that his own tenth wedding anniversary was an occasion to be recorded. Sentimental, insincere rubbish. But in the meantime, Mona, whose concept of life was so added up, calculable, practical, so much everything he otherwise lacked. She was absolutely what he needed in his inescapable and accepted situation. Including her ignorance. Ignorance of what his life was and ignorance, too, of any subtlety and insight except that two and two makes four. Four in hard currency, he thought cynically, and turned to go downstairs.

PART TWO

CHAPTER VI

FROM THIS window there was nothing much to be seen of the outside world: there was the grass of the lawn, then the tall beech trees or rather their trunks, the grey of battleships or of elephants, that ringed the whole garden. Not even a pathway that might lead to somewhere else. There were paths, but you did not see them from here; here only the brilliant green of grass always damp, scattered with the tawny leaves that formed a floor under the bare trees farther out. Little grows under beech trees, there was no undergrowth to diffuse the stern cathedral pillars of their trunks rearing up to the bare branches, all starting out at the same high level, each forming a repetition of the radial pattern and together a ring of rings. In winter, that was, when no sentimental prettiness of foliage obscured the pure lines and there was no Solomon's-seal, no patches of bluebells, none of that meagre, low-growing pale weed—herb, was it?—the name for the moment escaped her. Then, the whole expanse looked like the prints in various watery aspects on the wall of the elderly ladies' tea shop in the town. Later still the grove darkened, returned to its real self of withdrawn secrecy as the leafage matured, shadowing everything underneath it and slowly turning to a deep, brilliant rufous brown. The sound changed too, from fluttery, bird-calling swishing to autumn rustling and the rattling of rain on dry leaves before they slowly fell from the branches and settled into the carpet. At this time of year the ground note of sighing, almost moaning, that never stopped for more than an hour or so was the only sound, and that could be heard here inside the house all the year, whether it was overlaid by other, seasonal music outside or not. The hill on which the surround of beech trees enclosed the house was prominent enough to have its own winds; it was the highest hill hereabouts, and was locally called The Hill. All around, from here invisible, rolled cultivated moorland, but within the ring of trees you only knew that the countryside was there, it did not form a part of what you were conscious of; that was circumscribed by the grove. Inside the grove, the house and between the two, only a somewhat uneven, not closely cropped grass patch on this side that could not properly be called a lawn; farther left there was a sweet chestnut of quite different form and colour, and still farther some fruit trees yet more alien to the beeches, where the garden was firmly fostered in man-made bounds of growth. The beech grove and the grass ring within it had been there before history, and the house, familiar and old as it was, was merely a late superimposition. And you could feel sometimes, in winter, that the house was only tolerated there, allowed to be there. If it fell back into the almost ruinous disrepair of a generation ago before it was rescued, that would essentially change nothing except for herself.

The house was very old as houses go, even in that part of England where not much changes from one lifetime to the next, but built as it was by a pensioned servant of the first Elizabeth it was still only a child's toy built of grey stone blocks compared with the grove, the first seedlings for which must have been planted—or found?—in the Celtic haze of unrecorded time. Tenaciously, new beeches had seeded and old ones toppled or slowly faded away, so that the aspect of the trees on the hill remained just the same. The hill was Beech Grove Hill and the house, Grove House; her father left the names unchanged, as he left whatever else was possible to leave as it was in and about the house, when he bought it at a moment when nobody thought of buying such an image of permanence. The price of the entire hill was then a sum that would, at the moment she stood there, hardly pay for the house itself; her father bought it as a great gesture of choice, as a vow that this would all survive, in the late autumn of 1939. It was an affirmation for him then of passionate love for England, of deliberate choice, of a devotion to something glimpsed that could hardly be understood by a native. Coming as he did from a far place and carrying a strange name, he chose to be there, to stay there. England had not then adopted him; he had adopted England. Not for want of an alternative. He could have gone back home and worked for the enemies of these people; or he could have gone farther, to American safety, since the division of his family, once enforced, could hardly have been made worse by the added distance of the Atlantic.

Often he talked, as she grew older, of the feeling he was captivated by at that moment of decision. That feeling of the mass of the mainland from the far side of which he had come, where distance measured by water was related only to the great river and its outflow into a still enclosed sea dominated by enemies. From the far side he—they—had come to England, but it was by a long way not the far side. Only in the sense of Europe, that vague, sadly ineffectual but living concept was his homeland the last stop. The land mass itself went on and on past the landlocked sea, past crags and mountain ranges, past open spaces so great that the horizon was not an idea but was actually to be seen, and so level that it could be seen disappearing. The mainland rolled off round the world to its other side. It was here, a short jump from the Atlantic, that one was and could feel oneself to be, on the last outpost of Europe and of the civilised world. Here, jutting out into the sea, threatened from the land mass. Threatened by extremes of passion, hatred, anger, savage conflicts of power that took no count of human beings and were only words to people here. The people here, a phrase he often used, were in a state of happy ignorance inconceivable to himself at first; he thought it an affectation in the face of danger. But it was no affectation. They really believed in their safety, that they could never be subdued even if attacked; and attack itself as a physical onslaught was just a notion to them. Children, they were; he felt himself immeasurably older and experienced in ways they could not evaluate and he could not tell them of.

They had tried to help him in a way so generous that at first he did not believe it was genuinely meant. In the midst of their own perplexities—which, to be candid, were not so terrible to them as they were to him, for they did not believe them to be real somehow—they had taken thought for his personal dilemma. That he never forgot. That no other kind of people would ever have done. So he believed and to his own experience so it was. They offered to send him home, and as they said in their odd slang, "technically" his country was not occupied, so that "theoretically" his return was easily possible. The terms technically and theoretically always meant what they did not believe in. The word "theoretical" had not before been used as one of comical abuse in his various languages; it conveyed respectful attention before that to him, and it was years before he could use the word to mean what does not actually exist, is not to be taken seriously, as they did; he spoke it in inverted commas and its use in the English sense remained a private joke for him to the end of his life.

What was real for him at that time and was never lost again was the sense of the isolation of England. These childlike unbelievers in the horrors of the world filled him both with gratitude and a sense that he must take care of them. He knew all too well what they did not and could not know. Useless to explain, the voice rising to shrillness, the vocables becoming wilder; the only possible thing was to do anything that lay in his power to help them in what was to them still some immensely dangerous but exciting game, although they conceived of themselves as serious, just as children do. It was perfectly clear to him that their allies and friends were going to fall like clay pigeons shot on a range; that they were going to be stuck here on their Island all alone, having challenged the best-organised and most finely precise machine of conquest in the history of the world.

And as things turned out, he was right, for it took the entire world, apart from two beautifully coordinated military complexes, to destroy that machine, and even then it took five years of—afterwards—unimaginable effort.

From inside the ring of beeches the sea was not visible by several miles of rolling country, but it was there. Her father had never lost the sense of the sea, which was to him of an absolute foreignness, much stranger than the newly learned language. That language was only for him the fifth in a series, two vernaculars and two languages of culture, in which he could think and move his mind easily. But he felt the great open seas, the possibility of going out upon them forever, of being not shut in by them, but of loosening, of shaking off, of escaping spiritually rather than of being intimidated by their beautiful, savage, endlessly changing and never-changing indifference. This feeling is contained, he decided, for of course he formulated his ideas about the sea in the tides. The tides pulling outward and drawing in, endlessly renewing, endlessly the same, wandering the world, carried England for him, like a splendid, perhaps absurdly splendid, old and magnificent ship. For him the Island was not anchored, was hardly land as the mainland was land and was landbound. Nothing in the world of words gave him so much pleasure and understanding as the English phrase "the Ship of State," an image of a high and ponderous galleon bearing royal arms, balancing, surviving in a wilderness of waters. He, as terrified, seasick and unhandy a landlubber as ever confided his life to a gnarled, crazy old sea dog, was privileged to sail in her on a voyage of life and death and he never lost for an instant the sense of the romance of that voyage.

With delight he discovered the quotation of Kipling and used it many times during her childhood until she quite believed it must be, if not from the Bible, then at least from Shakespeare: "And what should they know of England who only England know?" And although she herself came here as a baby to stay for her lifetime, she, too, knew England as only those who have seen other lands can know the Island. She knew it as quite a different country from any other through her father's eyes. She knew it, too, as by no means the ideal kingdom it never ceased to be for him. He could to the end of his life read *King Henry V* without the slightest intimation of irony, and read it aloud, too. Having been at school in England, she could never do that.

Ah, if only that aeroplane had never fallen out of the sky, if only he could have been here now. With her father in the background, her life with Vincent must have been entirely different.

She was still standing at the window, still staring out at the grass and the ring of trees, which were losing colour now as the long dusk drew in. She had stood here just the same ten years ago, with the news of her father's death in the air trembling slightly in her hand, as she stood here now at the fresh blow. But now she was totally and irrevocably alone.

There was nobody to turn to. There was not even the actual scrap of paper in her hand to give her evidence of it. Words in an unknown voice on the telephone, apologising, commiserating, were as unreal as the fact. In fiction, and as Jenny understood up to now, in real life such news was brought either by telegram or by a policeman on a bicycle. Well, her father's death came, as it were, correctly by telegram; Vincent's, without evidence, unofficially, by the disembodied voice of a stranger who was, it appeared, not sure of his identity. Was she Mrs. Vincent Cheyney and was her husband just then motoring on such a road and did he drive a Rover, and so on. Even as the voice proceeded, breaking into its series of questions with constant reiterations of apology, someone else interrupted at that unknown end of the line to explain that they now had Vincent's wallet.

Jenny was practiced at covering the recurring fact of not being quite sure where Vincent was, or what he was doing, and evidently it passed without notice that she didn't know on this particular, and as it turned out fateful, day that he was really motoring on such a road. In fact, if the truth were told—but she did not mention this—she was under the impression that Vincent had been at the factory today only twenty-five miles away. But no, he was between Chester and Wrexham, apparently, when the truck hit the Rover head-on. Only the fact of putting Chester first gave the impression that he must have been driving south; perhaps back through Bristol. But from where? It was definitely in her mind that his three-day absence on this occasion was because he was meeting a customer from abroad in London and would return to bring the results of his meeting to his fellow-directors at the main factory, coming on westward and home, tomorrow. Westward, where Jenny stood looking out of the window, was where her father a generation before had set up the original factory; the testing shop, as it was still called.

It was quite in the general nature of her life that Vincent's sudden death should be so very tenuous a piece of news. Quite possibly she was mistaken as to where he had said he would be, coming from whence and going where; he was always having to put her right. Somebody would be coming up from the testing shop outside the town to tell her properly, and would

90

be covertly astonished that she knew something already. Perhaps she ought to go out and speak to Mrs. Foster or find Foster in the garden and tell him. But better wait until she was told a second time, just in case it was all a mistake in some way. There was a period when she was always making mistakes. That was after her protest about Vincent's secretary, when it was firmly lodged in her mind that Mona was a good deal more than a secretary to Vincent. The scene when she made this accusation heralded a bad time; it was still not at all clear what was wrong with her then. For months after that, almost a year, she was constantly making those silly mistakes.

Once Vincent was going to Warsaw about a contract for spare parts and she was so certain he had said he was going to Prague that she told everybody who asked. This led to complicated misunderstandings and arguments, for she was—at the time—perfectly sure Vincent himself had told her that Prague was his destination. And when Vincent came back and the mistake was cleared up, he asked her why she had told this silly story. "But you said so yourself, that you were going to Prague. You even had a ticket on Czech Airlines, I saw it," she wailed, almost in tears. That must have been an old ticket, he assured her gently, one with a credit outstanding on it so that it needed to be kept until it could be used up. He explained how that sometimes happened with people who travelled a great deal; this confused her still further, for even a quite easy procedure like that was beyond her at the time. Because she recalled clearly seeing the ticket—and it was a new one—with the morrow's date filled in but with the return date, as usual, left blank. It was obvious afterwards, of course, that she had imagined the whole incident about the ticket. She must have done, she knew, because that was only the first of such queer errors. Once a parcel of books came for Vincent and she left them, or thought she did, on the hall table as always. Foster found them in his potting shed two days later after the whole house had been turned upside down to no purpose in search of the books.

That was the first time Vincent looked at her so oddly, puzzled and worried, and answered Mrs. Foster's queries rather sharply to stop her talking. That sharpness, although it was meant to protect Jenny, did not quite have the effect

Vincent intended really, because Mrs. Foster was a sharp-witted woman and obviously noticed his embarrassment. Jenny was so touched with gratitude at her husband's protectiveness that she went quickly out before she should burst into tears. She wept a good deal and the fits of crying got more frequent as the mistakes and forgetful episodes went on, until she was almost hysterical half the time. Vincent was unfailingly kind to her then. It was agreed that her nerves were run down and that the Fosters and Mona between them should take care as much as possible of things like household bills and entertaining so that she need not trouble herself. And this arrangement continued after she was better; it was rather difficult to say to Mona or Mrs. Foster that though she'd been a bit jumpy for a time, she was all right now and could take on the household duties again. Besides, she was not quite sure that she was all right; probably Vincent was right and any strain would make her nervous all over again, so things were better left as they were. She lacked confidence, as he said, and must be spared all those responsibilities with money and such things that other people could quite well take off her shoulders.

This made her wonder whether she had at some time done something nonsensical about money so that it was better for everybody if she did not need to cope with the bank. Especially when Vincent was so much away. Vincent was firm about that, and certainly it must be worrying for a man to have to travel and not be sure things were in good hands at home; and of course he couldn't know that Mona made things rather humiliating when she came to the house to pay bills and talk to the Fosters. Once she said, "Oh, here's your pocket money, Jenny," in front of Mrs. Foster, and just gave her the money without even an envelope, and when Jenny's eyes filled with tears, Mona shook her head and gave Mrs. F. a quick glance, at which Mrs. F. shook her head too. So after that day Jenny tried not to appear when Mona came to settle the household books and see about repairs and such things, and that worked out better. Only, naturally, Jenny then did not know what was going on and began to feel a little isolated as well as unsure. She would come across a workman perhaps, and not like to say she didn't know what he was doing in her own house. And for a time, until she got much better, that way of running the house actually caused her to make some of those awful mistakes, like the time when she got the date of a cocktail party wrong and had to run upstairs quickly and change her dress when Vincent pointed out that the guests would be arriving in ten minutes. Jenny was sure the party was for the following Wednesday, and since she was in her "studio" all afternoon, did not even see Mrs. Foster getting out glasses or the caterer's van arriving with the canapés. She'd even written the wrong date in her diary because of mistaking what Mona said. You must try to concentrate, darling, when people are telling you things, Vincent said about that day. He became very worried about her, Jenny could see that, and would frown and catch his lip between his teeth when she seemed about to say something in front of anyone from the company that would cause even more talk.

The worst thing she ever did, though, was that original stupidity over Mona, for Mona never forgave her, she felt, and always spoke to her with exaggerated carefulness as if Jenny might break out into violence if anyone upset her—and that made people talk. Several friends at that time hinted that she ought to see a doctor, but she made excuses and pretended to laugh, because she was afraid of what a doctor might find. She kept her fears very much to herself, telling nobody. They would only think her odder than ever, and you couldn't expect people not to talk, as Vincent often warned her, even close friends might gossip without meaning any harm. His sigh, the first time he said that, expressed just what Jenny herself felt, that things were quite bad enough without a lot of strangers knowing. But he need not have worried about that, for Jenny was much too afraid of being thought mad to say anything. She did not mention that even to Vincent; in fact she never spoke of her nerves except when something tiresome happened, when she did something silly or failed to do what she was supposed to be doing. He always tried to encourage her and assured her that the whole thing would clear up in time.

And it did, too, that was the strange thing. That terrible hysterical fit when she screamed and beat the walls and threw a cognac glass at the bookshelf and was then suddenly still and calm, that was some kind of a crisis or catharsis. She was at one moment screaming—lucky that it was the Fosters' day off and they'd gone to the pictures—and the tears were pouring down her face so that she could not see at all. The next minute, the crying fit ceased as if by a tap turned off; there was a break and she was absolutely normal. That was the moment at which she returned to herself. She found the courage to admit to herself that she really was "ill." Very well, she said, in her ordinary voice, this can't go on; I will go to Doctor Limmert tomorrow and get him to find me a psychiatrist. The next day she could not get to the doctor, who was in the town, because Vincent developed influenza and she must stay at home to nurse him. And that was fortunate, because she didn't need a psychiatrist after that. She was perfectly well, never suffered any of those weird aberrations again, when she was sure someone had told her one thing and they'd said something else entirely; when she lost letters, mislaid all sorts of ordinary things that were later found in crazy places. From that day on she never got her appointments mixed up, and although for some time she did often want to cry, she never had another hysterical fit as if she were going insane and would have to be put away.

She was not only well, as if a devil had been driven out like in the Bible; she knew she was well. She knew she was all right and she was. Vincent was very careful and gentle with her for a long while after. It was as if he were holding his breath; and in order not to remind her or frighten her, he never once mentioned her illness again. Jenny could feel his reasoning that as long as things went well and she got stronger and more controlled, it was best to leave matters alone.

His having the 'flu was a good thing in more ways than one, because Jenny didn't take her sleeping pills for the next few nights in case he should need something while she was dead asleep. And by the time he was well again, Jenny found that she could sleep quite normally, and the pills, which made her feel dizzy and undermined her self-control, were not needed; they were pushed gradually to the back of the bathroom cabinet and gathered dust there. Jenny knew that this effort of will-power was a considerable part of her victory over her illness, and besides she felt much better without them. The bout of 'flu was a good time altogether. Vincent wouldn't let her call the doctor, it was quite unnecessary and he loathed doctors anyway, he said. Everyone knew what to do about influenza and he'd rather be looked after by Jenny. So they were at home by themselves for four days, and apart from a few telephone calls, she could have him all to herself for the first time in years. Vincent looked very white and shaky for a day or so, and Jenny realised how much his health had been affected by his worries over her; that helped her, too. She could make the effort to seem normal for his sake, and the responsibility of relieving his mind gave her a strong motive to control herself. As she gained control of her nerves the mistakes were less and less likely to happen and, since none did happen, her confidence grew quickly. She was proud of that, and glad to have achieved the victory for Vincent's sake, even more than for herself. She felt now, as she had felt then, that it was all for him, the whole strange period much more connected with him than with her own mind.

Considering it with the usual smattering of popular myths about modern psychology, Jenny guessed that this attitude on her part was some kind of transfer of responsibility, something to do with not wanting to face the fact of her having shown signs of mental ill-health. Just as, in the immediate shock of this incredible news, she had longed for her father's presence and help as she had not done for years past. Jenny thought of this longing as a weakness of which she should be ashamed. She was of an age when she ought to be able to rely on herself, stand on her own feet. The moment some crises faced her she ran for comfort to the companion and provider of her childhood and stood here dreaming out the window of a distant period of time that belonged to her father's life and not her own. She, Jenny, was hardly seven years old when he bought this hill and the house with it, and that time had no relevance to the present. The present. She would have to live here alone now. She would get rid of the Fosters. What a shocking thing to consider at such a moment, she thought, but she was not genuinely shocked. A small pocket of secret relief in that prospect was securely lodged in Jenny's feeling, a positive sensation of pleasure, almost of glee.

A sound from the hall penetrated, a sound recognised from

her whole life's familiarity with every detail of her home: the house door closing. Instantaneous panic made Jenny grip her hands together and move quickly as if for flight. Of course it must be Mona come up from the town to tell her the news. Of course, it would be Mona who would be entrusted with that task. Idiot that she was, why had she not thought of that in time to escape into the ring of trees. Now she was trapped, she was going to be obliged to face Mona, be talked to by Mona. Without considering what she was doing, Jenny turned to face the door, her hands still clutched before her, in the posture of one shrinking, a frightened creature, almost at bay, it might well have appeared to an onlooker.

That is exactly how Jenny did appear to the two persons who now opened the smoothly aged door and came into the room. She gave an almost audible gasp at seeing, not her husband's secretary but the Managing Director's wife and, behind her, nice, jolly teddy bear Teddy himself. Eileen Sandford was a big-built woman well into her forties with a strikingly pretty face in the Irish style. Black curly hair, a creamy tint to her skin and dark shadowy grey eyes corrected something florid in the carriage of her tall, voluptuously developed body, something flamboyant in its generous proportions that should have been majestic but that failed aesthetically. Her husband was shorter than she, a man round in every particular, of a russet redness in general and with a loud, fruity voice.

This voice was to be heard as the door opened, over his wife's slow contralto, for they both began to speak as they came in.

"My poor child," said Eileen richly.

"Jenny, my dear. We just had to come at once."

Jenny realised from this that it was already known that she had heard the news, and since she did not know what to say and therefore did not answer at once, there was time to wonder about that.

"The police telephoned and we were at the testing shop today, so we came straightaway. At least we're better than strangers at such a time. Such a shock, so terrible, the hospital just ringing you up like that."

"Out of the blue! I can't think how it could happen."

96

"They told me how," said Jenny. "There was an envelope lying on the back seat of the Rover, addressed to Vincent, here." The implication in this, which only now struck Jenny, of the condition the body must have been in, made her stop speaking. Her already pale and strained face grew paler still, and Eileen moved quickly towards the window, thinking the figure that swayed in front of it was about to fall. But Jenny did not fall. The brumous light from the window hid her face until Eileen was close enough to take her hands and see that the features to which she downwards bent her gaze were rigidly still and almost expressionless. If Jenny looked anything at all, she looked puzzled.

"The doctor ought to come," Eileen pronounced. "The poor little thing is completely shocked."

"No wonder, no wonder at all. I'll go and telephone, the housekeeper will have his number. I'll tell him to bring a sedative." He was already out in the hall and the word sedative floated back half audibly.

"I don't want to take any sedatives," argued Jenny uncertainly, and then stopped. No point in arguing. She would simply refuse, and Jenny felt a wan surprised pride in that determined thought. "Could you . . . Eileen, do you think you could tell the Fosters? I don't want to talk to—"

"I'll go as soon as Teddy comes back, and tell them they are to leave you in peace. People can be such a trial with their chatter." By people Eileen meant servants, although the Fosters were not exactly servants.

"Oh, they'll leave me alone, you need not worry. I hardly see them when Vincent is away from home, except when Mrs. Foster brings meals."

Eileen's magnificent eyes widened, her lips parted to speak, but Jenny had already remembered.

"Ahhh," she moaned, a frightened little cry. But no sob followed. She was suddenly unnerved by her own lack of sensation.

"It's all right, Jenny. It often happens with great shocks. It may not seem real to you for days, but you mustn't upset yourself."

"Perhaps it won't ever seem real," Jenny said under her breath. She slid quickly on to the window seat and stole a quick glance for reassurance at the tall trees whose tops swayed in the February weather. It seemed now to be raining a little, in the wind. Eileen gave the turned head a quick, sharp glance and in spite of Jenny's calm, or perhaps because of it, she felt that she was incapable of telling this quiet, almost flimsy, withdrawn creature what she had come to say.

"I'll just see what—" she said uneasily, and retreated. Outside, she held the panelled door in a large, managerial left hand, to keep it closed and said in an undertone to her husband, "It's out of the question to tell her now. I don't know why that didn't occur to us. We can't possibly."

"But she's bound to find out," he whispered back, holding a pudgy fist over the telephone mouthpiece, at which he waited for the doctor to be fetched. "We agreed it was best for us to tell her. Someone's got to." He gave a shamed, almost scared look at his wife's face and saw she was about to break down. "Think what it would be for her to hear it from a stranger. It's a miracle those fools at the hospital didn't mention it. If we tell her now before the shock wears off she may not realize quite what it means."

The doctor's voice jarred the telephone and Sandford began to speak. Eileen turned, still holding the door. With her back to him, she bent her head, and tears overwhelmed her.

"Oh, God," she sobbed helplessly, angrily. She almost flung the heavy door away from her and marched into the room, made brutal by anger and fear of what she was about to do.

She swallowed her tears and spoke loudly.

"There's something else, Jenny. There were two bodies taken out of the wreck. Mona was with him."

Jenny turned from the darkening, rain-flecked window. Her eyes in the half-light were dark emptinesses in the pallid blank of her face.

"Was she?" The voice was flat. "I wondered why Mona didn't come to tell me." She accented the name and left a most curious impression hanging in the air between them. She doesn't—didn't—like Mona, then, thought Eileen, defending herself from another thought that she believed could not be true. It came into her mind, but Eileen rejected it, for much discussion over the last year or so had issued in the certainty that Jenny did not know about Mona.

There was a still, undemanding dignity about the figure in the window that reduced the general opinion of Vincent's friends—that his wife was a sad failure and that he was hardly to be blamed if he found Mona's energetic gaiety seductive —to a somewhat mean and vulgar expediency. The notion that they all put up with the irregular situation and the constant implied lying it entailed, not out of kindness but because Vincent was a valuable sales director and nobody much cared for his wife, was very unpleasant to Eileen. Normally she kept such unwelcome ideas quite easily out of her consciousness with a well-developed self-esteem. She could not understand why something that never before occurred to her should now make her so uncomfortable. Another thought restored her. Jenny would surely want to sell the house now, and perhaps her old envy of it could be satisfied quite legitimately, almost as a favour to its widowed owner.

CHAPTER VII

"I'M SURE it would be much better for you to come home with us, Jenny. For a day or two. Until, well, just for a few days."

"I couldn't leave here." Jenny was so decided, now that the suggestion was made, that all the sound arguments in favour of the idea languished in a silence that rapidly began to seem to Jenny like rudeness on her part and to her visitors like a snub. This rather surprising turn took a few moments to develop, and by that time Jenny had spoken again.

"You are very good to me. I'm grateful, I can't tell you how grateful, that you thought of me. But I couldn't possibly leave here." This in a quite ordinary tone, the blankness of her face was what gave the conventional phrases the quality of indifference, which once again came over to Eileen, if not to her husband, as dignity. Teddy Sandford was surprised because it was rare for anyone connected with the company to argue with those suggestions of his wife's in the social sphere, which were in reality something more like orders than the expression of an opinion susceptible of discussion. He forgot for a second the meaning of their presence here and began to speak rallyingly, persuasively, almost jokingly, as if it was obvious that Jenny was just protesting politely and could not mean what she said. Jenny turned to listen to him with her normal aspect of rather submissive acquiescence, but she did not retract her own words, and a disagreeable impression gradually presented itself to Sandford that he was bullying the girl. This was disconcerting and he stopped speaking without finishing his sentence. It's almost as if she were not there at all, he thought, and would have been startled to know that this was visible in his expression. The thought was too much akin to the idiom that Jenny was not quite all there for it to be a happy implication; Sandford realised too late that this was not only his interior thought but had been produced by his manner of speaking to Jenny.

It was gradually impossible for the subject to be taken up again directly. Sandford glanced across at Eileen for guidance but received none. Eileen was not only unused to being argued with, she was also so accustomed to having good sense on her side that argument would usually have been foolish as well as rebellious. She was disconcerted by a genuine conflict of opinion, because certainly it was debatable whether Jenny could leave the house when so many arrangements would have to be decided in the next few days. Eileen was taking it for granted that someone would be deputised from the offices of the company to make all those arrangements, but evidently Jenny had not yet thought of it.

"You aren't worrying about all the business that will have to be done, Jenny?" she asked. "Of course, we'll send somebody over to sort papers and so on. And all the other things have already been ordered from the hospital in Wrexham."

"Yes, they said so," replied Jenny. "But it's not quite that. I just couldn't go away."

It was now almost dark in the room, the glooming, rainy dusk from the tall windows hardly entering. There was a lamp standing by the chair in which Mrs. Sandford was seated; she put out her hand to reach the switch and then drew it back again. Jenny's eyes followed her movement, saw the intention and the polite hesitation, and rose to switch on the lamp, an action that caused her to come into the centre of the room so that she stood before the big chimney piece of bevelled stone that reached above her head. The fire was not burning. Her father designed the heating system himself and had somehow managed to get it installed before war put a stop to such personal provisions of comfort. They rarely lit the fire in this or other fireplaces; it made extra work and meant that if the fire burned on an evening not followed by the cleaning woman's appearance from the nearby hamlet, then Foster would have to sweep back the ash and stack logs afresh. And the Fosters, it was always understood, had quite enough to do and, if it came to that, so had the cleaning woman, who was intended as a help to Mrs. Foster specifically.

Now, with a curious little air of deliberation, Jenny reached up to the sill of the stonework, which was at the height of her outstretched arm, and found a box of matches there, which she shook to make the characteristic rattle before taking out a match and bending down to apply its tiny flame to the edge of a sheet of newspaper under sticks and logs. The fire caught at once with a pleasing roar, and in a few moments she could contemplate with satisfaction a flickering play of flames.

Watching these movements, Sandford found himself remembering a fact not thought of for years. Like his own wife's, Jenny's situation here and within the company was an inheritance from her father and not the result of marriage. Curious, he thought, one hardly considers Jenny as the owner of this place or yet as the heir of her father's invention patents, but she is the owner. This led to a logical second thought: Jenny was now the sole owner of those patents. In point of fact, Jenny had been their owner all the time. Jenny was now the undisputed possessor of various devices and procedures, upon the secure use of which he and the whole company and everyone employed in it, to a considerable extent depended. Vincent's death removed a control over Jenny's actions which, until this second, had never seemed even to be necessary. Sandford found himself wondering with a mixture of guilt and curiosity whether Jenny herself had ever become conscious of this fact. Did she even know—she seemed often so detached from worldly concerns—that she always was in this position of power, ever since her twenty-first birthday? He rather doubted it. It was nevertheless now a matter of some importance that this should not be pointed out to Jenny by any one of a number of potential rivals before he himself had a chance to have a serious chat with her, as he put it to himself. He would speak to his fellow directors the very first thing tomorrow, and to Jenny as soon as possible after the funeral was over. In the interim it was essential that nobody should, with less concern for the decencies of life than his own, be able to approach Jenny while she was still in a state of lost and dazed shock.

"My dear girl," he said to his wife, "Jenny's right, of course. To go away would only add to her misery. I hadn't thought of it like that, but naturally you must stay here with her rather than us taking her home with us." Before Eileen could answer he turned again to the widow. "I'll ask Folliot to come over tomorrow to help you, sweetie."

The endearment was unusual enough for his wife to perceive that something more was involved in his words than a difference with her own opinion that Jenny should stay in their home. She at once fitted her own authority into whatever it was that had occurred to Teddy, and the mention of Folliot, who was the company lawyer, gave her the clue to his thoughts.

"Of all the idiots," she exclaimed cheerfully. "I just didn't see it like that, but naturally, you're right, Teddy."

Jenny became aware that this solution of the difference, although now past correcting, was almost as unwelcome to her as the original suggestion; she wanted no company. But a proper concern for manners as well as a genuine recognition of the great kindness she was being shown, made her smile and express her thanks. Eileen would manage for one night and Mr. Folliot would come tomorrow and bring with him a suitcase for her. The decision made Jenny aware of hospitality and she proposed a drink. She consulted with a look to make sure from Eileen's expression whether this was a proper thing to do in the circumstances, but evidently it was, so they all with relief took their favourite refreshment, from the silver tray that always stood against one wall of this room, agreeing without words not to ring the bell for ice. However, this need had been anticipated, and a few minutes later Mrs. Foster entered with a tweedy bustle and the ice container, not without casting a hasty and curious glance at her employer's widow, now her employer.

There was nothing in the nervous, "Thank you, Mrs. Foster," from Jenny to bring this thought to mind, and it did not come to Mrs. Foster's mind. She graciously allowed herself to be thanked, as she always did, as if whatever she had done was really outside her proper duties.

It was Foster, on her return to their own sitting room, who pointed out this rather important detail, and who pointed out as well the very good reason why they should in the future bear it in mind in dealing with Mrs. Cheyney. It would not be easy, even in present-day conditions in their profession, for them to get another position as easy as the one they had held for the years of Vincent Cheyney's marriage. The reason, or rather, the two reasons, were that Foster was partially disabled from a war injury, and Mrs. Foster, although a good cook, was not a trained housekeeper. There was also the matter of Foster's release from the army, but neither of them touched upon that. It did now occur to Mrs. Foster to wonder whether Mr. Cheyney had ever divulged this matter to his wife and to hope that he had not done so. If "she" knew about it, it might not be so easy to maintain the stance of condescension to Mr. Cheyney's widow as it had been while the master was there to subdue his wife; so Mrs. Foster thought of it. She may get a bit independent, left to herself, considered Mrs. Foster; this judgement showed Jenny's opinion of her housekeeper as a sharp-witted woman to be correct, for Jenny was already turning in her mind thoughts of dismissing the Fosters.

"He must have been killed instantly," suggested Foster, turning the newspaper with a rattle to the sports page. He gave a grunt of satisfaction at seeing that the horse he intended to back for that afternoon's meeting at Truro had not even been placed. He had been prevented from telephoning the bookmaker about it by the overheard news of Mr. Cheyney's accident. He leaned forward to stir the blazing fire that always burned in the Fosters' room, and added, "What's for dinner?"

"Mind yours," replied Mrs. Foster agreeably as she reached over the table to pick up her glasses, and then was struck by the thought that clearly was also in her husband's mind. "I think I'll roast the ducks you got from Harry. I meant them for 'him' when he got back, but tonight will be better, now. Mr. Sandford likes his grub. Nice bit of applesauce and the tops of the sprouts you brought in. We could have potted shrimps first. You better get washed and get your jacket on, Foster. You can serve tonight. Show a bit of sympathy. It's only proper."

Foster grunted again at this but this time without satisfaction, and rose to his feet, stretching and yawning.

"You're right," he said, and with a final glance of regret at the fire and the evening paper, made to leave the room.

"Put the paper in the hall when you go through," Mrs.

104

Foster reminded him. "And fold it the right way round. That Mrs. Sandford's a very noticing woman."

As she left the table, she turned to watch her husband carefully folding the newspaper to look as if it were freshly delivered.

"It doesn't seem possible, does it. We shall never see him again. Shocking thing, when you think of it."

"I can't believe it, myself. Haven't taken it in yet."

"No. Neither has she, you can see that. Dazed, she looks."

"Well she might be. What she'll do without him to look after her!"

His wife answered snappishly, giving way for a moment to a generalised dislike of her husband's sex, which normally she kept to herself. "She won't have to put up with that Mona about the place, anyway. 'Oh, Mrs. Foster, dear,' here and 'Oh, Mrs. Foster, dear' there."

"Ah. Sharp with the book, she was. I caught her counting the eggs once in the fowl house. Saucy bitch."

Their resentment of Mona's prying ways was justified. Mrs. Foster's self-righteousness made her as honest as the day, and Foster was too lazy to be anything else. This made him easier to live with than his wife, but they were both of them even-tempered and unexacting so long as they were comfortable, which is as much as can be expected of people living together in the same house. Jenny's dislike of them was unjust; they were not responsible for her humiliations, and many people in their situation would have made her feel them far more than the Fosters did. In fact, Jenny was largely responsible for her own inferior status in the household, but that was something that did not occur to her. Like most women, she accepted the climate of her life as something settled by circumstances outside herself, and even the constant example that others impressed themselves on their surroundings, rather than being modelled by them, was not used as a reference point to her own life. The very woman then sitting in the side room, as the living room was usually called, might have inspired Jenny with this ambitious thought, but did not. Eileen was to Jenny almost infinitely more capable in every way, including looks, than she was herself. Eileen's looks, in fact, were a good example in Jenny's view of her friend's capacity for dealing with the world, for Jenny's strong aesthetic sense, which she kept secret, told her that Eileen was not beautiful. Her outer envelope was handsome and impressive to almost everyone about her, but it lacked inner reality and structure; Eileen's appearance and manner were the result of her talent for imposing her wishes on the world, not the cause of her success in this accepted state of affairs.

"You're going to be here for a few days, Eileen," she said, making a suggestion without previous invitation, which was unusual for Jenny. "I could model your head, you've often said you'd like me to."

Then it struck her as wrong to think of such a thing at that moment and she caught her breath.

"Oh, dear, I suppose we couldn't . . ." she added.

"I don't see why not," objected Teddy. "Good for you to have something to take your mind off things, I should say."

"It isn't the opportunity we could ever have wished for," agreed Eileen with her air of authoritative consideration. "But since we shall be bound to stay at home . . ."

Sandford was about to say that perhaps Jenny would now in her changed circumstances take her hobby more seriously than she ever seemed to do. Realising in time that this would be an invidious remark, he said instead that in his opinion she had a considerable talent. What he really meant was that if she were to model his wife's head, that proved her talent existed, since anything connected with Eileen must be successful of its nature.

"Of course, I suppose I don't know anything about these things," he added humourously, and since this was quite true, Jenny hastened to deny it.

Presently they dined, and very well. Soon after dinner Sandford left, for he would be driving alone all the way back home that night.

"Do, for heaven's sake, drive carefully," said his wife as they saw him off, and they then both froze for a second at the tactlessness of this injunction. Jenny was staring at the pattern of the headlamps illuminating the gravel, lifting small scraps of yellowish stone into relief in an agreeable assortment of shadows. The thought that she disliked the yellow gravel, which made an ugly contrast to the grey stone of the house, and wanted at the time it was ordered to protest at the choice, went not for the first time through Jenny's mind. I can have that burnt porridge changed now, she said to herself and gratefully, with relief, began to weep.

"Mona ordered it without even asking me," she wailed. Fortunately neither of the others heard what she said, for it would have been unintelligible. Probably they understood her to cry out some complaint against a cruel fate, and as Sandford drove quickly off, glad to escape emotion, Eileen drew the weeping girl into the hall and closed the door, locking it decisively with the massive, ancient key. She was about to switch off the light over the door outside, but Jenny put out a shaky and wet hand and stopped her.

"I like it to burn at night," she whispered, and to Eileen's astonishment she seemed to be almost smiling through her tears.

Left alone at last in the guest room, still a trace chilly though the radiators had been turned on in the afternoon, Eileen thought of that strange look. These old stone houses, she thought, lovely and warm when they *are* once warm, but bitter cold if they're not. They ought to heat this room regularly. Mrs. Foster is too mean with the boiler. You know, she addressed herself as she always did, turning over the events of the day, that girl really is a bit touched. I do believe she refused to go away because she feels they will come back here. They, what do I mean, they?

But it was not Mona who formed the plural in her perception; she was not thinking of Mona, it was the girl's father. I wonder what an Oedipus complex is called when it's a woman, she thought, and inspected the row of books displayed for guests in the hope of seeing a good thriller there. Ambler, she said aloud, jolly good show; I ought not to use that expression, she added silently, it dates me. The thing about thrillers is that one always forgets what happened, so one can read them again. Just the same, Jenny is distinctly odd. She's what? Nearly thirty, but she seems like a kid. She married too young, never got control of the situation with Vin. Hm, not an easy chap to control, after all, I didn't manage it, either. That bitch Mona did, though. Vin found his match there. I wonder if he ever tried to get rid of her, before she really took over his life. But she was too bright to try to marry him; he would have lost the house and the patent royalties. She must have hated Jenny. I never thought of that before, but I bet she really put Jenny through the hoops. Why on earth did the wretched child put up with it? She's really quite defenceless, you know. Rather maddening, these helpless people. Well, she didn't know, but that's pretty crazy too; and there are ways and ways of knowing and not knowing.

With this wry piece of wisdom, Eileen settled herself in bed with a sign of gratification that it was so comfortable. With such a hostess as Jenny it might well have proved to be hard or not to have enough pillows. Not that Jenny furnished the house, any more than she ran it now. I suppose most of the furniture was here, and Vin just moved in. Or did Jenny keep house for her father? I can't really remember. Strange man he was, no wonder his daughter isn't quite normal. But brainy. If he'd lived he would have opposed that marriage. I always felt he knew about Vin and me. Let's face it, my girl, Vin was a stinker where women were concerned. That's why it took a real tough bitch like Mona to keep him under control. Your prejudices are showing, she admonished herself complacently, you just think like that because Vin was too clever to continue an affair as dangerous to him as to you. But it was I who got rid of Vin, he didn't leave me. I didn't give him the chance to do that.

Eileen opened her book and began to read. The curtains were closely drawn.

Jenny stood again at the window of her bedroom directly above the side room. The trees looked quite different from the increased height. Once used to the dark they were visible but mysterious presences, always there. It would be blasphemy to attempt to shut out their presence by drawing curtains, and of her own choice Jenny never did draw them. Pointless blasphemy at that. They were still present. Old gods, conquered by Christ, gone underground before history began, inhabited them. Jenny knew no fear either of the beeches or the imagined deities who haunted them. They were her friends, her protectors, and she loved them; it was of

108

people that she often felt fear. And she only submitted to authority when she "imagined" the old gods or spirits out there. Certainly Christ was the living God, but the older ones were there and she never had the slightest doubt of that.

A simple trick of gentle cunning had allowed her to reconcile the two concepts, and she confounded the priest of her own faith by expounding her notion to him as a young girl, of the vanquished ancient beings allowed to continue a shadowy existence through the mercy of the triumphant—but later —Victor. She could not know that the long-dead incumbent of the older confession to whom she had revealed this, and whose presence in the town was one of the reasons for her father's choice of this and no other house, had spoken of her "fancies" to her father. They agreed that, provided the fancies did not become an obsession, nothing ought to be done to admonish Jenny in a way that could frighten the child. She would grow out of it and, in a being of such delicate sensibility and perception of beauty, it would be dangerous to inhibit her imagination by frightening warnings. The imaginings never did become an obsession; Jenny was and remained an accepting child of the Church, but she did not grow out of them either. As their own existence was secret, so they remained secretly for the child as she grew: real but held in control.

After her marriage, after both her childhood mentors were dead, Jenny slipped somewhat from the embrace of religion, for Vincent was, if anything, Protestant and not very much of anything. But the ancient beings were still there. In ten years she never once spoke of this to Vincent. For him the house and its hill were a matter of possession and of the prestige brought with it by ownership of a place so eminently desirable. Jenny knew this and adopted the view because Vincent was so much more at home in the real world than she was. It must be true, and carried with it the advantage of something she could give her husband, something not only he but everybody they knew thought to be enviable. She gave the possession so totally to her husband, and he took it so completely, that only the shadowy presences were left to her after the passage of a very short time; nothing else, either of the house and land or of her own life, was hers any more.

So changed was all her surrounding world after her mar-

riage that her old fantasy companions—the reality, the being
of the house itself—withdrew into memories. Jenny left
childhood behind; at least outwardly she grew up, and that
was normal and to be expected and wished for. Yet on that
night Jenny felt her former companions to be there after her
long absence. They returned to her and she to their company.

CHAPTER VIII

MR. FOLLIOT was a stern, short, spare man with not much liking for words, who had spent his whole professional life with the company. What Folliot didn't know, as Sandford said on the telephone when announcing the lawyer's departure, was not likely to be of any consequence in a business way. And Jenny could trust his discretion; he would find the will, if there was one, and sort out personal from commercial papers so that the painful job of clearing up would be much simplified. All Jenny would need to do was go through the private stuff at her leisure. Or alternatively, but this Sandford kept to himself, just leave it alone to lose any power to disturb the widow, which would certainly be the wiser course. He supposed he could leave the outcome to Jenny's dilatory ways.

"I won't trouble you with any more questions than I must," said Folliot as soon as the conventions of the occasion were respectably dealt with. "I take it everything Vincent kept at home is here? Or did he have a desk downstairs?"

"No. Only my father's desk and that's not been used for years. I think almost everything would be at your office or the testing shop."

"But your father's papers. They would be here?"

"I don't really know. The originals of the patent certificates are in the safe deposit at the bank. You mean things like leases of patents, renewals of licences, that sort of thing? I think those all went through the office."

"One or two things Vincent kept under his control, you know. That is quite usual. There were a few procedures kept confidential, things other engineers might copy. That sort of trick is not unknown, unfortunately. I daresay that in the last years there was not much left that has not been independently

111

found out by inventors other than your father. But one or two of his instrument designs were of such brilliant simplicity, you know, that they remain very valuable. He was, after all, a genius, your father."

Mr. Folliot said this in a disapproving tone as if Jenny might be inclined to deny her father's value, but Jenny knew that this tone came from his dislike of saying anything in the least extravagant, such as using the word genius.

"You didn't inspect royalty payments and that kind of thing, yourself?" he hinted cautiously.

"Oh, no. I don't think I'd understand them. Vincent did all that."

"Well now. There's just this desk, the cupboard here and that's all? Nothing in the loft, is there? Old papers? You would think them junk, I daresay."

"Vincent was terribly, I mean wonderfully, orderly. I think you'll find everything in this room. There may be something in this funny little cupboard in the panelling here. It's the original panelling on this wall, my father had to have the rest stripped in here; it was full of dry rot."

"Sad. Sad. I remember what a ruin the house was when he bought it. Yes, indeed I do."

Jenny pushed the inconspicuous fastening on the door cut in the woodwork.

"It's locked," she said, incuriously. "But you have the keys? Vincent's ring?"

Mr. Folliot frowned at the thought of the state of the leather key holder given him by the police last night. He had cleaned the keys himself, after taking them from the mangled folder inside the sealed official envelope. No need for Jenny to know now that the car was half burned out. She looked quite drawn and ill enough without details being forced on her.

"Well," he said, "I'd better get to work."

"If there's anything you need, we shall be about," Jenny offered, looking about the room as if she did not know it. "We'll see you at lunch, then? One o'clock, will that be all right?"

Folliot watched her back as she drifted away. Extraordinary woman, asking if her lunchtime would be all right for me! She doesn't seem to understand any of the ordinary relationships

112

of life, somehow. And that isn't shock; she always did act as if she ought to apologise for being there at all. He corrected himself pedantically. Not always, perhaps, but since she was grown up. Probably her father's death, he surmised. That was a terrible blow to everyone who knew him. A good thing for her she had Vincent to take care of her. How she would manage now, that was another question. Shocking business, this. Dreadful. Well, all of them in the company did as much as anyone to add complexity to the machinery of living. And for a man constantly travelling, like poor Vincent, the risks were always there. Still, a bad business, and the woman secretary with him, too. No relatives, no nothing. Nobody will come to her funeral; from the personnel department Mr. Folliot knew that Miss Laver was quite lacking in family. He stopped sharply in the act of opening the middle drawer of the desk. I must telephone the funeral director about that, without fail. It would really be most unfortunate if they made an error of judgement just because nobody thought to let them know, and the two funerals were allowed to take place at the same time. From the window Mr. Folliot could see that Jenny and the Managing Director's wife were strolling across the grass towards the stables, unused for many years except for the makeshift studio where Jenny practiced her little hobby of sculpture. He reached for the telephone on the desk and dialled the number of the undertaker in Wrexham. Having called Wrexham twenty times in the last twenty-four hours, he knew the relevant numbers by heart. Added to everything else, he thought crossly, the accident had to happen so far away. Talking quietly to the obsequious voice at the other end of the line, he observed that bank papers and cheque book were neatly arranged in the middle drawer. With sedate approval of good business practice, Mr. Folliot picked up the folder of statements without interrupting what he was saying.

Two hours later the approval was lost in bewilderment. Puzzlement was already giving way to astonishment, astonishment to disbelief. By the time Mr. Folliot at length used the key to the cupboard in the panel he was in distress. In the cupboard was a thin leather document folder and only one other thing: a small steel cash box with a numbered opener instead of a key. He knew the type and the maker. They made these little cassettes to order, as well as in the usual commercial series. This was one of the special orders, whose number would have been proposed by the client and known only to himself once it was set. Even the man who set it, dealing constantly in such combinations, would hardly recall it for more than a day or so, and no record would be kept of the number in the files of the maker. Mr. Folliot set the almost square box of fireproof steel, painted in a mottled blue enamel, in front of him in the exact centre of the now bare desk top. He sat in Vincent's chair and stared at the object, the little barrel of numerals from one to nine and nought in his narrowed sight. He was as silent as the numbers, and he sat there for a long time. He was not considering what he must do. That he knew. He was considering the various implications, among them how he should explain himself to the two women at luncheon. Wisely he decided that the best method was to explain nothing.

"I have not found a will, though that is not of immediate importance. But there is a good deal of paperwork that Vincent evidently was accustomed to do for himself at home. More than I can oversee in one day, and most unfortunately we are in the midst of preparing a large contract. The estimates, the calculations, are of some complexity and I am bound to supervise the work myself. The best thing will be if I take such papers with me as I can manage and send an assistant over for a few days to do the rest."

Mr. Folliot then addressed himself to the food and to the two ladies and quickly found that Mrs. Sandford proposed to stay until the day of the funeral and would then return home for the half-term holiday of her sons. Mrs. Cheyney would return here after the funeral; she had no present intention of going away from home. The funeral would be held in three days. After that the coast would be clear.

"Oh, one thing. I'm not sure that we have your birth date, Mrs. Cheyney. It may come up in the—ah—formalities. Would you mind?" He passed an open notebook across the table with his pen, an old-fashioned fountain pen, and, with her typical incurious docility, Jenny wrote the dates down. Most people who used the special-order cassettes chose numbers based on the birth dates of one or other members of their families. Vincent's, he could, of course, obtain.

"Don't you need the marriage date as well?" asked Mrs. Sandford inquisitively.

"Ah, yes. Slipped my memory." The notebook passed again across the table. "Perhaps you could find time to go to the bank in the next day or so? I take it the papers you speak of would be at the bank you use in the town here? The will, if one exists, could be there."

"You know, Vincent never spoke to me of making a will—I'm not sure he ever did. I did, when we were married; I think it may have been you, Mr. Folliot, who said I should do that. But I don't know that Vincent did. Can't you recall?"

Vincent's will, if any, was not of the slightest interest to Mr. Folliot any more. But his memory clicked into place and he nodded.

"Yes, I remember your making a will. I remember Vincent saying that your property should be clearly regulated in the case of children arriving."

"Children?" Jenny asked. "Did he say that?"

Both Mr. Folliot and Eileen Sandford became aware here of some deviousness in the conversation, and both of them thought they understood it.

"I don't want to ask you about details that may be painful to you," said Folliot primly. "But you might just take a look, if you're going down."

"It's not a joint account, you see," said Jenny, now breathless. "I am not sure they would open the deposit. Perhaps you'd better give me a paper to show them?"

"A paper?" said the lawyer; in a less controlled man the sound would have been a gasp. "My dear child. I mean, forgive me, my dear Mrs. Cheyney, this is your own personal property we are speaking of. Of course you have access to it. You ladies, you are so unbusinesslike—" Here, unwillingly, Folliot caught the eye of the Managing Director's wife and the proposition of feminine lack of business sense became so clearly absurd that he stopped, unsure how to go on.

"D'you mean you have two separate accounts at the bank?" asked Eileen. "What a complicated arrangement!"

"Oh, no. Just one." Jenny's colourless face was now taut with nervousness. They were going, any moment, to know and then they would guess that the bank affairs had something to do with the time she was so odd. Then they would think she was mad.

Eileen showed again that unexpected brutality which had been so useful the previous day.

"You're not going to tell me," she demanded, "that you have no way of drawing money from the bank, Jenny?"

Jenny stared hard at the polished table top, dimly reflecting snowdrops and crocus from a bowl in the centre. She was unable to speak, so she nodded.

"But who did . . . then . . . Oh." There was a silence, as the saying goes, that could have been cut with a knife.

Mr. Folliot looked at his watch.

"I have time to go the bank before they close," he said, ending the discussion. "There will be no difficulty. They can send the signature forms up here to be signed. They know who you are, after all. Just use the cheque book upstairs in the desk."

They had finished, and just as the coffee tray arrived, the telephone rang and Jenny excused herself and went out into the hall, leaving her guests for a moment alone.

"You don't believe all that, Mr. Folliot? It can't be true. I just don't believe it's possible. You know, she always did have a bit of a tendency to be sorry for herself. It's just an act, sort of self-pity brought on by the shock."

"We shall see," he said, holding out a hand to indicate that the lady should leave the room in front of him. "But I agree with you so far as to hope—to be sure—that you will give Mrs. Cheyney some help in the next day or so." They understood each other perfectly.

Jenny accepted a signed receipt for sundry papers thought by Mr. Folliot to be better dealt with at the office, as he said, without showing curiosity or even interest. At the bank Mrs. Sandford's view was proved wrong. The position was that the account had been changed some years before from a joint account to a single-signature one, with drawing rights up to a certain amount in any given month conceded to Miss Mona Laver, secretary. This made Mr. Folliot feel sympathetic and concerned for both Jenny and her dead husband, for he had, naturally, heard all the current rumours and gossip about Jenny's febrile state of health and, as he thought somewhat disapprovingly, matters that flowed from it.

These rumours, established as they were by custom and habit, seemed to him, as they would have seemed to most people, to explain the strange arrangement. When he came to explain everything that had happened in the last few days it did not occur to him to put any other interpretation on the matter than the one that seemed so obvious. Indeed, although he spoke only of facts, and of those in the most discreet and scrupulously careful fashion, what he said and still more what he did not say, left the impression in his hearers' minds that his account contained the whole content of the domestic and legal affairs of the Cheyney household and property. There was no reason on earth why anyone should even consider any lack or flaw in his version. Mr. Folliot was a most trustworthy and proper person to manage financial and legal matters; it was impossible for anyone to imagine that he could ever knowingly either add to or eliminate from a reckoning any germane fact. It was not his fault that he did not tell the truth. He believed, and so did his hearers, that he spoke of persons he had known, in the one case all her life, in the other since he left the army and joined the company. If Mr. Folliot did not know them, who could? And Mr. Folliot did know them as far as any man lacking in imagination and insight can ever be said to know any human being. Mr. Folliot had spent forty years in the service of a large company, and human nature impinged on his career only in contracts and conveyances; he never dealt with personnel matters, as he would somewhat stiffly have explained, had anyone questioned his competence. Staff affairs were another branch of the company altogether. Worse even than this, Mr. Folliot's wife was the very plain daughter of a colleague who had the good sense to know that she was extremely lucky in her husband and took care never by a lifted eyebrow to imply any criticism of his view of anything. For thirty years nobody had ever argued with Mr. Folliot except in the board room, and there his briefs were invariably impeccable. The personal nature of his wife and five children was as carefully kept from him as men are kept from an Arab virgin; he was a happy man but a misleading witness.

But he was not happy at that moment. What he had found in Vincent's papers could lead only to investigations. But what he found gave no indication of who exactly ought to be investigated or even as to what. It was clear that something was wrong in some way that affected the property and finances of the company. Only the Chairman could decide. Folliot went to Lord Tantham and they talked the matter over until the air was blurred both with tobacco smoke and possibilities. Lord Tantham then decided to do what Folliot had all the time known was inevitable and necessary.

Being in London, Mr. Folliot lost no time in putting his problem before the competent authorities. He knew where to go and whom to see.

"As I don't need to tell you, complete discretion from start to finish is of the essence. Five persons had constant access to these papers, and a large number of others had potential access or potential knowledge. The matter may be large or insignificant in *your* sense; at the moment one simply has no knowledge of its extent and importance. But you will be aware that some of the company's products are devices of national and international concern. In spite of appearances, too, it would not be wise at this stage to eliminate from involvement any of the persons who could immediately, or at various stages removed, be concerned. There is the matter of the inventor's original nationality, for instance. Nothing could be more unjust than to allow even the least hint of any suspicion attaching to a dead man on that score if it were not relevant. You take my point, I hope? Julius Maculan was a famous name and still is, and his fruitful association with my company is a matter of history as well as the traditions of the firm. Some of his strokes of genius helped to shorten the Second World War and have had no less effect on military and other events since then. I suggest that whoever you propose to commission with this investigation should come in the first instance to my office, where he can learn what he needs to know of the technical side of the matter before beginning the real researches. There are people there who can be delegated to give him information without knowing why he needs it or what he is doing. I leave

118

all that side of the work to you, naturally; you have experience in covering up such enquiries with convincing masquerades. But whoever you send ought to have some smattering of technology, as we say nowadays. Otherwise he must sooner or later expose himself."

They went into details for some time before the question of the strong box arose. The niceties of this object's ownership and fate would have been a pleasure to Mr. Folliot at any other time and, even in the present circumstances, he could not help enjoying the neat little problem.

"You understand me, I hope? If the box is not opened until there is some official direction for its confiscation and opening, that is, until you have evidence, you may never get that evidence. Or you may get it at some length of time that would make it useless. You cannot ask for permission to open the cassette without giving yourselves away. I, however, possess a covering receipt for it as well as other things—papers your official will need to see. The present owner showed no sign of a special interest in the box when she signed for it to be taken out of her house. It may, of course, be empty. Or it may contain something personal and, for us, meaningless. I propose the following: *I* will open the cassette. If it is damaged, I will also order another of the same type to replace it. If it proves not to be necessary, nobody need even know about my misdeed; if it does become necessary, I will take the responsibility."

Mr. Folliot produced the box and they both sat staring at it as the lawyer had stared the day before. Every number combination Folliot could think of—birth dates, the more important patent numbers, historical dates connected with the uses to which those patents had been put, the founding dates of the company, the land transfer of Beech Grove Hill and Grove House. The official now thought of some other possibilities, but none of them served to open the box.

"The owner's name ought to be Pandora," he said at last, "instead of Johanna Maddalena."

"Mrs. Cheyney has always been addressed as Jenny since her babyhood," corrected Mr. Folliot, smiling politely at the joke. "Her father wanted her to be quite, quite British."

"But she was, in fact, born in what is now Rumania?"

119

"She was, yes. As you see from her papers. She was born at Cluj or Kolozsvar or Klausenburg. So were her parents and all their ancestors for at least six hundred years."

"And her mother? When did she die?"

"Dear me. That I don't know."

"But she is not alive? You said Mrs. Cheyney had no living relatives?"

"I did, but that was unconsidered. I should have said there are no relations in this country and none that I know of anywhere else."

"Well, it amounts to the same thing, I suppose."

"Not necessarily," answered Mr. Folliot slowly. "You have reminded me of an event I have not thought about for twenty years. Maculan came to this country and to our company in 1939. He elected to stay; we had already used some of his patents, you understand. His wife went home in August to collect whatever belongings they wished to have with them, leaving the child with her husband. Of course, we all knew war was imminent. That was the basis of Maculan's decision to stay here, for his own country was already under diplomatic pressure from Germany and he preferred us. What nobody then knew, of course, was the fearful speed with which events would move. I recall the then Directors offering to send Maculan home to fetch his wife. But before he could even leave here, it was too late. Maculan's home was already on the far side of enemy Europe. I believe not then actually occupied by the Germans, but not far from it, either. I seem to recall that it was all dependent on the sudden collapse of Polish defences and the westward moves of the Soviets, but I should have to consult the history books to be sure of my facts there. What it amounts to, however, is that I do not know the answer to your question. And I doubt if anybody else does, either."

"And the child was then—let's see—about eight years old."

"That is so."

"It seems odd to have left such a small child without its mother."

"Not so odd. Mrs. Maculan was not intending to stay for more than a week or so, and I recall that she flew. That was not then such a commonplace as it is now. She proposed to come back by the Orient Express to Paris; I now recall it clearly

because of the ticket complications at that time: it was necessary to get Mrs. Maculan a new passport from the Legation
here in London because the child appeared on her original
one."

"You mean the Maculans were aware that the enemy might
put pressure on her if she took the child with her?"

"They may have been. That was not the point at issue then,
however. If the mother took her passport with her as it was,
then the child had no identity document of any kind. You see?
We were already making arrangements for Maculan's nat-
uralization. In some haste, as you may suppose, since if
Rumania was drawn into the war it would be impossible to get
the papers through as long as hostilities lasted. Maculan
would then probably be an enemy alien. As matters turned
out, he would have been."

"So Mrs. Maculan's original passport stayed here. Didn't the
Rumanian Legation object to that?"

"Hmm. It's a Balkan country, you know. And they had
other troubles at the time. I believe something was said to the
effect that the child had some infection, chicken pox or something of that kind."

"Extraordinary clear memory you have, such a long time
after. I congratulate you."

"It was impressed on all our minds. We were very conscious
of Maculan's distress and anxiety. With hindsight it all looked
shockingly reckless, ill-advised. But, if you remember, the
map of Europe changed very suddenly within a few weeks.
Nobody then knew the crucial factor, that the Russians would
move west to meet the Germans. Perhaps it ought to have
been obvious but it wasn't."

"Ah. Hindsight."

"From the present hindsight, but at the time, too. I blamed
myself very bitterly only a week or so after Mrs. Maculan's
journey. Because neither Maculan nor myself were at the
disadvantage of any sentimental notions as to how foreign
politics work. Either one or both of us should have thought of
the possibility of what happened, before the event."

"I'm afraid nobody did, then."

"I daresay the experts did. But publicity in such matters,
and not only in this event, might easily have put ideas into

heads that would otherwise not have conceived them. And if one can put oneself back into that state of ignorance, it seemed at the moment of departure just a perfectly natural thing to do. I mean for Mrs. Maculan to go home to collect personal effects."

"Yes, indeed. And never be heard from again . . ."

"Not quite that. Several letters arrived through Bulgaria, Greece, or somewhere of that sort."

"And the rest was silence?"

"The rest was silence. It was fairly clear that an exit visa was denied at that time. And the incredible disorder at the end of the war explains the rest."

"He never talked about it, I take it?"

"Not after the first few weeks. When the war ended without news, in spite of all Maculan's efforts, it was agreed amongst us all that for the child's sake it was better to preserve silence. Maculan made a point of that himself." Mr. Folliot stared for a moment in front of him. "Maculan and myself were friends, you know. We shared a common interest in local history and it was I who wrote the account of what is known of Grove House, which you can find in the local museum."

As Mr. Folliot left the office after further considerable discussion, the official said thoughtfully as they shook hands, "It's a pretty little problem. Yes, a very interesting situation."

CHAPTER IX

WRINGING OUT the linen, Jenny walked back to her work and laid the wet cloth over the plaster.

"I'll wet it again in the morning, before we leave. Then I can finish it the following day. I think I've got the features now, and the rest I don't really need you for. That is, I mean I can manage without you."

She corrected herself, returning as soon as she stopped work, to her habitual shyness, her fear of arousing disapproval.

"I feel quite excited about it. It's really very like me, don't you think? I've never been done before. Painted, but that was a commercial portrait. I mean, this is a work of art."

Eileen Sandford watched the modelled head as it disappeared in its wrappings with a respect only partly aroused by the fact that the bust was her own. She took it for granted with a naïve egotism that was hardly ever challenged that anything to do with herself was important, but she was impressed, too, by a quality in the work that she recognized as something she had not met with before. The head looked indeed like herself, even in its unfinished form; it might almost have been in some famous art gallery, as she put it to herself. And Jenny, too, was quite different when she was working.

"Where did you learn?" she asked as Jenny turned on the tap again to wash her hands, now red with cold, under the chill clear water.

"I was taken on by Connors as a pupil while I was still at school," she replied, gasping and laughing a little at the shock of cold. She shook her hands free of water vigorously, dancing from one foot to the other and wincing at the ache. "He lived outside the town, did you know?"

123

"Of course, yes," said Eileen who had not known this at all. "He was really famous, wasn't he?"

"Yes, indeed. I was terribly lucky. He didn't take pupils as a rule."

"Your father knew him, I expect," suggested Eileen comfortably. They were pulling on coats by now, to cross to the house.

"Well, he refused Father. But Father wasn't to be put off. He took some awful thing I'd modelled and left it at Connors' house with a card. I've got the card still. He wrote on it 'The girl did this.' That was so like him. No explanation, just the bare thing he needed to say to get what he wanted."

"Did you keep the model, too?"

"Oh, yes. It was the first attempt at the singing bird that stands in the hall. I did it again later, of course, I couldn't show the first try. But it's still up in the loft."

"You mean that figure of a bird was made by you?" Eileen was astounded. "I thought Vincent must have bought that from someone well known."

"No, it's mine." Jenny was not at all offended at Eileen's unflattering surprise. "Father had it cast for me just before he died."

They were strolling now in the dark, clear air in the lee of the tall beech trees. Jenny usually took a walk round the garden after working, and did so now.

"You don't mind if we stretch our legs a few minutes?" she asked.

"But Jenny, you ought to exhibit. You could sell things, I'm sure."

"I suppose I could," said Jenny indifferently. "As a matter of fact two people have asked me to sell the bird. But I couldn't sell that."

"I wish you'd show this bust of me, Jenny. I should love that!"

"If you really like it, I'll give it to you. When it's finished."

Eileen was taking this for granted and found the simple way Jenny said it almost funny; but she did not say anything more than the expression of thanks because a curious impression was growing on her of the need for caution in discussing Jenny's hobby. Like many others, Eileen disclaimed all

124

knowledge of the arts while convinced of her own innate good taste, but she possessed enough judgement, if not in sculpture, to beware of making a fool of herself. For the first time in her life she actually felt that she did not know anything about art. She also felt that Jenny was not only talented but that Jenny knew it without reference to any value an outsider might put on her work. It was a new—and was beginning to be a slightly inhibiting—idea to Eileen that Jenny measured physical objects and beings by some standard of her own to which Eileen had no key. While modelling the head now reposing in the stable, Jenny's look, her whole manner, her movement, even she herself—Eileen found it very difficult to express to herself what she meant—were changed; she became a different being. But not that she changed, she was herself. Her eyes were different, especially the eyes. They were directed to the object in view, which happened to be her friend's head, as that friend now thought not altogether willingly, with an immediacy and a candour that, on consideration, were almost unnerving. Did Jenny, indeed, always consider whatever was exposed to her view with that clear and direct inspection? Was that objective, detached stare an expression of a limited aesthetic training, and directed only to what she was doing with her hands in clay? Or was it the outward sign which the Jenny they knew, Vincent's wife that is, normally did not trust herself to show or possibly did not need to show, that her perception of what went on about her was of another quality from what was conventionally accepted?

No, it must simply be that Jenny was talented in a small way, Eileen thought in her somewhat coarse-grained fashion, because if she really saw things with a special clarity of her own she would have seen through Vincent. That perceptive stare could never have been turned on her husband.

Arrived at this thought—and it was a definite thought process, for Eileen Sandford, although unpracticed at thinking was by no means a stupid human being—Eileen stopped herself with a physical effort that stopped her feet at the same time. She stood still. The soughing of the tree tops penetrated, the intense black of the branches over their heads was scrabbled on a turbulent mass of late afternoon clouds. Her head flung back in the determination not to think what she was thinking gave her the aspect of stern adoration.

"Oh. I should get you just like that," said Jenny without interrupting Eileen's thoughts. "I'm glad you like my trees. Not everybody can see them."

We are going to bury that man tomorrow, thought Eileen, and I could have such dreadful thoughts about him. She was almost frightened.

"They're creepy. Like being in church."

"Yes," answered Jenny.

"But I'm not sure I like them. In fact, I think I need a drink."

"Oh, do let's. Let's go in and have a great big gin!" Jenny instantaneously retreated behind her protective colouring. The frighteningly real child took cover in the artificial childishness, but it was too late to rescue Eileen from her perception. She was not going to admit it to herself, but she knew that the objective stare was real and the silly Jenny with the little hobby who could not cope with the world was a travesty. Eileen knew about children and their realism; she was the mother of four sons. Jenny knew. Jenny knew everything there was to know. Jenny was only pretending, more than to anyone else, to herself. The whole story of the last years—"all that business" with Mona—was Jenny trying *not* to know.

"When I come into the house, I remember again," said Jenny as she closed the door. "He travelled so much that I keep forgetting."

"You ought to go away for a bit. A cruise. Or no, you're so artistic you might go to Greece. Why don't you?"

"I can't go away," said Jenny. The tone of conviction reminded Eileen of her fancy that Jenny expected someone to come back if she only waited. This whole thing is making me neurotic, too, she thought, and drank her large drink too fast. I shall be glad when it's over.

"Do you mean to go on living here, then? Alone?"

Jenny stared, the thought of her aloneness giving her face a melancholy bleakness.

"Of course," she said quietly. "Where else should I live? I've never lived anywhere else."

"I just can't imagine living alone, I suppose. You're a long way from town here, even a long way from the next house."

"I don't mind being alone," said Jenny. Then, aware that this was a most unconventional viewpoint and made her seem strange, she added a lie to it. "I shall have lots of people to stay."

CHAPTER X

JENNY DID not mean what she said about having guests to stay any more than Mr. Folliot meant to give a false impression of her situation when discussing it with others. In fact, Mr. Folliot was not aware that he was talking solely about Jenny's situation either to his Chairman or to the public authorities. He was reporting a problem of law, of responsibility; it was Jenny's situation because she was now the survivor. But Jenny's social lie became truth the very next week, just as Mr. Folliot's truthfulness became a lie without his knowing it.

Mr. Folliot came five days after the funeral to introduce a younger man as one of his assistants. This was the second visit by the lawyer since that sad occasion, the first having been devoted to the regulation of Jenny's relationship, as her father's heir to the company of which both her father and her husband had been directors. This had, as Sandford perceived, never before been necessary but was now an urgent matter of business. Mr. Folliot explained with great clearness to Jenny what her position was and what the view of the company must be. He advised her with scrupulous fairness that in her own interests she ought to retain an independent lawyer, and accepted her surprised but indifferent stare of incomprehension as typical of her unworldliness. Of course he would advise her, replied Jenny, and he should so arrange matters that their relationship would remain exactly as it was. If he thought some formal declaration of this continuation was needed, he would know what to do; he did know and Jenny was made a Director of the company on the understanding that Mr. Folliot would represent her in the normal way of business but that she retained the right, and understood that it was her right, to appoint another attorney if and when she thought it wise to do so.

Mr. Folliot also on that day deposited a considerable sum of money in what was now Jenny's bank account, which on his previous inspection had proved, to his great consternation, to be almost empty. He explained with something less than complete candour, but without telling an untruth, that the money was an accumulation of various royalties and outstanding dividends to which the Managing Director and the Chairman had added a sum to cover what would have been her fees as Director if the question of her right to a directorship had not—as it now seemed unaccountably—been overlooked. A businesswoman might have found all this strange, but Jenny accepted it as in the nature of things and, since she did not understand what had happened and hardly listened to Mr. Folliot's cautious information, she did not grasp the fact that at her husband's death she was almost penniless. Nor did she, therefore, look upon the sums given to her as either a bribe or as conscience money from those who now felt that her interests had been scandalously neglected.

From Mr. Folliot's point of view and that of the company, this interview was a great success. The company was protected from the possible whims of a woman whose notion of business was nonexistent; the lady was protected from penury and given her rights. Above all, the lamentable state of her affairs, of which she appeared to be ignorant, was for the future corrected. There was no reason of law for Teddy Sandford or Mr. Folliot to feel any responsibility for Jenny having been without money; she was a grown woman and might be presumed to be able to take care of her own affairs with her husband. That this had obviously not been the case was not their business. Yet both men did feel that somehow they ought perhaps not always have left those interests so entirely in the hands of Vincent Cheyney. A curious state of affairs, they agreed between themselves, but even if it had been known in Vincent's lifetime, it was doubtful if much could have been done to change it. Vincent's character clearly contained a streak of extravagance that nobody had suspected, because there was nothing about Jenny's own way of living that could account for her being practically bankrupt at his death. The house, though impressive, was not large; the land paid for its own upkeep, being leased to local farmers outside the ring of beeches, and the household was run in a way frugal if anything, rather than generous. Kept with any ordinary competence there was no reason why the Cheyney household should have to buy greenstuffs, eggs or poultry, nor was Vincent's salary low for such a home, considering his wife's private income. It was extraordinary that, for instance, there was no hot water supply in the outbuilding used by Jenny as a studio; this detail had not failed to impress Eileen Sandford.

On the second visit, Mr. Folliot spoke to Jenny of rents and taxes and was once more astonished when he found that she did not know what rents were paid for their land by the two farmers who lived on Beech Grove Hill.

"The rents should be enough to cover your own taxes," he told her. "If you agree I will arrange for the payments to be made into a separate account so that there is always a fund for your tax payments that I can use without constantly bothering you. If we are careful, I should think the upkeep of the house could be covered by the rents as well. But as to that, we shall see how it works out."

"I should like to have new gravel laid in the driveway," said Jenny with an air of inconsequence. "It's the wrong colour, don't you agree, Mr. Folliot? They should be granite chips, not yellow."

"I'll make a note of it," he said gravely.

"Well, I wouldn't want to bother you with such oddments," disclaimed Jenny with an air of wishing to be reasonable. "Your assistant could see to it, perhaps?"

"Young Vail will have plenty to do for a week or so," replied the lawyer, recovering from a sensation of shock. He glanced at his watch. "He should be here at any moment."

Vail also looked at his watch, and then up at the wooden signpost in the centre of the crossroads: "Gullion left." Gullion was the name of the hamlet below Grove House on the hill that the car now began to climb. The little roadway was almost hidden between high banks with hedges atop them, so overgrown with grass, ivy, and clipped bushes that the old stone walls within the banks were hardly visible. The local baker's van pulled into a five-barred gate to allow the Ford passage. This was Gullion: a tiny stone church like a toy, granite gateposts, a scattering of neat, small houses and cottages among trees and hedges, a triangular opening hardly large enough to be called the village green, one general shop. The road, one-track, swung here round the hill, so that for the first time the grove of beeches was seen as imminently near above, although they were visible as a landmark from some miles off. The road swung again and again, the hedges, as in the village, partly evergreen and partly blackthorn, spikily arid. Again two granite posts, smoothed and yet pocked from ancient times and soft weathering, patches of yellow lichen clinging and the same curious rounded tops on necks. Very old, these stones, and no gate between them. Tall old yews, shaggy and patchily grown, the sable and shiny leaves of bays and rhododendrons. The end of the road; it was now a driveway of yellow gravel. Suddenly, the stern, tall beech trunks disowned the evergreens, reduced them to insignificance, an afterthought of domesticity by centuries. A sharp curve in the drive having the effect of a ha-ha cut off the sight of the entry from the outside world. Grass on either hand, the drive ended in a small round before the oaken door. Some crouching shrubs that would bloom in spring, low, grey steps: the house.

Hmm, thought Vail, I see what the old boy meant. The beeches that enclosed the house framed it as well. They were all round the house at a distance that made them sentinels. The building was late Tudor, granite of course, in blocks; the windows on this side tall with leaded glass set unevenly so that what flecks of light there were on a cloudy day shot off them here and there. Not big, proportionately slightly squat against the elongated giant trees. The house was of a sound solidity, a spare elegance of age, an old, dim jewel in a unique setting.

His first impression was that here was a possession for which almost anyone would be prepared to undertake great efforts to obtain or retain. One might look upon it as aesthetically so pleasing that its intrinsic value was practically incomputable because it was unique; or one might put a philistine value on the place as being of immense prestige, a possession that would guarantee respect to its owners through its air of moderation, of not attempting to be a great mansion, of being

131

stubbornly itself. There was as well, since it was with successful businessmen that this matter was concerned, the point that the house and its land were of considerable and increasing money value.

As soon as Vail arrived at the massive square portal he saw, too, that the house had either survived the generations intact or had at some time been restored with great care to its original state. While the mounting stones half sunk crookedly into the lawn's edge argued the first, the iron bands and lock-facing of the door were handwrought, but not more than a generation old. And parts of the window near enough for him to see in detail had been reglazed with old panes of glass but in nearly new setting. He guessed, correctly, that glass had been taken from windows broken beyond repair and reset in those that could still be saved. Someone had cared about the old house, and cared with judgement as well as love.

A middle-aged woman in a baggy tweed skirt and an aniline green cardigan over her blouse, which failed to harmonise either with her own appearance or with the blouse, opened the door to Vail. He was evidently expected, for she greeted him with a nod and the statement that he was for Mr. Folliot. She indicated a solid door to the right and added the information that they were in the side room.

"They" proved to be Mr. Folliot and a woman in her late twenties who turned her head as he entered. The room was even more agreeable to the senses than the deep hall and its oak staircase, with massive banister and low treads and its perfect rustic panelling. The panelling here was later, the windows tall with deep window seats, and a stone fireplace dominated the space between them. Vail managed to get a quick look at the panels nearest as he moved forward. Yes, linenfold. And real. The room was furnished as a sitting room with comfortable restraint, neither aping a period nor refusing machine-made cushioning. The first impression of its unknown occupant, as greetings and introductions were exchanged, was of intense nervousness. Her hand was long and narrow, and although she hardly touched his, which he deliberately extended to be shaken, it felt dry, bony and quivering as it flinched away from his grip. The fingers were cold, although the room, like the hall, was warm and he could

132

now see the central heating radiators. The eyes were immediately veiled and seemed, like the hand, to flinch. The thin features were well-proportioned but colourless, spoiled by what was evidently an habitual trick of clenching her teeth, possibly to control herself. The dark and copious hair looked as if she cut it herself. Like her unnoticeable clothes, it was neat but at once conveyed that the woman cared nothing for her own looks, or perhaps had given them up as a bad job. Meeting her for the first time as a separate person, and not an attachment of someone better known to the observer, something was at once clear to Vail that had escaped both Mr. Folliot and the Sandfords: the woman was of a settled unhappiness. Not grieving, unhappy. In the dry, fine skin of a grey pallor, the jumpy, febrile movements and the eyes, narrowed as if to keep out the light, were the signs of recent crippling shock, but the aura of acquiescent depression was clearly much older than the bereavement.

They discussed, the three of them, what Vail was to do and how best to go about the work.

"I will try not to disturb you more than I have to, Mrs. Cheyney. But I suppose I shall have to ask you questions. There are bound to be a good many things I don't know."

"Is it all so complicated, then?" Mrs. Cheyney spoke to Folliot.

"There does seem to be a certain amount of confusion," he admitted. "As I said, but I didn't wish to distress you at that time by going into details. Mr. Vail is familiar with the situation, naturally, but the material is not simple even to someone who knows it, as he does. We want to get all your father's affairs tidied up, you know, as well as Vincent's. I'm sure you will find Mr. Vail as considerate as I could be myself and he won't waste your time unnecessarily."

"Oh, I didn't mean that!" She sounded quite startled at the implication that she might have been complaining. "I only meant, it sounds as if Mr. Vail will be here for days. Perhaps even several weeks. I mean, the hotel in the town is really quite primitive and it's three miles away, in any case. Won't it be best if you stay here in the house?" She spoke directly to Vail for the first time, but her eyes strayed away from his face with reluctance at a personal contact.

"Really, I couldn't possibly put you to such an inconvenience," he objected. "The hotel will be well enough, I'm sure."

"But it won't be," she said. "It's really rather awful. There is plenty of room here. The big room even has its own bathroom!" This was evidently meant to be a tentative joke. "Eileen Sandford said it was very comfortable. And you know, Mrs. Foster is used to coping with several people. She won't mind a bit."

"I really think you should avail yourself of Mrs. Cheyney's kindness, Vail," pronounced Mr. Folliot sedately. "These country hotels can be a severe trial to the temper. And probably cold."

"It is most kind of you, but I really cannot so impose on your hospitality," argued Vail and frowned quickly at Folliot to enlist his support. It would be most improper for him, in the circumstances, to accept such a personal kindness.

Unfortunately it never occurred to Mr. Folliot that there could be any reason to include Jenny in Vail's researches. It did not enter his mind in London with Vail's superiors, nor did he think of it now. His attitude was simple: Vincent's machinations were at least as much injuries against his wife as against Tantham and Maculan, and although it was obvious that one could not add to the widow's sorrows with such sordid suspicions, that she must be protected from the knowledge until she had at least partly recovered from her shock and grief, there was no implication in Mr. Folliot's mind of any deception of Jenny. He assumed, wrongly, that the authorities took this view for granted, as he did. Moreover, the possibility that some outside approach might be made to Jenny seemed to Folliot quite enough reason for a man to be present in the house who understood what was afoot; Foster was not a protection against business or criminal visitors who might even threaten a woman living practically alone in this out-of-the-way spot.

"I will go and speak to Mrs. Foster," said Jenny, not wishing to make protestations of her willingness to accept Mr. Folliot's assistant, which is what Vail was to her, into her home. It was easier to escape so that she could take it as settled without further discussion, and she went out quickly.

"Do not forget," said Mr. Folliot seriously, "that Grove

House is some way from even the nearest house and it is by no means impossible that some accomplice of Cheyney's may arrive here."

"That is quite true," agreed Vail, "but—" He stopped. What the old boy says *is* true, he thought reluctantly. This place is not like a town. The only way it could be watched except by someone inside is by visible police guards. That would be horribly public. And even if we suggested guards as protection for Mrs. Cheyney for some vague reason, they would certainly put off anybody who felt like approaching her.

"I understand your scruples, but I am sure you are wrong," said Mr. Folliot. "There may be some doubt in your mind about accepting hospitality in the circumstances, but unfortunately a good deal of dissimulation is bound to be present in such an extraordinary case as this. And on the whole, don't you feel that there has been so much deception somewhere that no blame need attach to attempts to clear it up? Or, if it comes to that, to prevent the deception from going further."

"I suppose you are right," said Vail, still dubious, "prevention is better than cure."

"We must hold to that thought," agreed Mr. Folliot.

Once more Mr. Folliot departed after lunch. Jenny, however, who very much wanted to get to her studio, where a new piece of work awaited her, found that she was expected to show an interest in what Mr. Vail was about to begin. She agreed at once, but finding herself again in the dressing room next to her bedroom, where Vincent's desk always stood, she found this revisiting so unpleasant that she nerved herself to make a suggestion.

"There's a much more convenient room downstairs," she said. "We thought it must originally have been the agent's office, when this was a manor estate, long ago. My father used it as a study or library and I'm sure you would be better off there. There's space to lay things out, you know?" she added vaguely, not wishing to mention her real objection to this room. "It hasn't been used for years, but I expect it's in order. Perhaps we might look at it. . . ."

Vail noticed the dislike of his being here with the objectivity of a professional who allowed the sentiment its various and different possibilities. It was next to her own apartment, as well as reminding Mrs. Cheyney of her loss. Both of these alternatives were just as likely as that the room or her own next door contained something he was not intended to see.

The study downstairs was indeed a much more convenient place for work. A small room, looking over what had once been the stable courtyard and connecting with it through a short passage by a side door, long unused. It contained a massive, roughly carpentered table as well as a desk, bookshelves, a gun rack and a fireplace installed in the Victorian age with a grate for coals.

"Nobody here shoots, I see," said Vail with otherwise approving glances round the office thus offered to him.

"No. My father hated to have wild things killed and Vincent wasn't keen. But the gun rack was left where it always was. Do you shoot, then?" She was conventionally polite.

"I like to go out when I have the chance," Vail said, "but the season is over in any case."

"It's a bit dusty in here."

"I expect I shall make it a good deal dustier," he dismissed this. "Very well, then. I'll begin to clear out upstairs and get everything down here. I understand from Mr. Folliot that the stuff from the bank and everything that was in the desk up there has been put back into the dressing room?"

"I'm afraid that is going to be a lot of trouble. Should I ask Foster to help carry things?"

"Oh, no, thank you. I shall sort things as I go along." He went over to the window and looked out at the cobbled yard, grass and moss between the stones except where a well-worn track kept them clear. "Peaceful here."

"It is quiet. Shall I leave you to work, then?" A note of hopefulness in the question; she certainly did not intend to supervise him. But naturally, anything she was aware of needing to do was already done. That is, if her manner covered not a real indifference and ignorance but some other state of mind. If so, this would not be the first time in Vail's experience that a recognition of defeat resulted in just this kind of useful dissimulation by creating an effect of uselessness. The suddenness of Cheyney's removal from the scene and the disruption it caused might, quite simply, be being used as a means of withdrawing from a situation no longer capable of being maintained.

If that were so, it would probably quite quickly be put to the test of having to become active dissimulation instead of the present passivity. Because those with whom Cheyney had been sharing his interests could be expected not to wait much longer before trying to discover what was happening. They must want to know with some urgency just what, so far, had been discovered.

That Folliot had so quickly arrived on the stage was due to Sandford's realisation that the widow was no longer under any form of control by his company and that this must be corrected for the sake of everyone concerned. That Folliot immediately reported the strange discrepancies he found, and at the same time reported the reason for his so quickly having found them, put Sandford and Folliot, for different reasons, "in the clear." But nothing so far did as much for the widow.

While these thoughts were going through his mind, Vail was looking about the room for a telephone connection, and Jenny stared with a not entirely melancholy nostalgia into the courtyard. The line of the stable wall there is very pleasing, she thought, propped up by that small buttress at some time to support it. It must have started to bulge, as walls do; I wonder when. "Something there is that doesn't love a wall." How true.

"Ah, there it is," he said aloud and she jumped. "I'm sorry, did I startle you? I was looking for a phone box."

"I think it has an extension plug in here. You could bring down the telephone from upstairs. You will need one, I expect."

"Thank you, I'll do that if I may."

Edging toward escape, Jenny murmured something about "if you need anything" and gradually effaced herself. Odd creature, he thought, she fades out like the Cheshire cat, without a smile.

Once in the bothy studio Jenny, as always, turned the key in the door, for Mona came up there once to find her, and since then the door was always fastened. If she heard someone approaching she could stay quiet until they went away again.

She removed the cover from her new work and stood considering it. It was years since she worked directly in stone and she was still rather unhandy and slow. I expect I shall do this half a dozen times before I get it. I ought to model it first, save stone. But she did not want to do that. It was to be a group of tall and meagre veiled figures, the grove. They must have the knottiness and angularity of extreme age, but be at the same time smooth as the real trees were, the harsh edges only suggested from the inside of the stone. She began to work with anxious care, aware that technically the group was well beyond her half-trained powers, and soon forgot everything but what she was doing.

It was dark when she returned to the main house. The afternoon post lay on the big chest and Foster was doing something with the curtains where a ring had come loose.

"You don't take the evening paper any more," she said to him, lifting her head to look up at him on the ladder. "Do take it. I know you like to see the racing." Foster was so upset to hear thus that it was known he took the paper that he almost lost his footing on the ladder.

"Thank you, Mrs. Cheyney," he muttered, round a pin held between his teeth. The hook was fast on the ring again, and he shook the red rep curtain to test its hold before retreating cautiously down the treads. There was no longer anyone in the hall and Foster took the paper from the chest.

Jenny dropped the letter on her dressing table on her way to the bathroom. Clean, and warmed by the water, she returned to pull on slacks and a fresh shirt and brush her hair. She turned the envelope over, wondering idly whose hand it could be. Then she saw that the postmark was Wrexham. For once it was quite clear, the stamp. Thinking it must be from the hospital, Jenny weighed the idea of passing it on to Mr. Vail. But she did not want the stranger to know what a coward she was, so choosing the lesser of the evils, Jenny tore open the letter.

It took two readings to understand it, two readings and a check at the heading with its illustration of a country tavern on one side 'and the miniature telephone under the address on the other. "We thought it over a lot of times before deciding to write to you," the letter said. "But you will understand that we only started the hotel side of the business a few months ago and there are all our expenses to consider. It was only when we saw our local paper that we knew what had happened. Otherwise Mr. and Mrs. Cheyney, as we thought they were, were supposed to be coming back for another night. We read about the accident but did not connect it until the picture of the funeral, with the poor lorry driver there with his arm in a sling and a Mrs. Cheyney standing next to him, that we saw what happened. Only you see there is our bill outstanding and the case is just overnight things, nothing we could realize on. The lady was wearing her fur coat when they went out in the morning. My husband said let it go, but we have our interests to think of, otherwise we would not trouble you when you have so much trouble. But it was dinner, too, and two baths as well as the room. And a lot of telephone calls to London and they all have to be paid for. We therefore take the liberty of enclosing our bill herewith." And there was indeed the bill, with the same cliché heading as the letter paper. Double room with heating charge extra, two baths. Dinner, special order. Breakfast for two. Reservation charge for one night extra. Four pink gins, two bottles vin rosé, two brandies. Even early-morning tea was listed and, of course, service charges. Telephone calls were on yet another sheet.

I wonder what they ate, thought Jenny. They did themselves well. She took the contents of the envelope and went down to the side room without thinking what she was doing.

Mr. Vail was already there, tall, slightly bending at the shoulders, dark hair with one strand falling forward over his rather prominent forehead.

"Here is another bill," said Jenny. "Unpaid. Can I give it to you?" She just wanted to be rid of it, but whatever he expected he was unprepared for what he got. He read the letter, looked at the bill, and lifted his rather long face to examine her. It was that search for guidance that broke the unreality.

"I thought you would know," Jenny said blankly and tried to take the papers back, but her hands began to shake so uncontrollably that she missed them. So she abandoned this idea and put out a hand to support herself against the stone of the fireplace.

"This is appalling," she whispered, her eyes fixed with a

blind stare on his without seeing him. She was unable to move, she could not even move her eyes to close them. She was transfixed with a dreadful knowledge, as if she actually had never known the truth, as if the shock of knowing was as new as the letter's arrival. What stunned her was that her old knowledge, the old accusation so effectually denied, was all the time the truth. Vincent not only denied it but went on acting the denial at the cost of her own belief that she was unhinged. And he took this course and kept to it, *knowing* that if she believed his protestations she must doubt her own sanity, the evidence of her own eyes, ears and understanding. Jenny did not think these thoughts, they were already there in her mind, covered up. Now they were, with savage and irreparable violence, uncovered.

Vail saw that he must say something to contribute a feeling of the ordinary to what was at any moment going to disintegrate into a scene that neither of them would ever be able to forget.

"I did know," he said, "but I understood that you did not."

This hard candour seemed to help her; at any rate the sound of a level and reasonable voice saying something she could understand, words that proved she was not wandering in an unpeopled void of unreality, gave her some reassurance.

"But you don't know what that letter means to me," answered Jenny. "You can't know that, nobody can."

Vail began to disclaim any desire to witness uncontrollable emotion with a conventional expression of regret, but Jenny was not listening and went on talking, not to Vail but to herself. It was perfectly impossible for her at that moment not to put into spoken words what she was now discovering. She must say it aloud to prove its reality. She spoke rapidly and without expression.

"Both Vincent and Mona behaved as if what I suspected was out of the question, ridiculous. I remember quite clearly how it started. I told Vincent that he was unwise to start an affair with someone inside the company because of all the social and personal trouble that would create. His affairs before were kept so discreet that nobody knew of them except me, and I only knew because his various girls always took up an attitude of condescension to me while they were in favour with Vincent, and that gave them away. You see, it was always agreed that I was not very satisfactory; even I agreed with that, or I came to. He used to say I was so artistic that I didn't understand about flesh and blood people. But we never discussed such things directly, the subject was avoided, until Mona became his secretary. Then I said this about its being unwise. Vincent said I was imagining things, it was all my artist's fantasy. He did not even pick Mona as his secretary, she was appointed to him. They meant nothing at all to each other; he found her rather unappetising and she was intimate with several men and was thinking of getting engaged. When they were obliged to travel together for the sake of work, they always used different hotels. And so on, and so on. Naturally, Mona gave the whole show away by being very offended and 'huffy' the next time I saw her; but somehow I agreed, as it were, to believe Vincent and to see Mona's changed manner to me as her understandable resentment at being suspected of deceiving me.

"And it was after that that all sorts of things began to go wrong. There was the business of Vincent going to Warsaw when he told me he was going to Prague. That was the first thing. Then the parcel of books that could not be found, and about a week later Foster found them in the potting shed behind a shelf. Then Vincent and the Fosters started to look at me oddly and I got frightened. Once the figure of the bird you may have seen in the hall was moved to the upper landing, and when I brought it back to its old place it was lying on its side every morning for weeks and nobody had touched it. Finally I told Foster to wire it to its base with copper wire; the wire is still there. You see, when it was something of my own like the bird, I knew, I knew inside, that I did not do it. But the other things I didn't know about. I became hysterical and did not know what I was doing sometimes, and I thought I really did behave irrationally."

"You modelled that bird?" Vail sounded interested. "I thought it very good."

"It got worse and worse. I forgot appointments or transposed the days. I did something strange about money, although I've never known what it was, but something, because Vincent had to change the joint account at the bank. After that Mona did the housekeeping money when Vincent wasn't here, when he was travelling. Then other people, outsiders, began to look at me queerly and some of them suggested I should see a doctor, but I was afraid to do that. The worse it got the more afraid I was, you can see how that would be, can't you? Then one day Vincent asked me where his hairbrushes were and when I replied that they were on his chest of drawers as they always were, he said, 'You'd better go and look so that you know they are not where they always are. I suppose you've done something crazy with them, too.' I went to look and there were no brushes, but I didn't know where they could be. Then I had a sort of fit. A crisis. I screamed and raved and threw things about. And suddenly, from one moment to the next, I was perfectly calm and sane. I realized that something would have to be done. I must go to a psychiatrist.

"Next day I did nothing about it because Vincent was ill and I took care of him and then I began to get better from that day on. None of the strange things happened after that. We never spoke of it again, but I got better."

Jenny stopped speaking. Her rigid stance relaxed, and she turned towards the fireplace and away from the listener, who remained perfectly still and silent. She took the box of matches from the chimney shelf above her head, as she had done the day of Vincent's death, and shook them. Then she took out a match, struck it and lit the fire. She gazed at the creeping blue flame until the kindling caught and brilliant orange-red tongues of fire flickered round the logs. Then, still looking down at the fire, she spoke again.

"Do you see now what the letter means to me?"

There was a long silence, but evidently the flood of words had passed itself away.

"It means that you were never unhinged," said Vail at last. "You were being lied to. Tricks were being played on you. Is that what you mean?"

"That is what it means," she agreed. "And at the very moment when I really believed the lies and said I must go to a mental doctor, the whole thing ceased. Do you see? That was a threat. If I did go to a doctor and he was halfway competent, he would prove there was nothing wrong with me. Then the whole plot would come out. But I never admitted all this to myself until I read this letter."

There was a question Vail very much wanted to ask her, so much that he could hardly keep silent; but to ask his question would be so ill-advised at this moment as to negate the usefulness of his knowledge of its answer. What he wished urgently to know was, if Jenny had previously condoned her husband's mistresses as she said, why was the affair with the secretary of such secrecy that he was prepared to go to these lengths to preserve its inviolability? To take measures that required the collaboration of Mona Laver, so that the doing of it put him in the power of a woman he already knew to be morally unsound. Not that Vail any more than most experienced men would have condemned either a man or a woman for an illicit love affair as morally unsound. But if what Jenny now told him, or rather as he was quite aware, told herself in his presence, if that were true, then both Cheyney and Mona Laver were of a coarse cruelty of nature that stamped them both as criminal. It is one thing to deceive a spouse and go to bed with one's secretary. It is quite another matter to drive one's wife to insanity in order to achieve that end. The first is a matter of private deceit and unhappiness that could or could not have some possible excuse and is so common that a general agreement can exist to ignore it. Like most men, Vail hoped that he would, if he were married, not do such things. But it is a peccadillo compared with what these two had done. If it were true.

So there were two questions: was Jenny's story true, and if so, why, why, why? To the first question, Vail had the means of finding an answer. And to the second he slowly groped towards a possible answer, at the moment only in his own mind, which could go far towards achieving his purpose in this house.

Jenny now presented him with an easy method of testing her own story.

"I've rather thought of mentioning to you something that you will now understand. I should like to get rid of the Fosters and find somebody else to run the house. Do you think you could arrange that for me? I suppose it's rather outside your scope, really, but it would be an immense help to me if you would do it."

"Good Lord," he said, dismayed. "Get rid of competent

servants in this day and age? Are you sure? I mean, I do see that they have unhappy associations for you, but . . . ?"

"Oh, if you feel . . ."

"Well, not quite that. I see your position, indeed. But you certainly need somebody here, and it isn't easy to find reliable people so far out in the country. Look, how would it be if I had a talk with Foster? He could get the impression perhaps that I am just gossiping along in the course of a fairly boring job here. I could find out for you what they feel and think?"

"If you think so," she agreed weakly. "I daresay I am unreasonable."

"Let me test out the ground and then we can talk about it again?"

"Very well, thank you," she said. They were called to the evening meal at that moment, and afterwards exchanged only such commonplaces as strangers do in the presence of other strangers.

CHAPTER XI

By COMMON consent they went their various ways after dinner: Jenny to the studio and Vail to the downstairs office. It was very cold over the stable, so cold that Jenny shivered in her heavy jacket. One convenience that did exist there was a powerful light trained on the center of the bare space, and Jenny switched this on and stood considering her work. Or, rather, she looked at it without considering it.

If her perceptions that evening were true, and it was now too late for any but a pathological cowardice to retreat again into ignorance, there were consequences she could not avoid thinking about. Vincent could not have loved her. Indeed, Vincent's feeling towards her must have been so far removed from affection that—since it certainly could not have been indifference, for that would have made the long deception pointless—then the word hatred would be nearer the mark. You didn't play such tricks on anyone for whom you felt a coldness less than hostility; and although Jenny had never even thought before this of such disingenuousness, the shock of knowledge removed from her mind at one savage blow the entire clutter of habit, intimacy and illusion that enfolds every marriage. It was a stroke of moral violence no less than the shock of the Rover meeting a heavy truck head-on was a stroke of physical violence. But unlike such a bodily crash, it could not kill. Instead, it did what the powerful beam of light did in the studio—the emphasis of shadows only smudged by the other lights in their inadequacy were sharpened into cliffs and crevasses, black masses and planes of yellow brilliance with clear-cut edges. What could now be seen was seen in implacable detail and clarity, and what was still hidden by the heavy shading of the revealing light was in even inkier blackness than the pervading shadows before the light was burning. Before, the differences in darkness of those shadows was graduated so subtly that they could be ignored, the eye could accept them simply as shadows. Now what could not be all too clearly seen was infinitely secretive, deliberately hidden.

Evidently, too, Mona Laver was of overpowering importance to Vincent. She was not by any means his first affair, but she had become *the* affair. Important enough for him to take risks involving his career, a carefully built and much-prized prosperity, the expensively acquired perquisites of success. But no. Naturally, the others knew. It was, then, accepted. Vail had said as much. That being so, why did Vincent not leave her, his wife, and marry Mona Laver? This was one of the harshly exposed areas of illumination, and Jenny held her breath as she contemplated the expanse of injustice, of having been used.

She was by nature unbusinesslike, and Vincent, as she now saw, trained her to be more so, gradually reducing the areas of her competence until she was little more than a child or a moron. She now felt some shame at her own weakness and stupidity, which were as unkindly revealed as the other facts. But wait, was she so very stupid? Did not a long series of careful constructions make her stupid, reduce her to childishness? Fascinated by Vincent at seventeen and quickly afterwards bereaved; not many people had much sense at that age, Jenny thought. The loss of her father, who was also her childhood intimate, nurse, and playmate as well as parent because of the unusual circumstances of their life, of their being here at all, that was where dependence on Vincent had begun. The playful and loving protection of the weeks of an engagement that presented itself as the secure haven from a great emptiness of grief and loss suddenly now brought memories of sharp clearness. The repeated murmur of endearment at her youth and loneliness somehow now seemed to have shaded into the implication of an incapacity to manage situations and people. Somewhere a sigh of weariness entered, at the bachelor simplicity of former domestic arrangements, at the central European emigrés who lived with her father and herself and ran the household, and who had, as Vincent often pointed out, rather taken over their lives. Cer-

146

tainly the house was not properly run, Jenny could now agree, looking back at the time after she was left alone. This was the moment of the Fosters' appearance. And, of course, of her marriage. There was even then a vague proposal that she lacked some necèssary common sense or competence; not that she would have to make an effort to "cope" but that she could not be expected to. At an age when other girls were going to university or learning skills of complex kinds, she was losing the tools of everyday life. Her father's papers, for instance, Jenny supposed were not more difficult to understand than the subjects any girl learns at a business school. Yet there was an almost physical memory of the files being taken from her hands, which might quite well be a real memory of a real occasion. Even clearer, the implication that it was pointless to continue her apprenticeship to the great sculptor Connors, with his abrasive contempt for what he considered the philistine world of business. Her own distress at this decision, reversing her father's, might have reached rebelliousness, but Connors himself resolved the matter by returning to his native Ireland. His disappearance did not end the recurring adverse comments on sordid hovels, laziness masquerading as the licence of the artist, the self-indulgence of such a life throughout the war and postwar difficulties; most often of all, the question of Connors' value as an artist. These ended only gradually as Jenny herself began to agree with them in a childish duplicity of flattery of Vincent that cherished his jealousy and possessiveness.

Vincent's possessiveness, the display of his jealousy, did not end with an almost sudden slackening of spontaneity and urgency in their intimate life together; these qualities retained their strength as well as their power to convince Jenny of his love long after it was agreed that physically she failed in some way never openly expressed but often implied. The guilt of this discovery, so wounding to Jenny, quite quickly dominated her feeling for Vincent; she was permanently and irrecoverably in his debt, and if he turned to other girls it was not because he did not love her but because she failed him in a way that reduced her to impotence. Obviously, lovemaking was something that the very simplest woman could understand, and indeed this was proved by the standards of those Vincent preferred to herself. But if Jenny found these girls vulgar and pretentious, that only proved her own lack of understanding as well as her inadmissible jealousy of them. She was painfully aware of her own need for humility and the need to retain Vincent's love in other directions, since she failed in this important one. She ought to be, and she was, grateful to her husband.

Mona appeared when this pattern was well established. It was precisely because the open secret of her own lack of sensuality and naturalness was absolutely agreed between Jenny and Vincent that Jenny mistakenly felt herself able to warn Vincent of the dangers of a liaison within the permanent frame of his life with the company and herself. She felt then a deep tenderness for Vincent because she for once had recognised, before he did, something that could harm him. The shock of having not only presumed to know better than Vincent, but of having in her inexperience been mistaken as well, shook Jenny now in retrospect and returned her, with a deep flash of anger and resentment, to her present knowledge.

For if she was, after all, right in her judgement of Mona Laver, she could have been right about other things and persons. And if her assumption that a love affair which must become common knowledge was not, as she judged, dangerous to Vincent, that was because his disloyalty had long before reached a point where he constantly hinted to others of her own inadequacy. Only because Vincent had carefully prepared the ground was his preference for Mona accepted by his colleagues as a second-best solution to an impossible situation with herself.

At this point the area of illumination fell off sheerly into black unknowingness. For there was nothing about Mona to distinguish her from any of the other fleeting fancies. There was no great charm of appearance or personality in her that gained acceptance for her among Vincent's friends and colleagues. They lived, all of them, closely allied in their social as well as business lives; Jenny herself was further outside their circle than Vincent's secretary, and she now allowed herself to recall without her habitual insincerity a number of small instances when Eileen Sandford or Mr. Folliot, among others, showed that they did not think of Miss Laver as an equal.

148

Jenny always allowed herself to assume that this was local snobbery or an internal company rating of position. But even Jenny's unworldliness was obliged to admit that secretaries do not come into the fixed categories of business hierarchy. Some secretaries, including Mr. Folliot's own, came from the landed gentry of the countryside and were socially more prized than far more senior members of the company. If Mona Laver was treated as an inferior, it was because she was lacking in the graces of a refined sensibility as much as because of any snobbery in her circle. Mona Laver was in fact as commonplace as any other of the girls Vincent wanted at one time or another to take to bed, as unimpressive but not as docile. Jenny had been right in her judgement that Mona was dangerous; she was hard and ambitious and Vincent had made a serious mistake when he became intimate with her. The kind of mistake Vincent never made.

It was inexplicable. Or at any rate, inexplicable to Jenny, and having come to a place where the light failed out of her own sheer inexperience, Jenny's attention switched and she grasped with a sensation of shock that she was quite mistaken. Mona became a mistake for Vincent only when they were killed together in a motoring accident. It was as simple as that. Their situation was completely in Vincent's control; the two of them, as well as all their acquaintances, perfectly understood the form, as Vincent would have said. It was the brutal chance of geometry, the wing of a sixteen-wheeled truck slightly out of its permitted path at the single moment when the Rover, too, was out of its track. A few inches, the combined speeds, their total weights very slightly miscalculated—that was the only misjudgement.

At the dreadful realisation of this fact, Jenny put out a hand to touch the stone of her block and felt with its chill how very cold she was, standing there in the hard light of two hundred watts. The lamp itself made a small circle of heat behind her shoulder, but everywhere else was so bitterly cold that she was shivering from head to foot. This shaking came as much from her inner confusions of emotion, her inability to think logically about her predicament, as from the surrounding atmosphere. She had missed the perfectly obvious among the many facts of memory, so perhaps all her other conclusions were as false as the one that Mona contained some special importance

149

for Vincent? Yet she had come to this thought slowly. And come by herself, without outside help. One mistake did not reduce the whole sequence to nonsense. Jenny went back to the early part of her marriage and now she felt sure that there *was* some deliberate intention in its course, some calculation steadily held to in the accumulated details of her own loss of confidence. Jenny supposed now that any girl going from the schoolroom into marriage with a man ten years her senior would hesitate to challenge her husband's authority. Did everyone who married young become so totally subservient as she had been? But most girls had mothers, fathers, siblings. She could recall thinking on the day of Vincent's death that things would have turned out differently if her father had not died. Perhaps she would not even have married Vincent?

The thought became vague. Jenny leaned forward to examine the etched lines in the stone block where as yet only outlines of her concept existed. Her attention now caught, she narrowed her gaze and scrutinised the point at which the chiselling of one of the figures began more deeply. She moved a step sideways to see how the light fell. Then she pulled at the sturdy board and trestle on which the block was raised, to turn the whole stone slightly. A sensation of profound distrust and doubt filled her to the exclusion of all other thoughts. I cannot ever have believed this was going to be any good, she thought, almost in panic. Those lines there—sentimental, unreal, a craven humiliating appeal to the immediate sympathy of the viewer. What would Connors say to that—he would throw the whole thing into the dust bin. Connors! What would my father have said to it?

Her father would hardly have credited that Jenny, however technically inept, could have committed this kind of artistic vulgarity; she knew that as soon as she looked at her work with the different view newly forced upon her. Her father always believed in Jenny's inheritance of his own talent in another form. Essentially that talent was the naïve, direct look, the diamond eye that for Maculan had cut through surface or incidental accumulations on a mathematical or engineering problem to its inner question of just how to do what was required, no more and no less. Not to adapt but to see afresh.

Jenny sank down on a low bench that stood near the block and stared at her own aberration with a now implacable eye. It would have to go, of that there was no question. The only question was how far she had allowed her perception to be corrupted, for how long and whether it could now by stringent and honest work be corrected. She must inspect the bust of Eileen tomorrow to decipher in it her loss of integrity, to decide whether this new attempt *was* only an aberration or a real inability to see clearly. She would be able to judge that from the unfinished head, but for this evening she lacked the energy to put it to the test.

As to how the downfall came about there was never any doubt. Jenny had become an habitual liar to herself and to others, out of cowardice, acceptance of humiliation, lack of a decent pride. She had allowed herself to believe that she was useless and helpless, and naturally she became so. The time for blaming Vincent was as quickly past as it came; it was herself she must blame now, if only because there is only one character that can ever be changed and that is one's own.

For tonight it was enough; she was as exhausted as if she had pulled the ruined stone block by main force up from the town by herself. A few minutes of walking among the beech trees and she would go to bed.

Once outside and moving, Jenny felt the night to be less cold than the unheated stone building. The air was brisk but not unfriendly and so windless that the trees were still and soundless. Somewhere a small animal scuttled, outside the grove a heavy bustling betrayed the presence of a cow at the edge of the hill meadow. As Jenny moved towards the house, she hoped that Vail was not about. By the morning her outburst before the evening meal could be ignored, but she had no wish to face anyone tonight. In circling the house Jenny bypassed the courtyard or she would have seen the light still burning in the downstairs office. In the hall only one lamp glowed as she let herself in and locked the door behind her.

The thought about Vail recurred, once safely in her room, for she had run up the stairs quickly, so that if he were about, she could disappear without meeting him. All very well, she thought, to assume that by morning no comment on the scene she had so untypically made to a stranger would be needed. Or would even be possible unless she mentioned it herself first.

She did not know Vail. He was a man of about thirty-five and, she supposed, trained for the law. Rather tall, with shoulders that appeared to be thin and angular, and slightly bent, he was dark-complexioned, with somewhat deep-set eyes and hair that, although tidy, was long enough to allow a lock to fall over his high forehead. She thought his forehead was narrow, but could not now be sure. His voice and clothes were so neutral, ambiguously so it now seemed to her, that she could tell nothing about his possible upbringing. If he were what was formerly expressed as "badly brought up," he might feel himself entitled to comment on an incident that, after all, included himself as a participant. It seemed unlikely, but Jenny began to worry about the possibility and what she could do to cut it short if it happened. In the middle of cleaning her teeth her concern struck her as ridiculous and she lifted her bent head to frown at herself in the glass admonishingly. You are not to worry about such stupid details, she told her reflection. If he is unfeeling enough to mention something so clearly bound to be unwelcome to his hostess, tell him you would rather not speak of it and make it clear that you expect him not to discuss it with others; he is, after all, an employee of the company and must look upon you in some way as his employer. This idea, the first time it occurred to Jenny, made her giggle slightly, and she looked so absurd with toothpaste foaming round her mouth that she laughed aloud at herself and felt better. Still, it was uncomfortable having this total stranger about, and she could not think now why she suggested it in the first place—unless she wanted to assert herself?

Nobody can ever see the expression of their own eyes, so Jenny could not appreciate how much this notion conflicted with the timid, lonely look that even laughter did not drive out from her face.

152

CHAPTER XII

Vail was not at breakfast and Mrs. Foster said, in her own characteristically disapproving fashion, that he drank his coffee very early.

"Said he would take a walk," she added, as if that was something Mr. Vail was not entitled to do. "He keeps all those papers locked up. Nothing at all on the desk when I went to dust."

"I'm glad he's tidy," said Jenny, pouring coffee. "Lawyers always lock things up. That's what they are for."

"Norma's up from the village this morning. Says her mum's leg is bad and she'll help for today."

"Is it all right for her to work?" asked Jenny. "I mean, I thought she was still at school?"

"School! What she ought to be is working. Nearly fifteen and hardly spell her name. I'd school her if she was mine. Foster saw her the other day in that little café downtown. Coffee bar they call it now. Never turn the noise off, howling and yelling, they don't. With a boy."

Privately Jenny thought that the boy was probably one of Norma's brothers, but she did not say so.

"Cat's going to kitten again," added Mrs. Foster with a slight sniff. The implication was clear.

"Oh, good. We'll keep the kittens this time."

"I got a little bit of pork for lunch." Mrs. Foster suppressed the desire to argue about keeping kittens, since she would just get rid of them when the time came without saying anything. "So you'll have something cold for tonight."

"Is something good on at the cinema?"

"I didn't look," disclaimed Mrs. Foster untruthfully. "Foster says he's going to have a look at the point-to-point at Mainter.

153

He thinks of nothing but horses, that man." She was gloomily gratified by this; horses were the sport of kings. "I shall go and have a cup of tea with Mrs. Bound at the House. Can't stand about all afternoon in this weather. She's quite a nice person. In her own way. Lady Mainter is going to get her her own telly as soon as she gets back from abroad." Mrs. Foster collected a plate used by Vail and transferred it to the sideboard. "Nice to be some people. Well, can't waste all day gossiping, can I?"

"I'll ask Mr. Vail if the company can get a rebate on a set. Then we could have a television." Jenny cunningly left the exact position of this much-desired luxury uncertain; she had known with dread for months that it would have to be bought, and only the tragedy put it out of her mind. Might even buy two, she thought with wild extravagance. I'd like one myself. Vincent refused to buy one because popular programmes caused the dinner hour to be moved from evening to evening and Jenny agreed with him; only at this moment did it occur to her that she did not in the least mind at what time she ate.

"Well, everybody has it now," pronounced Mrs. Foster defensively, in case she might be expected to express thanks. With an indistinct remark about greens and Foster, she left the room to tell her husband of the victory just won for him.

"Well, we're going to get the TV at last," said Foster a little later to Mr. Vail as he accepted a cigarette. He pushed back his sweaty garden hat and sighed heavily. "He would never have it. Ought not to mention that, I suppose. But everything was always done the way he wanted here, you know. Strict about meals, he always was. Dead on time, like the bloody army."

"You didn't get on well with him?" Vail sounded so casual that Foster did not pick up the implication of this familiarity.

"Well, Mr. Vail, I'll tell you. He was all right, but he never forgot to come the officer with you, if you know what I mean. The Missis reckoned he wasn't a real gentleman, he was always so conscious of everything, she says. But it isn't just that. I had an officer once, was his batman. I was a regular you know. Oh, yes. Well, this Captain, before the war, he was a proper one, his father was something at Windsor Castle, one of those hereditary jobs for the boys. And I never—never in my life —knew such a man for rank, he was a real snob like you don't

154

meet nowadays. Always asking if you was comfortable, first take care of the horses and then the men he would say and roar with laughter. Officers come last, like hell they do. Foster's devoted to me, he'd say, because I take good care of him. I could have killed him sometimes. Well, I didn't have to. The Jerries did. Well, Mr. Cheyney, he wasn't like that quite, you couldn't say that. But he did stand on his dignity a bit. Never let you forget it if he did you a favour. Of course, he did take me on when I came out of the army, quite true he did. With my leg, you see. But he was fussy, like a woman, the smallest thing. You forgot something and he'd keep on and on for days."

Foster squinted up through cigarette smoke and the brilliant sunlight from the log he sat on, to see Vail lounging against the side of the shed as if he were too tired to stand upright.

"Yes, keep on, he did. A nagger, you might say. She didn't have it too easy, I'll tell you that. I don't mean the girls. Don't think she minded about them. Though naturally she didn't care for this Laver. *Mona!* Now her I couldn't stomach. I could have danced at her funeral, all right. No, I was sorry for her sometimes. Mind you, she asked for it, tremble if he as much as looked at her. Mrs. Foster was really the one for him. She's got a real talent for not caring about, you know, looks and hints and that."

"Yes, that's the way. I didn't know Cheyney took you on. None of my business, of course, but I thought you were here before then. With old Mr. Maculan."

"No. Never knew him. Well, I'll tell you. I was Rhine Army, you see. I knew I'd have to do something straightaway because the day I was demobbed, as you might say, the quarters was *kaputt,* as they say there. Mr. Cheyney rang up the very day, I often wondered how he knew, and offered us this job here. They weren't even married then. She was here alone, the old man was just dead a few weeks. They say down in the village she was a pretty girl, before. You'd never have known it then. But I must say, she's all right. I always got on with her, myself."

"Do other people not get on with her, then?" Vail sounded apprehensive.

"Oh, yes. Far as I hear. I meant him. They didn't hit it off!"

"Ah," said Vail quietly. He made a slight gesture and strolled away so slowly that it was not clear until he was out of sight whether he was going or not.

Crossing the corner of the courtyard Vail saw Mrs. Cheyney opening the door to the stable. Upstairs in the house when he entered the vacuum hummed. A wood dove cooed from the beech grove, a singularly inappropriate sound to come from those sentinel trees, Vail thought, as he went in by the side door to his so conveniently placed office. If anyone listened by his door, they would not have heard what he was saying on the telephone, yet he did not seem to be keeping his voice down. His numbers came through without any waiting and he knew at each one who to ask for. Within half an hour Vail knew what he guessed from their conversation, that Albert Foster was dismissed from the Army in 1948 on the grounds that while on sentry duty at the regimental ammunition depot he left his post and repaired to a local inn, where he drank three glasses of beer. This military crime would never have been discovered if three men with black stockings over their faces had not overwhelmed the other sentry during that half hour and got clear away with "a quantity of weapons and ammunition." This was the second of such raids, and the Army was obliged to make an example of Foster and two other men who took their sentry duties with equal lightness. Departing from the somewhat slack practice of the Rhine Army at the time, they were dismissed from the service with ignominy, losing their pension rights. A serious matter, even in what for want of a more exact term was called peacetime. The only note Vail made was the date of the court-martial, for he took this to be a useful date for Mrs. Cheyney to know. He needed a little longer to get the details of the quite commonplace army career of Vincent Christopher Cheyney. Further questions revealed that Foster was once in Lieutenant Cheyney's platoon, but was transferred rather suddenly. Altogether, Foster had quite a list of transfers in his military career, always the sign of a bad soldier. Cheyney himself was demobilised in 1946 with the rank of Captain, acting Major. He then went to Berlin as a civilian on the Control Commission staff, but returned to England a year later.

"That's the point," said Vail aloud. "Some time in that year."

156

To ask once again for detailed security records about Cheyney would, Vail knew, be useless. There would be none, and there was no reason for there to be any. People who get away with things, thought Vail, don't have records. Then he narrowed his eyes at the date written on the telephone pad. At what point did he decide that he was, as he put it in his mind, on Mrs. Cheyney's side? It was his job to be very conscious of what went on in his own mind and he thought about the question seriously.

He thought at first that it was at some point during the previous evening's events, but then the moment moved back to the scene in the living room. That flood of burning words was real; it would have needed a highly experienced actress to reveal the anger, the old insults remembered with such pain, the sheer outrage of voice and look of those moments. No amateur could have made them convincing; they must have turned into melodrama, even bathos, if acted. She must have suffered, he thought. Even if there is nothing in this story but dishonesty about money, the man deserved his fate.

His own sensation of anger surprised Vail. It was no part of his business to pass judgement in any sense. His job was to find facts, and that was quite enough. Facts, he reminded himself. Facts only. The only real fact they had at the moment was a list of number groupings, now with the cipher "translators." There was not much more hope of discovering anything useful from that enquiry than of researches into Cheyney's brief career in Berlin. There are narrow limits to what can be done by hindsight, and records from after the war were, from the point of view of Vail's profession, unfortunately easygoing in the matter of checking on the real opinions and attitudes of officers who might almost by chance become the holders of secrets. And in fact, as Vail knew only too well, such checking does probably as much harm as good. Vail did not believe in the ideological grounds usually discovered to be responsible for treachery.

In his experience, the repetition of political faiths produced to explain the various acts of treason he had brought to justice showed themselves to his firmly pragmatic mind as rationalisations. Certainly, rationalisations put forward as often as not by the criminals themselves, who thought they believed in them; but men must always find respectable reasons for the things they do wrong, and what could be more worthy of respect than love of peace and concern for the brotherhood of mankind? A man who betrays a narrower concept of loyalty in the name of humanity may be put in prison and, in some countries, be executed. But he attains thereby a kind of martyrdom; a darkly romantic aura accompanies him that subtly turns those who discover his crime into the evildoers. Traitors are the Byronic heroes of our times, so Vail considered, the modern equivalent of the corsairs, the bandits and pirates of other eras. He was philosophical about this, having become used to it, but in the course of getting used to the unexpressed odium that attached to his profession in the popular mind, he had thought a good deal about it. His work made him intimate solely with those whose treachery was discovered, sometimes by chance, as in the present case, and sometimes by long and patient investigations, which only very occasionally were helped by irrefutable confirmation.

The normal conclusion of an investigation was confession. The desire to unburden the mind was quite simply induced in the suspect by repetition of questioning, which in the end became more oppressive than the prospect of trial and imprisonment. Almost all suspects allowed themselves to be drawn down into this spiral of fear and loneliness by answering the first questions, which usually seemed to them to be harmless. They were sure they could deal with them. But their answers always contained the seeds of more questions, often about extraneous and even pointless matters unconnected with the real subject. Only patience and curiosity were needed, nothing more, as personal qualities in the questioner; the techniques of interrogation were a matter of collation. In the finish the criminal wanted to confess, not because he was badgered and still less ill-treated, but because the hard lacquer of conceit was cracked and splintered off his mind by the gradual discovery that he had, after all, made mistakes. To Vail it was axiomatic that traitors always possess the same characteristic of an arrogant vanity that allows them to be sure they are entitled to make decisions for others. Not the choices in personal life that everyone makes, but large judgements that involve other people's lives—sometimes many lives. This it

158

was clear, was a childish characteristic; an adult knows that there are huge areas of experience he cannot judge because he lacks the knowledge. Only adolescents are convinced they know everything.

Whenever Vail was asked to help in forming an opinion on whether such and such a person would be "safe" in a position on which the lives of others depended—and this happened with increasing frequency as he continued to be successful —he would advise the responsible man to concern himself in the first place not with the opinions of the candidate but with the manner in which those opinions were expressed and, above all, in the instinctive attitudes of the candidate to those about him. The man who always knows best is dangerous, especially if education and training have given him skills not commonly attained. The variant of this arrogance is shown by the inferior who believes that he is not being given his due by society; he may steal to gain a spurious superiority that gives him the secret advantage of laughing at those who trust him. Once a man allows himself to do what he knows he will be punished for—not what is wrong, because he does not believe he can be wrong—he builds constructions that will make his crime worthy of respect. These notions lie about waiting to be picked up and are adopted by millions in their formative years and then let drop; only the infantile arrogance of those who lack even the sense to be afraid of being caught causes them to be actually trapped into doing things that will make the constructs vitally necessary. And the further into deceit such a man goes, the more tenaciously and passionately he believes his own excuses. They are his justification; they must be true.

In Vail's opinion, human beings rarely believe anything with all their minds. In this he was no doubt superficial, for although our age is one of disbelief, in other times men have had strong and abiding beliefs. The very excitability with which opinions are debated seemed to Vail a proof of their unreality. Men rest in a deep belief with peaceful confidence and only when it is in question does passion enter, out of fear of losing the confidence that enables them to live their troubled lives.

A cynical man, then, who did not believe in anything much.

159

Yet he behaved as if he did rest in some sure foundation. Vail was unaware, as Mr. Folliot was unaware, that his present conduct was at odds with what he thought he was doing and saying. Just as Mr. Folliot, out of lack of imagination, had left a doubt as to Jenny's own honesty, so Vail disposed of that doubt by a stroke of insight he would have laughed at if accused of trusting to it. Indeed he would have said that his belief in Jenny's soundness was founded in the conviction that she was not clever enough to dissemble, a discovery made so quickly that it could not possibly be safe for him to rely on it. But rely on it he did, and was right to do so.

"Oh, blast!" he now said aloud, stretched himself and got up to walk about the room, which was not large enough to accommodate more than a few of his long steps. It was boring to sit here for hours, supposedly examining papers that were all clear as daylight and in no more muddle than Vail's own modest bank account. He turned to the bookcase, with titles in half a dozen languages, only two of which he understood and only one well enough to read for pleasure. And the English books were largely treatises on engineering and mathematics, including a handful of unbound lectures and analyses by Julius Maculan. Vail tried to read one of these, and although its style had a strain of almost naïve directness and modesty mixed with a humour that was very attractive, the subject was so esoteric that he was no more able to understand it than if he were again ten years old. He pushed them back into the row and then saw a pamphlet with Henry Folliot's name under the title. This was precisely the opposite of Maculan's work. Written with a stolid precision that showed not the least desire to engage the reader's interest, its content was not only intelligible but fascinating. It was, in fact, the history of the house he was living in, written years before by Folliot at his friend's request for the local museum. Vail began to read and turn the pages with increasing speed. It was not very long. As soon as he finished reading, Vail pushed the little volume into his jacket pocket and set out to explore the outside of the house and its surroundings, quite forgetting that if his hostess met him he could be accused of slackness.

He made a picture as he walked rapidly towards the entrance gateposts, of a man hot on the trail of some intriguing

160

secret, for curiosity was a major characteristic of Vail's; he could hardly have been much good at his job without it. Of course, old Folliot was quite mistaken. These tall stones were much older than his talk of ancient Britons and King Arthur's times. Iseult and the Duke of Cornwall, my foot, thought Vail with delight, these are Celtic fertility deities, or whatever they are called. There must be human blood on these, if only generations of stupid hands hadn't touched them for heaven knows how many centuries. I must find out about prehistoric Britain; I wonder if she has any books of her father's on the subject. Balked by lack of knowledge, Vail set off again, first walking round and through the beech grove and then going back to begin examining the contours of the ground. Presently this process became useless without a great deal more precision than he could at once give it. A survey, a map, that was what was needed. No, a camera.

He turned quickly and, if he were given to exhibitionism, would have cried "Eureka!" to find himself face to face with Mrs. Cheyney, who was considering his curious conduct with astonishment.

"Look here," he began excitedly, and pushed the lock of hair off his forehead. "This place is absolutely fabulous. Well, really fabulous as well as in the slang sense. D'you know anything about it? Have you any books about it? You haven't a decent camera in the house, I suppose?"

"A camera?" She countered his questions with a blank surprise.

"Yes, a camera," he cried, frowning now because the slanting sun of late winter was shining in his eyes. "Look, these mounds and humps probably have other stones buried in them, like the gateposts. There may have been a whole ring up here, the circle of trees argues for it, don't you see!"

"But I think the posts were brought up from Gullion. There's another pair by the church there, you know."

"No, no. Those down at Gullion were taken from here. That's quite obvious."

"There is a camera," she said slowly. "I'll get it for you." He followed her, still talking.

"If some were dragged down to the village, and I'm sure they must have been, they may be strewn over half the county.

But there must still be some here. Those humps couldn't only be fallen tree trunks; they would have sunk with time. I mean, only some of them would still show, d'you see?"

Jenny hurried her steps, his vivid curiosity infecting her, until they were almost running. The Leica was in Vincent's chest of drawers with a number of rolls of fresh film.

"I suppose you can use it?" she asked dubiously. "I certainly can't."

"Oh, yes, I've done a bit of photography. Is it all right, though, for me to borrow the film? Your husband seems to have been a keen photographer." There were several extra lenses in the leather case, as well as the camera itself.

"He used to take it with him a lot. For professional work, I believe."

Jenny wondered why this made Vail stand still for a moment, holding the contraption in his hands and staring down at it.

"It's perfectly all right for you to use it," she assured him awkwardly. "It was a present from me, as a matter of fact."

Like everything else he possessed, thought Vail grimly, but said no more than smiling thanks for the loan.

"You'll need some covering shots first, to parcel out the area," began Jenny again, speaking quickly to cover her embarrassment. "Let's see. Every two paces, perhaps?"

"Ah, I was just worrying about that. Must get complete cover with no gaps. Start at the right-hand gatepost, hm? And move clockwise round to the left-hand one, a pace or so at a time. Or should we use a proper measure?"

"Not straightaway," she urged. "Just clear enough to identify the detail shots, especially profile shots from the ground up, don't you think? After all, it will have to be done by an archaeologist if we're to do any serious research, won't it?"

They were halfway down the stairs already, Vail glancing up at the sun, and at the same time screwing in the wide-angle lens by touch as he went. They went through to the outer edge of the ring of trees hard by the gatepost and Vail paced it to the inner edge.

"Eight paces here, as near as makes no matter." He ran his eye frowning as far as they could see the grove. "Mysterious how evenly the trees grow. It seems to be almost exactly the same depth, at least the part that's visible from here."

"It is all the way round. In the old pictures it is too. They just seem to grow that way."

"Weird, isn't it?" Vail stood staring up at the crowns of the beeches, touched by some awe for a second that pierced his interest with a deeper tinge of meaning. "You feel you'd better not meddle unless you take it seriously."

Jenny nodded. "My father always meant to explore; he put it off until the war was over and then because there was so much work still, and then it was too late. He used to say this was the centre of the Island. Symbolically, not literally. Heartland, he called it." She checked with a glance to make sure that Vail did not find this funny and went on: "He loved expressions like that. It wasn't his native language, you see, and all the worn-out phrases were fresh and beautiful for him, as if he'd found them for himself."

"I expect he did, too."

"It used to bother me when I was at school. I was afraid the girls who came home to stay with us would laugh at him. But somehow, people didn't laugh at him. Only, the way he talked of England, nobody really understood."

"Patriotism, you mean? Well, the war rather killed all that."

"It wasn't quite patriotism, you know," she said seriously, following Vail as he paced away from her. "We were once German-Hungarian-Rumanians. So if he could have felt patriotism it would have been for King Carol and not for King Arthur."

"King Arthur?" he said sharply, almost crossly. "This place must go back long before King Arthur."

"Yes, he was sure of that. But I meant—you know, a figure." She moved with him farther to the right. "What made you want to know about the grove, all of a sudden?"

"What? I suppose—I just saw it. Saw it for real, as the Americans say."

She said, almost complacently, "It does get people, if they really look at it."

"At first I just saw the house, and that's splendid enough. The light has changed."

"It does every few minutes here."

"Do you think it was the grove that made your father pick this house?" asked Vail presently. "It's rather an odd choice for a complete stranger, somehow."

"Partly, yes. I don't really remember, but he told me, often. It must have been a combination of chances, in fact. They were looking for a small subsidiary factory, I expect you know that, at the beginning of the war. There happened to be a big workshop-factory in the town here, that made some sort of parts for racing cars. The owner was retiring from business, and clearly motor racing was not going to be much in question while the war went on. It was just what they wanted, trained mechanics and everything. So my father was looking for somewhere to live nearby. Somebody must have told him this hill was up for sale—or perhaps he asked about it. You can see it for miles round, as you know. Then, there is a Catholic church here, too."

"So he was religious, your father?" Vail sounded surprised.

"I don't think exactly that. But there was me, you see." She was silent and then added, "And perhaps because of my mother, too. They say women are more religious than men. But she never got back here."

"I heard that. Frightful thing to have happen to him."

"Yes. It was kept from me, but I knew always that he blamed himself."

They were now far enough around the ring of trees to be circling the cultivated garden, where Foster's back could be seen bent over a vegetable bed.

"He must have done, even if it wasn't his fault. . . . I say, you don't mind talking about it? Tactless of me."

"No, I don't mind." This was an understatement; it was in the nature of a long pent-up relief to Jenny to talk openly about her father, she having been silent for years on the subject.

"It's interesting, you see. I mean, one can see how he felt but not feel it, not inside how it must have been for him."

"I suppose not, for born Englishmen. You'd have to know how he felt about the Island. History and all that and being so settled for*ever,* everything having been the same right back into history and before history."

164

"He felt safe here, I suppose."

"Safe?" She laughed a little, involuntarily. "That's just what he didn't feel. He thought the British were crazy to defy the whole Continent. It included the Soviet Union then, of course. He thought we were all going to be swept off into the Atlantic. He was very conscious of the open sea, naturally."

"Just here, one could hardly not be."

"No, not 'just here.' Because of where we came from, right over there in the middle of the land mass, where you can't get out. Here you can always get out, all you need is a ship. That was how it was for him."

Vail did not understand this, his concept of "ship" being something one absolutely did not think of in terms of getting out, for that meant disaster and Jenny was certainly not expert at explaining a complex state of mind. With a long familiar sensation of inadequacy, she was ready to give up the attempt before it was well begun. However, her persistent companion continued on his own track of misconception.

"Then, if he didn't feel safe here, he must have stayed because he wanted to fight the Germans? The war must have been a tremendous personal fight for him. He must have hated the enemy."

Jenny did not want to answer this, she felt that Vail was thinking along a line so different and yet parallel to her own that they could talk for hours and arrive no nearer to each other's view, as if they were to circle the ring of beeches, one walking inside and one on the outer circuit so that they could never meet in spite of acting in the same manner by the same means and for the same purpose. She was oppressed not only by this inability to induce Vail to move towards her own knowledge; she was made reluctant by the memory of the habitual warning that she spoke of something that would not please her husband. Vincent did not like her to talk of the past, and Jenny was so used to avoiding the subject, where possible, and dismissing it as quickly as she could where it was unavoidable, that she did not trace her unease to its source. But reply she must, not only out of politeness but to remove an impression that her father would have rejected with indignation.

"He didn't hate anybody. That wasn't his nature at all. And

how could he hate Germans anyway—you can't hate yourself. But he didn't think of people as nations, masses. People were people to him, and mostly unhappy or frightened. What he did hate was ignorance and people being misled by untruths: expressions like 'no good Hun but a dead one' or 'Bolshevik hordes' made him absolutely furious! He knew that the war had to happen because of the first war, because everything and everybody was in such a terrible muddle. And all the lying; he used to say 'the lies, the lies,' and put his hands up to his head. Of course, he could hear on the wireless all the different languages and he knew what awful things, poisonous things, were being spread all over the world. He would almost weep with rage when he heard Goebbels make a speech. But he wept as well—I remember it because it frightened me—when Cologne was destroyed by air raids."

There was silence, on Vail's part because he realised that a serious mistake had been made, and on hers from the consciousness of a far too vehement tone. Jenny felt miserably that she wanted Vail to understand her and also to understand, to sympathise, with Maculan. Vail was aware of a mistake that he ought to have foreseen, but aware, too, that his questions were improper and deceitful. Fortunately, they were engaged in doing something they could continue to do without words, and presently Jenny spoke again, her voice trembling slightly with the effort of sounding light.

"I've made him sound solemn and pompous. He wasn't like that a bit. As a matter of fact he was a very funny man." This statement came out with such a woeful air that Vail could not repress a quick smile. Jenny caught his smile and was able to laugh at herself so that her mood was lightened by the feeling that it was not necessary to explain, after all.

She was quite wrong in that notion, but it comforted her.

CHAPTER XIII

THE VOICE of Foster calling and waving an arm towards the house interrupted at this moment, and, following his signals, Jenny saw Mrs. Foster leaning out of an upper window and shouting something about the telephone. By the time she went in and returned from her message, Vail, advancing on the far side of the house, was already in sight of the gap in the grove where the drive ran. To Jenny's astonishment it was nearly one o'clock, and as she came up with him she said as much.

"Can you finish before lunch?" she asked. "We can't keep it waiting because it's their day off. Well," she temporised, "I wouldn't dare anyway, but specially not on a Thursday."

Vail noticed, not for the first time, Jenny's almost neurotic concern with sticking rigidly to the facts when making factual statements. With a quick glance at his watch, he assessed the remaining space.

"Five minutes," he said, "we'll just have time for a drink before eating." Then he pulled his lock of hair with a self-consciously comic air and added in what he supposed to be the regional accent, " 'Scuse me for taking the liberty, Ma'am."

"Not at all," replied Jenny in a haughty, affected voice, imitating Eileen Sandford's as she heard it just before on the telephone. "That was Eileen. She wants to drop in this evening. She and Teddy have been to see their youngest son. His prep school is quite near here. He's got chicken pox. I hope you've had it?"

"Oh," said Vail and sounded somewhat glum at the news. "I'll disappear, then."

"Not unless you want to. I expect he'll want to have a word with you, won't he?"

"Can't think why he should," answered Vail, and Jenny was a little surprised at his offhand tone. "Just one more frame." And he took the last photograph. As she turned to go back to the house, he added, a little shamefacedly, "Er, unless you feel you must, perhaps it would be better not to mention our researches to the Sandfords."

"Of course," answered Jenny with a quick look at his face. "A good thing you mentioned it. I'd be sure to blurt out something and then they would think I'm wasting your time."

With a pleasingly conspiratorial collusion, they went indoors to pour out the proposed drink. But Vail was thinking to himself that for the second time within a few minutes Jenny had made a remark that accused herself of some fault. However carefully Cheyney had trained her to blame herself for everything that ever went awry, this streak of childlike honesty, a weapon given direct into the hand of anyone who wished to use it against her, must be a trait of her own nature. As Foster said, she asked for it, and this showed a shrewdness in Foster as well as indolence and irresponsibility that he would do well to bear in mind. Not only that; Foster, according to his military record, must have some experience of the executive branch of the law and might, perhaps without defining his recognition at all closely, see something in Vail that for the moment should not become public. There was also in Foster's disinclination for hard work and its accompanying rejection of decisions the certainty that he would, in a moment of choice, gravitate to whatever seemed likely to guarantee his easy life, his bread and butter; in plain English, Foster would tend to be open to bribery from anyone who could show him that Vail was a threat to his comfort. From the very little Vail had seen of Foster's wife, she would not be friendly to any such offers; her self-righteousness would suspect them. But, unless Vail was much mistaken in Foster, his wife would not be told. Anyone casting about for a means of communication to the house on the hill would be much more likely to scrape an acquaintance with Foster when he was in the town with his three-wheel carrier and his wife's shopping list than to try entering the prickly hedge of the housekeeper's preserve.

Indeed, the use of Foster as a messenger or agent might have been a possibility always kept in reserve, and this calculation was hinted at from the beginning by Cheyney's having, at the moment he did, decided to employ the couple at all. The chief motive would clearly have been to make sure that every occupant of this house was entirely under Cheyney's control, but the choice of a man known to be unreliable was not altogether explained by that consideration unless Cheyney also knew that Foster would do almost anything—should the need ever arise—for a quiet and comfortable life. It was therefore quite likely that Foster would be approached in the immediate future. His manner to Vail, supposedly an employee of the Maculan company, was too open and casual in their talk that morning for an attempt already to have taken place.

During the course of these thoughts Vail replied to one or two remarks from his hostess of the kind that may be answered without much thought. But as they moved into the dining room on the other side of the central hall, Jenny said something that made Vail abruptly return his concentration to her.

The dining room was on the north side, and usually there was a certain chill about it, from its sunless aspect rather than from change of temperature. Jenny's place at table was changed. She faced the windows instead of sitting at the round table with her back to the door and sideways to the light. Altogether, it was noticeable that Jenny liked to face not only the light, but to face outwards, to look out of windows.

"I got Foster to help me turn the table round," she now said. "I like to see the garden, don't you? It's pretty on this side, with the fruit bushes and the kitchen garden. So neat."

"Useful, too," he agreed, and remembered to hold her chair, which seemed to surprise her faintly. "But why didn't you always sit there?"

"My husband liked to face the door," she said simply. "So the bell was under that side of the table."

"This vegetable soup is good," he said, before craning his neck to see what Jenny meant about the bell. Sure enough, the electric bell cord came up through the carpet a few inches from where his own feet now rested, and was stretched from there to the centre stand of the table and pinned under one of its four claw feet to rise at a sharp angle to the underside of the table where Jenny sat.

"But you could still have been placed opposite the windows," he objected. "I don't see you as being so conventional that you must sit opposite the other person at a table. In fact I don't see you as conventional at all."

"Oh, no, not me." Jenny stopped whatever she was going to say and could be observed deciding to change the subject. "Do you really think we can find something like a Druid ring in the grove? Or something even older? After all, lots of people might have thought of it and found nothing of interest?"

"Not at all," said Vail, watching Mrs. Foster as she carried in the promised roast pork with various succulencies. "Not stuffing? Marvellous!"

"Well, the sage grows in the garden," replied Mrs. Foster, resentful at being accused of taking trouble. "Onions, as well."

Vail made a face suggesting a strong desire to embrace such a cook, and got a most unpromising look in return which, to the surprise of all three, not least of Mrs. Foster herself, turned into an unpractised sound like a giggle. Mrs. Foster raised her shoulders and pulled her chin down as she made this sound.

"Mr. Vail. Really!" she said, blaming him for her lapse of self-control, and having now placed the dishes on the hot plate, got herself out of the room in a mixture of annoyance and gratification.

"I never thought to see the day," said Jenny, having allowed time for Mrs. Foster to cross the hall. "Getting round Mrs. Foster, that really is a triumph."

"It's easy," he disclaimed. "I'll sell you the recipe, if you'd like it. But about the stones. If any exist. Far as I understand it, which is not far, nobody really knows much about Druids or how long ago they existed, or even whether the word is not just a sort of general cover for what is unknown about British prehistorical customs."

"Yes, but that doesn't prove nobody has looked at the Ring before now."

"No, I suppose not. But it's not awfully likely. I don't think—again, as far as I know—that popular interest in archaeology goes back very far. A couple of generations, perhaps. And don't you think it must be pretty much a matter of chance whether somebody in any given place took an interest? Someone like your father, d'you see, obviously he'd have excavated the whole Ring by now, if it's there."

"But I've just thought of something. Perhaps most of what remains of the stones, if Father and you are right, are under the foundations of this house? Perhaps some of them are even among the stones of the house. The builders may have used them in the sixteenth century?"

"That's a fascinating thought," he said with his mouth full. "They could certainly be identified, if that is so. I say, one wonders rather what effect that would have on a house. I mean, they went in for human sacrifice and all sorts of larks in those times. I suppose you haven't any ghosts, have you?"

"Ghosts?" said Jenny, and he was startled out of his joking by the extraordinary change in her expression. "Not ghosts, not in the house, but I've often felt . . ." She stared, not frightened but awed. "How did you know? Nobody else has ever felt it, except me. And I haven't spoken of it since I was a child."

Vail did not want to confess that he was only inventing a comical supposition, something in the style of an *Ingoldsby Legend*. He hesitated, with a strong reluctance to admit that he was, up to this moment, not taking the subject with much seriousness.

"I don't feel anything," he admitted in a quite different tone. "Hadn't you better tell me what you're talking about? That is, if you want me to understand. . . ."

"Oh, but you have felt something. Of course, being a lawyer, you wouldn't want to admit it, but you must have done."

"Felt what?"

"That there's something in the grove, of course."

"Something more than trees growing in a ring? Yes, there's a knowledge that they are very, very ancient; have 'always' been growing there. By some action of the prevailing winds, always seeding themselves in the same area afresh. Because undergrowth can't prosper under beeches, the small animals don't frequent them much on the whole. So the mast isn't carried about. And being heavy and hard, the seed is no good as bird food and isn't transported in that way. And I daresay if I knew about husbandry I should be able to add that pigs don't like climbing hills, so beech groves on a considerable elevation would hardly be pig-breeding grounds; pigs, as you know, like to eat beech mast. That's why the grove continues as it has and will grow forever just the way it does now unless some ape cuts the trees down. But that's all perfectly rational and has nothing to do with the supernatural."

"Yes, yes, certainly. But just because the trees grow so symmetrically, people in ancient times believed there was some purpose connected with them." They were both stubborn and inventive in defence of their differing views. "Some mystery. So the grove became a tabu place or a holy place."

"Probably both. But you don't believe in that ancient myth any more than I do. That wouldn't be reasonable."

"Not believe in it, no. But there's something." The word Vail used in a protesting tone was just the one to make Jenny withdraw defensively, and the thought of being unreasonable did produce its usual sensation of fear and of wanting to hide her inner self. Yet to her own surprise, she answered and even continued. "Don't you think places where many generations of people have worshipped, felt themselves dedicated, keep some atmosphere. . . ."

"Ah, now I see what you mean. Sorry, I misunderstood. Yes, certainly, places do keep atmospheres from the past. But the awe is in our minds, knowing—or in this case guessing —what power the place once wielded over men. Mustn't mix up the place with what goes on inside our own heads. As a matter of fact, it doesn't have to be either ancient or religious; I once saw Lenin's mausoleum and got a real shiver of superstitious fear thinking of the huge changes in the world made by that one waxy little head when it was alive and thinking. And, as you know, it's said it isn't even Lenin lying there, only an effigy."

Mrs. Foster reappeared with an apple pie and thick cream and began to pile dishes up on the wheeled tray to remove them.

"Leave all this, Mrs. Foster," said Jenny. "I'll put the things in the dishwasher. You're all ready and Foster won't want to miss the start."

"Well, I have made the coffee," replied Mrs. Foster, conceding a point. "So if I could put it on the hot plate?" She did this, having never any intention of doing otherwise than as Jenny suggested. "It's quite black towards the west. Looks like a storm coming up."

"I hope not. Have a good time and ask Foster to put half-a-crown on a likely horse for me."

"He's quite bad enough with his betting!" With muttered farewells Mrs. Foster disappeared, to enjoy the prospect of a ruined point-to-point.

"Why is it in the afternoon?" Vail asked Jenny.

"They do sometimes; when it's a big market, that has to be in the morning, of course, and most of the farmers stop for the horses afterward."

"Ah. Country life indeed."

"Well, if you shoot, as you said, you can't be so very ignorant of country life," Jenny smilingly challenged this affectation.

"Only as an occasional visitor to bucolic scenes. I'm the complete townee. As a matter of fact, I've hardly even been in this part of the country before."

They finished their pie and Vail rose to fetch the coffee pot and the cups.

"I meant to ask you about your sculpture," he said as she poured out. "Yes, sugar please. Have you given it up entirely? I've directed a shifty glance or two about and there is nothing of yours except the singing bird visible. Or do you keep them in a private gallery away from the piercing artistic eye of the likes of me?"

Jenny wondered a little that Vail should feel such discomfort at this question that he must make a heavy joke to cover it.

"I do, yes," she said. "But you can come over with me and see, if you'd like to." Then it occurred to her that he did not want to refer to the moment when she herself talked of the singing bird, and was satisfied. "I'm going to the studio. Unfortunately, nothing has been cast in the last year or so, so there are only models. But if you're interested, of course come with me."

"It really does look stormy," he commented as they emerged later from "his" side door into the back courtyard. "Hadn't you better bring an umbrella?"

"It will go over, it usually does. The black wind comes up from the sea, there's a little shower and then the wind changes

173

again." She looked up at the piled and drifting clouds. "The light changes every hour here, and the countryside with it. Perhaps that is why we don't produce many painters?"

"Maybe. Poets instead."

He shivered as they went into the unused stable, but Jenny, used to the chill, did not notice and opened the door at the top of the rough stair into the loft, where it was even colder. A bleak northeast light drained in from the enlarged window. The place having been built as a hay loft, there was no fireplace. The studio window was not even finished, Vail noticed. Roughly cemented and plastered, it had never been painted; the wooden frame was still as bare as the day it was carpentered. Jenny saw his look but did not explain.

"The light really is very bad," she said doubtfully. "I'm afraid you won't see much. The big lamp would only make a crosslight."

Miles away, out over the invisible ocean, a great rumble of thunder faintly reached them. Vail hoped Foster had not left uncovered the seedlings he was planting that morning as they were talking. Then he directed his attention to Jenny's work.

There were a dozen or so models, arranged along the wide window ledge. Others stood on the far side on a trestle table. One head occupied the work stand, covered in unbleached linen. Jenny took this in her hand and said she must wet it again, she wanted to do some more work on it. Vail saw the head of a woman, which could have been finished.

"What do you want to do with it?"

Jenny did not answer, but instead offered him the earlier work. By the time Vail had examined this and progressed through the more recent things, he did not need to ask what further work was still to be done on the portrait head. The figure showed a distinct trend of slackening talent, a loss of the grip of vitality and imagination. He returned to her early work, turning one or two of the figures about to see them in the round, since he was unable to walk behind them. By this time Jenny was already working on the woman's head.

"I've got the likeness all right, but flattery has crept in, there's no doubt." She was muttering to herself, not to Vail, and seemed to have forgotten he was there. He leaned against the sloping wall by the window and watched in silence, smok-

174

ing a cigarette. Silence inside the loft stretched into time while out of doors the west wind began a shuffling in the beech trees, raising their sigh to a moan that rose and fell. A thin whistle piped through some angled gape and was gradually joined by many voices of wind. Somewhere a wooden door slammed heavily and a beam creaked in answer. Unlike the previous observer of Jenny at work, Vail was not surprised at the change in her aspect; it was not the first time he had watched someone doing what it was born in them to do and what they knew they could do.

But the change was certainly very striking, striking enough to be a revelation. Even the hands were different; the flinching, thin, uncertain movements were sure and decisive now. The hands ceased to be feminine; they were professional. The eyes were hard and clear so that the brilliant hazel of their colour was to be seen for the first time. More than anything else, the mouth relaxed from repressed effort of control into a pushing of the lips as if the worker would treat the clay by chewing it, or was perhaps talking silently to the clay and persuading it to submit to the strong, boyish fingers whose joints and muscles could be clearly seen. As the face, especially the jaw, relaxed into its natural lines, the whole shaping of the head altered, or rather could be seen for the first time, and Vail could now recognise a likeness to Maculan's head from pictures he had seen and from several of the models that he guessed correctly to be products of memory. Not only the inheritance of talent was visible, but the gift as it could develop, as it showed already in the singing bird and one or two of the figures Vail had been looking at.

How long he stood there, absently smoking one cigarette after another, Vail did not know. Uncharacteristically, he did not look at his watch or even feel time passing.

The storm came closer, piling up a purple threat with majestic energy. Flashes of lightning lit the hut so that Jenny looked round irritably and narrowed her eyes to see in the gloom. The thunder boomed and rattled. Only Vail was aware of a moment of total silence outside. The trees were for a breathless instant still, the chattering birds gone to shelter in fear. With an earsplitting crash the storm broke directly over their heads, a blaze of light turned them and the modelled head into effigies in a wax museum, hail came down with tremendous force in a rattle of annihilation. Jenny started in terror and her lips opened for a cry unheard in another crash instantly following the first, so near that it deafened them both.

"That one hit something," he said and swung towards the door. Dazed, she reeled toward him and he caught her arm. "It won't hit twice," he cried. Her eyes were terrified.

"The house!"

They stumbled together, panic-stricken, through the door and down the uneven steps into the open where the wind was like a hurricane and hailstones fell in a solid, slanted mass. They both turned their backs to the wind to see the house. In a moment they were drenched, and Jenny's hair, blown in the first blast of the opened door, was plastered across her face. Then they saw the blaze, which survived for several minutes even in that downpour. But it was not the building, the lightning had struck over the garden. They leaned against the wind and staggered out of the courtyard, where they could see the chestnut tree split as if by a tremendous axe and the already blackening burn running down inside the breach.

"Oh, thank God," wailed Jenny, beside herself with anguished relief. She sagged against Vail. He thought she would faint and put his arms round her to support her, almost carrying her slight weight across the court and into the side door.

"Are you all right?" he asked her anxiously, still holding her, propped against the passage wall.

"Oh, God," she said, trembling wildly. "I thought it was the house."

"It's all right," he said, "it's all right. You're wet through as if you'd been in the sea. You'd better go up and have a bath or you'll get cold. Catch your death, it's turned much colder."

They were both shivering. As she turned towards the hall he held her elbow still, not trusting her ability to stand upright. It was almost dark in the house and the howling of wind betrayed an open window somewhere. Vail reached for the light switch at the entrance to the hall. Nothing happened.

"Power failure," he said angrily. "Just what we needed."

She began to laugh at this and then burst into tears.

"Look here, you're all in. You go up and have a hot bath and then rest. Those wretched people are coming later."

"I'm so sorry," she wailed, putting up a hand to her mouth to keep from sobbing aloud. "So childish of me. I'll be all right in a moment."

"You've had about enough, lately. Go on, up you go. I'll go round and see that everything is closed."

There was a small square space between the main hall and the kitchen, now cut off by a door padded with artificial leather, and there a window was open. Vail closed it; the floor near it was spattered with water but since it was stone it did not matter much, he decided. He continued through the house, but was relieved to find everything closed and in order.

The storm was already drawing away, its fury spent. He went to the door of Jenny's room and called through it.

"Everything's battened down fast. Are you in the bath?"

"Yes. It's lovely and hot. You have one. And change your clothes." He heard the splash of water as she raised herself and turned round. Not a bad idea, he thought, it's as bad as the North Atlantic round here.

As he unstrapped his wristwatch he saw that he was shaking. This happened sometimes, the result of being torpedoed for the second time, years before.

CHAPTER XIV

"THERE'S A TREE down just below the village," announced Teddy Sandford. "They said it would be an hour before they could haul it away so we went back to the town and had a drink." The voice came nearer and Sandford entered the room, looking as round and ripe as his voice. "Hallo, my dear chap, how are you?" This greeting was issued with a wealth of hearty familiarity enough to warn a child of five that Teddy did not know the person addressed as well as he wished it to appear he did; Jenny did not hear it, for she was following Eileen, and Eileen, too, was speaking.

"We tried to telephone you, naturally, but the tree falling brought the lines down with it. It must have been the most appalling storm ever!"

"It was indeed," said Jenny's lighter voice as they came in. "Eileen, do you know . . . ?"

"Of course I do. How are you, Mark?" The contralto voice did not falter, but the name received an unintended emphasis from a very slight hesitation and a flicker of the eyes before the self-confident smile took over Eileen's expression. This gave Jenny the impression that Eileen did not like Vail, whose Christian name she now knew for the first time.

"We had a thunderbolt in the garden," she said with pride. "I thought the house was struck and nearly died of shock. But it was the chestnut tree."

"Good God, how frightful! Is there much damage?" Teddy sounded really concerned. He included Vail in his question, so Vail answered, looking quickly at Jenny first.

"I went out to look, after the storm," he explained. "I don't know how hardy chestnuts are, but it looks to me as if the tree will die of it. Its trunk is split almost to the ground and badly

178

burned." Jenny went to the drinks tray, hiding a helpless smile. He evidently did not intend the Sandfords to hear the whole story, and this gave Jenny an odd feeling that the two of them were keeping a secret. It was so pleasant that she felt almost excited for a moment, and bungled two glasses in her hands so that they clashed musically together.

"I have to go and get the ice."

"I brought it," said Vail. "Hope you don't mind my interfering."

"So you did. Thank you."

We're all overacting like an amateur dramatic society, he thought, annoyed with himself. And I ought not to have gone for the ice. This Sandford girl is everything Jenny is not, and will draw all manner of conclusions. The first of these suppositions was clear to Vail from the first glimpse of Eileen's person, and the second made him even more annoyed with himself than he was already, because he no sooner thought it than he perceived that the conclusions Eileen could draw would be, at least in intention, correct.

"There were bits of branches and twigs scattered all over the seed beds," he said. "I fear they won't survive, either. Proper mess."

"Poor Foster, he'll be furious. That means all his plastic covers are ruined, too."

"The hail would have done for the seedlings, anyway," pointed out Teddy. "He put them out a bit early. Not like Foster."

"Good Lord, I'd forgotten the Fosters being out!" cried Jenny. "Do you think they'll be all right?" She turned to Vail, and only when it was too late to change either direction or tone did both strike her as ill-advised. She was handing a glass to Eileen as she made the exclamation, so that even concern for the Fosters getting drenched did not serve to disguise her preoccupation with her house guest. There was the glass, extended in a hand quite detached from any hospitable intention, while her whole body was turned away from Eileen, to whom it was directed. With dismay Jenny felt herself blushing from the modest neckline of her dress right up to her hair; in the confusion of her feelings it did not occur to her that the shaded lamps in the room would not expose her change of

179

colour but the self-conscious eagerness of the smile with which she sought to divert Eileen Sandford from noticing what she wished to hide, betrayed her more than the flush.

Fortunately for both of them, Eileen took the matter in hand and began to talk about her son's ailment and the tea shared with his headmaster after the visit. She sat comfortably half-turned towards the room in an armchair by the fire, which blazed energetically, and gave a perfect performance of the correct way to behave when other people are determined to make an exhibition of themselves. This successfully transferred Vail's annoyance, first with himself and then with Jenny, to a neutral object, and from that moment he disliked Eileen Sandford.

In a few more minutes they all four began, for different reasons, to enjoy themselves, and by the time Jenny went to set out dishes for a modest supper they were a gay party. The meal made them even gayer: Jenny's salad was praised, the cold pork was finished, the cheese pronounced perfect, and Sandford poured the wine with a generous hand. He went down to get the bottles himself, being knowledgeable about wine, and came back with a mysterious Provençal rosé. None of them had ever heard its name before, but it was both light and potent.

"How like you, Jenny, not to know the wines in your own cellar," said Eileen, as her hostess asked about the bottles.

"Oh, cellar!" disclaimed Jenny. "It's hardly that. I expect Vincent brought this back from some journey or other. Or it was ordered from a business friend . . . don't you think, Teddy?"

"Probably," agreed Sandford, rolling the wine around in his mouth in the approved fashion, an honour it hardly deserved. "But as to calling it a 'cellar'—you have quite a bit of stuff down there. You must keep it up a bit, you know. Don't let things run out. You're a careless little thing, but one must keep a decent drop of wine in good condition, y'know."

His wife gave him a sharp look at this tone, which betrayed an interest in Jenny she would not have suspected him of. It came to her that Jenny, in lonely possession, had acquired desirability and she automatically wished to reduce her again to nullity.

"I see you've changed this room about," she commented. "I'm not sure I quite approve. It's changed the symmetry rather."

"Do you think so?" asked Jenny dubiously. "I just wanted to face the window. . . ." She was at once unsure, almost as if she had no right to change former arrangements. She knew, of course, that Eileen felt her small changes to be an impermissible objection to Vincent's dispositions; but Eileen, having made her point, was inclined to be kind and continued with sly jokes about the buying of wines until they were all happily exchanging tales of wine snobbery experienced at one time or another.

Altogether, Eileen's efforts to rid the evening of tension were so successful that in their laughter the return of the Fosters went unheard. She was such an exact opposite of Jenny and so very much what Vail disliked in a woman that they argued happily and took up a prejudice against each other so comfortably that a benevolent onlooker might have decided that if Eileen Sandford had not existed she would have had to be invented to provide Vail with half a dozen excellent reasons for preferring Jenny. She discoursed on food and wine, she condescended with compliments to her hostess, she overruled her husband's opinion twice; above all she was large, high-coloured, voluptuously rounded and pleased with herself as she was. Presently she turned to the subject of the head of herself that stood almost finished in the studio over the stable.

"It's such a good likeness, you'll be astonished, Teddy," she assured Sandford enthusiastically. "You've seen it, Mark? Don't you think it's excellent!"

The storm had effectually put the sculpture out of Vail's mind and he now recognised its original for the first time; for although he knew Sandford from his visit to the company, he had met the Managing Director's wife for the first time that evening. For a moment he was startled out of his composure by this failure on his part and, since Jenny was looking at him, she saw this and was puzzled by it.

The pretence that he knew Eileen Sandford already made Mark unkindly dislike her more than ever. It also exposed to him how sharply he felt averse to deceiving Jenny. He faced

181

the prospect of finding himself in a difficult, in fact an impossible situation. Because he was by now aware that of all possible faults in a human being, deceit of any kind was the one most likely to alienate Jenny's sympathies. This perception was keen enough to cause a momentary constriction in his solar plexus, a sensation of suspense that he resembled Eileen in at least one way, and that was in being pleased with himself as he was, but certainly the idea of being displeased with himself was as unfamiliar as it was unpleasant. And he abruptly realised that the possibility of Jenny's being disappointed in him, of his making her unhappy, was even worse.

It so happened that Vail's career up to then was concerned with persons who were already under suspicion and were identified. That is, they recognised investigations, and in particular Vail's questioning, as what they were: opposition to their own actions. The surveillance of people without their knowledge was unusual in Vail's specialised professional experience and had been confined—as it was in the case of Jenny—to those such as colleagues or neighbours who were connected in some way with a suspect but who could be assumed to be on the side of the law. It could easily have happened that Vail was obliged to entrap some near friend or relative of a suspect who would not willingly give evidence against him, even if they knew of his unlawful activities. In fact, this had not happened to him. Nor did he believe that this was the position where Jenny was concerned; he judged her disillusionment with her husband to be so complete and so justified that she would not attempt to deny other misdeeds of his if she knew of them. But Vail also judged that Jenny's neutrality would not go further than that. Asked for evidence against her husband, he rightly guessed that her answer would be that no matter what Vincent might have done, it was certainly not his widow's affair to prove his guilt. He was so sure of this that he could almost hear her voice saying words to that effect. And those words, if pronounced, must inevitably be followed by an accusation against himself, that he was in her house under false pretences.

As long as the complete detachment that was the foundation of Vail's training and practice in his job was maintained, nobody could call him dishonourable. The chance of his being present when Jenny was faced with the unavoidable proof of her husband's deception had removed that detachment. She became intimately a human being to Vail after that moment. And not only objectivity was maintained by professional reserve; the self-respect of the officer was secured by it. The loss of a genuine detachment turned Vail at once into a spy, a peeper through keyholes and a listener at closed doors. His newly found feeling of sympathy for Jenny could only appear odiously false. Either he must declare his true function to her or she must discover, sooner rather than later, that he was not an assistant of Folliot's or an employee of the company. She would hate him for it because she would relate it in her mind to the deceptions from which she had suffered in other personal relationships.

He must tell her the truth. But first he must get the permission of his superiors, which meant giving explanations that would convince them that Jenny was not implicated in Vincent Cheyney's secret life. This would take a little time; during that time he must remain here or risk an attempt being made to get in touch with Jenny without his knowing of it. Such a complete dereliction of his duty was unthinkable; he would have to risk at least another twenty-four hours' silence.

During this time Sandford was discoursing with Jenny on a newly rebuilt country house hotel on their road a few miles away. Here they proposed to spend the night, driving early the next morning back to their home. The preempting of a possible invitation to stay the night at Grove House was intended, as Sandford explained, not to overburden Mrs. Foster's patience, and doubtless the Sandfords were quite sincere in that. Only because the real atmosphere in the household was unavowedly changed did the gossiping remarks acquire the nature of an emphasis on the aloneness of Vail and Jenny in her home.

Less than a week before, none of the four persons at the round table could have dreamed that such an implication was possible; now suddenly it was not only possible but so obvious that in Jenny's "official" state of recent bereavement, the presence of a guest living in the house became an impropriety. It goes without saying that no such implication was even hinted at by a glance, but it was very noticeably present. It was not remarked upon until the Sandfords were alone in the car on their way to the hotel, when Teddy observed obliquely, in the homely phrase, that Vail seemed to have got his feet under the table at Grove House.

Vail himself at the same moment was wondering just how his intimacy with Jenny could have deepened suddenly enough for him not to be aware of it. His answer lay not in the various chances of their acquaintance but in the circumstance that he had not up to then been professionally concerned with a woman who was at once young and alone. In other words he felt himself and not Jenny to be responsible. However, Vail felt that his need not to pretend to be a member of the household, not to presume to move from his status of the guest who is only there for a particular purpose and not solely out of hospitality, did not relieve him of the obligation to help domestically. Modern life has its own conventions, he thought, and older customs do not always help with small problems of behaviour. He piled dishes on the wheeled tray with a wry sense of the advantages of former times when considerations for personal staff did not exist in the physical form of plates and cutlery disposal.

Jenny came back from waving good night to the red lights of the Sandfords' departure and at once began to help with this work. Its being obvious that the dining room could not be left untidy until the next day removed anything personal from their actions as they stacked the dishes from the evening meal into the machine. As she switched it on, she yawned.

"There are people who call this thing materialistic," she said. "It seems the very opposite to me."

"It's the latest cliché that household gadgets are not materialist capitalist tricks to make the money go round faster," he corrected her. "You must keep up with your truisms. This complicated and handsome machine is nowadays a liberator." He patted the shining white casing of the object under discussion while it hummed and then broke into a subdued but fierce lashing of water inside. "Excellent device it is—somebody should write an ode to it."

"You don't even have to stand around until it's finished. It actually switches itself off." She yawned again, putting up a hand politely. "I shall go up. I'm tired."

"Goodnight, then."

At the door—Vail was opening the kitchen window—she turned and said, "If you want a drink, you know where everything is."

"I probably will take a whisky, if I may."

And on this mundane note they parted, each congratulating himself on having managed what could have been an awkward moment with complete urbanity.

It was not late. Vail laid a couple more logs on the fire and brought his drink to the revived blaze. No news from Sandford, he thought, automatically arranging the present state of his enquiries in his mind. No letter, no telephone call had arrived to indicate that Vincent Cheyney operated his second business life from his office.

Mr. Folliot's original suspicions were founded on notes and order references which showed that patented processes belonging to the company had been divulged to some person or institution with no connextion to the firm's offices. They were notations, not letters or formal documents, and Vail assumed they were merely the current record of what was being dealt with at the moment of Cheyney's death. In themselves there was nothing to arouse the suspicions of Jenny or the Fosters if they should have seen them. Folliot knew they did not refer to legitimate customers of the company because, from a lifetime of memory, he knew exactly the state of affairs in his own business. To anyone else these papers would appear to be work Cheyney was in the process of completing during his journeys, papers he would, like all senior sales representatives of large firms, have in his possession during the negotiations. Vail took it for granted that Cheyney would have destroyed these papers after finishing the transfers they recorded. He must always have done so, because there were no files of such transactions in the house; the discovery of such records, if they existed, was one of the things Vail was here to establish, and he was pretty sure by now that, by no means unexpectedly, they did not exist. Only the list of seven-digit numbers was direct evidence of illicit business. Alive, Cheyney could probably have accounted for the other papers in some way that might have been difficult to disprove. Dead, he was unable to do so.

The efforts of his own colleagues had produced nothing that could refer to these numbers. All that was known was their illegitimacy, for someone must have recognised them if they were part of the normal work of the firm. There was not even any indication as to whether the message contained in the numbers was one coming in, or one Cheyney was about to send, or had sent and not yet received an answer to. Since they were almost certainly based on a book code, their solution by the cipher department, if it ever succeeded, might be a long job. Those brilliant strokes of deciphering known to Vail as almost legendary were all achieved during wars, when inspired mathematical geniuses took a hand in such work out of patriotism. In the dull days of peace, inspiration played a smaller part. The numbers were related to none of the many code systems at Vail's disposal. Any book among millions and any edition of any of those books might have yielded one page to Cheyney and his contact. Grove House was not, Vail was happy to recall, one of those houses in which books lie about everywhere. There were several hundred of them, it was true, but not more titles than he had been able to dictate on one roll of recording tape.

It was now several weeks since Cheyney's death, and Vail was beginning to wonder if his "friends" were not content, on hearing of the tragedy, to let well enough alone and reconcile themselves to the loss of a useful ally. The detail that so puzzled the conventional mind of Mr. Folliot was not even interesting to Mark Vail. That Cheyney was out of funds at his death he assumed to be caused by the transfer of whatever money was not immediately needed to maintain a front of normality for Grove House, to some safe bank account to which Cheyney could retain access if his position with his company, or even with his country, became untenable. He assumed with near certainty that this state of affairs over money dated from the beginning of the deceptions so successfully practised on Cheyney's wife and were connected with the same cause. Probably, too, the woman was provided for; their liaison was several years old and it was unlikely that she had resigned any hope of marrying her love without some compensation. If Mona Laver saved her money in an ordinary way, that would soon be discovered; if she bought property with it that would soon be discovered; if she bought property with it abroad, that, too, would appear with time. Vail was quite sure that some such funds existed in Mona Laver's name, whether or not she knew the kind of business she was involved with, and he was equally certain that the nest egg was separate from her lover's "insurance." Such patterns of behavior were axiomatic. Vail found himself thinking how much more intriguing this case would be if Cheyney had only been injured in that road crash and not killed. That might have been an instructive meeting. Although, of course, the successful domination of such a submissive wife as Jenny Cheyney was no great proof of character. Or even of high intelligence. A mere child, he thought, and with a strongly artistic nature, left alone in the world to be married by the first fortune hunter who presented himself. Even if Jenny were not naturally as weak as her husband had trained her to be, she was notably unworldly, and insulated by the artist's temperamental shield against the everyday world as well.

Curious chance that just the kind of man who could easily fascinate and then control such a young girl should come along just at the moment she was left alone. Did Cheyney gravitate to the girl or she to him? He was, at any rate, on the scene before Maculan's tragic death, for Folliot and others had told stories of tennis parties and picnics, the sedate pleasures of a fairly close community welded somewhat abnormally together by the secrecies of the war just past, in which its role was important but unpopularly civilian.

The newly demobilized young engineer-officer would have been as much an exciting addition to that little society as Maculan's only daughter would be a prize for the ambitious newcomer with the aura of one who did not tamely produce the means of warfare, but with heroism implicit, used them in the field. If Cheyney might be assumed to be aware of Jenny Maculan's position as heiress there was nothing disgraceful about that, but somewhere in the accounts given to Vail was the flavour of an almost forgotten disapproval. Probably unfairly, he reminded himself; those who had stayed at home in safe jobs might have envied the returned soldier, and Maculan must have been jealous of his only daughter, his only love.

Cheyney must have been a handsome man, and after a major war a front soldier of twenty-seven is a middle-aged man in experience. Anything denied to him by a prolonged celibacy in the desert must have been more than replaced by months in Italy before he went to Berlin after the end of the war. Vail had learned his own lessons of corruption in Athens and the heady mixture of civilian despair and military power to relieve that despair, which is the reward of the warrior in victory. But he was prepared to believe that even the practised decadence of Greece in 1944 was child's play compared with postwar Berlin, if only because depravity was so much more at home in that climate and that ancient centre of Balkan laxity than in the stern capital of Prussia. In the ruins of Berlin and the shameful abasement of a once proud and stiff-necked people humiliated by the knowledge of their world-advertised infamy beyond any hope of sympathy in defeat from their conquerors, an intoxicating power was within the reach of the most junior or untried soldier. Power of the most corrupting kinds, where the pleasures of sadism were added to every conceivable form of bought or enforced sensuality, where starvation and a savage climate ensured servility in the defeated, and encouraged, almost enjoined, insolence in the victors. Where half a packet of cigarettes could buy food for a family, and where in thousands of wrecked homes the mother or a daughter were the only means of wheedling those cigarettes out of men very conscious of their currency value. Vail had a shrewd assessment of the sinister effects of such an atmosphere of venality, where sudden wealth was there to be picked up, no former ownership was felt to be valid, where alcohol was in effect free, and women were instantly available, and not just any women but beautiful and cultured women, socially superior to the man and through whom he could and did insult and humiliate not only the woman and her own menfolk but a whole nation in her person. Only men of high character or extreme timidity could be proof against such all-pervading corruption; weak or flawed personalities quickly lost all sense of proportion and control. Vail had seen this happen, he had himself felt the pressure of temptation and had not entirely resisted it. The period in his own life was a remembered lesson of the ease with which all standards of decency can be lost, and a lesson that he would have been

188

afraid to face again even with all the added stability of fore-knowledge.

He received a powerful insight now into the obsessive motive to achieve a more lasting power that such an experience must give to a man already ambitious and lacking—as his later history proved—in consideration or concern for other people. A man who was really ruthless might well accept any means of furthering his ambition, once he knew the joys of such a powerful and privileged position. And he would also know, from the war itself as well as its aftermath, how easy it is for a determined and intelligent ambition to disguise its own harshness, provided it maintained a civilised exterior.

And such a veneer Cheyney evidently had achieved. In all the conversations engaged in by himself during his visit to the management offices of the Maculan company, as well as in the records of the investigations of other officers, there was no hint that Cheyney was felt by his companions to have come up from the ranks. To mention this would be contrary to the fluid conventions of the time, and even the expression that rose in Vail's mind was self-consciously denigratory of anyone capable of using the outdated form aloud. Even much less explicit snobbery would be felt to reflect rather on the person who admitted to it than on the one who was spoken of. But still, without any condescension, Cheyney's friends might possibly have felt, and therefore shown, a sense that his social achievement was as respectable as his technical and commercial attainment. There was nowhere in Vail's excellent memory any such implication. Even the old soldier Foster was perfectly at ease with the idea of Mr. Cheyney as his employer while being, typically, the only informant to draw a distinction between one who was previously an officer because he mastered a technical arm of the service and one who commanded troops, whose father "was something at Windsor." But there, too, in the memory of Foster's remarks, some lack was now visible. He did not say a single word, did not make even the most perfunctory claim, to any grief or loss in his memory of his dead master. Quite prepared to admit Cheyney as his benefactor ten years ago and the source of his secure living ever since, Foster evidently felt not the least personal warmth towards the man with whom he had lived in the same house for a decade. This now perceived gap in Foster's mind became a discovery. For once noticed, this lack of feeling could now be felt in general among those from whom Cheyney had disappeared with such shocking and upsetting suddenness. The normal reaction of friends to an accidental death begins in the superstitious fear of personal mortality, thus savagely dragged out of its hiding place, and then moves into sorrow for the loss. The common phrase so often used precisely expresses this sensation of loss in its simplicity: we miss him, we say. Nowhere could Vail recall either the phrase or its mime in a shaken head, an unbelieving sigh, an abstract eye as the lost friend was recalled with a word or a gesture often used by him. When Sandford took Vail for the first time into Cheyney's office he did not say how empty the room seemed, or that he could hardly credit Vincent's death. As a matter of fact he didn't say anything, Vail was sure. He was embarrassed, that was all. Neither did Folliot or Sandford, the only two with any suspicion, express the view that the strange state of Vincent Cheyney's affairs would quickly be cleared up. They had not protested that there must be some innocent explanation of the discrepancies in Cheyney's papers, no instinctive loyalty made them doubt their feeling. And none of the people Cheyney worked with every day found it necessary to express to Vail, in his sketchy disguise as Cheyney's lawyer, any personal loss. Every remark of the kind, without exception, referred to Cheyney as a professional man, not as a human being.

Cheyney seemed to have been admired professionally, and there were the usual envies of a vigorously pursued success, but no liking and no intimacy. He would hardly have had much time to form deep friendships; both in the Army and at Tantham and Maculan he worked too hard towards his own objectives. In a few years he acquired proficiency in a far from simple branch of knowledge, made more difficult for him by lack of theoretical understanding. At the same time he was getting a social education that removed him safely from a half-finished manual apprenticeship through the thickets of military customs into the Directors' Room of an internationally renowned business. It was an achievement that argued talents of no small order.

It would not do. Vail looked back himself over a career not very different. He, too, proved himself in war, advanced himself by persistent hard work, and made his own success. But he knew he was not deluding himself when he felt sure that the men he worked with would miss him as a man, and not only as a colleague who would have to be replaced, if his car hit a truck.

The difference was the deception, of course. Cheyney had been living a complex deceit as well as learning his life as he went along. To mislead his colleagues and—in some ways more difficult—his rivals, he maintained a constant distance from them. But he lived his double role as well into the most intimate and instinct-laden details of his private life, and that with a girl whose intellectual and aesthetic standards were imbued with those of the acknowledged genius who formed her. No matter how childish at first the still plastic sensibility he worked on, that was a remarkable feat. Cheyney must have forced his wife's mind into his own pattern without delay, and Vail now felt an inkling of that process which made him almost shudder.

Here, altogether, was emerging the outline of a personality of consistent and calculating hardness. Not active cruelty; it must have been a cold unfeelingness, the operation of an egotism with the consistency and resilience of tensed steel.

And Mona Laver was the safety valve. There was something about that young woman in the depositions. Vail went quickly and fetched his papers from the locked desk that had aroused Mrs. Foster's annoyance. A small echo from the past somewhere was there, something said by Sandford. Yes, here. "Miss Laver replaced a girl who got herself involved in the Watson case, about five years ago." Vail remembered well the Watson case and the report from the County Detective Inspector, among many other reports. If only I'd come down myself then, he thought bitterly. It must have been the shock of Cheyney's life. I might have tripped him then, when he was off-balance for a moment. The miserable creature who sent the anonymous denunciation of Watson actually worked in Cheyney's office! I recall her distinctly now. Tear-stained, indignant at the loss of her job, but with not the slightest remorse at what she had done. Yes, we had her in London.

There was nothing we could do to her, she's probably still sneaking on some young fool like Watson. No wonder Cheyney decided to trim his sex life after that. And the Laver just suited his needs, evidently. No doubt he tested her discretion thoroughly, before committing himself that time. But the intelligent calculation of the man! To use the very moment of danger to build greater safety. Because of course he had to have his known, accepted, condoned excuse for any little discrepancies of time or place; they always do have if they are successful. Oh, the swine, the clever swine. Clever, but morally an idiot. Meaningless statement. In all probability Cheyney was never taught any morals. The Ten Commandments heard in school in archaic language, lacking any relation to his grubby boy's life. Who would ever have put the fear of God into Cheyney, so that he might hesitate to lie and cheat? Not that slummocky mother of his, Vail was sure. So let us leave the self-righteousness on one side. And go back to his friends and bedmates for evidence of what he was really like. He took the direct evidence with him, as one might say. Mona Laver—was she christened Mona? But other women, before or since, there must be someone, other than the anonymous letter writer—someone with a bit more sense, a bit of a standard of comparison. Would Sandford know?

Somewhere out of the evening just over, a hinting suggestion surfaced, a little misty trace of unadmitted tenseness in Sandford, a flick of the eyes towards his wife, caught before the movement was quite made as if he felt an apprehension that she would expose herself. Married people were aware of things in their lives for years without ever formulating them, and certainly without speaking of them. Was Sandford aware of some current in his wife that might only have become traceable since the shock of Cheyney's death? Her reaction might have been stronger than their relations would account for, for certainly, thinking over Sandford's manner, there was a slight firmness about the way he turned the conversation to wine again. Yes, there was some flavour in the talk—when was it—something to do with the room? The remark about the wine cellar? Yes, that, but more than that. Something in the dining room. "I see you've changed the room about." A faint challenge of disapprobation, a little more than a casual preference for the arrangement as it formerly was. As if Eileen Sandford took Vincent's decision as to how a table should stand to be absolute. He was not imagining it; she was startled almost, as if at quite a new idea, the idea that Cheyney's dispositions and tastes were not untouchable, had been touched, a faint, distant possessiveness, a connection direct to Vincent in Eileen's memory. In a woman of Eileen Sandford's entrenched satisfaction with herself, that could only mean that at some time she had adopted Vincent as hers and thus put him beyond the criticism of others.

The conflict within her mind between her assessment of anything belonging to herself as valuable, even long ago and fleetingly, and the hard facts of Vincent Cheyney's long deception, must produce a breach in Eileen's self-confidence into which Vail would slide the scalpel of his trained, suspicious intelligence.

CHAPTER XV

VAIL HELPED himself to another whisky and soda; the ice was almost melted. Old houses are never silent and this one made small sounds about him that, combined with a sight of the ice-thickened wash in the bucket as he tested it, reminded him of ships at sea with their creaks and rattles and slight abrasions of invisible parts that move incessantly against each other. Here the sounds were of wood, perhaps of stone but not of metal, yet they brought with them the old memories— sea and wind. The storm, with its abrupt and indifferent violence, was still present in his mind, his perceptive but unimaginative mind. His fear of the sea, in the aspects in which he had known it, was something he had learned in the harsh winter of North Atlantic war to control, but he would never lose it, although it was now a scar in his being many years old. It was grown over with hardened tissue, but it was still there and alive. Human beings do not "get over" the great wounds and fears that set up the mind's frontiers with barriers beyond which skulks the knowledge of mortality. And men who experience their own deaths at nineteen can never recover the unknowingness that is youth.

With a deep shudder of his consciousness, Vail recalled the moments of the second time his ship was torpedoed. The first time he was stunned by something as yet unknown, but the second time he lived it as his coming death, the horror of *knowing* that the great wash of dark waters must now crash over the frail shell of his head, bearing him down with its roaring pull and swing into the depths from which he could never struggle back breathing into the black howl of wind. The instantly sinking mass of the ship pulled him with fearsome force downwards in its race. He did not struggle, he was a straw, a scrap of matter, and the explosion that immediately followed, killing many of the crew, was a huge shock inside his head. It threw him up and out, breaking one arm against the timbers of a boat as it disintegrated, leaving only flotsam he could cling to with his good hand. He and the boatswain were left, the other man naked as he was born, in the roaring waste of inky night. They were not only alive, they were not alone, they had each other. Those who have experienced such disasters retain for the rest of their time on earth an instinctive, an absolute perception of loyalty: that is, of dependence on each other. Everything in nature, including man himself, is against the survival of man, and only by each belonging to the other can he save himself from the outer dark. These obscure and terrible thoughts oppressed Vail; he could not understand why they should now overtake his mind, when the pattern from that wartime fear had been set for years in his choice of a profession.

To reassure himself he moved across the room, harmonious and warm, washed in subdued and coloured light, and saw something not before noticed. On a small table, out of direct light from any of the lamps, stood a small bronze head that Vail recognized as Maculan's. The broad, magnanimous forehead gave a kind of innocence, almost childishness, to the slightly frowning eyes, the rather broad but inquisitive nose and the humourous and sensitive lips; it could not be mistaken. One could see just from the head that this was a man of small physical stature but large in every other sense. How I should like to have known him, thought Vail, staring at the classic metal, warm and intimate before him. That man, too, fell from a frail security into the thrashing chaos of waters, the crippling cold wildness of destruction; he, too, fell to his death, but the death stayed death, he was not exploded back into living. But that can only have been for Maculan a confirmation of a lesson learned over ten years before, he thought. The lesson that in the midst of life we are in death, that defeats occur for which there are no defence. That he must have learned—and oh, learned by rote, by repetition like learning Greek roots at school—from the shocking event of his wife's disappearance just before the war. That is, before our war. The continental war was already raging, Maculan's war, his original war; or it had broken out again after a twenty-year cease-fire. What must a man feel who, through a mistake of judgment, sent everything that women mean to men, sent soft warmness and the comfort got from protecting responsibly an even more fragile weakness than his own body, sent all the complexity of intimate and irritating reality, away from himself into an inferno of hatred and fear? He was too busy, so his wife went and never came back. How would one feel about *that*? Not the Judas feeling of a man who betrays his fellow-men, but the ultimate treason to the mother and wife. The wife taken for granted, the wife used, the wife already a little boring, the wife on the border of one's important life, the wife important just because of all that. The background to which is owed rest, calm—disputed wordlessly by her—from that lap or bosom flies the inventive spirit, and to preserve its right to fly the spirit of invention sacrifices its essential womb. How would one feel about that?

One might feel, in the moment of falling into the endless tumbling waters, a kind of justice in death. Or on the other hand, such a man, a genius of invention, might find time only to ask how the beautiful air machine, the conqueror of time and space, came to fall as this one did.

Behind Vail, his construction of logs added to the fire was now burned through and fell together in a shower of bright dust and sparks with a small plop of sound, a soft implosion of heat and light that startled him slightly, so that he turned away from the bronze head. He was in the act of turning, poised on a heel with one hand swinging an almost empty glass, when the question penetrated as if a telegraphed message were coming over a wire: How did that aeroplane come to fall just as it did and when it did?

Oh, come now, he said to himself, now consciously thinking. A sudden storm, mechanical failure, there are so many flying accidents. Maybe by an oversight in Gander they ran out of fuel. Maybe a member of the ground-service crew in a hurry to get off simply left a screw unturned. Yes, maybe, and perhaps a mechanic, not out of haste but out of design and paid for it, just did not tighten that hypothetical screw, maybe such a mechanic actually loosened the screw?

"*You've* got a screw loose," Vail said aloud to himself with emphasis. He moved over to the fireplace and drank the last of his whisky, tipping up the glass sharply. Whatever his outer thought said to him, he was aware, somewhere down in his consciousness, of having received a message.

Could it be? he asked silently, with fear and anger. Could it have been planned so far back? He stared across at the bronze head, so small to carry such a load of meaning, not more than eight inches high. Before his death? Before, that is, the marriage?

He looked past the fireplace and out through the window, which reflected as in a subdued dark mirror the colours and shapes of the lighted room. Dimly through the reversal, when he went close and peered, could be seen the outline of the trees. This wretched girl and her "influences," he thought, she's got me doing it now. Flights of schoolgirl fancy. But really, it could be that this thing was planned so far back. The idea might easily have come to me before this, and only because of the storm and that atmosphere during the evening with the Sandfords being so golf-club hearty does it seem strange now. Only I doubt rather that Maculan's inventions would be irreplaceable enough to justify such an elaborate and vulnerable plot. Valuable, yes, but not all that valuable. And to murder him would mean no more inventions, after all.

But if Maculan was in a position to expose something? It wouldn't be the first time murder was done to protect a useful source. Vail's scowling face pictured in the old, uneven glass was grim with shadows, a gargoyle come to life, a cobbold peering in at human habitation. He moved his head and jutted his chin to make an even more impressive image, and the window moved the lights about in pools and runnels like water. He could himself recall two cases where murder had been committed to cover treason, and he knew of a number of other examples from the hearsay of colleagues; these cases rarely came to justice or were even known about until a good deal later. In the nature of the world in which such things happened, disappearance and death were always possible from various causes.

And there was the curious fact about Maculan that among all the papers in the factory offices and at the bank here, not to mention in the house itself, there was not one old personal

197

letter, no diary, no notebooks, no photographs from his youth. There were plenty of papers, but they could all be classified as designs or documents; they were not personal. True, Maculan's tragedy was ten years old, but it was not as if these people lived Vail's kind of life, often moving and throwing away things as they moved; they had lived in this house for twenty years and intended never to leave it, but there were none of the dusty boxes full of rubbish, none of the rarely used drawers of cupboards standing in passages with forgotten letters pushed to the back. It was an extraordinarily tidy house, now he came to think of it. He would not have expected Jenny to be so orderly. There were papers Vail could legitimately inspect, and he had done so with trained thoroughness but no success. That there was almost nothing belonging to Cheyney was not surprising, but he understood from what he was told that Maculan's household was in some disorder at his death. Folliot had spoken of the muddled and makeshift housekeeping and the disorganized refugee couple who failed to keep the place properly clean. Small wonder, Vail thought: the wife was a child psychologist and the man a neurologist, although neither of them could then practice. Maculan was evidently more benevolent than efficient in domestic matters; a good thing the child went to school or they would probably have tried their crazy psycho tricks on her, poor little soul, as well as ruining her digestion with their foul goulash.

Having restored his sense of proportion with this piece of healthy insular injustice, Vail felt ready for bed. He turned out the lights, and went out into the hall where one light on the upper landing faintly lit the stairway. He went over and tested the front door, which was locked. Presumably there was a routine by which Foster locked up, even after an afternoon out, but perhaps he ought to make sure about "his" door to the back courtyard, which was rarely used. It was indeed unlocked, and Vail opened the door and stepped out into the night drenched with fallen rain, windless but with a ragged heaven, with the moon in its last quarter. Up there was wild weather, here on the ground all was still. He could feel the great trees breathing their cold freshness into the night. Trees, he thought, with an outgoing like joy towards them.

Moist scent that was not quite spring blew gently against his body, a soft buffet that hardly moved but swelled up and round. His foot slid a little on the rounded cobblestone on which it rested. As he stepped back into the doorway his heels sounded clear, startlingly clipped, and the big key in the mortice lock scraped loudly. But inside once more, the slight sounds of the house could be heard again, shifting secretively, creaking like faint old footsteps. It was intimate now, cosy, it accepted his being there.

In the process of going to bed it occurred to Vail that this problem was going to be solved by the others concerned with it, and not by himself. He was, in fact, only sitting still here and waiting for something that every day became less likely: a direct attempt to discover what had happened to Cheyney and any unfinished business he might have had in hand. This thought annoyed Vail; he thought by now of the Cheyney affair as being his job and he wanted to be the one to finish it, tie it neatly together. He felt a distinct possessiveness about the matter. He suspected himself of being slow and clumsy about it simply so that he could stay on here. Both the suspicion and the idea itself were so foreign to Vail that he again accused himself of adopting fanciful notions from outside, allowing himself to be influenced by an imaginary atmosphere.

He was almost asleep when a perception startled him awake: he was being devious with himself in blaming some vague ambience; he knew quite well that it was for Jenny that he wanted to stay here. Yes, and he could feel her living presence a few yards away from his own and imagined her sleeping quietly, her head turned sideways into the pillows with dark hair almost covering her face. You can put that notion out of your head, he adjured himself. Saddle yourself with a young woman ruined by a disastrous marriage—which she almost certainly invited—an artist at that, and, final impossibility, probably a spoiled artist. . . ? He sank back again into sleep, knowing himself awake but just about to become unconscious, to drown in sleep. . . . Drown? He was instantly awake again.

It was only the storm, he assured himself, using a method which had worked well for years on the fewer and fewer occasions that the memories came back. Just relax, it can't happen again, there's no war now and it's all years ago. Just don't allow yourself to think about it. The trick worked, he began to slide again into sleep and even when some small animal squealed in the distance he aroused only enough for the thought "fox" to explain the cry in his half-dreaming mind. He slept, but was aware of sleeping, of lying in bed, of the curtains at the opened window billowing slightly; he turned over and his pyjamas tangled, restricting his movements. After what seemed a few minutes he turned again and pushed the covers down from his shoulders, sweating. At once he was cold and turned again, reaching blindly for the blanket, which eluded him; with a smothered groan he half-raised himself to catch the cover; the bed was now disordered. He tried to construct a fantasy to cajole himself into sleep, but it would not capture him and he began to count over the various facets of the job he was engaged in, moving without rest in and out of sleep for hours. It is not hours, he told himself wearily, but minutes, and in another few minutes you will be fast asleep. But it was hours, for the next time his eyes opened he could see the faint light of first dawn past the curtains; less than half an hour had gone by since he last looked at his watch. He turned for the fiftieth time and lay sprawled until he realised that he was not now even able to pretend sleep. He might as well get up.

He rolled out of bed muttering curses and pulled on slacks and a heavy pullover. But once out of doors he felt better and strode away from the house with a feeling of needing to shake himself up. Through the beech grove he ran a few steps down the slope and then began to circle the hill, breathing deeply in the soft moisture-laden air. Two fawn cows lazily following the rest of the herd were in his way and he gave the nearer a friendly clout on her hindquarter. She turned her ridiculously shaped head and stared at him, softly chumping on her cud. Her eyes were so beautiful that Vail stopped to stare back at her; she very slowly and with a perfect dignity turned her gaze from him and lumbered away, unperturbed. The ground here was almost saturated, he could feel it spring and give way to his tread, and the rich grass, which was not grass altogether but a myriad of green herbs of all different shapes, bunched down under his boots and sprang without bruises back again. His ankle boots were already darkening with a wet stain, and strands of various leaves and grasses clung to the suede. He shoved his hands into his pockets and then, seeing a fanning out of light, looked up. By moving to the east, he now looked over a spread of valley below him, cut up into many small sections by hedges studded irregularly with trees. It was misty with yesterday's rain, here and there a sparkle, but in general of a bluish green mistiness. As he stood still, seeing what Maculan once saw, the sun rose over a far hillside and flooded the whole world with a mild, benign and joyful yellow sheen.

Hearing a slithering sound he turned, expecting another bland stare from a Guernsey cow, but was not in the least surprised that it was Jenny in slacks and a heavy black jersey that might have been a copy of his own. Vail swept out an arm, indicating that he would like to embrace the entire landscape, and Jenny came closer, so he put both long arms round her shoulders and kissed her instead.

"There are a few primroses and violets out already in the hedge here," she said quietly. He kissed her again, this time with more purpose, and she sighed deeply and kissed him back. After a moment she said, "Couldn't you sleep either?"

The "either" gave her away completely and he felt he must protect her from such innocent candour.

"What a talkative girl you are, to be sure," he said and returned to kissing.

But as everyone discovers in their teens, standing up is no position for making love. It also occurred to both of them at the same moment that if anyone else was about they were startlingly visible. This quite alarmed Vail, who being a Londoner, was accustomed to having as a human figure in its surroundings, a lack of uniqueness that amounts to invisibility. There were some trees about twenty yards away, there was a whole company of birds and there were the cows, now disappearing, rears pointing upward and tails flicking, over the turn of the ground down towards—he supposed—their byre. The landscape was anything but empty, but they were the only humans. He looked about in the way people do who have something to hide.

201

"Anybody about at this hour is too busy to notice us," Jenny assured him with a pleasant feeling of knowing more than Vail did. "I'm glad your name is Mark. I used to play tennis years ago with two brothers called Matthew and Mark and they were so nice, I've always liked the name."

"How odd," he said, his voice wobbling with laughter. "My brother's name is Matthew."

"It isn't odd really. They belong together. You seem so different. I don't see how I could not have noticed how good-looking you are."

"People usually do seem different when they begin to kiss each other," he pointed out. They started to walk together round the hill.

With various side excursions to look for early hedge flowers they spent about half an hour or so circling well outside the beech grove. There was blackthorn thinly budding along dark, spiny twigs, primroses in first bud, low-growing violets of a piercing darkness and, in a place more spongy than the rest of the hill, celandines.

"They have very pretty leaves," Mark said of these, "what are they called?"

She told him, with astonishment. It was like being a child again, telling the names of flowers, but it was the feeling of not being apprehensive or careful, which was also like being a child. By common consent they began to move up now, to strike through the trees towards the house. Looking down at the hundredfold variety of plants at their feet they did not notice until they were nearly upon it that the storm had uprooted one of the beeches. An outer tree, very old, had fallen inwards, forced by the wind coming from the west. Its great spread of roots faced them as a barrier and they could see that its fall had brought down branches from other trees in its track, as it now lay pointing towards the house. They stared at the hollow from which the tree had been wrenched and the tangle of snaky roots still covered with clumps of earth. Many were broken, exposing whitish muscle, others ranged into the alien air, reaching for their hold.

"Mark. Look," said Jenny and pointed into the raw hole. Clutched all about with broken roots was a long stone of roughly square section.

"You see!" he cried triumphantly and jumped down into the depression. "It's another of those fertility symbols. Or whatever they are." He began to pull impatiently at the jutting corner sloping up at them, but it was too deeply and solidly embedded to be moved so easily. Mark clambered up again and they stood staring at this so timely piece of evidence, he brushing damp earth from his hands and she looking up to see how much damage the fall might have done.

"We must get in touch with the county archaeological society," Jenny suggested. "Don't you agree, Mark?"

"Oh, not yet," he urged. "Let's keep it to ourselves for a bit. We don't want solemn old men in deerstalkers tramping about—do we?" As he said it he meant it simply, but at once it occurred to him that for another reason he would rather not have strangers inquiring about the place for the next day or so. With local worthies who might know a good deal about Maculan and the company, he would have trouble keeping up his deception. The thought of his own dissembling depressed him, and then he was thunderstruck at the definition he had used in his mind of his position in this house. It was the very reverse of the real situation; he was engaged in putting an end to deception, and one so base—he reminded himself—that almost any means possible to a civilized man were justified. That he was now worried and puzzled was visible in his face, but his use of such words as "ourselves" and "we" was so delightful to Jenny she hardly noticed the change in his expression until afterwards.

Jenny was laughing at the thought of solemn old men in deerstalkers, and the matter of professional investigation was for the moment shelved for both of them.

"Let's come back and photograph it later," she suggested. "That is, if you have time."

"After breakfast, you mean?" he asked.

"Are you starving too?" It was so easy to understand him that she felt for a moment quite dizzy with the blissful feeling of intimacy. They struck through the grove and walked up the path through the kitchen garden, where the aroma of y strong tea and toast met them as they came to the rear door.

"Oh. They're up," said Jenny, disappointed. Then remembering, "Of course, it's Mrs. Godolphin's day today. If she's better, that is."

"The cleaner? Her name can't, it just can't be Godolphin!"

"It is, though. Lots of people about here have terribly grand names. Mr. Folliot says they may be descendants of old families who came down in the world, married beneath them . . . you know? There's a man keeps an oil shop in town, his name is Drake and he believes, if nobody else does, that he's a descendant of Sir Francis Drake's brother who moved east into this district, it's said."

"Oh, Lord, Plymouth Hoe, and Captain's sleeping down below. The steady trade winds blowing. All that?"

"All that. I don't even know if Francis Drake had a brother, do you?"

"No. I wonder if he did have? How fascinating. One could spend a lifetime exploring local records."

"We must go in, I see Mrs. Foster's form through the window and she's looking at us. Well, records, you know, it could be a brother the wrong side of the blanket."

"You mean one can never really know. . . ? Maddening thought. Why did you say Mrs. Foster's 'form'—it sounds affected."

"I thought of a fox's form, I don't know why. Or is it badgers who have forms?"

"Foxes have earths," he said firmly. "I thought you knew about the country." Holding Jenny's elbow, Mark opened the door and perfidiously pushed her in before him. He could feel in the thin, little sinews of her arm the reluctance of her movement and then a stiffening of resolve.

"Good morning," she said, sounding that terrible cheerfulness with which only the feared are greeted.

"Hi, Mrs. Foster," said Mark from over Jenny's head, "we've had a splendid walk and we're starving." Mrs. Foster turned an early-morning face that promised no good of the day, and stared at them, muttering good morning but not otherwise quite knowing what to say. Faced with Jenny's usual apologetic manoeuvering she could have blandly ignored the hint, but Vail's manner took something for granted: she would naturally be glad to hear of their appetites. Without having time to think of what she was saying, Mrs. Foster replied.

"If you'd be satisfied with tea, Mr. Vail, I'll put this lot on the trolley for you. Eggs and bacon all right for you, Mrs. Cheyney?"

"Oh, we don't want to steal your breakfast, Mrs. Foster," disclaimed her employer, with an aspect almost of terror.

"I do," contradicted Mark cheerfully. "Now I smell the bacon I can't wait another minute."

"Two seconds, it's just done." Mrs. Foster was actually smiling, although her expression only a minute before was weighted with the accusation of yesterday's spoiled outing, which must have been somebody's fault. "Here we are. Marmalade and honey are in the dining room, there's a toast, milk, tea, oh, butter I've forgotten. Here we are, then. You won't mind the eggs and bacon straight on the plates, will you then. Now Mr. Vail, you're a big, strong gentleman, you'll push the trolley for me, won't you?"

The trolley had rubber-tired wheels to manoeuver over the uneven stones and floor boards; it made a pleasing, slight clatter as it ran, and the dishes touched each other. Jenny was towed behind it by the same invisible pull of confidence that had so signally succeeded with Mrs. Foster. And with her astonishment and admiration she felt a distinct pang of jealousy that Mark could find enough sympathy with her housekeeper to effect such a change in her.

She wanted, she recognized that, all his attention for herself.

"You know," said Mark presently, when half the bacon had blunted his hunger and he could eat the rest less eagerly, "she's perfectly all right. Just wants to be treated like a human being, that's all. Your nervousness with her is almost as bad as being rude—don't you see that?"

Jenny stopped with her fork halfway to her mouth and stared at him.

"You mean, I suggest that she's . . . you know, I never thought of it like that."

"Of course it's none of my business," he went on, reaching for more toast. "May I have another cup of tea, please?"

"You don't quite understand how it was," Jenny began to defend herself, and that in itself was something quite new. But she felt urgently a need to be understood by Mark, and that

205

was worth making an effort for. Still, she flushed slightly with the unaccustomed self-assertion. "I was always so scared of anything going wrong in the house. I mean, so many things did go wrong at one time . . . And . . ."

"And he nagged? That was it, wasn't it? You can tell me, my father was a nag so I know what it's like. Just keeping on and on and on, always the submerged self-pity, the implication that nobody cares about him which masks a bottomless egotism. Constantly picking on things whether they matter or not, and never letting up. And even after you know quite well that it's all a confidence trick to get his own way, you can't do anything because you can't stand the eternal nagging. Is that how it was? Or did he have another angle?"

"You *do* know how it is with people like that. Yes, that's true, and you go on feeling that it's all your fault, even after you know . . ."

Mark now helped himself to tea from the large, dark-brown kitchen pot, since Jenny had not responded to his request.

"Some people go on feeling it's their fault," he said with bitterness. "My brother did. I rebelled before I was fourteen, but then my mother and Matthew got it even worse: my attitude was their fault, as well as everything else. So rebellion didn't work either; the only thing was to leave as soon as I could. That's why I went into the Navy, I could go as an ensign at thirteen to the college then, before the war."

"But I couldn't leave, you see," said Jenny sadly. "I don't mean I thought of going, because I never had the courage. But it wouldn't have worked. The house and everything . . ."

"You mean you'd have had to chuck him out? Yes, and of course, he just wouldn't have gone."

"I can't honestly say I ever got as far as thinking that. Mostly I just tried to hide it from myself. I can see now, hiding things takes up all one's energy. But I did always feel, no, I mean in the last year or so I felt, that there was no way out. I knew I could never put over my point of view, and there was the company as well as the house—you see? The scandal, the trouble, the explanations. . . ."

"You must have thought of it sometimes, though? Not only in the last few weeks?"

"Not quite consciously. But in a shadowy way, like a kind of day dream. With a frightful feeling of remorse at being so disloyal. Even when it was in dreams. I have a recurring dream. I'm escaping from somewhere, I don't know where, just trying to get away."

This was familiar. A notorious traitor with whom Mark dealt for months on end once described the same kind of dream to him. This man did escape in fact; he committed suicide just before his arrest could be made. The memory made him cautious now, and Jenny added something to her hesitant explanations that sharpened his apprehension.

"What makes me so bitter, now, is the feeling of having been used. The deception was so crude. And I allowed myself to be deceived, knowing really that it was my own cowardice that he used. The injustice of it—I can't forget it."

"Tell me something: did it never come into your mind that these affairs—this affair with the Laver girl for instance —were really immaterial to your husband. That they covered up something else?" She looked so puzzled that he was drawn to say more, hoping that her suspicion might have gone so far. "I mean, covering something in his business life. Men do use affairs to account for absences, aberrations in their lives that otherwise would look suspicious?"

Jenny stared blankly at him.

"I don't understand," she said, shaking her head. "How do you mean, in his business life?"

He could not now say he did not quite know, for in the next hour or so he would explain to her exactly what he meant. He shrugged and frowned.

"As you say, the deception was crude. Elaborate, too. It makes one wonder."

Mark changed the subject successfully, the moment passed.

But as they rose to leave the breakfast table he said that he should make some telephone calls as soon as the working day began, as soon as people were in their offices.

"And then we'll have a talk, about business and all that. You will be in? Not planning to go into town today?" There was a note of anxiety in his questions that made Jenny very happy. "I mean, before I pack up and leave."

"Leave?" she cried. "Not today?"

"Well. Soon anyway, I'm afraid."

207

Jenny did not like to say that they could postpone his departure for a few days without Mr. Folliot being annoyed. It seemed to imply that Mark could employ a dishonest trick. It also suggested that she, Jenny, was trying to involve him. Since she was doing just that it was important not to say it; any words on that subject must come from Mark.

"It's quite clouded over," she said instead. "We shall have to wait a little to take any decent photographs of the stone."

She herself was aware of how ingenuously disingenuous that sounded and, suddenly out of her depth, made some excuse and ran upstairs.

CHAPTER XVI

THE SLEEPLESS night, shared as it now seemed companionably with Mark, was filled for Jenny with memories that seemed in retrospect sordid, intimately unpleasant. For some reason, Eileen Sandford's comments on her rearrangement of the dining room belatedly annoyed her. The hypocrisy of it, she thought, staring out of the bedroom window sightlessly. They knew, Eileen knew, but they still kept up this convention that Vincent's dispositions were under the protection of some piety, that it was somehow improper for his widow so quickly to change anything once ordered by the dead man. Even the bleak indecency of Vincent's dead body being still accompanied by his mistress was not enough, it seemed, to change their views. They did not know, she realised, about the hotel bill having been forwarded to her to point up the true situation like an unpleasant joke; but they could not really suppose that Jenny was not now aware of the liaison, even if they still thought it was news to her three weeks ago. They themselves had told her that Mona Laver was with Vincent in the car. The occasion of the funeral, pushed to the back of all their minds as soon as it was over, had been made hideous instead of grievous by the fear that somebody—the lorry driver, the nurse from the hospital, the undertaker—might say something that could bring the second burial into their obsequies by some unconsidered word.

The very thought of that other funeral, unseen, unspoken of, was of a meanness, a scrambling secrecy that made them all shifty and ashamed. One elderly aunt, it was reported, witnessed it in the morning before they all so respectably assembled in their expensive mourning array at noon. It was so arranged that what was in fact a luncheon party should take place at two o'clock at the best hotel in Wrexham. The private room, the company discreetly relaxing from the duty of grief, seemed at the time and even more now, like a gathering of masks. The shock of suddenness was the real cause of their awe, certainly of Jenny's pallid stillness that passed for anguished self-control. And that, at a funeral, had its own propriety; the dead, in a very real sense, buried their dead on that day and only a clown would have found anything wrong with carrying through the inevitable ceremonies with the dignity of convention.

But afterwards, surely. . . ? Even a day or so afterwards, Mr. Folliot distinctly showed an implicit agreement to a washing of hands, an unspoken statement that they need not pretend between themselves to anything but a quiet reserve that should present a neutral front to the view of the world—but no more. Considering now his manner on those two visits, Jenny was struck by Mr. Folliot's exact measure of what was due to decency while drawing a line at which hypocrisy could and should halt. He had pretended to nothing. His enquiry as to Jenny's health was correct and no more; he had neither pried nor pretended, and she now liked and respected him for that stiff-necked honesty.

The marked kindness of the Sandfords since the accident was built on a falsity elaborate enough to be playacting. It was disgusting, and Eileen's show of surprise at Jenny's changing the seating arrangement of her own table was not only a piece of impertinence; it was a kind of toadying, a keeping up of appearances in private, where such deception was unnecessary, that reduced them and Jenny with them to small-minded conformity. It was, on the other hand, not quite the matter of the table but a general unspoken proposition that they should agree to this make-believe, to a show of respect and grief that none of them could really feel, which now made Jenny resolve to say something to Eileen at their next meeting that would put an end to this vulgarity.

Jenny began to construct the proposed conversation; her fantasy carried her into a retrospect of miseries and humiliations that she presented in her imaginary explanation to Eileen Sandford with a resentment long buried, banned as much from her own mind as from the sight of others. She

210

would tell Eileen what she really thought and felt about Vincent with a clarity that should make it impossible ever to mention him again.

Whether or not she would ever find the courage to do anything of the kind, her inner dialogue banished any hope of sleep. Memories crowded back, and the more Jenny thought of the past, the more she recalled of it—and all bad. Bitterness and anger mastered her mind and she walked to and fro in her room rehearsing everything she might bring forward to what was now no longer one listener but might have been a whole group, or gradually might have been the dead man himself whom she never accused in life. She recognized indignantly that the very event which had freed her mind of servitude made it impossible ever to face Vincent with a new-born independence; it was too late.

Feeding her own rancour, Jenny dredged up vile details that certainly could never be told to anyone, moments when she tried to please Vincent, to seduce him, and was repulsed with an amusement so cruel she almost cried aloud to think of it; and even worse was Vincent's pretended kindness after those moments, when he advised her not to ape sensuality, for she would never be a voluptuary. Sometimes he excused his indifference with the suggestion that Jenny was unhealthy, that even the most penetrating of Paris scents could not remove the sickliness of her person. Sometimes he accused her, always gently as if with pity, of wanting only to conceive a child, a design he frustrated by the simplest means on the grounds that her health would not allow her to produce a sound baby. That Jenny had never been ill except for normal ailments was not allowed as an argument, and even when a specialist found nothing in the least out of order, Vincent said with scorn, as if stating a fact generally admitted, that gynaecologists were empiricists who knew nothing.

The very perversity of these attitudes, their standing normality on its head with a confidence that in retrospect appeared almost pathological, was what disturbed Jenny with a late-night clarity. Granted her youth and ignorance at her marriage, which ensured Vincent's unassailable and continuing influence over her mind, it was still a most astonishing thing that she should have accepted the notion that it was

211

unusual, still less blamable, for her to want children. It was stranger than her feeling inadequate because she was no expert in the techniques of love. Did husbands always want their wives to behave like the *grandes horizontales* of Paris in the last century? The example came easily to mind, for Jenny had been reading Balzac, but its old-fashioned air did not make the question any easier to answer, for here her ignorance was so great that she could form no opinion. Even books and films, which, apart from the whispering of schoolgirls and occasional jokes, were really all she had to go by, gave her little actual insight, and when she came to examine the question she found that she didn't know what and how—as she put it to herself—other people did. Imagination might supply some exciting possibilities, but she just did not know about anyone but Vincent, and her husband had never liked her enough to vary what he called, and frequently, the routine. He made it clear in many small ways that with other girls before his marriage it had been quite different. Later it was not only before his marriage, but his new experiences were, from the very start, clearly her fault. Later still, her supposed nervous instability was discovered to be the root cause of the inadequacies, and Jenny believed that too.

She could now understand that this belief was what cut off all chance of her either rebelling or changing herself in any way that Vincent said he wanted. The occasions of her gawky attempts were so humiliating that the longing to reach Vincent gradually died altogether in helpless failure. At the time it did not occur to Jenny that since Vincent knew so much about physical love, he was in a position to teach her. But it occurred to her now, and she knew that it was one of the many details that had been for years buried as unwanted knowledge in her own mind and body. She now knew with confidence that a man faced with an entirely untried girl ought to be eager and delighted to initiate her into all the amorous pleasures; she was sure of that without knowing why she felt so certain. It was just obvious. That was the not quite stated point of half the love stories she knew of. From popular films and novels to the greatest works of art, quite half of them took it for granted that men acquired knowledge, usually but not always by unstated means, and found it satisfying to communicate that knowledge to innocent and amorous wives. It was the lawful, allowed debauchery of marriage with ignorant but loving girls that was clearly supposed to be the greatest of pleasures: from the *Ladies' Home Journal* through Mr. Knightley to Othello, that was the agreed upon masculine idea of exquisite joy. And it must, moreover, be true in general in the real world, or why else had a world of men until now always kept the women they meant to marry in a state of virginity? An answer at once presented itself that the real reason must be the security of fatherhood. That made Vincent's attitudes even more strange; whether for reasons of property or the longing for immortality, men everywhere wanted children.

It was not she who was abnormal, she decided. Not only history and literature but the people about her as well proved that even where there was little or no feeling between the partners of a marriage, possessiveness and love for their children was a powerful and almost universal emotion that dominated the lives of millions of people.

Then why had Vincent ever thought of marrying her? There could only be the most base and crude answer to that question. He took on something he did not want to get what he did want, and afterwards, to keep his ascendancy, convinced his wife of her failures to keep her subservient. The difficulty here was that Vincent was not in any other way neurotic enough to be forced by not understood inhibitions into making his marriage empty and sterile. He was a competent and well-organized man in other departments of life. Perhaps his personality was abnormal only in sexual matters? For Jenny was not quite so foolish as not to know that many men and women married for advantage and still fitted their own desires into the pattern they had chosen without serious unhappiness. In other words, most people kept the implicit bargain, men as well as women. Somehow it would not fit with Vincent's character in other directions to suppose that he would not get what pleasure he could out of his marriage. The only logical explanation was that Vincent never liked her or desired her, that she never was "his type" and that he never would have thought of her at all but for her property. That she, her person, was a definite drawback from the start. That

213

he wanted property very badly, it was clear. But a man of his looks and war record, his competence, could find any number of women who united a fortune he lacked with a person he did not actually dislike. So: he wanted *this* property?

But why? There was no point. That must be all wrong, she had erred somewhere in her reasoning. And her father did not particularly like Vincent, Jenny remembered, so that must have presented another disadvantage from his point of view. She did not recall a strong feeling of disapproval on her father's part, but enough of reluctance to take Vincent's attentions to his daughter seriously to account afterwards for Vincent not wishing to see or hear too much of his memory. Her father was a little jealous, she supposed, and afterwards Vincent was jealous of his influence. Vincent didn't like the sculptor Connors, either. Neither was regular churchgoing popular; it came in for a good deal of teasing until Jenny stopped going, although it made her uneasy. These evidences of possessiveness were the strongest proofs of Vincent's love for her, she believed for years, and in the last period of her marriage they were the only proofs. They still presented a difficulty in her mind . . . unless there was such a thing as a generalised jealousy? Perhaps there were people who were mistrustful of every influence apart from their own, who saw any interest or concern outside themselves as a threat? That seemed quite possible; Jenny was prepared to accept the idea as a possible solution. But it did not quite fit in with Vincent's personality as she remembered him; it fitted his words and actions but not with—here Jenny could not express quite what she meant —not with the "feel" of Vincent.

Jenny abandoned her efforts to work out a reasonable explanation of her past life; it was too puzzling and she supposed she was just not clever enough or knew too little about people to understand what had made Vincent behave as he did. But there remained a feeling, a strong feeling, that she needed to understand; it was essential to her future peace of mind to know *why* the things that had happened in fact came about.

Dissatisfied, uneasy, she lay down at last and tried to sleep. After half an hour rest was no nearer than ever and she switched on her bed lamp and opened the novel lying half-read on the table beside her head. A pity *Lost Illusions* was finished. Even in the bad translation, Balzac was a whole world of his own; this novel was amusing but it did not tell her what she felt Balzac might if she could grasp the key to insight. Even the most comprehensive and profound of books could not teach her much, she feared. What she needed was more experience, direct living, so that she could recognize the wisdom of what she read. Even the teachings of the Church, however true and eternal, were no help with adult questions unless they could be related to what actually happened, what people, including oneself, actually did. The Church decreed what one's attitude to the world and other people ought to be—not a set of rules but a measure for any rule, any person, and any situation which, once adopted, would show clearly what one should do and be. But the gospel might as well be propounded in the original Aramaic if one knew nothing about people, including oneself, and about the world; it was like telling a blind child about colours. Jenny sat up in bed, struck, as well she might be, at having made a discovery. Of course, that was what made the lessons of Christianity so often seem stern and uncompromising; they were framed for people who were living lives full of intractable problems, not to be considered in a vacuum of inactivity.

What I need is experience, I must go out and do something, know people. So Jenny addressed herself. But how? A job was an impossibility, for she had no training. Travel was just another form of looking at life. She was too far from large centres of education for her to take up a course of studies in some formal way. Local affairs? The local charities? Human beings, it was a saying of her father's, can never be dull, and Jenny could imagine that the unknown quantity of "local affairs" might be full of excitement and intrigue, once taken up. Yes, she would ask about, go and see people like Lady Mainter. Nothing important at first, of course; she would have to start by addressing envelopes and making lemonade for bazaars, but at least there must be something she could do. The notion of actually setting out to do something on her own was at once so stimulating and so unnerving that Jenny was further than ever from sleep. By the time she had turned over every possibility that occurred to her in her own neighbour-

215

hood, and from sheer weariness fell asleep, it was well after three in the morning.

Even then it was a half slumber and as soon as the sun rose it woke her up through the windows at which she had forgotten to draw the curtains. She was too alive with energy, a feeling almost forgotten, to want to sleep, in any case. She jumped up and pulled on slacks and a pullover warm enough to make a coat unnecessary, for she distinctly did not want to be hampered with heavy clothing. Walking rapidly she cut through the garden and the grove, coming out into sunshine and mist together. The mist was shifting and rising thinly; it was almost warm. Rounding the isolated row of hawthorns Jenny came upon Mark Vail, who was staring out over the valley to the east of her hill. Hearing her he turned; she realised that the mild domestic beauty of the valley was as touching to him as it was to her; she knew that at once from his expression. To emphasise his enjoyment, Mark made a comprehensive gesture that included herself in the pleasure he felt. Jenny moved the two steps needed to approach him and in the most natural fashion in the world Mark enfolded her shoulders in his arms and kissed her.

"There are a few primroses and violets out already in the hedge here," she said, to express the wonder of the morning. He kissed her again and this seemed so much the natural thing to do that she returned his kiss, and although they exchanged some more remarks Jenny could never afterwards recall what they were because she was dazed with sleeplessness and joy. His lips tasted of fresh air and toothpaste, his cheeks were rough, unshaven, the pullover rather harsh as his arm touched her ear. The kisses were testing, not quite amorous, but promising, with sensations Jenny had almost forgotten. She felt shaky, the uneven ground made it difficult to keep her balance and while standing still the pre-spring chill of the air became noticeable. So they began to walk round the hill, without needing to discuss their movement.

They would make their own breakfast, she thought. Mark was very funny about flowers, he didn't know any of their names, and she looked about to find new things to tell him. The hollow of the fallen tree with its naked and broken roots startled her and she was suddenly afraid, as if at a dereliction

216

of duty, that its fall might have damaged other trees in the grove. Then she saw the stone, and Mark jumped down; his spring was graceful, neat. She wondered if he played games much, and which games; perhaps tennis; she could imagine he was rather good at tennis and would look well in white shorts and shirt with his dark skin and hair. In fact, Mark had not played tennis since leaving school. He was up again now, beside her, the stone much too heavy and long buried to be moved by one impatient tug. Jenny could see that by a lucky chance the tree trunk had fallen between the other trees, grazing one high up and breaking several branches but not hitting any of the trunks hard enough to bring another beech down with it. Jenny felt that this good luck was something granted to her; she hadn't felt this childish gratitude for a long time or felt the sensation of knowing just what another person meant even when he did not speak. She was delighted afresh with the picture of stuffy old men in deerstalker hats; she could see them, moving like Groucho Marx among the tree trunks, searching for something, and at once decided that they didn't want anyone about in the grove.

The scent of tea and toast, an outline of movement behind the windowpane returned Jenny abruptly to here and now; of course, the Fosters got up early on Fridays because of Mrs. Godolphin coming. She only thought his joke about Drake funny, it did not really amuse her, not when she thought of insisting on getting their own breakfast over Mrs. Foster's equal insistence that it would be no trouble, of course she would do it for Mrs. Cheyney, and Foster's breakfast could wait for a moment or two, it wouldn't really get cold. Jenny was still going over this inevitable wrangle in her mind as it became clear that the Fosters' breakfast was going to be theirs and Mrs. Foster really did not seem to mind and she was so surprised that she let slip the often thought-of opportunity to say she really preferred tea to coffee in the morning.

Later, by the care with which Mrs. Foster avoided looking directly at her when giving Jenny a message from Foster, Jenny knew that her early morning walk with Mark was the subject of discussion. The cleaner being at the house meant that whatever was said would be carried at once into the village and, within a day or so, into the town. This thought worried and confused Jenny; she was embarrassed and showed it. But it was high time that spring gardening plans should be agreed upon with Foster, and this provided an escape from her room, where Mrs. Foster proposed to clean windows, or rather to supervise Mrs. Godolphin doing so.

With a feeling that she was being chivvied from one place to another, Jenny went down and out of the front door, leaving it open. She would walk round the house to get an idea of what was needed for the borders, and then have a look at whatever Foster had in his glass-covered frame. Zinnias, she was sure. Petunias? That dark-blue stuff, Foster liked that for edging mixed with stonecrop.

Foster was in fact then bending over the frame. The seedlings were just what Jenny expected.

"I think I'll go down to the town and get some rose catalogues," said Jenny, abrupt with determination as she came up. "The drive borders would be pretty with low-bush roses."

Foster straightened up and pushed back his gardening hat in a sketch of politeness.

"Roses?" he asked as if he had never heard of them. Jenny knew what was in his mind. Money was not spent on the garden; they used perennials and what Foster could produce himself for the borders.

"I don't really like mixed borders," she said, trying to ignore both her own and Foster's implications. "And roses would suit the house better in any case. And while we're at it, why don't we get a couple of climbers to grow up over the chestnut that was struck by lightning? If it dies we can use the trunk as a support and if it doesn't, so much the better."

He was staring at her rather blankly. Had she spoken with too great energy, as if expecting to be argued with?

"I'd like at least one of those climbers with dark red flowers. I don't know what it's name is, there's one on the churchyard wall at Gullion—you know the one I mean?"

Foster said very slowly, "Matter of fact, I've got some rose catalogues. The nurseryman sends them by post. Lives in hopes, I daresay."

"Good," she said. "His hopes are going to be fulfilled this year."

"They're in the potting shed. I'll get them. Of course, it's the wrong time for planting, you know that."

"It doesn't matter. We can use fertiliser," she said recklessly. "Lots of people put roses in, in the spring. I've seen them."

"Well, they're hardy things, roses. We can always try. Just a minute, Mrs. Cheyney, I'll fetch the books."

It was easy. Jenny felt elated. She walked over to look at the ruin of the vegetable seedlings under the torn plastic shelters, scattered still with broken branches and twigs. A large black currant bush was smashed too. She clicked her tongue at that. The leaves were budding, and she pulled off a shoot to savour its aromatic smell.

"You could ask Harry at the farm if he can let us have some horse dung?" she said, accepting the gaudy and shiny sheets from Foster's earthy hand. "I seem to have heard that's best for roses."

They enjoyed, both of them, the rose catalogue of the previous autumn and picked provisionally half a dozen names, pencilling the quantity in with a stub of carpenter's pencil Foster proved to have in his pocket for marking seedlings.

"I hope they still have them," said Jenny, flipping through the pages again.

"I'll tell them we're thinking of doing up the garden here a good bit," suggested Foster. "You know, hint at a lot of bulbs and that. That'll fetch 'em."

"Bulbs?" she said. "Foster, what a good idea!" She was aware that Mark was approaching and felt rather than saw for the first time with what a gradual and sloping effect he seemed to appear, hands in slacks pockets and head down, apparently concerned only with the small shooting points of green in the beds. "Bring back a spring catalogue if they have one, why don't you?"

"Well," he said, rubbing his still rough chin without embarrassment. "It's late but we could bed them out for this year, well, tulips anyway. And start properly in the autumn, then?"

She said excitedly, "We could have the grass full of daffodils!"

"I didn't know you thought much about flowers, Mrs. Cheyney."

Jenny looked at Foster's little grin. She made a statement of policy. "Well, I do," she said definitely. She had lived with Foster for ten years and never found it comical that his nose was crooked and pulled sideways when he smiled, which he did only with the right side of his mouth. The slightly bulbous tip of his long nose bent towards the smiling side of his face and gave him the look of an elderly and wise bird.

"What are all those smallish trees around the other side?" asked Mark with his air of not yet being quite with them. "Fruit trees?"

"Trees!" Foster struck his ear briskly with the ball of his hand. "I'd forgotten. There's a beech down in the storm, Mrs. C. Did you know?"

"Yes. We—I saw it this morning. What should we do?"

"Better be sawed up. We can burn it. Harry's got a proper 'lectric saw he'll lend me. There's an apple with the mange of some sort, too. That smells good in the open fireplace. Wants stacking properly, of course, 'til next winter."

"You won't cut down anything without asking me first, though? I don't like trees being felled."

"I'll show you now," he said, and they strolled away. They all took on the casualness of Mark's lounging gait.

"Saw an orchard once when I was a kid. There were a lot of geese and ducks in it, eating the fallers. I was scared stiff of the geese."

Foster looked at Jenny. "Mr. Vail's a great one for the country, isn't he?" he said slyly.

"You can't keep ducks without a pond," Jenny informed him.

"Oh," he said vaguely. "Pity."

"Little China geese. Pretty they are," mentioned Foster. "Keep the grass down, too."

They contemplated in silence the aged apple tree, misshappen and knotty, grizzled with great age.

"I suppose it ought to go," said Jenny reluctantly.

"You could always replace it," suggested Mark softly. "With one that bears fruit."

"We've got more fruit than we know what to do with," she said.

"If it was any good we could do something all right," said

220

Foster, betraying some annoyance or scorn in his voice. "Needs a bit of expert attention. Then we could have the jam factory up to collect the fruit and pay for half the garden, I shouldn't wonder."

It was clear that Foster had at some time carried an approach from the jam manufacturer's buyer and been refused.

"But why don't we do that? Expert attention? You mean the nurseryman would have to come and prune properly . . . show you how?"

"Mr. Cheyney would never hear of it," said Foster. "Sorry, Ma'am." He never addressed her as Ma'am except when there were fashionable guests present. It was evidently an apology for reminding her. "He would never have people about, you know."

Instead of answering, for she did not know how to do so, Jenny walked round the old apple.

"All right," she made up her mind. "Let's have it down when Harry can come. Listen, Foster. Why don't you ring up the garden people and say you'll come down on Monday? Let them know so that we don't have to wait about for delivery. You can arrange what needs doing at the same time."

"I could go this afternoon, really. Ground's boggy from the hail still. Can't do much with it today. Well, they can't prune or anything until autumn."

"No, but someone will have to come up and have a look? And there's quite a few things to do?"

"Well, there would be if you meant . . . ?"

"To do things properly?" She took him up. "I don't want to change, but we ought to keep things up. Mr. Sandford was saying that. Look, you could take Mrs. Foster down for a cup of tea, perhaps the cinema. She had a rotten day yesterday, after all."

Foster stared blankly at this.

"I could ask her, then?" he collected himself. "If she's finished in time."

"I could take you out to dinner," suggested Mark. "Time I repaid some of your hospitality."

"Oh, but the hotel in the town is impossible. We'd have to drive ten miles to Withen St. Columb! It's quite ten!"

"You seem to forget the invention of the internal combustion engine. Ten miles is no longer a day's journey, even hereabouts."

"You're dreadfully facetious sometimes," she said.

"You invite a rather childish sort of teasing, you know. Why Withen St. Columb? Though the name is enough, really."

"There's an RAF station of some kind there near there. A quite good hotel with restaurant and bar and everything, even dancing at the weekend, where the officers go. It's very old, older than this house, they say."

"Ah, that would be Withen Camps? I've heard of it."

Mark had indeed heard of the station. That was the exchange through which his telephone calls were discreetly routed for security reasons, without Jenny's knowledge.

"They do something odd there," Jenny dismissed Withen Camps. There was a secret delight in the thought of being taken out to dinner by Mark, so strong that she felt a fibrillation of the nerves like a constant very delicate trembling, almost palpable, perhaps almost visible. This sensation reached her solar plexus, and the nervous system, long unstimulated, began its magical process of stimulating the blood to flow faster and to fire the inhibited imagination with coloured but unspecified images as bright as the photographs of flowers in the seedsman's advertisements.

Not only was it years since she had been taken out as a special occasion for herself rather than as a duty to some guest; it was the first time in her life anyone had taken her out to dinner as a first stage of courting her. She left school at seventeen to live in the rather remote but not unsociable countryside, going from a conventual if healthy life to a place that retained not only the manners of former times but was isolated by the recent war. In that district, so far from any large town, there were no fundamental wartime changes except those that took people away; that is, villages became more self-contained than for several generations. Because they were producers of food, the rigours of rationing and the hardships of a self-imposed and puritanical "austerity" were unknown to them, but their abundance, although natural, was looked upon with disfavour and envy by outsiders. This attitude of the townsmen was not understood by the country people, and it caused resentment and a defensive secrecy that created an unnatural barrier between towns and country.

Moreover, Jenny's father, though not Jenny herself, was unchangeably foreign. Their household was run by foreigners for the years of the war, and Maculan never spoke English without a comical accent. While his prestige ensured their inclusion in local life, his intellect almost more than his strangeness made Maculan unlikely company for the local worthies; he could have entered their interests in his serious, consistent fashion, but they could not even envisage his concerns. So until her father's death Jenny lived on a footing of uneasy heartiness with the owners of the larger houses round about who viewed the owners of Grove House rather as generous subscribers to local hospital and cultural funds than as friends. Her father's real contacts were with distant colleagues and the faraway world of high affairs that Jenny herself never entered.

This was a situation peculiarly suited to Vincent Cheyney's needs and he took every advantage it offered him. The dead Maculan's reputation was raised into a barrier against all spontaneity; this Jenny never overcame. Vincent's journeys formed an obstacle to the acceptance of hospitality; he confined his own entertaining to those who suited his purpose. Thus with her marriage to a director of her father's company Jenny lost any warmth or familiarity from even those neighbourhood acquaintances she did retain.

Thinking of Foster's remark that Cheyney would never have people about, Jenny was aware, as if from outside herself, that the isolation of the household was unnatural and she wondered if people gossiped locally of them as recluses. She realised suddenly that not a single neighbor had been to see her after Vincent's death; a small stream of friendly condolences came by post, from Lady Mainter by telegram from Rome, and that was all. Bitterly she thought, they felt that writing a note was all they could manage.

"I never did *learn* gardening," Foster was saying. "Well, my dad kept his bit of allotment when we were kids. I like the work though. Seem to have a green finger. Keeps you out of the house, too."

Mark appeared to get on with everyone, thought Jenny, both enviously and admiringly. I'd better try his method on some of the neighbours. Whatever his method is.

"If you'll excuse me, I'll go and telephone this ancient restaurant at Withen St. Columb. What's its name?"

"The Lion. I'm not sure whether Red Lion or White. I haven't been there for ages."

CHAPTER XVII

"YOU MEAN the *Black* Lion," said the clipped voice at the other end of the connection. "How very nice. We've got a big party on, Wingco's anniversary in the Service. Why don't you join us? Y'know, representative of the senior service and all that, glad to have you. Oh. Guest in mourning, sorry to hear that. You'll want to be private then. Well, just call Withen 224 and ask Mrs. Slocum to give you a table in my name. That'll be all right, you'll find. Not at all, m'dear chap. See you later. You'll have to drink a glass of wine with us, you know that? Can't let you out of that, y'know, mourning or no mourning. Eh? Ciaou!"

Of course, thought Mark, he was at the NATO base at Acquileia. I suppose he calls bints, bambine nowadays. The particular net of convention of the services, each with its own special flavour, both caught and annoyed him. Asses. Spectacular young men, not so young any more, in their flying machines. With their electronic gear. I suppose they use developments of stuff Maculan invented. I'll bet they do.

"No glasses of bubbly tonight, my dear fellow, I fear," he replied, catching exactly the idiom but with a different tone. "You will be good enough never to have seen me. Clear?"

And that calls itself a security officer, Mark thought, dropping the receiver back and at once picking it up again to telephone the hotel at Withen St. Columb. The distant man so brusquely cut off returned the compliment. He turned to his Flight Sergeant and said crisply, "Bloody copper."

"These deep-set lanes make one feel there is nobody else within miles," Mark said as he drove rather slowly down the hill in the fleeting dusk. "And I suppose there isn't, either."

"Don't count on that," warned Jenny. "We may meet a herd of cows."

"What an **extra**ordinary light this is. Perfectly clear, startlingly clear, but darkening, everything looks unreal. I'm beginning to find this part of the country fascinating."

"I'm afraid we are in for some more rain," said Jenny prosaically. "This still, clear light, it isn't light but there really isn't a word for it, often means rain coming."

Her voice sounded musically pleasing and he glanced sideways at her pale, small profile and was jolted to see it so neat and pretty, framed in the hood of the black coat edged with soft fur. It was the only black coat the one "good" shop in town could offer her when she bought in haste for the funeral, and was much more elegant than she would normally have ventured upon. It certainly did not look like mourning clothes, Mark thought. It was like the things the women he knew in London wore to go out in the evening, and therefore brought Jenny into a closeness not felt up to now.

This movement towards a possible relationship more familiar to Mark than that presented by Jenny's real situation was continued by the Black Lion. It was a country hotel that positively begged to be called a hostelry, so self-consciously aged and picturesque was it, so frequently did the rooms and passages turn corners, trip up or down steps, expose beams, lower doorways so that even a moderate stature might feel the need for a precautionary duck of the head. The various public rooms carried fanciful names; apéritifs were drunk not in the Bar but in the Smugglers' Cave, the Grill Room was the Ox Roasted Whole, and the main restaurant, incredibly, the Baronial Hall. Mark stared at this last with unbelief. Panelled Hall, yes, he thought, they could just get away with that but no, not Baronial. His attention was further delightedly caught by the Coffee Room, the door of which carried a panel—they were all rough-edged tree sections with the bark still adhering but the cut surfaces varnished over crudely painted lettering, announcing Lavender Parlour. Finally a small off-licence was indicated by a suitable drawing of a fat monk with wine measure in hand, Simon the Cellarer's Store.

"This is a perfectly splendid place," he said with great

satisfaction. "I can't wait to discover what they call the lavatories. And do the bedrooms all have names?"

"I don't know," she said, "I've never stayed here." She looked about her with fresh perception and began to laugh. "I never saw it as funny before!"

They went into the tiny bar, hung and cluttered with every conceivable piece of nonsense from a never-never world of the past, from billhooks on the walls to torches in sconces from behind which peeped electric wiring and red bulbs. The seats were, of course, cut-out barrels, and there was an inglenook without a fire, since the space was needed for a table. At this table sat three junior RAF officers but otherwise the bar was all theirs. The drinks were, however, of today and there was even plenty of ice, for many of the officers stationed at Withen Camps had served abroad for years.

Vail almost expected a notice offering them genuine Olde Englyshe Meade and felt cheated for a moment by being reduced to the normality of pink gin and salted peanuts. The smuggling atmosphere was provided by a print of a lugger painted all-over black and lurching through threatening seas on one side of the bar itself, and by a Customs Cutter on the other side. Over the bar were several muskets. The centre of the bar shelves was occupied by a nautical chronometer in a battered and well-polished brass case.

"So long as they don't mix the drinks with salt water, I'm prepared to put up with it," said Mark in an undertone to Jenny so as not to offend the pride of the barman behind the counter. Two young women now joined the boys in the inglenook, amid a chorus of cries of joy. They were both pretty and both of exactly the stamp of conventionality to be expected of junior Service men, one wearing a dress of scarlet chiffon and the other, as she informed her escort, her "slinky and sophisticated cocktail dress" of lilac metal brocade.

In contrast, Jenny's plain black dress took on a distinction that, in Mark's mind, hardly belonged to the wearer. He found himself not sure that he liked her new resemblance to other women he knew well, nor the view of her as she might fit into a metropolitan scene rather than this riot of countryfied quaintness. In fact, Mark took in what Eileen Sandford had already called to herself a kind of dignity in Jenny. Underneath the impression that she might at any moment return to her manner of wincing nervousness, he could see now that the Jenny who worked on the bust of Eileen was not one aspect of her nature but its fundament; she possessed a secret scale of measurement that was confined to her studio only because its use in the outside world had been ruthlessly forbidden by systematic bullying. In a moment of insight, Mark understood, as clearly as if he had been present during the long process, just why Vincent Cheyney was obliged to reduce his wife to near slavery; an objective viewpoint was not only a danger to his hidden life, it was also a threat to the arrogance that was one of the constant characteristics of people who did what Cheyney did. Mark knew from experience that an inflated self-esteem could be taken for granted in Cheyney's makeup, a self-centredness that could not help being affronted by any independent judgment. So he would be forced to do instinctively what expedience would have made him do in any case: kill Jenny's confidence in her power to make comparisons and draw conclusions from her own observation.

During their drinks and Mark's thoughts, a gray-haired woman approached who introduced herself as Mrs. Slocum. She evidently knew who Jenny was and offered polite condolences, not without a glance at Jenny's host. Her detailed explanation that their table would be in the Grill Room, since the main restaurant was reserved for the party Mark already knew about, was clearly designed to give her the opportunity of inspecting the stranger. With the advice that baby lamb was roasting for dinner the gray-haired woman then withdrew, her elaborate formality leaving behind a distinct impression that she did not approve of a widow of three weeks dining alone with a man, even if he was a business associate.

"Hmm," said Mark under his breath, "as to that . . ."

Jenny laughed with delight at the recognition that Mark did not like Mrs. Slocum and that she did not need to hide her own opinion of that lady's unspoken criticism, which drew into the open a promise in the evening hidden up to that moment, at any rate for Jenny.

Mark was asking the barman for the wine list, and over the shiny, dark folder and the movements of their hands, Jenny absorbed with poignant but still unfocused amorous joy the shared joke of illicit secrecy from his eyes.

"With roast infanticide we will drink a lordly Hock," said Mark, still looking not at the list but into Jenny's eyes. "You don't mind that I can't afford champagne?"

"I don't at all *like* champagne," disclaimed Jenny truthfully, and so utterly changed was her apprehension of sensuality that she did not even remember the cause of her dislike. There was not the least shimmer of connection between this evening and Jenny's only comparable experience. It might have been, and of course it was, happening in a different life.

"But let's not think of money. I can't think of you as a businessman at all."

"Neither can I, I fear." Mark pushed the thought away. "Although it's so necessary."

"It may be, but not this evening." Jenny supposed he might wish to discuss some routine matter belonging in her mind to Mr. Folliot and was determined that he should not. "Tell me about the Navy."

"Not the war!" he cried, laughing at the incongruity. "That's worse than anything."

"We'll talk about nothing, then. Just nonsense. Everything can wait until Monday."

This admission of Jenny's, expecting the atmosphere of an outing to last the whole weekend, made Mark's heart turn over. It was not so much the words as the look of brilliant, smiling triumph that accompanied them that disarmed and almost frightened him. She was so sure she knew what she was doing; it would have been naïve in a girl of eighteen so to expose her innocent little plan. She means to seduce me, he thought with a sensation between laughter and shock. She's made up her baby mind to assert her freedom. She may even be aware of it. But she may not be.

Jenny saw his expression change from startled amusement to something that might have been caution.

"Oh. You were thinking of leaving before then?" She stammered a little with returning shyness.

"No. *I* wasn't thinking of leaving, or rather I don't want to think of it. But I'm not my own master, as you know. There are other people involved."

She misunderstood him completely. She stared down at the glass before her on the bar and said nothing because for a moment she could not speak calmly, nor find the words to extricate herself.

"What is it?" he asked almost irritably.

"Nothing. I mean, it didn't occur to me. Of course, naturally, you have other things to do."

"You think I want to leave?" He could not possibly ask if she suspected him of being married. Even to a girl as silly as Jenny that would be too obviously an answer to what she had not said.

"Oh, blast," he said helplessly, entangled in his own double-dealing. "Let's go and eat."

But even in the short distance to the Grill Room the strong current of emotion swirled away Jenny's self-distrust and Mark's uneasy conscience; even his momentary annoyance advanced their feeling of intimacy in its assumption of their being close enough to each other to show their feelings. And by a transfer of his dislike of his own deviousness to an area less intransigent than duty, Mark began to talk about London, his flat in Holland Park, his constant but casual companionships with several young women, his dislike of the idea of marrying, which he rightly attributed to his father's difficult temperament. It was only very gradually that the sense of some discrepancy entered Jenny's enjoyment of this covert statement of Mark's position vis-à-vis herself. She attributed this hardly perceptible unease to a small guilt she expected to feel at the pleasures of the evening and the expanding consciousness of delightful anticipation that spread through both of them behind their small talk. Not a word was said that Mr. Folliot—but not Eileen Sandford—might not have heard, but during the following two hours Jenny and Mark progressed from a perceptible but still easily retractable appeal into a state of quite definite intention.

Through amusement at the pretensions of the Black Lion, and enjoyment of the food, which was adequate, and the wine, which was excellent, they moved into a pervasion of amorous feeling as real, as invisibly but palpably real, as if they were seated not in a somewhat ridiculous public room but in a secluded garden full of scented flowers. A delicate and powerful tension formed itself which seemed to Jenny at least, since her perceptions were the stronger for being so much less experienced than the man's, like a cord that vibrated between them.

It began to seem intolerable that they must drive almost ten miles back to the house. On the road they were forced to stop at a railway crossing, and to the accompaniment of an express train roaring and rattling over the rails, Mark kissed Jenny with a lover's kiss. Afterwards this was the only thing either of them remembered about the drive.

The house was silent, and but for the lamp over the main door and the dim light burning in the upper hall it was dark. They did not exchange a single word. The slightest pull from the hand holding hers drew Jenny to the guest room as she was already turning in the direction of her own room.

Only for an instant did she feel a fear of her own inadequacy, and this fear proved to be quite misplaced.

In fact Jenny found her thoughts of the previous night strikingly confirmed. Mark seemed to expect and want nothing from her but lovingness expressed in physical terms, and this was the easiest thing in the world for Jenny to give him. Indeed it was so easy and so pleasing that they made love most of the night, waking and sleeping, talking and caressing in a natural and lovely intermingling until five o'clock, when Jenny slipped away to her own unwelcoming bed in the chill of a rainy dawn. She slept instantly and deeply but awoke as usual, so eager to lose no moment of Mark's presence that she was not even late for breakfast.

An extraordinary change had taken place in Mark's appearance. This, too, was quite natural and it did not strike Jenny as strange that his hair now gleamed like a starling's wing, that his eyes slanted a little upward with a grey-green shimmer like the sea moving with sunlight as his glance moved with laughter. His lips she now saw were rimmed in a clear outline, a symmetry delightfully altered by the quirk of his smile as he gave her a sly grin of conspiracy with his formal good morning. And his movements were so graceful, as he half rose. His head was set neatly, with an air of suppleness on the strong throat, and the slight bend of his shoulders forward was not now ungainly but the only way for a tall man's height to be at once emphasised and diminished in a charmingly modest and self-confident effort to be the same size as everyone else. She even knew where this bodily mannerism came from; he was too tall for a sailor. As a boy at the naval school his name was inevitably "Lofty" until he was commissioned, and this title distinguished him, Jenny was sure, by more than the chance of long legs.

A similar situation having repeated itself for Mark many times, he could no longer experience this crazy or magical transformation. But he, too, felt a distinct change into a grateful ease mixed with something he was less used to, the knowledge that this vulnerable and guileless creature must not be trifled with. Simply having made it clear to her that for him this was a slight affair was not enough to free his conscience, because his greater experience saw that Jenny did not have—he put it to himself as her not *yet* having—the knowledge of such affairs that would enable her to believe his warning. To a woman on the one hand chaste and on the other moved by all the flood of erotic happiness and gratitude that follows the end of a long starvation, the idea of a slight affair was quite meaningless. Jenny, Mark was now deeply aware, was not a girl to have affairs. It was not something that could be discovered without the very acts being undertaken which must bring the ban on frivolity into effect; Jenny's lover could not be sure of her essential seriousness without doing what committed him to be careful of her. It is a danger always open to adventurers, which is why philanderers who have caution or moral sense learn to leave virtuous women alone. One can only assert one's freedom after the fact of love by using a kind of brutality that Mark had never yet needed to use and that he did not feel himself capable of when he looked at Jenny's blissful and adoring eyes. He thought for a moment of the two or three women normally available to him whose terms of reference agreed with his own, and was aware with a shift of deep unease that none of them provided anything to compare with the delightful sensations of mastery and total exclusiveness that belonged to the night just past.

Mark had deliciously debauched a woman who might almost have been a virgin, and he knew himself too well to believe for a moment that he was going to let it go at that one night; the initiation of Jenny into love was much too exciting to be cut off short.

"There's a big parcel of books come with the post," said Mrs. Foster as she came in. "Addressed to you, Mr. Vail. Shall I bring them in? I could bring some fresh coffee, if you'd like?" This last to Jenny, who accepted the offer with pleased surprise. "Being as it's Saturday, I mean."

"Ah, from the library," said Mark, taking the bulky packet in dark paper from her. "I asked them to send a few things on British archaeology. Probably complete gobbledegook, I suppose." He was unwrapping the packet and rolling up the wrappings neatly for the return of the books. So besotted was poor Jenny that this commonplace routine of library users appeared to her as evidence of a most superior mastery of the business of living. Mark was so *at home* in the world, she felt.

"Do you use the library much?" she asked respectfully.

"A good deal. Sometimes even for just reading, but we often need information on all sorts and kinds of things from philately to—um—the Aztecs and back again."

This time the discrepancy between what Jenny knew Mark's job to be and the things he said did strike her. But she was quite willing to believe that she did not know at all how wide were the problems presented to a lawyer retained by a large engineering firm, and assumed that in any case his examples were simply a manner of speaking. But it did occur to her now, for the first time, that Mark was not at all like any lawyer she knew. But that seemed perfectly reasonable, because Mark was unique and did not resemble anyone else in any other way, either. She had not known, for instance, that the company kept a law assistant of Mr. Folliot's in the London office, but this, too, was clearly something she ought to have known and she was glad now not to have exposed her ignorance by some comment yesterday when Mark was talking over dinner about his London flat.

In fact, the examples Mark produced were genuine, but some alchemy must have been at work in Mark's mind too, for he did not notice his own inconsistency. Only a day or two later he thought of this lapse with a feeling of disquiet that approached fear in its strength; how could he have been so unthinking? What was the matter with him that he should

233

make mistakes so contrary alike to temperament and training?

They retired happily to the side room to consult the treatises on ancient British remains, looking up everything they could think of in the index of those that seemed helpful, poring over the maps of their own district, and putting marking slips in chapters or references to read later. It was about eleven o'clock when Mrs. Foster called Jenny to the telephone.

"Some wretched man I've never heard of wants to come and see me," she said on her return, consulting a slip of paper on which she had noted the name. "He did not want to talk to you, said it was for me personally. Odd man. Said he must see me, he even wanted to come today but I said that was impossible. He's coming on Monday morning. What d'you think he wants?"

She was not intrigued, not even interested. If anything, noting Mark's instantly restored watchfulness, she was annoyed that anybody should be coming to interrupt their colloquy. But for Mark a switch was keyed in and it wiped all intimacy from his face and manner; the neutrality of professionalism took over. So it was going to happen, after all.

Jenny took what she privately called his official look to mean that the call was from a rival company who would make her some offer to buy out her father's patents; Mr. Folliot had apprised her of this possibility.

"I don't see why this man needs to come here," she said crossly. "I could just as well have said on the telephone that there's nothing doing. But he absolutely insisted."

"Well, I suppose one doesn't discuss business on the phone," answered Mark quietly.

"That's what he said. I said he should talk to you, but he refused." She sighed. "Well anyway, he's coming. We shall just have to get rid of him as quickly as possible."

Her simplicity, her assumption that Mark must share her own unwillingness to be interrupted, pierced her friend afresh with a desire to protect her. Her character was far from having been ruined by her marriage, he saw. She was just as ready to trust him, Mark, as if nobody had deceived her in her whole life; and their short, their so new, intimacy gave her already a confidence in naturalness that might well have been lost forever. Mark was not this time amused or beguiled by the childish candour, the unwomanly openness with which Jenny gave away her real feelings. It struck him now at first as imprudence that approached idiocy, and then as something near unconscious blackmail. As if she were, without knowing it, defying him to treat her with anything but the most refined scrupulousness. But he knew as well, having returned now to a normal shrewdness and self-knowledge, that it was his uneasy conscience that caused the sensation of annoyance.

I've got myself into a fine mess here, he expressed it to himself.

"Let's go out and have a look at the hollow where the tree is uprooted," was what he said aloud. "See if there's anything more there, now we can check what we ought to find."

The rain had stopped about an hour before, but it was wet enough to make them pull on rubber boots, Jenny her own and Mark a pair borrowed from Foster. Under the tall trees the ground was not affected by the morning's drizzle; it was, if anything, a little drier than the day before. They cleared the sloping stone without much difficulty with garden spades, but it was too heavy to lift without a forestry crane. Mark brushed at the crumbling, damp earth clinging to the exposed remnant, with his hand in a driving glove.

"There are cuts in it," he said, "gashes or perhaps . . ."

"Oh, how marvellous if they were signs," cried Jenny. "Runes, would they be called?"

There did seem to be slanting lines cut fairly deep into the stone.

"Mind," he warned, as Jenny lifted her spade, "we mustn't damage anything. That's about all I do know, that incrustations could be important evidence. What we ought to do is hire a jack or something and lift it out—we could wrap it in sacks."

"Harry at the farm has a little crane thing for logs that he can attach to a tractor. But could we get a tractor in here without touching any of the trees?"

"We must measure the approach width. Could we get Harry up to look? He could probably tell, from using the tractor all the time."

"I'm sure he'll come. Perhaps not today, but we could go down and talk to him now. Mr. Blane won't mind, if they aren't frightfully busy, I'm sure."

"Harry is the farmer's son, is he?"

"Nephew. The Blanes haven't any children of their own. But he's like a son. You'll like him. Let's go now, shall we?"

"Shall we tell Foster first? He won't want to be left out of the arrangements. He was talking of getting Harry up to saw the logs, you recall?"

"Yes. Yes, I suppose I'd better."

As they came up with Foster in the orchard Mark was pleased at his thought, for Foster was standing there talking to a stranger. But what might have become a suspicion, if he had only seen the man, was resolved at once by Jenny's greeting him as an old acquaintance. Mark saw that it was the owner of the local nursery come to inspect the chance of considerable and continuing orders from a house which, although one of the larger properties in the district, had never made use of his services. It was visible in his slightly cautious manner to Jenny that the family was considered strange by the local people; the bluff, stocky man did not quite know how to treat her. He would know without thinking about it exactly the right tone for dealing either with the Mainters at their beautiful mansion with its famous gardens, or the neighbouring farmers and their quite different needs. But Jenny was not only an unknown quantity, someone who took no interest in the land, she was a suspect outsider. And really, Mark thought, although to him not suspect, she was living in a world that was not modern England. An outsider she was, not only because she was protected by money and a house of her own with land round it so that today's world could not get in. Or, rather, she was an insider. He wondered suddenly what Jenny would make of television advertising when she bought a set—he knew she would buy one because she was doing everything that was the opposite of what Cheyney wished or needed. He nearly laughed aloud at the idea of Jenny staring at the pop world in which the only motive was to wheedle the high wages out of everyone's pockets so that no one ever bought anything worth having and therefore resented, not the wheedlers, but the world. The tree man, as Mark thought of him, was an enemy

236

of that world, no doubt. But he was an enemy of something he knew about that could encroach on his life if he did not defend it. Jenny did not know that world existed.

Mark recalled suddenly a still-juvenile army signaller whose facility with numbers advanced him to a certain signals' unit at twenty-five, none of his superiors noticing that he was in fact still a child. The warnings he received that the work he did was secret and the code books to be kept under lock and key by a routine he was required to learn by rote, did not impress him with their seriousness because he had never been serious. They stimulated him instead to copy something he saw in a film; he took the inside of one of the books out and replaced the bulk with the inside of a novel he found in his landlady's bookshelf, for he was living in billets. Then he took the real contents of the code manual and hitched a ride to London, taking the driver's camera off the back seat as he left the car. He looked up the address of the Cuban Embassy but was stopped before he could negotiate the sentinels at the gate by a policeman who recognized the type of camera; the car driver was unfortunately a professional cameraman and his equipment was worth a good deal of money, so he reported the theft at once to an acquaintance in the police (all press photographers have acquaintances in the police force).

When questioned later by Mark as to his motives for trying to sell the ciphers, the young man explained that he had tried for weeks to win enough money at Bingo to buy himself a transistor radio "like the others have," but the numbers at Bingo proved unreckonable, being random. So he took the cipher book. Mark did not even trouble to ask the boy whether he recognized that what he did was wrong. He knew the answer would be a repetition. The money was not obtainable from Bingo, the lad wanted a transistor set, and that was all. At the trial the judge thundered about treachery, the prosecution alleged delinquency, the defence produced a psychiatrist who explained that the young man was retarded in a polysyllabic fashion. As a matter of fact, Mark knew, the trouble was none of these things; the boy simply did not know that if he stole things he would get into trouble with the police, and the reason he did not know was that nobody had ever told him so. He was apparently grown up and supposed to understand the warnings of the company sergeant major, but these warnings made no connection in his mind with childhood precepts about honesty or fear of the consequences; there was nothing to which a connection could be made, for he had no childhood precepts. But he did see stories about Che Guevara, a romantic-sounding name, and a faraway country in the sun, and the heroic figures of his comic books were always taking things and being praised for doing so. So he went and did likewise. Mark wondered if, should he tell Jenny that story, she would understand it any better than the boy understood the judge's strictures at his trial. He doubted if Jenny knew what Bingo was. He was sure she would not understand that the boy did not know what he was doing, in the normal meaning of those simple words.

During the minute or so of these thoughts, Mark was taking a bystander's part in the gardening conversation with Jenny and the two men. But he then began to drift away from the group, to inspect the other fruit trees—they were standing by the half-dead apple—to give himself time to fix the reason for that story coming now into his head. The meaning of that memory was the likeness between Jenny and that wretched boy who never understood what was happening to him, who was so uncalculating that it did not occur to him that by saving his specialist's pay for three weeks he could easily afford what he wanted. The likeness was that the signaller was innocent. Morally, he was innocent in the literal sense of being unknowing. There was no guile in him. Sentenced, he showed a real, unforced blankness of incomprehension.

CHAPTER XVIII

ON A DROWSY Saturday afternoon, Mark discovered, a well-ordered household is essential to privacy. Having lived alone for years he was used to another kind of private life, but if one knows where every member of the community will be at any time, one is just as alone as if the house were empty. What had been necessary for other secrets was now used for better purposes, and Mark and Jenny retired to her room by the simple trick of going first to the studio-stable and leaving it again by the unused fodder door invisible from the Fosters' sitting room.

Talking was almost as satisfactory as making love, at any rate during intervals. The room was quiet and warm, there was no sense of any other presence in it for it was very much Jenny's room, which Vincent had rarely entered in recent years. Panelled walls, thick carpet and interlined curtains embedded sounds as well as emotions.

Mark, exploring the house's beauties, passed a hand over the silky, pale grain of the unpainted wood. It was slightly in relief from its great age, the loops and squirls of a tree's growth long ago could be followed by his fingertips.

"It's really exquisite," he murmured, "what absolute bliss to live with this living wood and stone. It's a whole life in itself. Didn't you say some of the woodwork had dry rot upstairs? Panic if it had!"

"Not now," she said dreamily. "Not for years now. If you like the feel of the wood, try the window sills."

These were of silvery, dressed stone, smoothed by generations of wear.

"Nobody knows where the original builders got that stone. It's not even English. So they say."

"Who says that?"

"Oh, some chap who came once. He was writing a History of British Domestic Architecture. But he said he knew even better examples of the period. So we didn't get included."

"Good."

"That's what I thought. Vincent was furious."

"At not being included?"

"After all the introductions and fuss, you know?"

"I can imagine. How strange it would have been . . ."

"To be in a book?"

"No, I meant . . . Never mind, it doesn't matter."

"But what?"

"If I'd come here and Vincent was here. If I'd met him here."

"It doesn't seem very possible."

"I shouldn't have said it. I'm sorry."

"You can say anything. That's the whole marvellous thing."

"Only a few days ago I thought it would be interesting."

"But not now."

"Not now. That's strange, too. I've never felt before how much everything is changed by making love."

"It would be even more strange if . . . How could love not change everything?"

"Yes. But only yesterday I would have thought you childish to say that. Now it seems obvious. And wise."

"You must have known some very odd women. I think I'm rather shocked."

"I almost am myself. Perhaps I'm regaining illusions instead of losing them. I see you've been reading Balzac!"

"Well, he is supposed to have been writing about real people. So the reverse of that experience might be true, on another plane at another time?"

"I hope you don't always take what you read so literally."

"Why? Oh, you're looking at Donnerstein."

"*Human Psyche for the Layman*. God, what pompous rubbish!"

"Rubbish? Donnerstein? But he's famous!"

"Notorious. Crapulous old fool. Knew less about human beings than your cat, let alone Balzac!"

"But don't you believe in psychology?"

"This tripe? As much as I do in numerology or astrology.

240

You speak of the subject as if it were some sort of magic!"

"But surely it's science?"

"It's a mishmash of various unproven theories and insights, and that's all. How on earth did you get hold of it?"

"Vincent got it for me. He thought I should understand such things—my own mind."

"He did, did he? Yes, he would! I suppose he thought it would cure you of respecting your father! Or detach you from your religion?"

"How did you know that? Mark, that's just what Vincent said!"

"And did it?"

"N-no. But it made me feel a bit guilty."

"Now tell me. Why should you not admire and respect your father? He was a great man, and you had the luck to be his child. As for the Church, I'm not a believer myself but who the hell was Vincent to decide that two thousand years of belief was nonsense?"

"Well, not if you put it like that! But . . ." The long habit of accepting Vincent's views collided now openly instead of furtively with Jenny's lifelong belief, and when Mark challenged her she could not push the discrepancy away with vague taradiddles about Vincent being more experienced than herself; for Mark's robust scorn was so phrased that it now occurred to Jenny in so many words that the creed rejected by her husband was unknown to him. She doubted, now considering the matter, whether he could have repeated the opening phrases of the formal creed and still less have understood them. This thought, paradoxically, made her laugh.

"Oh, Mark, how absurd! I just never thought of it. But how right Vincent was to keep me from the influence of other people!"

He was pierced suddenly by a sharp jealousy, the physical anger of a threatened lover. The sensation itself was not unfamiliar, but he never before felt it so strongly, nor with such a pain of responsibility. If he, Mark, disclaimed Vincent's right to tamper with his wife's faith, how much more must he accept his own lack of any right to interfere.

"Don't talk about Vincent!" He was almost shouting at her. "The man was a monster."

241

He gripped her so hard that for a second she paled with the memory of fear and shrank together. He released her instantly and she swayed.

"Oh, God," he begged, "Jenny, you're not afraid of *me*?"

"Of course not, how could I be, I mean . . . I don't know what I'm saying."

Mark dropped onto the edge of her bed and put his head in his hands.

"I wish I knew what was happening to me," he muttered. "This is getting quite out of hand."

"I can't understand why you're so upset. We were so happy, before. Have I done something stupid? Tell me!"

"You haven't. I have. Worse than stupid. Oh, why did this have to happen? No, I don't mean it like that . . . don't cry, baby. I'll explain it some other time."

He was kissing her and she him and it was too late to worry about ethics for the moment.

But later, Mark saw the unlucky book again on the chair where he had thrown it in rage and he actually took it with him when he went downstairs and tossed it into the back of the fire, an action he would have laughed at, at any other moment of his life. He had put himself into a quite indefensible position, one he could find no excuse for, and the angry confusion of this thought was made worse by the scorn with which one side of his mind treated his new seriousness about a matter up to now anything but serious. By allowing a "purely personal" affair to impinge on his professional, his masculine, standards, it was brought into that area of behaviour where how one behaved really mattered. He was breaking the most primitive law of hospitality, accepting friendship under false pretences. It was just what Cheyney had done. And not only could he not extricate himself by simply going away, he knew he did not any longer want to. He wanted things to go on as they were, so that Jenny need not know what he was doing here in her home.

It was also quite clear and to be expected, that the Fosters were aware of a great change in the atmosphere between himself and Jenny. Indeed, their altered looks would have been impossible to disguise from a blind man, for the difference was in their voices, their gestures, it penetrated the air about them. Especially an almost instantaneous change was noticeable in Jenny; the blood that ran faster coloured her cheeks, brightened her eyes, made her every move elastic with the vitality of stimulated nerves. Jenny was, in the true old saying, a different woman, and nobody now meeting her for the first time could have thought of her as a child. At the table she laughed, she talked spontaneously instead of answering what was said to her; they talked of the archaic stone uncovered by the fall of the beech tree, of plans for further exploration, of the forestry crane with its mechanical arm that appeared to act like a living creature, moved as it was by unseen switches and levers. They discussed the Blanes from the farm, who were as interested as they were themselves in the finding of the stone; even the nurseryman stayed on late into the morning, watching and helping and giving them all advice, while Foster clambered with Mark into the pit to make sure that the stone was not scraped or banged in its removal.

"It's sad that it won't be our stone any more, now that half the district knows about it," said Mark, laughing at his own possessiveness. "All your neighbours will be up here to look at it."

The thought of strangers reminded him again of what he wanted badly not to think about. At the latest tomorrow, he assured himself, and then we can have the whole story out in the open. An urgent message to his superior was as yet not answered, and Mark expected impatiently that the telephone would ring to give him the permission that would release him from his deception. He needed to be rescued, he admitted to himself that help was necessary; he could not bring himself to break the rules of his job without that releasing word from authority. If only that boneheaded Folliot had not misled them all with his caution, his failure to commit himself to Jenny's innocence, this tangle could not have happened. Mark could not know that the possibility of Jenny's involvement in Vincent Cheyney's secret affairs was so remote from Mr. Folliot's mind that he naturally neglected to say what he himself took for granted. Poor Mr. Folliot would have been astounded to know what blame was being laid at his door for something he never thought of. Mark even dimly grasped the real trouble, for once he met Jenny, on the very day of his arrival, which now seemed so remote, he wrote her off as being of no interest to him professionally. His actions and his conscious thoughts at that time remained suspicious, but there was not much reality in the routine caution of his unbelief. He recognized that now; he had ceased to consider Jenny capable of such a sustained nervous strain of self-control and forethought even before her outburst when the letter from the hotel near Wrexham arrived. But there was no mention of this in his reports; they recounted only the facts without his deductions from them. Those deductions depended essentially on Jenny's person, which was not evidence for men who had never seen her. Indeed, such outbreaks frequently form part of defence structures for those who feel their secrets threatened. And the injured innocence of the guilty is often at least as real in their own minds as it would be if it were sincere.

"Is something wrong?" Jenny asked him, fearing a return to his black mood of the afternoon.

"Thinking of the neighbours. I'm in a false position here and putting you in one, too. It's beginning to bother me."

"Oh, but Mark . . ." she was dismayed. "The neighbours! How could anybody know?"

"Darling," he protested, "the veriest idiot would know in five minutes. We might as well go down to the town and carry placards about like Aldermaston marchers."

The telephone rang in the hall and Mark was forced to grip his chair to cut off the sharp movement he made to leave the table and rush to answer it. The ringing bell choked; Foster was answering it in the kitchen.

A moment later Foster put his head in at the dining-room door.

"It's Colonel Bartle, Mrs. Cheyney. Shall I say you are still having dinner?"

"Oh no, I'll answer it in the hall. Thank you."

Halfway to the door Jenny stopped and turned back to Mark.

"I see what you mean," she admitted, smiling ruefully. "Colonel Bartle is the Chairman of the County Historical Society."

"I knew it!" Mark cried dramatically, half to cover his impatience and half laughing. "Can I come and listen?"

"Mrs. Cheyney, my dear girl, I hope you got our letter? We were unfortunately away at the time, or should certainly have come to support you at the funeral. My wife said you wouldn't mind, although it is a Saturday evening. I really could hardly wait to ask you about the find at Grove Hill. Would it be too much to impose myself for a few minutes tomorrow morning? Hey, what's that?"

A ghostly male whisper in the background of the old man's voice said, "Withen Camps here. Who's calling, please? The lines seem to be crossed, sir."

"Get off the line, whoever you are," ordered the Colonel.

"This is an official line you're speaking on," said the unemotional operator's voice, now quite clear.

"Of course it's an official line, you fool. And I'm speaking on it to a neighbour of mine. What does he mean, official line? Even nowadays we don't have pirate telephones, do we?"

"I'm sorry, sir, I'm trying to get through."

"What do you mean, get through. I am through. Get off the line."

"I'm not addressing you. Please clear the line."

"How dare you. Say sir when you speak to me. What's going on here! Mrs. Cheyney? Are you there?"

"Yes, sir, hold on. There's some old local on our line, I'll get him off."

"Are you referring to me as an old local? I shall report this to the supervisor. What was that you said? Service line? Don't believe you. You're a lout. Get off my line!"

"Can you hear me? I thought you couldn't. So sorry." Some switch was pulled with a loud clack and the voices became instantly much clearer. "I've cut him off now, sir. But I still can't raise your number. I'll come back on in a minute."

"Well, hurry will you?" said another voice, at once unconcerned and authoritative. "I've got to tell this booby he isn't cleared for takeoff. These special duty calls are becoming a blasted nuisance. I shall put in a complaint about it."

"Takeoff, sir? There's no flying tonight, it's socked in with fog from here to Land's End. Even the owls aren't out tonight."

"Not literally, you fool. Oh, sorry, that was rude of me. I mean I have to tell somebody he can't do whatever he had in mind. Christ, this is getting involved! And I have to be duty officer the night we have all this farting around!"

"You watch your language, sir, there's a lady on this line." This the Colonel, now shouting.

"Who the hell was that, Corporal?"

"It's that gremlin in the line again, sir."

"Sounded like an American. What's the *matter* with the telephone tonight? We'll have the flaming Russians cutting in next."

"That wouldn't surprise me either. Hang on a second, sir."

"An American," cried the Colonel in anguish. "I'll have you for libel, give me your name, rank and number this instant!"

At this there was a breathy silence for several seconds. Then a wild scrabbling. The unfortunate operator was pulling out all his plugs and the line went dead except for a high singing tone.

"The music of the spheres," said Mark as Jenny put down the receiver.

"What do you think that was all about?"

The telephone rang again.

"Yes?" said Jenny cautiously.

"Colonel Bartle here. I'm terribly sorry. You haven't got any Americans there, have you? That fellow said there was an American. I thought he meant me, but he can't have done. He can't, can he?"

"Oh, I don't think so," said Jenny pacifically. "Hardly."

"That's what I mean. I mean, if it wasn't me there must be somebody else about. Foreigners, I mean. He said something about Russians, I distinctly heard it. I'm not sure if I ought not to report this, you know. Do you think it can be an emergency? Of course, you're much too young. But there were those nuns in 1940, I haven't forgotten them, with bicycles. We had to turn all our signposts around the other way, you know. To confuse the enemy, in the Home Guard, you know. Of course, in my active days we didn't go in for all that sort of thing. Spreading alarm and despondency, that sort of thing. Mind you, my dear, I remember when I was first commissioned —that was sixty years ago—we had the Boers after us then, and there was a lot of queer talk about, very queer talk. But that's the Stone Age for you, of course. Ah, Stone Age. Yes, your stone. Now, I wonder . . ."

"Why don't you and Mrs. Bartle come up tomorrow morning and we'll have a look at this stone? Then you can make a proper report to the Society . . . I don't think I could quite manage to . . . for me?"

"Well, my wife will be at church, you know how it is. If I might? But not if you're entertaining. I don't want to butt in. Sunday, too."

"Oh, no, not at all, I'm not entertaining. I shall look forward to seeing you. About . . ."

"But of course you're not entertaining. I'm so sorry, I quite forgot for a moment you're in mourning. So if you *haven't* any Americans staying with you?"

"Absolutely not, I assure you."

"Well, it's most kind of you, about eleven suit you? Just you know, just to have a look at this most promising find of yours?"

"That will be splendid, about eleven then?" Jenny was now breathless. "Thank you for suggesting it. We'll—"

"Yes, indeed. I'm still not sure I shouldn't report this American hanging about, one never knows. In this weather, too. I assure you when I took the dog out I couldn't see my hand. Not even my hand. Well, tomorrow then, Mrs. Cheyney?"

"Tomorrow. Goodbye."

"He was still talking, poor man," she said, putting the telephone down with a look of dismay, as if it might start ringing again.

"Is he cracked? Or senile? What was all that about Americans?"

"I think, you know, because he said there was a lady on the line to that other . . . who could it have been?" Jenny was laughing helplessly. "Americans do that."

"Do what?"

"Call people ladies. No, he isn't dotty at all. It's the telephone, you know. When you talk to him, I mean himself in person, it's perfectly all right. Only it just sounds funny on the tele— Help! Again!

"Hullo?"

"Mr. Vail there, please?"

"It's for you this time." Jenny gave Mark the receiver.

"Vail," said Mark in a tone that brooked no nonsense this time.

The apparatus squawked and rattled.

"Thank you," said Mark, "goodbye." He put the thing down very carefully and turned away towards the side room. "Bloody thing," he said gloomily. "Oh, sorry, Mrs. Foster."

"Just the coffee tray. I think the phone service gets worse every day, don't you, Mrs. Cheyney?"

"It's certainly a bit blinky tonight," agreed Jenny, still laughing.

"I'm afraid I shall be leaving on Monday," said Mark. Mrs. Foster, in the doorway, turned and saw the two of them, standing one on either side of the fireplace looking at each other.

"Was that what the call was about?"

"Not quite. But yes. I shall have to."

Mrs. Foster, who was really a tactful woman, pulled the door to without clicking the catch.

"I'm behaving like a clown, not to mention a bastard," he said. "You know, I've never felt like this before. I'm out of my depth, suddenly." He sounded surprised at himself.

"I don't understand," said Jenny.

"No, you don't. That's just it. I wouldn't want you to be that kind, either. That's just the trouble."

"But can't you tell me?"

"It's not what you're thinking. Not personal at all, it's professional. It's my job. I ought never to have stayed in the house. That's so pikestaff plain now that I can't fathom how it wasn't perfectly clear from the start."

"Mr. Folliot seemed to think it was all right?"

"For him it was. Then. But you've changed, I've changed. Everything about us has changed except one thing."

"You mean, the reason you are here?"

He could not even grasp at that half-understanding, and shook his head helplessly.

"It doesn't seem at all important to me," said Jenny, smiling a little nervously. "Compared with . . ."

Then she was silent, trying not to think that Mark was

concerned about his reputation with the company, regretted his new involvement for that reason of expediency.

"That old man," said Mark suddenly, jerking his head towards the door to indicate the telephone conversation. "Like something out of a popular play in London. 'Retired Colonel' in person. I didn't know they really existed. But what d'you suppose a man like him, brought up in another age, would say about me? He'd call me a 'cad,' I shouldn't be surprised. All very well to laugh, the idea's the point, not the way he would say it."

"Do we have to care what old Bartle would think?"

"I think we do. The way things are, d'you see, he'd be right. If it were not so, I couldn't be worrying about it. In a manner of speaking."

"No darling, that's going too far. The world has changed and everything in it."

"Put in another way then, since this old fossil is destined to be comic, being a retired army man in a pacifist age. If your father were here, what would he think?"

"Ah," said Jenny with a bright look of triumph, "that just shows you! If you think Father would have cared about you being Mr. Folliot's assistant, you're way off the track. He would just be glad I was happy." She stopped, her honesty made her hesitate. "Provided, that is, neither of us was committed to somebody else. What he couldn't stand was deceptions."

"God," groaned Mark, entangled in impossibilities. "That is just what it is!"

"No. What you're talking about is conventions, and Father didn't have any. As a matter of fact, though I've never said this to a living soul, Father lived with the housekeeper when I was a girl." Jenny said this with great pride, as showing her worldly knowledge.

"He can't have done!" Mark countered. "Her husband was here!"

"Yes, he did. They'd been separated for years. Hardly spoke to each other. But they were refugees and they couldn't get proper jobs then, being enemy aliens technically."

"But they stayed after the war was over?"

"Mrs. L. did, but Dr. Limmert was practicing again then, he

still is, in the town. He had to take all his exams over again. That's what he spent the war doing."

"And what did Mrs. Limmert do when your father was killed?" Mark was greatly interested now.

"Didn't you know? She's Frau Professor Anny Limmert. She spends six months a year at Berkeley in California and six in Berlin at the Free University. She's famous—in her own line, of course."

"So she stayed to be with your father?"

"She must have done, mustn't she? He'd been good to them, you see. That's what I'm talking about. But she didn't just stay here, she was writing great books all the time. I mean, big fat books, I don't know whether they are great."

"The household must have been a picnic!"

"Well, the cooking was sometimes a little bizarre. You never knew what time meals would be."

"Was the cleaner here then, Mrs. Godolphin?"

"No, we had a cleaner, but not Mrs. Godolphin." Jenny stopped, drew a breath and took courage. "The old one Vincent got rid of. She was a slatternly old girl and her family was always cluttering up the kitchen."

"So you were alone here with a slatternly old cleaner after your father died?"

"Yes, but the slatternly bit, that was Vincent. I liked her. Though she was a bit casual. But then, so were we. I had all my modelling mess in the drawing room then."

"You never seem to use the drawing room."

"Hardly. We don't need two sitting rooms, really."

"You could come back into the house, now," he suggested.

"I don't know. D'you think so? Vincent had the drawing room all done up by an interior decorating studio in London. And . . . I'm not sure I want to be eccentric. It puts people off, rather, and I don't want to do that any more."

"One of the bedrooms? A north one. How many are there—apart from the Fosters'?"

"That's an idea, Mark. There are six rooms up there, not counting the attics. One used to be my schoolroom, but it hasn't been used for years, and the other two empty ones are just bedrooms, dreary, deserted sort of places. We hardly ever had guests in the house to stay."

"He was a rather unsociable person, your late husband," hazarded Mark, and then wished he had not spoken.

"You see," she said unhappily, "I was supposed to be delicate and nervous, and so . . ." She stopped and her eyes cleared with a suddenness that reminded her companion of the startling changes of light in the country about there. One moment all was darkling, thunderous, and the next a gleaming sun washed pale gold over the landscape, changing colours and outlines in a few moments. "But I don't need to feel that any more, do I? I know better now."

His answer was to kiss her with great satisfaction. The bones of her shoulders were almost sharp, and he was already used to her physical being: the quality of the skin, the exact consistency and texture of her lean, fine-boned but soft person, the subtle, intense awareness in her and in himself of physical compliance, the unique way her upper lip lifted as she smiled. The fear and gratitude he could sense in her translated itself through nerve endings into a most delicate tremor both pitiful and exciting to him.

"You're so solid," she said quietly. "And warm."

"You aren't. I'm half afraid of breaking a bit of you off, I think."

"Don't suppose you will, you know. But you can if you want to."

"I don't want to. That's the point—you're just right as you are." He thought it over. "You're the absolutely rightest woman I've ever known. I think I may be in love with you. D'you think that's possible?"

"How could I know? I hardly know you well enough to tell."

"You might know because I say so?"

"Oh, hardly from what you say. . . . I wouldn't trust to words, I think, any more. Deeds would count to convince me, I mean there's a feel about what you do, that might be it—what you say."

"There, you see? What I say is what you go by, you said it yourself."

"No. That's just a pointer, the suggestion. But you have a feel—perhaps I mean I have a feel—of completeness or something."

"And you haven't had that feel before?"

"No. Have you?"

"I don't believe I have. Not like this. Perhaps men are different from women, at least so they say. Sometimes I've had terrific physical things with women I didn't even like much. But then one always has reservations, it mustn't go too far or mustn't last too long. Some of the most splendid sex girls would be impossible to think of living with; they wouldn't even know what I was talking about or I wouldn't know what they were all about. I can't explain it."

"The trouble is, sometimes you can't know that—before."

"Only by experience. I was lucky, I got a good deal of experience in the war, when there was no question of any real attachment. Strictly temporary on both sides."

"I was a bit too young. And then it was too late."

"Tell me, was there a moment, something you can recall as definitely a revelation that you would never really get along with Vincent? I mean, in the way we're talking about?"

Jenny moved away from Mark and stared into the fire, thinking seriously and pulling in her lip between her teeth.

"There were several things. But there's one thing I can actually show you—d'you want to see?"

"Of course. Show me."

She went to the door and led the way across the hall into the large drawing room.

"It was probably walled off from the hall in the eighteenth century," she explained. "Vincent's decorator knocked down a connecting wall over there so that it's now twice the size. You see?"

"Originally the hall was the living room, coming right across the house on this side?"

"That's it. Afterwards this was two smallish rooms, and only recently one big room as it is now." Jenny was moving about, turning on the overhead chandelier and all the lamps.

Mark received a distinct impression that, perhaps without knowing it, Jenny was using this room as a test of himself as well as of the dead Vincent. There could be no question of testing him for honesty here, except in the sense of his having the hardihood to say what he thought of his hostess's drawing room; the question must be one of aesthetic perception. So far, Mark had been watching Jenny as she moved about. Now

252

that she stood still and watched *him* from the far end of the room, he began to examine that.

"How do you know that was originally the ladies' parlor?" he asked, for she was standing in a space somewhat narrower than the rest and which was still panelled, like most of the house.

"There was a powder closet in it. You see? Here where the alcove now is."

"Part of the eighteenth-century rearrangement?"

"I suppose so, although the alcove may have been there before. I don't think the stonework—or brickwork—was really examined by Bellingford. To tell its age, you know."

"And what happened to the panelling of this end?"

"That was the worst infected by dry rot and various beetles. The old woodwork was taken out when Father bought the house, but then the war got serious and he couldn't have it replaced. He was actually thinking of having it done when he was killed."

The panelling here had not been remade. Instead, the various sections of wall space, as divided up by door and windows and by the fireplace, were formed into quadrangles outlined by raised stucco mouldings, which, with their outer spaces, were painted and covered inside with a pale green damask wallpaper of a design with shells and urns carefully matched to the period of the room. The panelling of the far end was painted cream like the other paintwork. The window curtains were of silk damask in the same design as the wall covering and the same colour. The fireplace was faced with white marble, a carved shell in its centre. On the wide shelf of this marble were one or two elegant pieces of porcelain and three photographs in silver frames. There were more pieces of porcelain in the alcove Jenny had shown Mark as the old powdering cupboard. In the wall above the fireplace was sunk a landscape with a river that might have been a Guardi or, as Mark supposed, a good copy of a Guardi. The furnishings were sofas and chairs covered in a cream shade of the same damask. These were modern, the various tables, a tallboy, a glass-fronted cupboard, the canterbury and other beautifully disposed pieces were of mahogany or rosewood and all of the correct periods, most of them being genuine and the others well-matched reproductions. Some were French, some English; all were pretty, a few valuable.

As all drawing rooms must be, it was a formal room. This is just as true of the "front room" of a cottage as of a great salon. There was nothing wrong with that, nor with the mixture of French and native furniture. Mark went over to a console table by one of the windows, the only painted piece there, of a curly feminine sweetness, gilded and with little medallions painted in simulated frames showing typical countrified scenes of city imagining.

"Venetian, it looks. Very nice too. Positively quite da Ponte. That's Venetian, too." He looked up at the chandelier. "But that's a real beast. I'd get rid of *that* straightaway!"

He was beginning to enjoy himself, a bland, malicious smile quirked the corners of the lips Jenny found so well formed.

"Ye-es. Even the books. I wonder whether Vincent ever read Richardson. Or was that the decorator, I wonder? Delicious, the whole thing. Love to know if the man saw the joke —he *was* following Vincent's instructions, wasn't he? Or was it all left to him?"

"Half and half. Vincent talked to him a lot, and then they moved things about, took things away, brought in others, until they got it right."

"Got it right for Vincent?"

"Got it right for Vincent."

"But it's an imitation of something he'd actually seen. Isn't it?"

"I don't know. You think so?"

"He didn't tell you?"

"Oh, no."

"I wonder where he saw it? Some place he was greatly impressed—by the surroundings? Or by the people there? Somewhere he was in love? Or somewhere he was 'put down' in a certain sense, or a certain fashion. Where he found he had much still to learn. . . ? Or is it really a stage setting, simply that? No, not quite, a little more than that. The foreignness wouldn't have occurred to him as so strongly a part of what he wanted unless he'd seen it, been in a similar salon abroad."

"What makes you think that—abroad?"

"The whole thing is unEnglish. But—perhaps the fireplace,

I think. That shell design—copy of 1790 about. Dresden? Würzburg? There's nothing French about it, it's purest middle-Europe rococo. Could be in Prague. Only not quite right, too little decoration, the shell wouldn't be by itself there in the centre. It would have trails and ribbons, squirls, curlicues. As it is, it's rather a nice derivation, but not a correct imitation. And the shelf is too wide. This type of thing would at home be fronted by a bronze or brass grill with a wood stove behind it; it wouldn't be an open fireplace with dogs. And no shelf, only a shallow ledge. The shelf is typically English, to protect the wall above from smoke."

"It was made by a stonemason near here," agreed Jenny expressionlessly.

Mark walked through into the other section.

"Nymphenburg," he remarked of the porcelain figures. "This pair is old, the others postwar. Now, I wonder where he got the pair?"

"He didn't. My father brought them with him from Rumania. They are the only things here that belonged to him."

"Ah. The only things, one may guess, that received the stamp of Vincent's approval. Good enough for his room. Very interesting."

Mark continued moving about, no longer examining with much attention any particular aspect of the room, but considering it as the projection of a man's embodiment of what he wished to be. Or to be thought to be, he corrected himself. If vulgarity is in its essence the use of things or people in some sense other than their own being and purposes, the pretty and tasteful room was vulgar. Certainly the upholstered furniture was intended for sitting upon, the windows for lighting and for their view of the flower beds outside that were naturally and very effectively framed by the dark barrier of beech trees in the middle distance. But the wholeness of the picture was that of a deliberate presentation of some desired attainment, a statement that the man whose room it was, was a certain kind of man. It was not really intended as a frame for social or personal intercourse; it lacked the pleasing atmosphere of cultivated hospitality that must always be the aim of a formal sitting room. Nor was it the expression of the interests of the owner, for if it were, there were bound to be oddities among its posed harmonies. There would be a record player or a piano, the books would include a few recent novels or travels, some biographies or political memoirs, objects that reflected what the people living here did when there were no guests present to occupy them and their apartment. Among the photographs and the ornaments would stand anomalies, those things given to families and kept for the sake of the giver and not necessarily what they would have chosen. But here were a wedding group and several well-known faces by well-known photographers signed with civilities to Julius Maculan, the eminent inventor. There was no hideous vase presented by an elderly aunt, no cushion cover happily cross-stitched by the child of a friend in her school handicraft class. The entering stranger could hardly imagine he would find a bundle of last week's newspapers saved because the crossword puzzles were not yet done. The canterbury held copies of some magazines, the *Director, The New Yorker*, not a single catalogue of a salesroom for one who occasionally bought something for his beloved and beautiful house, and the magazines were as smooth as the day they were delivered; nobody had read them. Mark did not open the sloping cover of the writing desk. He did not need to. There were no patterns of upholstery stuffs, no odd visiting cards, no bits of fishing line to remind of the needed replacement, no unanswered letters. It contained neatly stacked and sorted writing paper and envelopes in the conventional sizes with the name of the house stamped by a copperplate and never used.

What the real owner of this house wanted to do had been relegated to the stable loft. There was nothing here that indicated an artist in the house, or an engineer. It had not occurred to its designers to include a model of any device of Maculan's, the original, perhaps tentative, handwork of the genius. Maculan's prestige was used for Vincent's; as for himself, he was not represented by anything at all. And neither was Jenny. Even the wedding group was there as part of a statement about Vincent. It was this egocentricity that made the whole careful design vulgar. It was falsely presenting a picture, an atmosphere of someone who did not exist: Vincent as he wished to be seen. Especially the foreignness was anything but the reflection of a taste formed by much travelling, by the delighted discovery of charms other than those of England. It was not the escape from a provinciality clearly stated in the carefulness of the collection; it carried, rather, the aspect of a defiant claim to a status implicitly denied by the need to claim it. Using his knowledge of Vincent's travels and his former military history, Mark deduced that with this masquerade Vincent was not just imitating the elegance of some once-known place and people, he was demanding his inclusion among a kind of people and their atmosphere from which he had somewhere in the past been, or felt himself, excluded. This stamp of demand, the note of insistence, was the reality of Vincent's taste and was so strong that Mark found himself thinking that if he could discover when and where the impressions had been received that resulted—as soon as Vincent had the means—in this room, he would know what turned Vincent into a traitor.

"No," he muttered aloud, "that's a bit farfetched. But why—" he turned now to speak directly to Jenny—"*why* was he so concerned to present a complete picture? Not many people are so conscious of exactly how they want to show themselves. It's not self-expression, not even a perfectly respectworthy imitation: it's a show, a setting."

"You hadn't been in here before, then?" she asked.

"Once. I looked in the desk thing for any papers, and there were none. But I suppose I assumed that the emptiness of the place was because of there being no one to use it at the moment. Mourning, no guests, I must have thought. So I didn't look at it. Not really to see it."

"It's interesting, isn't it? The deliberateness of it. It made me sorry for him. I knew his family were poor, of course, and his mother had to beg for a free place at school for him. His father's school. His father having died, you see, when he was a baby."

"But his father is alive, surely! He's in Canada, isn't he?"

"Oh, no, he's dead ages ago. Where on earth did you hear that?"

Mark recovered himself with the unpleasant sensation of duplicity and shock.

"I think from Folliot," he lied.

"But how strange," she said, staring. "I've always understood . . . perhaps that was a lie, too. I've never met his mother.
They didn't write or anything. She didn't come even to the
wedding. Or the funeral, for that matter."

"You never met Vincent's mother?"

"No. I understood they parted with ill feelings years ago
and never communicated with each other. Vincent didn't get
on with his stepfather, I believe."

"Was she—or were they—invited to your wedding, d'you
know?"

"They weren't, no. But I know an announcement was sent
of the funeral and not replied to. I saw all those myself."

"So Vincent sort of constructed a family history? His father
died and his mother remarried—perhaps beneath her? Was
that how it went?"

"Something like that, I remember. It wasn't anything directly to do with his mother, but when Vincent told me he
didn't like old Connors—the sculptor, you know—he said
Connors reminded him of his stepfather, a coarse brute of a
man. He couldn't think how his mother could ever have
married such a man."

"But was Connors a rough chap? It doesn't sound likely,
he's a pretty famous artist, after all."

"No, of course he wasn't. But he could be rather harsh with
people who didn't know anything about sculpture, especially
if they thought they did know."

"I see. Perhaps they looked alike, Connors and the
stepfather?"

"They may have done. They were both Irish, I do know
that."

"I gather Connors ticked Vincent off at some time?"

"They had a fearful row. Connors told Vincent not to
interfere with my work and said he knew absolutely nothing
about the arts. He called Vincent a philistine. Vincent said
Connors was an old fraud practising a confidence trick on an
ignorant public. He also called him a tramp who lived in
squalor so as to look like an artist unconscious of the small
things of life like bathing or keeping the house clean."

"I wish I'd been there!"

"Heavens, it wasn't funny. It was dreadful. After that, of

258

course, I couldn't go to Connors any more. Then, a bit later, Vincent suggested I should take my mess to the stable so we could have a proper drawing room. So I did."

"Did you never go to Connors' house again? No more teaching?"

"It was a cottage, not a house. Vincent was right there, it really was a midden, but he didn't understand that Connors couldn't work in a proper house all neat and tidy with some woman always clearing up. That's what he said, but he couldn't afford it, either. He was hopeless with money."

"And Vincent was the exact opposite. Very orderly, very organized, precise."

"Very organized. I think, looking back, the thing I remember most strongly is the exact way every detail had to be worked out. He made a fetish of what he called 'Admin.' It was an end in itself, it always seemed to me. Not to make things more convenient, like most people, but for its own sake."

"And yet he had affairs, and that is usually rather a messy business for married men."

"Oh, they were organized too. What Vincent couldn't bear, what made him really angry, was being surprised, something happening that hadn't been planned for, taken into account. If people just turned up, for instance, as they do in the country, or came to call—at first quite a lot of people called in the old-fashioned way—he got so cross that he showed it. So people stopped coming. In the last year or so, only business acquaintances and colleagues from the company came here, and then only when they were invited."

"By then Vincent had got rid of all *your* friends, I take it?"

"Got rid . . . ? I suppose he did, yes. No, I think to be fair, *I* did. I thought of myself as unstable, you see, and I was afraid of others noticing it." Jenny's voice trembled and she was obliged to force herself to go on speaking. "At one time I thought if everyone began noticing and gossiping about me, I might even be put away. . . ."

"God, what an unutterable swine the man was," muttered Mark and put his arm round Jenny's shoulders to comfort her.

"I still can't quite believe it was all deliberate," she stammered, near to tears. "I mean, why would he? Why? He knew, because of other girls before, that he could get away with Mona. So why? Do you think he was afraid I should suggest divorce? But he can't have been, I'm a Catholic."

"Well, at first he made a good deal of fun of the Church, you say."

"But he may have regretted that later . . . Is that what you mean?"

"It could be, couldn't it?"

"I suppose so, but I don't feel it really. Though the whole thing did start up when I warned him about Mona, being his secretary, the company and so on. Yet—I don't know. The more I think about it the less convincing it seems."

"But have you thought, Jenny, although it all began with your protesting about Vincent's mistress being in the firm, that might not have been the real reason underneath? Look, consider—there must have been a scene, a quarrel. Wasn't there?"

"A scene!" she said shuddering. "It went on for weeks. I thought Vincent would never stop bringing it up. How I cursed myself for ever having said anything! And I thought myself so clever at the time, seeing a danger to Vincent that he didn't see for himself. But of course, he did see it and it was all planned and accounted for—Mona, I mean."

"Yes, but I'm thinking of something else. During this long quarrel, when Vincent wouldn't let you forget your tactless mention of his unfaithfulness. While he was persuading you that Mona and everything else wrong between you was solely your fault. Sometimes you must have answered back? You must have defended yourself at first—you weren't as cowed then as you became later. You might have said things in anger, right at the start, that Vincent took to be threats. Naturally, he wouldn't have mentioned them, if you did make them, and you forgot everything you said because since Vincent kept nagging about just one thing, you thought Mona was the only cause of his anger with you, and you attached it all to Mona, as he perhaps meant you to do. Do you see what I mean?"

"I see what you mean, yes. But I can't remember what I said. A great deal was said, I suppose, yes, I recall. But I can't believe I ever threatened Vincent. You forget I adored him and I already blamed myself for our failure, long before

Mona came into our lives." She turned, touching him with trembling hands. "Do let's go into the side room, away from here and talk about something else."

"Darling," he said at once. "Come along. You seemed to want to have it out, but don't think about it, it's all past."

He drew her to the door and pushed her gently into the hall, going back himself into that unlucky place to turn out the lights. As the switch by the door faded the chandelier into darkness, Mark thought unwillingly that Vincent's setting had after all become a test of his own honesty. And he failed the test, as Vincent did.

His disingenuous questions to Jenny depressed him more than the thought of the antagonist who would arrive on Monday, even more than the thought of leaving Grove House. The enemy he could deal with, he knew, and he knew, too, that he meant to come back again to this house when he could do so honestly. Monday, he told himself, would be not an end but a beginning.

CHAPTER XIX

JENNY HARDLY knew what she expected on Monday morning from the intrusive caller. She assumed he must be a businessman because Mr. Folliot had seemed to anticipate an approach by some rival with an interest in her father's patents. But in her entranced preoccupation with Mark and herself she felt only a disinclination to be disturbed by outsiders. Mark was to leave on the next day, he had told her so, and she was not sure how to make it clear to him that a quick return was to be taken for granted.

Whatever she vaguely envisaged, she certainly did not expect anything like the man who appeared from the local hired car as Jenny and Foster stood viewing with proprietary admiration burlap-bound rose bushes laid out in their future places along the newly turned beds bordering the entrance. It was a sunny, blowy morning with scents of earth and clipped grass, the green promise of spring in the still warm effluent of a heap of byre sweepings, which were the contribution of the Blanes to the planned splendour of summer.

The man bent into the car to speak to the driver and then stood looking about him as it turned and crunched over the new bluish-white of granite chips. He removed an aged brown felt hat and the breeze lifted his grey, untidy hair in wisps. The first impression of his being rather untidy was altogether incorrect, Jenny saw, as she jumped the width of the flower bed and moved towards him. He was, in fact, almost dandyish, but his clothes hung on an emaciated frame as if they did not belong to him, and his round-rimmed tortoise shell glasses were slipping down on a nearly bridgeless nose. He tipped at them helplessly on one side and waved the decrepit hat. It might almost be that neither spectacles, hat, nor the charcoal grey suit and the blue shirt belonged to the ill-coordinated frame that moved in jerky, only partly controlled, movements.

"Mrs. Cheyney?" he called in a high, precise voice. "My dear, the house!" He turned to take it all in, tilting his head and screwing up his eyes as if inspecting a picture. "Perfect. I'm almost afraid to go inside. That's rude of me, I know, but you do see that, if not too good to be true, it's certainly too good to go on being true?"

"Good morning," said Jenny smiling at his praise of her treasure. "How d'you do?"

"I do rather poorly, to be truthful. An unusual luxury, so one treasures the opportunity. And clearly anyone who lives in this house must be of an authenticity! One can risk truth with such a person, I feel sure."

"You are very kind," said Jenny, her formality softened by her delighted smile. "Come along in." And she opened the door to usher the visitor into the hall.

"Oh, la, la," he stopped once more inside the door to admire. "And to think that duty, miserable word, kept me from enjoying this all these years."

At Jenny's surprised look, he bowed slightly.

"Yes. You see, I knew your husband briefly, years ago. Such a brave, beautiful man, so unfortunate in his tragic fate. We live in terrible times, we do indeed, my dear lady."

"Yes," agreed Jenny, not knowing at all what he meant, but he talked, she understood that, in his own way. "I'm sorry you were kept from coming here before."

"Not as sorry as I am, I promise you. But until I retired it was out of the question. But my goodness, I haven't introduced myself. I'm Polter."

"Of course. I thought I recognized you, from the papers, you know. But I didn't like to ask in case I was wrong."

"From the newspapers? Then you haven't seen me making a fool of myself on the telly? My dear, you're an angel. What luck, somebody who can still, possibly, just possibly, respect me as a scholar."

"But surely everyone must respect the author of *The Great*

Elizabeth and *Nelson, Man and Hero*? Not to mention the other things, I mean the really great works that I can hardly understand at all. But Professor Peter Polter is a name—"

The caller interrupted her, waving a thin hand.

"Ah, a name. Well, let's not go into all that. Let us rather look at the stuff of history itself. You hear me? Tiny clichés, they just pour out!"

He walked over to the foot of the stair and looked up, slanting his head and crouching, to see up the line of the treads and the handrail with its turned supports in the light from the two-storey window up to the wide landing above.

"Oh, God," he said flatly, "England. The pale sun coming through that mullioned casement with the garden moving behind it all twigs and buds."

The joke did not come off; there was a note of distress in it, as if he almost meant what he said in spite of himself.

"Have you just come from abroad?" Jenny asked, wondering at his tone.

"Not quite from abroad. But from strange places, one could say. I've spent all my life whoring after false gods. That's a misquotation, I'm sure, but then, the Bible has not exactly been my thing."

"I don't think one can say any quotation from the Bible is misquoted," said Jenny, quaintly pedantic. "I don't know, of course, myself, but my father used to say we don't know for sure in lots of bits quite how the original was."

"The strange, quiet gentleness with which you say that! Are you by any chance a Believer?"

"I suppose I am," she said.

"You sound a little defensive there. But you mustn't mind me, I'm getting old and dotty, you know. Nowadays I'm allowed to say anything."

"Come into the drawing room. That was Vincent's room, very much his, so you'd like to see it."

"Myself, I've been a Believer all my life. But like Iago, I quite deliberately took the path of wrong. People do, you know. No, perhaps you don't know, I hope you don't. Out of sheer naughtiness, in my case."

Jenny did not take much account of his words. It seemed quite natural to her that he should toss words to and fro like sparkling points of glass in the light. It wasn't necessary to know precisely what the words meant; they formed patterns from which meaning would, in its own good time, appear.

He stopped again on the threshold; it was evidently one of his mannerisms.

"Ah, pretty room, nice proportions," he said, sounding intentionally false. "But really, quite frighteningly dreadful. Vincent's room, you said. Oh, my paws and whiskers. A disaster. Could have been 'done' by Bellingford."

"How did you know?" Jenny stared. "It *was* done by Bellingford."

"How did I know? But it carries his filthy paw marks, the mark of the beast. Dreadful man. How could he, in such a house. Total immorality, I assure you, total. Even for Bellingford, it's unbelievable. My dear, you must change it all round as fast as you can drag things. The doom will come upon you, said the Lady of Shalott, if you don't. Ah, no, it's really the curse will come upon you, I mean the curse *is* come upon *me*, said the Lady of Shalott. But really, one can't say that. Poor Tennyson, I do love him. What with Shalott—my sisters used to call it 'Lady of Onion,' the silly little things. That was in the days when everything Victorian was execrated. Where was I? Yes, with Shalott and the curse, really too mixed up, cooking and the lunar cycle."

"How did we get to Tennyson? Do explain," cried Jenny, laughing helplessly.

"Getting things wrong, don't you see? I don't mean Bellingford, he does this sort of thing on purpose. I mean poor Vincent. But I'm not joking about this room. You really must, absolutely, change it all round and put in one or two cosy solecisms to cheer it up. I'd get rid of those matching curtains and the wallpaper panels at once. They are simply too gracious for words. Can you afford to? If you can't I shall quite understand if you just take the curtains down, for the time being. But you can't leave it like this, poor pretty place, if only to save poor Vincent's reputation. He just didn't know, did he?"

"No, he didn't know. But I can't quite see why you should guess that I do? Oh, there's Polly at the window. Half a moment, I must just let her in."

"I don't even guess," he said, still staring about him with histrionically shocked looks and shudders. "It's just that I feel I can say anything to you and anyway I do say anything now, since I cut loose and I have no commitments to you, you see, or anyone here, or indeed anyone at all any more."

Jenny was at one of the tall sash windows, pulling it up a space.

"Come along, Polly my love. Gently now, don't exert yourself. That's the girl. She's kittening, you see. I think any minute now. Mrs. Foster rather chases her about, but she likes it in here because nobody comes. Open the log box, would you? You see, she's taken my old cardigan, I put it out for her, isn't that clever, my little one? Look, I shall just put a bit of wood here so that the cover doesn't shut down on you and you mustn't worry, I'll bring you some milk and things. I hope you won't mind, Mr. Polter, I mean Professor. But I think we'd better go into the other room, so that Polly has some peace and quiet."

"Yes, let's," he said, "anything to get out of Bellingford's horror chamber."

"Oh, I say, you are exaggerating. I thought you said you admired Vincent?"

"I didn't say I liked his taste. There, rude again. But you weren't quite his taste, were you?"

"Mm? She'll be all right now, I think. Mrs. Foster won't come in here before tomorrow. What did you say?"

The little cat was making a loud, metallic purring, moving about in the half-empty log box and rhythmically treading her white-tipped paws into the woollen heap of an old jacket while she looked up at Jenny with languishing, slitted eyes.

"All right, my love," said Jenny and touched the cat's flat brow with the tip of one finger. "You just mind your business and we'll mind ours."

Jenny locked the door behind them and led the way across the hall to the side room.

"Ah, that's better," said Polter. "Now I can tell you what —oh."

"This is Mark Vail. He's in the London office. Professor Polter, Mark. Mark is clearing up all the confused papers, you know. We had to get out of the drawing room because Polly is in a bit of a hurry. I shall have to think of something to tell Mrs. Foster about the locked door."

"You could just say the cat is kittening in there," offered Mark.

"Oh, dear, d'you think?"

"Have you come to look at the stone we found, Professor Polter?" asked Mark. "I didn't know prehistory was your field. I've been reading about Celtic remains and *Tuatha de Danann* and *Beltine*, but it doesn't seem to offer much."

"Prehistory? Celtic remains? What stuff! I've no idea what it's all about."

"Neither have I. That's just the trouble," agreed Mark. "I thought you might have."

"Never heard of a stone. You probably need to talk to Dobson. He's always digging up dreary old rubbish with runes on it in Greenland or somewhere."

"Oh, I dare say it isn't very interesting," disclaimed Mark crossly.

"I'm sorry," Polter said lightly. "Shouldn't have said that. I didn't know somebody else was here and we'd been talking, or were just about to talk. Forgive me." He moved to a window seat and leaned back into it. "It's disgracefully early, but do you think I might have a drink?"

He sounded all at once exhausted and resigned, so that Jenny was disconcerted. She looked into his face for a moment before going to the tray of decanters.

"Are you all right?" she asked timidly.

"No, I'm dying. But then, we all are."

"Whisky?" asked Mark, implying frivolous disbelief. "Or brandy?"

"Whisky please. Water, no ice, thanks."

There was a silence. Evidently Professor Polter's spontaneity had been dispersed by the unexpected presence of another man.

"Ah, that's good," he said presently, and drained his glass. "I almost have the feeling we've met before?"

"I think not," said Mark, "although I've seen you, of course, in your television lectures."

"Another?" suggested Jenny. "Do have a drink too, Mark." She was unused to people drinking so quickly, or at all during the morning, and concerned not to expose her uncertainty in the face of the evident lack of sympathy between the two men.

Mark took Polter's glass to refill it.

"Would you like me to go?" he asked Jenny.

"Oh, no. Why?" she objected. Then she turned to Polter to consult his wishes, but he had risen from the window seat and did not see her enquiring look. He went over to the round table that stood between two armchairs on the other side of the room and where a few small objects were laid out, including the bronze of Maculan's head. This he picked up, gazing abstractedly at it.

"It is my father," said Jenny.

"I know. I met him several times during the war." Polter took the bust to a window to study it more closely.

"Really?" said Mark, surprised.

"We were on one of the many Intelligence committees together, and some other things. He was one of the most remarkable men I ever knew. I remember discussing him with Vincent, just before his death."

"You talked to Cheyney about Maculan?" Mark sounded so astonished that the visitor noticed both his manner and the intriguing detail that for Polter to talk to Cheyney about Maculan was to Mark—and why to Mark?—significant.

"Vincent was fairly new with Maculan's company then," replied Polter, and a blandness overspread his tone that was as calculated as all his other mannerisms. "He was interested, naturally, to know I had met his famous chief."

"I see," said Mark, sounding again as if he did not at all see what Polter wished him to understand, but weighed some other consideration in his mind and did not mind Polter knowing it.

"This is good." Polter was still holding the bust and glanced at Jenny, now very much the guest speaking to his hostess. "It has quite authoritatively caught Maculan's inner quality. Who did it?"

Jenny answered, startled, "I did."

"*You* did? But I didn't know you were . . . that accounts for my not recognizing the hand, the style. If you did this you have considerable talent. But I suppose you know that. I don't think I have ever seen anything of yours shown?"

"I haven't done much in the last years, and nothing nearly as good as that or the singing bird."

"I think the head of Eileen Sandford will be good," interposed Mark quietly.

"Where is this singing bird? May I see it?"

"Of course. It's in the hall. Too big for a sitting room."

"May I, please?" Polter was already at the door and Jenny politely followed while Mark stayed where he was, leaning with one shoulder against the stone frame of the fireplace. His head came to just where the carved bevelling of the stone made its angle for the lateral stretch.

"But this is excellent," he heard Polter's voice. "For the age you must have been, amazing. The straining throat, the givingness of the line. My dear, you have inherited your father's genius in another form. You're quite wrong, though, about it's belonging in the hall. It should be in a much lighter place. The drawing room obviously, with all that charming fenestration, giving it floods of light. It is aspiring, the lovely bird, and needs space, shafts of sun."

"Vincent would never have thought of putting it in his beautiful room." Jenny laughed slightly but an uncharacteristic rigour stiffened her voice.

"Oh, my dear! Don't call that beastly affected salon beautiful. Sarcasm does not become you and you know very well it isn't anything but horrid. Quite, quite horrid."

"Vincent thought it lovely," she said.

Professor Polter was still holding the bronze head, and he looked down at it now and hesitated, looking from the bust to the bird and back again.

"I had better put your father's head back where it came from," he said in a curiously toneless voice.

He rearranged the round table, putting the bronze towards the wall and moving away from it an onyx box for cigarettes, so that the dim, quiet reflection in the polished surface was not interrupted.

"Like a forest pool, the wood. Perhaps in the Alps, not very high up. Not conifers but still leafy trees, where the leaves lie forever in the dark water. Perhaps in those chestnut groves above Bergamo. You know northern Italy, just before the hills become real mountains?"

Jenny shook her head.

"I climbed one autumn in the Dolomites," said Mark, "but higher up."

"Tell me," Polter asked him, "did you know Vincent well?"

"No, not well. I'm in London, you know."

"I came here today, being in this part of the country, to say how sad I was made by Vincent's death. But I'm even sadder now, feeling that I can't sincerely say that." He swung his small head with its wispy white hair around to take in the silent Jenny. "It's been one shock after another, the last few weeks. But I think, even without the other shocks, you would take away one's appetite for the customary insincerities."

"I don't think I quite understand you, Professor."

"No. I don't quite understand, myself." Polter looked at Mark. "From your presence here one must deduce some confusion. And, forgive my candour, there is not much air of mourning here."

"Accidents do often cause, or uncover, confusion," agreed Mark. "Although I don't know that you should assume much from the little you can have seen here this morning."

"Whatever I have seen, there is one thing I did not expect. Though perhaps I should have done, Maculan having been what he was. I did not expect to find an artist here, a talented artist."

"I understand you less and less."

"I rather think you were not intended to understand," said Mark slowly. "A certain mystification was the object, but you were not intended to notice it."

"Perhaps I am talking nonsense," said Polter lightly, "I've done a good deal of that in my time. And very brainy it's always been considered. Let us put it down to the ravages of illness and whisky."

"Very sad. However, I doubt that it was either of those misfortunes that led to your underestimation of Mrs. Cheyney. More likely, you have been misinformed. But don't you feel, Professor, that you are showing a certain lack of consideration for Mrs. Cheyney's feelings? You do not really know her well enough to pry into her relations with her late husband. I find your manner odd, for one who came to condole."

270

"I don't at all want to keep up any hypocrisy, Mark," interposed Jenny quickly. "Professor Polter is quite right. There is no mourning here, except for wasted time."

"And you clearly don't mean Vincent's wasted time."

"Did Vincent waste his life? I don't think he thought so."

"Well, he died while still in his thirties. But you may be right; perhaps he did, without knowing it, waste what life he had. Poor Vincent."

"Yes, poor Vincent. No matter what *he* thought his life was, I felt, even at the worst moments, somehow sorry for him. That is, up to his death. But now there is only the anger of deception, injustice, the knowledge of having been used." Jenny lifted her head, determined to make her statement. "And, as you said yourself in the drawing room, used in the services of such a worthless ambition."

"I didn't quite say that. I was shocked at the lack of his *own* taste. Which might have turned out just as badly, but being his could have offered the possibility of learning more. But to adopt the standards of others, such low, philistine standards, when he lived in a place and with people able to show him greater perceptions, a chance to grow—that is what is so sad."

"He didn't want anything more. You are quite wrong there. He thought that the only handsome room in the house, really. And Vincent was sure that he could, and should, educate me, not the other way about. Not that I think I have much to offer, but my father obviously had and this place was his choice. It was my father's plan that Vincent rejected for his commercial fantasy of gracious living."

"But Vincent started, after all, from such a level! I felt so much sympathy with his driving ambition, when I knew him. One could still just see then what he came from, the childhood, the youth that offered him so little of a hope of anything that matters. I remember well his telling me how he started on the course he took, the jolt of anger that inspired him, years ago."

"Ah, he told you what started him?" asked Mark.

"Yes, but that doesn't matter now," Polter brushed Mark aside with a frail hand. "I admit that seeing now the paltry imitation of somebody else's apish antics in which his ambitions issued, I was horrified, yes, horrified. But still sorry, deeply sorry for him."

"But the course Vincent took involved so many lies, such weary unhappiness. For a time I was almost unhinged and I can't forget that. Because it was all quite deliberate, you know. Vincent always knew exactly what he was doing."

"I don't see, in any case," said Mark, "why Vincent should be so much pitied. His background was not so very different from my own. I, too, was unhappy as a child; I, too, was sacrificed to a narrow selfishness. Vincent's mother can hardly have been more deadening than my father was. God knows, I don't pretend to much virtue or achievement. But we could all say we had a poor start. I daresay you yourself have not always been fortunate. And poverty is not the only deprivation. Consider Jenny. Removed from her home as a child, she lost her mother, was forced to adopt a new society, new language, new customs. And she was only a child when her father was killed and she was left defenceless for the first fortune hunter who came along, to use her for his own ambitions. And what ambitions! One might just as well pity that passiveness, as the one who acted and got what he wanted."

"All decision to act involves the risk of acting wrongly, mistakenly."

"But no suffering for his actions was done by Vincent Cheyney. Even in his death he didn't suffer. He was killed in an instant, leaving others to disentangle the results. And not only his wife. That is only the very worst. There are other consequences of 'the course he took.' "

"Oh, you mean commercially? His colleagues? One really can't waste much sympathy on a bunch of moneymaking, golf-playing hearties!"

"You're very frank, since you must include me in that bunch!"

"Certainly not. I can't imagine you playing golf."

"Or making money, if it comes to that," Mark agreed, almost grimly.

"But for other reasons, you are not a man to inspire pity, I would say." Polter eyed Mark with a sharpened speculation. "Though certainly not a commercial hearty."

272

"The modern cant."

"I daresay. No, for some reason I don't quite place, I find you somewhat formidable."

"Perhaps you are not used to others applying your own nerve-racking candour?"

"It may be that," agreed Polter smiling. He finished his drink and then drew in a sharp breath and his features contracted in a painful spasm. "These rheumatic pains are supposed to go away as the illness progresses, but I can't say I've noticed much improvement yet. D'you think I might beg another drink?"

While Jenny went to get whisky from the tray Mark remained leaning against the stone fireplace, hands in pockets; he did not try to disguise the disbelief he felt as to the seriousness of the Professor's illness.

"Let's hope that is evidence that the doctors are wrong, then," he said cheerfully. "Could I have a drink too, Jenny?"

"I tried to think that for a time," agreed Polter, accepting his glass. "But I fear it cannot be so. Two eminent neurologists are agreed that they can do nothing, and that really proves they are sure, don't you agree? They would hardly admit their uselessness unless they felt obliged to. No, no, the nerves are all shrivelling away, wilting. With the next attack I shall be crippled, if not paralysed."

He is determined to force sympathy from me, thought Mark, and he felt a rare consciousness of anger. He knew he would never get at this man.

"How terrible!" said Jenny.

"One is tormented, you know, not so much by thoughts of mortality, though they are bad enough. It's the childish feeling that one is being punished; these primitive superstitions gain power when one is faced by one's own helplessness."

"Punished?" whispered Jenny. "Oh, you mean what you said before about having given your life to evil? I didn't know you meant it literally."

"What a lovely, naïve realism! But *I* don't believe I was wrong. The thought just comes in from somewhere else. The old bogeyman morality condemns me."

"For what?" asked Mark.

Polter laughed a helter-skelter giggle of tortured sensibility.

"This is a very strange conversation, isn't it? One's life alternates, or has alternated, between total secrecy and perfect openness."

"I doubt if anyone whose opinion you care for would condemn you for your life."

"No figure that I can envisage, no. But some atavism produces an ancestral wrath. A fear creeps in that it is somewhere known—one knows it is not so—that talents, influence, work have been used always for something else, not for themselves."

"Whether that would be a nightmare depends on for what."

"For what, yes." Polter gazed down at his half-empty glass. "But even rationally sometimes, the influence over all those young lives that I enjoyed so much, now seems in retrospect to have been misdirected. I wish now—I'm becoming maudlin—that I'd told them all to go away and grow roses or write poetry, do things that are useless."

"Among those lives, Vincent Cheyney's?"

"Among them, Vincent, yes."

"But Vincent was never at the university," objected Jenny, bewildered.

"Oh, there were other things. I've done various things in what is called the public service: appointments' boards, recommendations and the like."

"You have been an influential man," said Mark.

"Yes, I've popped in and out of people's lives at crucial moments, and used to get a lot of satisfaction out of it too. What is called making oneself useful. But now I wonder how I could have thought that power—the knowledge of being able to get things done, knowing whose ear to catch—could have been all that important."

"But getting things done is important," Jenny urged. "Nobody can grow roses if others aren't willing to run the world."

"And if those others are running the world, your world, in the interests of ideas that would—that well may—destroy your world?"

Jenny did not, up to now, connect Mark with this kind of imprecisely "political" remark and she looked at him doubtfully. She did not in the least understand him, but the whole morning's incident seemed to Mark so glass clear and unmistakable that he felt a sharp impatience with her ignorance. Jenny did not understand him, but Professor Polter did. He and Mark had been crossing words from the moment of Polter's entrance in a way both of them had had much practice in. And one of the details grasped by both of them was that neither of them wished Jenny to understand them at this moment. It was just as clear to the Professor that Mark was acting without Jenny's comprehension in whatever he was doing, as it was to Mark that Polter was the key to an old mystery.

If Professor Polter did not challenge Mark's disguised accusation, he was left with no alternative to confession; a man so sharp-witted and sharp-tongued would not simply let so hostile a charge pass if he were blameless. The reply of a clear conscience could only be indignation. But with a grimace of scorn at such taproom slogans, Professor Polter shrugged and was silent. His silence rang and echoed in the quiet room.

Mark did not follow up his advantage. He did not wish Polter to become conscious of there being any more to fear than what must be already obvious: that Vincent Cheyney's employers had discovered his treachery to them. When Polter went away and thought over this curious conversation it would perhaps become clear to his highly experienced mind that Mark Vail was not a lawyer in the employ of Tantham and Maculan. There are professional characteristics that charge the atmosphere for sharp sensibilities, and Mark knew very well that he carried his badges openly displayed for those with reason to recognise them. He was as much a certain type of policeman as Polter was a certain type of university don, and if the visitor had not been confused by pain, fear of a creeping disease and whisky, he would have picked up Mark's wave length at once. As it was, Mark still retained the advantage of a delay, but it would not be a long one.

Holding that advantage for an hour or so, Mark could afford to enjoy his success. For years, for double the years of Mark's career, the knowledge had existed that a man or several men in fairly high places worked quietly, continuously, systematically at recruiting spies who would, when their overt careers were assured, be put to work against their own society. Those are crude words and nothing to match them was ever done or said by men like Polter. They worked with beliefs and ambitions, the names of which were never stated harshly; the moment in each case at which the already committed agent, who might well have forgotten years ago what he could think of as a youthful indiscretion, was reminded of his commitment was invariably handled by others. Some of those picked by the historian from among his students were never called upon at all, either because they never reached a position where they could be useful or because they proved cantankerous. In cases such as Vincent Cheyney's, where Professor Polter assessed the character, or encouraged the devotion, or confirmed the blackmail, where that method was in use, of agents recruited by others he was brought into the matter as an outsider and his identity remained unknown. This part of his work had ceased some years before when he became a well-known public figure; his usefulness was not lessened by the change. His influence was greater than ever. The only reason he was asked to ascertain the state of Vincent Cheyney's affairs, right at the end of his career when his retirement was already decided upon, was simply that he had known both Maculan and Cheyney and belonged to the social world in which it is unexceptionable for the acquaintance of an outstanding man to call upon his daughter years later.

Mark's presence in Jenny Cheyney's house was eminently justified by its outcome. His elation at this unexpectedly great success was so expansive that he was at once concerned to hide it. A glance out of the window provided the means of doing so.

"Speaking of growing roses," he said, pointing with the glass in his hand, "Foster is signalling to you. He evidently needs advice."

It proved, on their having drifted, or straggled, out into the garden, that Foster could not quite decide on which angle of the storm-blasted chestnut the climbing roses should be set. There was the prevailing wind to be considered, he pointed out, which would prove a hazard in a year or so when the trailers were tall, while on the other hand the southwesterly, or weather side, would get more sun. The question was compounded by the equally important consideration as to which side would offer the largest field of vision from the house.

They were all still standing with frowns of concentration about the burnt and torn tree when the hired car was heard returning to pick up its passenger. Its driver, alighting, took in at once what was going forward and came over to add his voice to the council, casting the decisive vote for Foster's proposal of the southeast aspect on the grounds that in a year or so the roses would have so smothered their support, if protected from the wind's buffeting, that the whole houseward side of the tree would be decked with dark red roses.

The driver then took the opportunity of asking Jenny about the newly discovered ancient stone, a matter of some local interest. Polter and Mark began slowly to stroll towards the car, Polter turning several times to look back at the house.

"Yes, it's Maculan's house," he said. "Just like himself. It doesn't need to assert itself, it makes no statement no matter how self-confidently quiet. It simply is."

"Sad that he had so little time to enjoy it in peace," said Mark.

"Really, just the war years, yes. He never even lived to know the war would not be continued."

"Or not in a noisy form." Mark smiled at Polter, an almost conspiratorial smile which he knew was unwise but which he could not resist. "Strange, his death. I didn't know him, but he is very real here. I've been thinking a lot about him in the last week or so. During this clearing-up process, you know. I suppose one sudden death always revives memories of other, former accidents, disasters. Once or twice I've had an odd feeling in this out-of-the-way place. It's so cut off here from the distractions of town that queer impressions come out of the air, almost. That's to say, naturally, there is time to think here. Nothing more than an unaccustomed quiet. But a feeling recurs as if there were an echo, like a note of music hanging in the air that I could understand if I weren't so damned modern. It's a sensation I've never had before. Not even at sea, and one has some pretty queer notions at sea sometimes."

"At sea?"

"I was in the Navy."

"Ah. I would not have expected you to be the type for queer

277

notions. But this is indeed a strange place. Perhaps it brings back the past, ghosts? I suppose, one might say, in the common phrase, it belongs to the past."

Polter now looked at his watch and then across at Jenny, still talking to the driver and Foster.

"You have other visits to make in this part of the world?" asked Mark.

"Not near here. I am going north, to Bridgnorth. Complicated journey, across country. Do you know Shropshire?"

Mark shook his head. "I'm a frightful ignoramus. Apart from naval ports, I hardly know England exists outside London."

"The true Londoner. Here comes the driver. My goodness, I must fly. I shall miss a train and that would never do. I am bidden to dinner with some terribly rich acquaintances who collect television personalities. As they believe, court jesters."

"Now what do you think that was all about?" asked Jenny as they stood watching the shabby old hat waved from the car window. "Wasn't he the strangest man? But attractive, didn't you think?"

"Yes he was, curiously attractive. But, I think, a wicked man."

"Oh, darling, how stern you are. Surely sad rather than wicked?"

"I wasn't referring to his private life," Mark said. "That was pompous. Sorry."

"To what then?"

"He said himself, he has used those who were under his influence for 'other things' throughout his career. He didn't mean making improper advances to innocent youths, though I've no doubt he did that too. Except, in my experience, that innocence is hardly the word for the adolescent state."

"You're putting up Aunt Sallys and knocking them down yourself," Jenny accused him, laughing.

"Yes, aren't I? His mannered dishonesty is catching, it seems."

CHAPTER XX

"YOU DIDN'T believe in his candour, then?" Jenny was puzzled by some hint of concentration in his look, and by the way he seemed to slide off her questions into answers that were not answers. As if, almost, they were saying things to each other in front of strangers and could not express their private meanings openly. Just as Mark said, the oblique fashion of talking in so apparently open a way, so confidingly taking an intimacy for granted that the person talked to was stimulated into the giving of an intimacy in return. That beguiling trick, which only seemed to be friendship, might be catching.

"I haven't yet heard *you* speak of candour, of truthfulness, in the time we've spent together," said Mark. "Could that be because of what Polter called your naïve realism? You don't speak of it because you don't even know the opposite exists. If you did, all this would be an open book to you." He stopped, angry and unhappy. "Doesn't he make you wonder at all? What d'you suppose he meant by 'the course Vincent took'?"

"Did he say that? I don't think I noticed. I mean, he talked just for fun, half the time, it seemed to me." Jenny stopped, trying to think, to please Mark by understanding what he meant. "But why don't you explain?"

"I can't explain."

"But you seem to have understood him," she ventured dubiously, not sure whether this was a continuation of a game of words or whether Mark was pushing her—she could feel a pressure—into a seriousness that rose about her like a thickening of the atmosphere. Like Mrs. Foster conveying her wishes by her manner. Like Vincent silently bullying by pretending to be hurt. Oh, no, not like Vincent, that was a shocking

279

thought. It was Professor Polter who demanded sympathy, that was what recalled Vincent.

"The Professor did say strange things. That about evil, but I think he meant being queer. I just felt sorry for him."

"Yes, he was collecting your forgiveness, all right. Just in case he should need it. They're all the same, those types, just like other kinds of criminals. They spend their lives doing other people all the injury they can and then, when it suits them, we must all be sorry for them. Polter is ill and old now, he is sorry for himself, so he comes here, to you of all people in the world, and begs for sympathy like a little boy who has scraped his knee coming crying to Mummy."

"That's putting it very—it's awfully exaggerated, Mark."

"It's far from exaggerated. It's not nearly strong enough. And I'll have my say with Master Polter before I'm done with him."

"But Mark," she begged, shocked at his bitter anger.

The telephone pealed in the hall, echoing. They turned their heads, waiting for someone to answer it. Then they both made a move as it became clear that Mrs. Foster was out of earshot.

"Listen, Jenny," Mark said as they reached the door together. He caught at her hand. "Listen. I know what that is. I should have left here before this, and that call is to order me back to London. I shall have to leave at once. It is even more urgent now, since Polter came."

"Order you?" she cried. The misgiving spreading through her nerves was now close to fear. "Order you? Mark, what are you trying to tell me? Why don't you say what you mean?"

They were at the source of the ringing, and Mark picked up the receiver.

"One moment please," he said loudly and held the ear piece covered firmly in his right hand so that the black shape hung down in his grip.

"You've got to think," he said rapidly and quietly, still in that tone of anger that was not anger but urgency and rebellion. "That man was talking quite openly in fact, and not just for effect. He thought you knew what he was talking about. You have to work it out for yourself. I see now that this *was* the only way to manage it. And not only because it has paid off. Nobody who didn't know you would ever believe you knew nothing, I can see that. And you have to, you must, come to it by yourself. Listen, I can't hold this up any longer."

He spoke now into the telephone, and then stood there listening, his head bent, his mouth set hard. He was in a moment an entirely different man.

"It's quite true, I've dragged it out, sir," he said at last. "But I was right. It's paid off. I've got the whole thing, and not only this one case but a string of other matters. Of course, I can't say anything on the telephone. But, if you could wait for me? If I leave immediately, I can be back sometime after midnight. Yes, I think it is urgent. No, beautifully, perfectly simple. I was just sure. I knew there had to be something. To make sense there had to be something. All right, sir, until tonight."

Mark was still holding Jenny's hand, gripping it tightly. He put back the telephone and the whole space of the hall was filled with his triumph and pride.

"Darling Jenny, try to trust me. No, that is just what you shouldn't do, don't trust me. Work it out. You have it all in your head, it's all there. Your father, Vincent, Polter, and what Polter said. Your own memories. It has to be there, in your own mind. Somewhere, at some moment, you said something to Vincent that started off a whole series of incidents, a campaign of intimidation. But it was not because of Mona Laver, though probably about the time of the trouble with Vincent over her. You remember what you told me when the hotel bill came? About that time, you said or did something that was a threat to Vincent, and you've got to bring it back. If things had not happened between us—no, I won't even say that. *Because* things happened between us, you have to understand, from inside your own mind, why I've done the things I've done. And you can't understand me if you don't know what Vincent did. You knowing, not somebody telling you."

He dropped her hand and moved hastily towards the corridor and the room he used as an office.

"I must go, I daren't put it off for a moment." He was speaking over his shoulder. "I'll just get my document case."

She heard, as she stood dazed by the telephone, the rattle of the door, the hasty steps, rustle of papers, wooden slam of a drawer, chink of keys, all familiar, often repeated sounds.

281

And then, a tread not familiar, belonging to the present, as he almost ran back into the hall. Only his footfall was different; the other sounds were as much recalled as other noises of her life, such as the particular way one tread on the stairs gave out a dark, old creak if anyone trod heavily on the balustrade side but not on the wall side. The sounds were recalled from hurried departures by Vincent, frequently repeated in the last years. The footsteps were different, for Vincent's going was always from upstairs, from his dressing room, and up there carpets blurred his steps to a muffled thud that was hardly noticeable, while Mark now came along the hard and uneven flags of the passage where every heel stroke echoed. So the clipped steps were Mark now, not Vincent and the past, but otherwise it was a repetition, so that for a moment Jenny felt her head spin with confusion as Mark appeared.

"But your case?" she protested blankly.

"My clothes? They can wait. Be sent on, collected. Something. That doesn't matter now. My coat is in the cloakroom, isn't it?" He was across the hall and in the washroom where outer clothing was hung, and he reappeared immediately, shrugging his arms into the waterproof driving jacket and slapping the pocket to assure himself that car keys were in it. It was like a recurring dream, and what made it so unreal was the sensation of something happening of which she was not told, was not meant to know about.

She turned stiffly to watch him and broke frantically out of the doubling of time and memory.

"But you're coming back, Mark?" she cried.

He stopped dead by the house door, his grip on the iron door handle and she saw now that he was deliberately keeping away from her, not touching her, not making even a hasty farewell.

"When you ask me to," he said. "You have to ask me. Then I shall know. . . ." He stopped and they stared at each other, as if accusingly, as if in anger.

"But—wait! I don't understand. . . ."

"I can't wait, I must go." He meant, perhaps, to say more, but at that moment the padded door opened with its familiar puff of sound and Mrs. Foster came into the hall and without

282

seeing them went over towards the drawing room carrying a vase, empty. In the second that Jenny moved her eyes to the housekeeper, Mark was gone and Jenny put out an imploring hand with a choked sound in her throat.

"The door's locked," muttered Mrs. Foster, rattling at the knob uncomprehendingly.

"I locked it," said Jenny, quite calmly. "Polly is kittening in the log box."

"In there?" Mrs. Foster's voice was as horrified as if the melodrama of the last few minutes had been hers rather than Jenny's.

"Yes, in there. Don't disturb her, please, Mrs. Foster. If there is any mess—there won't be, but if there is—I'll clean up."

"But, of all things! Oh, poor little thing, and I meant to get rid of them. I mean, the door's shut and she can't get out."

"I left a window open at the bottom," confessed Jenny.

"But we'd better look. See if she's all right?"

"Well, don't make a sound, then." Jenny brought the key out of her pocket and very quietly unlocked the door so that they could peer into the still room, where nothing moved, nothing made a sound.

"She's all right," said Mrs. Foster. "Asleep, I daresay."

"But you wanted to drown them," accused Jenny.

"Well, the kittens, that's different. I wasn't thinking of Polly."

"I do believe you're fond of Polly."

"Polly is all right, nice little thing. She's a good mouser, too."

"And we can keep the kittens, can't we?"

Mrs. Foster retreated from goodwill.

"That depends. There may be half a dozen."

"I'm sure not. Polly is so small," urged Jenny. "Then I'll take her to the vet. I promise, if we can keep the kittens this time."

"Well," muttered Mrs. Foster, "it's all according. We'll see."

"Oh, dear me," said Jenny suddenly. "I do feel funny."

"How, funny?"

"Only for a second. A bit dizzy." Having unwisely spoken, Jenny was now more concerned with appearing normal to Mrs. Foster than with a strange physical sensation quite new to

283

her, as if the centre of gravity had shifted inside her. She held herself rigidly upright and the sensation did, in fact, go away as quickly as it came.

"All this excitement, it's bad for you. You'd better lie down for a few minutes." Mrs. Foster scolded, sounding anxious as well as disapproving. This suggestion did not commend itself to Jenny, and she went instead to her studio where she spent the hour that remained of a restless morning chipping pointlessly at the ruined stone block in the fugitive hope of its becoming an abstract plastic form, which, she had already thought, she might call "Turning Point." Pointlessly because she knew perfectly well that it would not turn into an abstract plastic, and that she did not wish to move on to that easy path of egocentric forms which fail to communicate anything but what the artist determines they should mean. She knew well that if her work became less explicit it must be because she progressed towards greater command both of techniques and of her own understanding, not because the abandonment of organic form and anatomy was easier.

In other words, Jenny spent the next hour trying hard not to think, and above all trying not to think of the abrupt departure of Mark Vail.

She was greeted on her return to the house by Foster, who was evidently waiting for her.

"I can't find Mr. Vail, Mrs. Cheyney. Did he go off with that Professor? His car is gone."

"Mr. Vail has gone," she said, and felt again that slight, sickening sensation of some focus in her body shifting. "I expect he'll be back, but for the time being, he's not here."

"I didn't see him drive off. Must have been in the shed, fetching a new trowel. The handle's broken on the one I always use." Foster was looking at her, with a frown of nonunderstanding touched already with puzzled hurt. "You mean he's left altogether? But he didn't say goodbye."

"It was very sudden. He rushed off after Professor Polter Something urgent, he said. He asked me to say goodbye for the moment to you. But he has left his things here. So he'll be coming back."

This confusion of half-truths came out with a notable lack

of conviction that left both of them unsatisfied. Jenny moved uncertainly towards the stairs.

"I must go and wash my hands before lunch," she said, looking at her hands.

"Well, that's awkward. There was a telephone call for him and I said he would call back for sure before lunch."

She stopped halfway up the first steps, hand on the banister, and turned round to face Foster but not quite looking at him.

"I had better call, then," she murmured. "Have you got the number?" And she gestured vaguely toward the telephone table where a message pad lay.

Foster followed her across the hall, pulling off his old gardening hat. It was, thought Jenny, like Professor Polter's hat only rather older. It showed a wavy sweat line on the frayed band. This was deeply familiar, though she did not recall noticing it before. Out of his pocket Foster brought a slip of paper and looking just past Jenny, offered it to her.

"They said it was Withen Camps speaking," he said reluctantly. "That's the RAF station."

"Near where we went to dinner," said Jenny slowly. "It must have been a mistake."

"I don't think it was a mistake, Mrs. Cheyney," Foster said, still looking up at her, his nose pulled sideways by an anxious twist of the mouth, pulled just as it was when he smiled his crooked smile, but he was not now smiling. "I heard it quite clear, and the officer's voice in the background, too."

"Like Saturday night," said Jenny, staring past him with an uneasy surmise of trouble coming.

"Mrs. Cheyney," he said. "The officer's voice said, 'Haven't you got that policeman on the line yet?' and then the operator said, 'They're just fetching Mr. Vail, sir.' So I don't think there was any error, Mrs. Cheyney. Not on the telephone."

"I don't mean you made a mistake, Foster. But there must obviously be a misunderstanding somewhere, mustn't there?"

"Well, you would know that better than me, Mrs. Cheyney," he replied. The insistent repetition of her name warned Jenny that Foster was much upset; everything seemed to be happening very slowly, even their voices were much slower than usual.

"I'm as puzzled as you are," she denied the implication. "Are you sure that's what they said?"

"Sure as I stand here. What was it, Saturday night?"

"When Colonel Bartle telephoned. The lines were all crossed. All sorts of different voices. Mrs. Foster noticed it, too."

"Yes, the wife did say something, now you come to mention it."

"And Mr. Vail had another call immediately afterwards. It's really very odd. Perhaps our number is almost the same as Withen Camps? Although it's never happened before. Or has it?"

"Not that I know of," said Foster. "And the numbers can't be much alike. It's a different exchange. And Withen Camps would have its own exchange, a big station like that."

"And this morning," said Jenny frowning, "Mr. Vail had a call just before this crossed-line one. That was the telephone call that made him decide to leave in such a rush." She shook her head in bewilderment as she turned again to go upstairs. "What could they have meant—policeman?" she muttered to herself.

This inevitable speculation was naturally not confined to Jenny, who failed at first to take it quite seriously. Faced as she was with the abrupt loss of a companion who, in the short space of three weeks, had become indispensable to her, a small matter of crossed telephone wires was only an interruption of what she could no longer avoid thinking about. In the studio she could do without Mark, but that was the only place where an empty space was not painfully emphasised at every moment, every movement.

Mark was palpably not in the side room when she went in. The glass of sherry before luncheon, which was already a fixed point of each day's progress of the communication between them, tasted sour. The silent dining room, laid with only one place at the table, was made miserably chill by the glum and sideways looks of a Mrs. Foster not yet prepared to commit her suspicions to words.

The moment came soon enough, and the next day Jenny

286

was interrupted in an unhappy reverie of loneliness by the reality of what she imagined, only a short time before, as an improvement in her life. The Fosters wished to leave.

"But why?" she asked, blankly staring at Mrs. Foster's averted face.

"I don't like it, all that business with Mr. Vail. The police and that. We've talked it over and over, and I'm sorry but our minds are made up, Mrs. Cheyney."

"I see. And I can see you are sorry. So am I."

"We feel we ought to have been told, if there was something. It's uncomfortable, not knowing what's going on and then being faced with it, by accident. We might never have known."

"I wish to goodness we never had known."

Mrs. Foster gave her employer a sharp, covert look at this and sniffed unbelievingly.

"You can't suppose I knew Mr. Vail was a policeman. Surely you don't think that? Why, I do believe . . . You don't think, if it's true, that it is anything to do with you two? Or me either, if it comes to that?"

"How can we know," she said. And of course, Jenny was bound to admit they could not know and Jenny herself did not know. She sat down with a weakening sensation, trembling a little, in one of the armchairs with the upholstery Professor Polter had so disliked. Mrs. Foster had followed her as she went into the drawing room to look in on Polly and the baby kittens in the log box. There were, as Jenny guessed, only three of them, delicate curls of damp fur making faint mews and half-hidden under a proud and anxious Polly.

"I suppose I ought to have discussed it with you as soon as Foster told me about that call. But, you know, I can't help feeling it was some stupid mistake. I mean, we did have crossed lines a day or so before that, didn't we?"

"Yes, we did. But that's just it, Mrs. Cheyney. It's a nasty feeling."

"For me, too," said Jenny sadly.

"You see, you didn't call them back, did you? To find out?"

There was a long and embarrassed silence. Jenny could see that her failure to investigate the telephone call seemed to Mrs. Foster like proof that she knew what it was about. And really, why did she not telephone Withen Camps and ask them what they wanted? She tried to pull herself together in a crisis that she now recognized as about to become a disaster for her and said slowly, "I rather felt, recently you know, that you looked upon this as your home now."

"Well, but it isn't our home, is it?"

"Evidently not. But ten years is a long time. And specially since...." She looked up. She stared straight into Mrs. Foster's eyes, abstracted with thought. "It's obvious that whatever it is all about, and I don't know any more than you do, whether you believe it or not, it must be something to do with Vincent's death."

"*Mr. Cheyney?*" The emphasis on the name told Jenny that the Fosters had not struck upon this possible explanation. Like most people, like Jenny herself, events in their immediate circle were always interpreted as having something to do with themselves.

"Mr. Vail was brought here by Mr. Folliot. You know that. And Folliot came here to clear up our papers, the confusion left by Mr. Cheyney's death."

"The police? Mr. Cheyney?" Her tone made the connection impossible.

"If Mr. Vail is some kind of policeman," Jenny felt her way in this obvious and so strange idea, "then the reason for his coming here must have something to do with the time he came. Mustn't it?"

"But Mr. Cheyney!"

"I must think," said Jenny.

"But if that's what. . . . Why didn't anybody tell us? Why didn't you tell us? But what could . . . ?"

"Nobody told me anything, either."

That Jenny should be told nothing of what went on about her was to both of them not surprising. Only now, in the consideration of a new situation was this factor in it, which was seen by Mrs. Foster as a constant state of affairs stretching back into the past, into the time of her own introduction into the lives of the Cheyneys, shown to be startling; only now did Jenny's ignorance seem extraordinary. Nobody ever did tell Jenny "anything" as far as Mrs. Foster knew, but in the light of the quite easy and rational way they had managed the household together since Cheyney's death, this old-established fact looked strange and sinister, lit up as it was by the new context of Mr. Cheyney and some kind of policeman. Indeed it was literally staggering, so that Mrs. Foster's knees gave way and she sat down.

"If all this is not some strange mistake, you must see that it can't have anything to do with either of you two or with me. Nobody has asked me any questions. Has anybody questioned you or Foster?"

Mrs. Foster shook her head.

"That's what makes it so peculiar," she pointed out.

"No. That's what makes it certain that it is nothing to do with any of us directly. We just happen to be around." She said this with a deep, sad bitterness.

"But can't you find out? Mr. Sandford or Mr. Folliot must know?"

"I shall have to find out. You see, it didn't quite strike me until now. I ought to have thought of you and Foster, but it just somehow didn't seem real."

Jenny looked down at the cat and mechanically bent to touch its head with one finger. I shall have to live here alone, she thought, and perhaps Mrs. Godolphin won't want to work here if the Fosters leave. Shall I be forced to go away, leave here myself? For a time, anyway? This shocking thought gave her an idea to grasp at.

"Let me talk to Mr. Folliot," she said. "Don't make any final decisions now. I can't believe you want to go, and as for this not being your home we can work something out, I'm sure. But if you really want to go, you can still do that when we have cleared all this confusion up. Look, you and Foster didn't have a real holiday last year, why don't you take one now? Take two months and we'll see what happens. You could go and visit your family? Or go on one of those lovely holidays abroad, like in the Sunday papers. Everybody does now."

Two days later the Fosters departed, leaving behind them trunks packed and labelled, on the very day that the long-awaited television set was installed. Jenny, with a consciousness of anticipation compounded of anxiety and relief, was left quite alone.

It was raining heavily as the hired car disappeared in the middle of the afternoon. Jenny closed the front door, locked it and lit the porch light as if it were already night.

The bust of Eileen Sandford was finished, after much thought and work. Early that morning Jenny had walked round it once more, trying to see it afresh, and not too ashamed of it. Then she scratched her signature, "Maculan 1958," on the back where the base began, and smoothed off the base itself with a spatula for the last time.

Now in the silent hall she went to the telephone and made the long-distance call needed to arrange the casting. It was years since anything of hers had been cast and she was surprised that the man she spoke to remembered who she was. He went to consult his work book before naming a date, and she stood idly, holding the receiver and looking about her at the dim, shadowy hall in the rain-soaked dusk of a day that never really became light. It was hers altogether now; there was nobody with any claim to share it, she possessed it inwardly as if it were alive, as if she could physically embrace it in her arms. This at any rate was hers. She absorbed the house as waiting for her and of it having been freed from some heavy restraint; now that she was alone she could grasp with buoyancy the relief that Vincent Cheyney would never again inhabit her house or her spirit.

The telephone clacked and, as she lifted it, she saw that it was hanging in her hand as it hung in Mark's hand on the day of his going.

CHAPTER XXI

THE STAIRWAY jutted into the hall, asymmetrical and only more or less in the middle. After five steps, a little square landing made space for a right-angle bend emphasised by the handrail with its massive flat upper surface worn by hundreds of years of hands sliding up and down its length. The uncarpeted stair treads were uneven, and up the longer flight this could be seen if one looked, as Professor Polter had done, from the turn up to that big and high window, the sight of which seemed to have pierced him with some nostalgia, so that he had cried out, as Jenny now recalled.

"Oh, God," he had said, "England. The pale sun coming in through that mullioned casement with the leaves moving behind it." And surprised at his tone, Jenny asked if he had come home recently from abroad. As his exact inflexion rang now in Jenny's head she could hear the histrionic attempt at derision in the hackneyed phrase "mullioned casement," which indeed was inaccurate, as Polter certainly knew, since such stairway windows were not made to open at all, whether by hinge or sash. She was quite clear about the sneer in the words and about the protesting love of the exclamation, "Oh, God. England." The sarcasm denied some claim. Claim—to what? How could Polter, an Englishman, be conscious enough of a claim on his feelings by his own country for it to come to mind so sharply, as if this old house's survival made him bitterly aware of some contrast it offered? Why here? He had spent his life not only with history—and British constitutional history was his subject, Jenny knew—but lived among historic courtyards, towers, cloisters in an academic rank itself part of history.

Jenny was well acquainted with the buried depth of English

"nationalism." That word, itself a little foreign, she used to herself. Among those with whom she spent her school days, at first as a stranger, it was an unconscious reaction and emerged only as a joke. Only those who knew the English intimately from one degree off-center, from one step outside, could be unaware of what they were aware of. It needed a touch from some other place, from another state of being, for that deep source to well up to the surface. The house itself did offer a contrast—she accepted this from her father—to any other place, simply because nowhere else did domestic continuity reach back without a break of war or revolution far enough for dwellings of this middle sort to have survived as homes. Cottages too small for plunder could survive, mansions and palaces great enough to be deliberately preserved or restored would be cherished. But yeoman country houses like this one were confined almost entirely to England. This generalisation in Jenny's mind was not exact, but it was near enough to reality as she understood it for her to grasp by intuition what had been at that moment in Polter's mind.

But why should Grove House so touch Polter? And why, ill as he was, make this long journey out of his way to pay a small tribute of memory to a man he knew only slightly ten years ago? For he did not come to commiserate, nor did he write at the death of her father, whom he had known longer and better than he knew Vincent; of that Jenny was sure. She did not quite believe that either the blank wall of age presented by retirement or the knowledge of an incurable illness would account for a sentimental journey attached to his heart by such a slender thread. And certainly this could not explain the strong undertone of rejection permeating those words. There is no question of denying the claim made implicitly by a place and a history that are one's own, as this place was essentially Polter's. Faced by mortality, one would, rather, be glad, if bitterly glad, for that window's survival in this house. One would not reject it as a painful accusation. Accusation? From where did she get that word?

Drawn by the staircase, Jenny mounted slowly, drawing a hand along the almost black, unvarnished sheen of the hand-rail, which was wider than her hand span. The joints in the wood had been almost eliminated by time and use; ages of dust and wax had filled them up. Reaching the wide landing that was once a gallery, of which the side opposite the big window had been walled in as a passage during the eighteenth-century rebuilding, Jenny was faced by four closed doors. They were unevenly spaced, two more having been walled up in her father's time to turn small side chambers, once children's rooms, into bathrooms. On the window side to her right was her own bedroom. Then came the door of Vincent's dressing room. And well over to the left at the end of the landing was the main guest apartment with its own bath.

It was so quiet that Jenny could hear the gutters running full outside, and if she listened intently even the cool spatter and slip of rain could be heard against the tall window. She opened the nearest door, her own footsteps no longer audible because the gallery landing was carpeted. It opened with a slight creak, one of the many familiar house sounds, and swung gently back. She stood and stared into Vincent's dressing room, where he had slept for the last three or four years. It was narrow, with one window opposite the door, and Jenny could see beech trees veiled in clouds of rain billowing slightly in the wind. The glass was not streaming, for the rain blew laterally past this tier of windows. To the left the wall was panelled, where a door led into a tiny chamber, now a wardrobe; farther down towards the window the cupboard halfway up in the paneling was almost invisible from the door, the opening being one of the inner panels. Only by the new safety lock could one see there was a cupboard there. Under the window stood a flat table where the telephone once rested on a blotter backed by a long inkstand never used and a modern reading lamp. The desk chair was precisely in the centre of the writing table, pushed under its middle drawer. At the window end on the left was the door that led, past the bathroom dividing their rooms, to Jenny's bedroom. Rebuilding had made almost a narrow tunnel there, or it would have been like a tunnel but for an odd little window, high up. Then came Vincent's chest of drawers, the looking glass tilted somewhat forward, nothing on its surface at all. All of Vincent's personal effects were gone, collected by a local charity. Between the chest of drawers and the threshold, where Jenny stood, was the bed in the corner. All was neat and trim, the clothes stand, the armchair, the reddish carpet: empty, spotless, inhumanly reserved.

The bedcover, with neatly arranged corner flutes, and curtains were of a dull fawn, not a colour at all but emphasised neutrality, and the braid edging was precisely the red of the carpet. That reserve and neutrality, that careful matching, were to Jenny infinitely depressing. The lack of anything left over, any stack of paperbacks, a personal telephone list, even a pair of shoes forgotten in the collection, all were expressive in their denial of evidence, of Vincent himself. By contrast with the sense of a continuing conversation with Mark when he was there, and with the change in her relations to the Fosters, it struck Jenny forcibly now that a central characteristic of Vincent was that he never expressed a definite opinion. He never committed himself. Everything about him, including his control of Jenny herself and his methods of getting his own way, were continuously, deliberately oblique. Unlike everybody else Jenny had ever known, Vincent, by a now clear contrast, had somehow carefully held his own self aside, out of the line of sight and hearing, as it were, and she searched her memory in vain for any direct statement or any clear answer from him to a question. Even now, when the table drawer and the drawers of the chest, like the cupboard in the panel, were quite empty, they were locked up from habit, with locks and keys put there by Vincent.

Coming back to this state of affairs, so long taken to be natural, this inexpressiveness and secrecy were to be felt as heavily meaningful, extraordinary. The hasty departure of the Fosters and Mark's departure, together with the strikingly untypical refusal by Mark to say openly what he meant, were suddenly reactions to some quality of Vincent's; Jenny's realisation of Vincent's uncommunicativeness as a significant, a major characteristic became, by contrast with these others, a discovery. She discovered that what Mark did once, and in connection with Vincent, what had alienated the Fosters so that they fled, Vincent had done all the time. Vincent hid things, hid himself. But not because of his adulteries. The police do not concern themselves with private sins, and unless Foster was as crazy as Jenny was once thought to be, Mark stood in relation to Vincent as some kind of policeman. Jenny was obliged to put this to herself vaguely as "some kind" of policeman, for Mark was clearly not like any ordinary policeman. A special kind of police, then? Arriving so soon after Vincent's sudden death, after a life now seen as excessively secretive.

Jenny moved into the room, now looking at everything in it with speculative curiosity. On the inkstand lay a bunch of keys with several loose ones. A large, ancient iron key to the wardrobe, Vincent's house and car keys on a ring from which the leather holder was gone, the brass ones with decorated grips belonging to the chest of drawers. One after the other Jenny slipped them into their proper places and turned them. The drawers were empty, there was a bitter smell of seasoned oakwood with a faint hint of lavender. Next she opened the wardrobe and walked in to the hollow rattling of empty hangers on the rack and a grey reflection of her own figure from the unlighted mirror. She swung a door open; behind its looking-glass front it was as bare as on the day of its installation. There was just enough light to see that the whole area was dusted out, uncluttered by as much as a dropped collar stiffener. Even the suitcases had been removed with the contents and given away with them. Not even an airlines tag remained as evidence of ten years' occupation by Vincent, ten years of constant travel, work, secrecy.

Those journeys. It was a journey, hastily postponed on Vincent's falling ill with "influenza," that ended what Mark called a campaign of intimidation. The door with its mirror front fell into its frame with a thud when she pushed it and her reflection swung again into the glass as if she were moving: a swoop and a hand falling to the side of a form dark and almost featureless.

On that other afternoon more than a year ago, Vincent was in his dressing room, his suitcase half-packed, Jenny hovering anxiously about trying to help. He turned towards her and asked for his hairbrushes, making a gesture of one hand to indicate that they were not in their usual place on top of the chest of drawers.

"I suppose you've done something crazy with them, now," he said.

295

She looked at his face and then at the gleaming wood where the long shoehorn lay, the tray for cuff links, the bottle of shaving lotion, the electric shaver. No hairbrushes. Clothes-brush, but no hairbrushes. So strong was the immediate impression of those commonplace implements of masculine convention that Jenny walked out of the wardrobe and stared again at the uncommunicative surface of the chest of drawers. Now it was quite clean, everything, including the brushes, was gone. And now Jenny stood quite still, concentrating in a way not at all like her behaviour on that other afternoon.

Then her eyes scored in turn every angle of the dressing room, even the neatness of the bedcover, but in there she did not touch anything. She ran, already sobbing wildly in the recurrence of panic, through into her own room and began pushing and throwing things, beating on the walls, crying out unbelief and searching frantically with a nerve-draining terror of unreality for what she knew perfectly well was not there. Vincent followed her through into the doorway, where she could feel him at her back, and stood watching. Since his death Jenny had not seen his face so clearly as she now saw it in recall. His regular features were as real as in actual vision, the brilliant blue eyes somewhat obscured by the drawn eyebrows, which were so unusually straight and regular. She must have turned to look at him, for she could see his expression now; he looked sorry for her but neat, detached, above all under control, as she so often and lamentably was not at that time. That controlled, watching look drove her, taunted her.

She grabbed at the glass he was holding, his after-luncheon brandy that he always referred to as a postprandial *digestif*, and flung it with its contents at the row of books on the back of the writing desk. It hit two volumes of some history with red leather spines and gold lettering that disappeared in the dark spread of cognac. As far as Jenny knew, Vincent never read history and she found she did not know what those two books were; they were no longer there and neither were several volumes of the paperback series of *Famous Trials* that stood next to them and which Vincent did read. They could perhaps have been books by Professor Polter, it suddenly occurred to her. Why did she throw the glass at the books? She did not know. Perhaps to avoid the temptation to throw it at the panes of the window. And the journey Vincent was about to undertake, the reason for his packing; where did he intend to go? She rather thought it was to have been Prague, but that might be a memory of other occasions; at any rate he did not leave, and there must have been various explanations made —cancellations that, typically, Jenny did not know about.

No, it was a projected journey to Prague which *began* the series of increasingly weird and frightening things that mysteriously went wrong. That was not the afternoon she threw the brandy glass; that was more than a year before.

She made now a forced effort to remember just what happened after she threw the glass. She must disentangle this rank growth of briars and bindweed that so nearly strangled her; it was not enough to know that it had once been growing up and round her understanding and now was dying away.

Vincent stood there in the doorway watching her as she searched her own room, pushing and pulling at objects, fighting them. She was not genuinely looking for the hairbrushes because she knew they would not be there any more than other mislaid or misused things, times, spoken words, were what or where they might be expected to be. There was dismay in Vincent's attitude, one hand raised as if it still held the glass and his body in a slight crouch that sketched a backing away in fear of her furious onslaught. And he might well really have felt fear of what the ladylike little girl of a few years ago had become. But his eyes, as always, were under control; they did not share the cramp or tension expressed by muscles. He was, she knew it now, waiting to see what she would do next, what would be the effect of this repetition, of the terrible again-ness taken on gradually by the meaningless and unheralded changes in perfectly ordinary things and circumstances.

In many households the tools of daily use have no fixed places and their untidiness is not fearsome, just as times and appointments for many people are more or less elastic so that an hour or even a day transposed is not strange and, still less, sinister. But Vincent's things, especially, were always ordered with obsessive neatness in a household where, in general, rigid order reigned. For those brushes to be lying on the left instead of the right of his chest of drawers would be unusual and

297

would cause an automatic move to rearrange them. Just as a meal ten minutes late was not a matter for mild irritation but an outrage causing panic haste.

It must have been Vincent's expression, outwardly half nervous and half resigned but inwardly watching and waiting, that broke the last reserve of Jenny's control. Her sobbing wail became a scream, the voice, hiccuping and choking, rose to a howl.

"I'm going mad, I shall do away with myself. I shall commit suicide. I shall follow my father, gone, gone like him out of this horror. It isn't true, I didn't touch them, they are here, they must be here. Somebody else does it, it isn't me. But I won't be put in a home, I'd rather die and I will die. I shall kill myself."

It was ludicrous but it was pathetic and terrifying too. She saw herself turning in headlong flight. Did she mean to throw herself out of the window, which would be quite ineffectual? Or was it instinctive flight away from Vincent? But as she moved she saw herself in the glass on the dressing table and the movement was arrested instantly, as if of itself, by the sensation like a crash inside her, an inner blow of great force. She stared, seeing herself slobbering at the distended mouth, her teeth clenched, howling, retching, inhuman, insane. Her hair was half over her face and that in itself was terrifying. An uncared-for hand that shook violently crept over her wet mouth, and with the other hand she pushed the hair out of her eyes and smeared the tears off colourless cheeks while she stared into her own eyes, lost, dolourous, despairing. She gave a great gasp to catch air and sank, shuddering in every nerve, into the low chair before the mirror. She recognised as a stranger, standing away from herself, the dreadful distortion of what once was Johanna Maddalena Maculan. There seemed to be a long wait there, a silence and unmovingness, before she recalled her voice speaking shakily and huskily but in a normal pitch.

"Very well. I am ill. I can see that. I shall go to Dr. Limmert and ask him to recommend a psychiatrist. He'll know what to do. I've known him most of my life and I can trust him."

She was shivering now and clasped her upper arms with her crossed hands in an attempt to warm, or to comfort, herself.

"I am so cold," she whispered, "so cold." And hardly waiting to slip off her house shoes, she pulled the flowered cover half off the bed and slipped in under the down quilt to hide, to be warm, to curl up tightly and slide into exhausted sleep.

That, with not more than a word or two of difference in the exact speech, was what happened. It was not the first scene of its kind, but it was the most violent and it was the last. Jenny then came to a decision, that she would fight. She determined to save herself and then she could sleep as she had not done for months. Even more startling, she ignored Vincent as if he were not there at all; the shock of recognition killed her fear of him in the moment that she became aware of it and challenged it in herself. Him she did not challenge and she was still a long way from admitting to herself that she was afraid of him. When she awoke it was evening and Vincent, too, had retired to bed, alternately shivering and burning with a raging fever. By the time the Fosters returned from the town, for luckily it was their day off, Jenny had retreated again far enough into her self-deception to protect herself. She reassumed her disguise towards Vincent, felt concern, gratitude, affection and fussed him with hot-water bottles, hot drinks and aspirin.

It was not her loss of control, not her slide away from reality, that shocked Vincent into collapse that day; those were what he needed and expected to see in her. No; she threatened him and the threat was the moment when she recognized herself. Vincent saw in that instant that, essentially, Jenny knew she was sane. She was able to apprehend that something terrible and irrecoverable was happening to her and she was able to decide that it must stop. When she said in that strange flat voice of reason that she would consult Limmert she not only called on the objective and outside help of reason in the form of a doctor; she appealed to the past, to what she knew she could trust. For Dr. Limmert had lived in Grove House throughout the war with Jenny and Maculan; the old fool, as Vincent always thought of him, knew Jenny's mind from childhood and knew it as a neurologist. To consult him was within a hairbreadth of saying that she did not trust Vincent. Vincent must have reeled back from the precipice of having gone too far, so far that the slightest further pressure on

Jenny would force her, not into a lunatic asylum but into the admission of what he was doing to her. That *he* was doing it.

It was still unlikely that Jenny would allow a suspicion into the surface of her mind, for to suspect her husband without a motive of bewildering her out of her wits would have been only one more proof of her own instability. She knew of no motive stronger than promiscuity, and in the present state of social customs, nobody need go to such lengths to cover a scandalous plurality of beds. Once Jenny made up her mind to resist Vincent, it could be only a matter of time before she either left him and escaped altogether from his control, or put the question to herself *and others* as to why he should play such tricks. His illness, the collapse of his nerve, put off—as it proved for good—the moment at which Jenny would actually consult a doctor. It gave Vincent time to reconsider his tactics, and the outcome of that breathing space was the abandonment of Vincent's attempts to undermine his wife's ability to make sensible judgments.

The change in Vincent was so striking during his attack of "influenza" and after it that the short break in living made by four days in bed could neither account for it nor disguise it. For weeks after that he did not nag her, never once warned her to try to control herself, never offered her tranquilisers or sleeping pills. He watched her incessantly, but the relief from constant reminders and expressions of concern as to what she might say or do was so lightening to Jenny's spirits that his unspeaking concentration hardly oppressed her. The terror of her mistakes, losses, forgettings, faded as they no longer occurred. The wild confusion of her own certainty that she did not herself commit these actions went as the actions failed to recur; and that certainty was a large part of her fear of insanity, for the unknowledge of her own acts, which was how the certainty appeared to her was the actual state of alienation. She held a growing hope, which she hardly dared to feel, like a long-drawn breath: she thought she had "pulled herself together." She had, but not by herself. Vincent cured her, not by needing her or being kind to her but by ceasing to torment her. What remained was for him to see whether she would take her instinctive rebellion further, and his silent watching was directed to that end. She did not; she compounded with fate and they entered upon a period of stalemate, a truce. On her part Jenny agreed tacitly that her reason had been and could still be in danger and that her life should be managed for her. On his part Vincent pushed her no further so long as he could be satisfied that she did not face the implication of that crisis. He must have spent months of nerve-racking suspense lest something should inspire Jenny to penetrate further into reality. There was not much risk of that; shattered nerves ensured a peace of exhaustion, and she was cravenly content with the humiliating compromise she had attained.

memories of terror much worse than the state of limbo she was in kept her from seeking professional help. She still believed that her reason was in danger, but as long as that fear, locked away like a monster in a dungeon, kept her passive, she was safe from renewed attacks.

Except for the extreme defiance of doctors, there was no one to whom she could go. She was quite isolated from anyone not under Vincent's control by a process that began when she first knew him. Once Maculan was dead, and after her marriage, the Church and the sculptor Connors must go, and gradually childhood friends and neighbours dropped off under constant discouragement until there was not a single soul round Jenny not chosen by her husband. This appeared perhaps to others as the natural process of interpenetration of influence and personality that forms marriage; in actual fact it was the strangling of one human being in the service of another who, in turn, was himself in the grip of some sombre and menacing obsession. Towards what aim Vincent's driving demon had been directed was of little interest to Jenny; she recognized instinctively that it literally did not matter. A hidden drive in Vincent's psyche would have found some totem to worship, some gloomy and inhuman idol to which his pathological urge to secret domination, his tortuous lust to destroy would have attached itself. If Vincent had found himself on a paradisal island of the South Seas, he would have discovered a bleak puritanical godhead to torment and frighten human beings with, some ugliness to cover beauty and turn spontaneity and laughter into the cataleptic rituals of devil worship.

CHAPTER XXII

THESE WERE strange thoughts, and only a month ago, before the accident, they would have filled Jenny anew with the fear of madness. She faced her thoughts now, shocked by her own hatred, but with only a rational tremour of nervousness in the face of a mystery, because it was a question which actually existed and not the fabrication of a sick fancy. Mark's existence was proof that she was sane, and because she now knew she was sane, there had to be a reason for Vincent's actions. Yes, Mark. There was some detail that connected Mark with her reconstruction of that horrible scene of hysteria.

It was in the repetition of a journey about to be embarked upon, the mirror image of Mark's own hasty departure a few days before, when his collecting of keys, papers, coat echoed former perfunctory leave-takings, so that Jenny almost expected to see Vincent, not Mark, emerge from the passage downstairs.

Jenny's head swam with the confusion of that vision, but the clue was somewhere there and she must think it out. Mark came rapidly out of the corridor . . . no, before that. He was holding the telephone, the decision to leave was just made, he was urging her to work it out for herself, recall what started the mysterious repetitions of queer happenings. He was about to go on a journey of which she knew neither purpose nor goal, and that connected with her efforts to bring back Vincent's journey on the day of her outburst and his own reactive illness. She had thought he was about to fly to Prague, and then decided that she was confusing that memory with another occasion, another departure to Prague—or was it to Warsaw?

That was over two years ago, and she found it difficult to

re-create, even approximately, what was said or done. It was, she thought, not more than a few days after her interference in Vincent's affair with Mona; it must have been, for she always connected the start of those errors and displacements, those transpositions of timing, with the conversation about Mona.

But it could not have been that day, she clung on, shocked into recall, for the affair with Mona was then at least two years old. By that time Mona was a fixed feature of their lives and already encroaching on Jenny's home as well as filling Vincent's desires and needs.

Jenny clutched at her head and sank down into the armchair into which Mark had flung the work of popular psychology on that Saturday afternoon in her room. She shut her eyes tightly in a passionate concentration of all her spiritual forces. Was it possible that she was transposing one incident with another, more than a year distant from it? The discussion about Mona could not have been when the "queer tricks" began to happen. Or had Vincent put that idea into her mind as the first of those tricks, like a cerebral operation, the success of which showed him that he could use the method as a weapon? Think, she adjured herself, think, and Jenny groaned aloud at the agonising effort of memory.

She had already once this afternoon clutched at a point of recall. Vincent had been about to leave for Prague, or Warsaw. She produced that memory this afternoon because that was the point at which the former scene, now two years old, began. Yes, she could remember, she could and did now know that Vincent almost shouted at her, accusing her of a sick jealousy over the innocuous secretary, which induced hallucinations in her so that she began to question everything he did, confusing her insane hatred of Mona with his other activities, journeys, work. Something was there; she must pull it out very gently, like Ariadne's thread, and it would lead her back to what Vincent had actually said.

He had seemed, startlingly, to lose his temper, something he never did. Apparently on the subject of Mona Laver. So Mona must have been mentioned; Vincent would not have chosen a peg to hang his nagging upon that would not hold Jenny's believing attention, both at the time and subsequently.

Yes, faintly she recalled, like the darkened reflexion just now in the wardrobe mirror, Vincent's voice saying that Mona would know of his return plans and would let Jenny know. He did not yet know exactly from where and on what day he would be back. And Jenny, not wishing to hear the news of her own husband's arrival home from his already interfering secretary, protested.

"But surely you know where you are going to be," she said, "and more or less for how long." She knew enough about the countries Vincent's business took him to, to be sure that firm arrangements must be made—visas, bookings, appointments must already exist, together with the exact length of his stay.

"It isn't quite certain," Vincent replied with his usual vagueness, his dislike of committing himself, which contrasted so strikingly with his insistence on precision in other people's arrangements and which Jenny now found so full of meaning.

As soon as she remembered clearly what was said, Jenny remembered also why she had protested on this of many possible occasions. She could feel again now her qualm of superstitious fear at Vincent setting off on some only partially known voyage on the anniversary of her father's last departure, from which he never returned. Training had made her reluctant to mention her father, but the sensation of foreboding at the coincidence was too strong to ignore. Trying to match Vincent's deviousness, in which she had little experience, and made nervous by anticipation of his certain annoyance, she said the very thing calculated to bring down his anger on her unlucky head.

"Father always knew exactly where he was going and when he would be back. He never needed to let me know through secretaries." And then, keeping it up to put off the evil moment which she saw approaching in the warning lowering of Vincent's level brows, she chattered anxiously on. "Except, that is, the last journey he made. And that was changed at the last moment. He was meant to fly straight back from New York and they changed it—I never did know why—to a stop at Gander."

"They needed to pick up another flight engineer," Vincent

304

said sharply, defensively. And they stared at each other in an echoing void of astonishment, she at his knowledge of this fact and he at his mistake. There was no reason why Vincent should not have picked up this important detail from his colleagues, but there was still less reason why he should never have told the person most concerned.

"Oh," she said blankly, "was that it? But why did you never tell me?"

And round this question there gathered again the echoing silence of dismay.

Then, in Jenny's increasingly clear hindsight, Vincent gathered his resources together and began, with that assumption of controlled patience that covered his long disappointment in his marriage, to speak. She could almost hear again the sadly indrawn sigh.

"Jenny, why do you try to be clever? It's always so obvious, like a small child making sly excuses that only *he* doesn't know have been used a million times before. You know quite well you were not thinking of your father. That's just one of your usual pretences. The whole point is your insane jealousy of poor old Mona. Ever since you got that wild idea into your head about her and me, you've badgered and carried on about it at every opportunity. Can't you see that you ought to try at least to control your crazy hatred of the poor girl? It's an obsession with you, and you know quite well why. But if I'm prepared to live like this with your coldness and strangeness, I can't see why you can't accept what is, after all, your own nature. I do wish you'd drop this constant pretence that you are ill-treated; it would make everything so much easier for both of us. And the way you drag in your father, it's almost indecent sometimes. We all know you adored him, really in a rather unhealthy sort of way, and it's quite clear why you connect him in your fantasies with Mona, since you've got this notion about her stuck in your head. You can't see it, of course, but everybody else can, that it's all your father's fault, the way he brought you up. If you could see that you might succeed in getting away from him, becoming more normal. You'd rather live with him than me, that's perfectly obvious to everyone but you, but at least you could try to hide it, appear

305

more like other people. And why take it out all the time on me? I'm just the unlucky fellow who isn't your precious father. . . ."

His voice rose gradually, losing its patient tone, losing resignation and slipping from self-pity to anger, hinting at a pathological relationship during her adolescence, suggesting an incurable inability in her to maintain an adult relationship with him, with anyone. It went on without pause for a very long time, interspersed with that "everyone" who was called in to be witness to her instability but who was never identified, and with talk of Mona, who was always poor Mona or fat old Mona or blousy Mona. It went on longer than she ever remembered at one time, until Foster came in to say the car was waiting and Vincent turned to the door, shrugging, and went without saying goodbye.

She held it fast now. He must have made telephone calls between leaving home and taking the connecting flight to London, because several people, including the Sandfords and the Folliots, came to see her to make sure she was all right, as they said, mentioning that Vincent had asked them to do so. And she recalled the conversations, in which they covertly observed her and she said anything that came into her head to keep off her relations with Vincent, talking of his journey to Prague, for which she had seen the air ticket. On his return it appeared that he was in Warsaw and not in Prague, and then it all began. A few days later the parcel of books was mislaid. A few days later still the singing bird was found, incomprehensibly, up here on the main landing and then, morning after morning was lying on its side in its usual place. And the Fosters began to look at her askance and to pretend, with heavy tact, to notice nothing. Other people, too, began to ignore things carefully, things that did not exist but which Vincent had, it was now obvious, warned them to expect. She supposed they had found what they were told they would find. Once she said abruptly to Teddy Sandford at a party that she could hardly lift the singing bird off its base, it was so heavy, so she could not have carried it up the stairs, but that proved to be one of the things Teddy had not been told about, for he stared and shuffled and suggested kindly that she should go away for a rest.

It must have been a week or so after his return that Vincent produced sleeping pills which he said were recommended as reliable and would keep her from being so restless. They were followed, after the first fit of hysterical weeping, by daytime sedatives, accompanied by repeated cautions, warnings, reminders that she should not forget to take these medicines, should watch her tongue, try to control her imagination. The rest was repetition: quiet, relentless repetition hammering at her growing fears. Pretended concern and sympathy became pity, pity became anxiety and gradually turned into hopelessness in Vincent's well-thought-out playacting.

It was now no longer possible to avoid the great question of why. Nor was it any longer doubtful what the answer must be. Jenny rose slowly from the armchair and drifted to the window on the weather side, where streams of water ran like a torrent of inconsolable grief, distorting the vision of trees increasingly green. Now everything could be seen to be budding, not only the early shoots on the lilac seen days ago by Polter through the hall window. That lilac was showing points of flower buds as well as leaves; it stood in an especially sheltered spot.

The pouring rain, shimmering and shifting, filtering her view, was lovely, with a clean sluicing and, gazing out at her world of solitude, there was no single moment at which Jenny reached the truth. But presently as she turned into the room once more, she knew that nothing had been an accident up to the crash that removed Vincent from life. All was planned, all calculated, except for the second of misjudgement on the main road near Wrexham, far away to the north of here.

A depth of baseness opened up before Jenny's dazed senses like a crevasse in great, dark rocks. A tumult of knowledge, of discovery, shook her whole soul. Hundreds of details clattered round her as they fell into place, making a clear, tidy pattern out of chaotic ignorance: the pieces of the puzzle slid together. Now the mirror held up by a sorcerer for her to stare into for the ten years of her adult life was shattered and she could see clearly past it into a gulf of perfidy in which her own life had been swallowed up and, but for a merciful chance, almost lost. She had not even been a tool in the hand of a magician but simply one of his requisites. Not even for use: a piece of property on the possession of which depended Vincent's opportunity to deceive and betray. He needed to be married to Maculan's daughter in order to use Maculan's work and to cover a crime.

She sat still for a long time, until after dark, unable to move, lamed with exhausting thought.

CHAPTER XXIII

ALMOST EVERYONE would deny the possibility of such a situation as Jenny Cheyney's continuing for years in the modern world, although the same people can see about them those who live their whole lives in similar states of deliberate ignorance. As a generalisation about others, the elastic adaptability with which subjective conceptions cover hard fact is easily agreed to; it becomes threatening only where the circumstances are anything like the observer's own. Since most people are married and since most marriages are very different from the realness of them felt from inside, any suggestion of long deception or self-deception in marriage is normally greeted with indignant disbelief. The denial is always the strongest from those who most deceive themselves or allow themselves to be deceived.

The instinct to defence by ignorance is very strong, but it brings with it its own inherent danger. Jenny Cheyney first allowed herself—and then forced herself—to see the facts of her life because she had lived with a gibbering mask of that danger for years; the danger is that unreality about one group of facts, as soon as it becomes difficult to maintain, can flood into other areas of the mind and eventually submerge the mind altogether. The fear of insanity was stronger in Jenny than the fear of facing reality; she knew from experience how inexact are the boundaries between one unreality and pervading, uncontrollable loss of reason. Most people who live in self-deception never discover this danger, which hardly exists in lives where very little ever happens except what is expected and can be absorbed. The conflict between real life and expectation is usually artificial and caused by belief in continual and mostly commercial assurances of a possible perfection; the real circumstances of the majority of nervous patients are not unbearable, as the sufferer supposes. They simply cannot be made to fit an impossible perfectionism.

Jenny was fortunate in the physical circumstances of her life, which were easy and settled; since the lies in her life were real deceptions and not fantasies, she might otherwise have gone mad. The accident that forced her to face reality was the same event that saved her: she came gradually to the realization of her good fortune, but the immediate effect was a desire to escape her own researches and a great, bleak, heavy weariness. It was almost dark, the downpour had set in for the night when at last Jenny switched on the lights in her bedroom and an image of the scene indoors instantly appeared from outside the windows against the rain-laced evening. She became aware of intense loneliness at the sight of that reflexion hanging in the dark air, coloured, warm but inhabited only by herself. She went downstairs, turning on lights as she reached them until in the side room there bulked the unfamiliar shape of a new acquisition that promised release from solitude. She turned on the television set, trying to remember what the installing mechanic had showed her, and was at once included in the bluish flashing wonderland of visual advertising.

This was delightful, a pleasure increased by its unreality. Jenny was quite without desire for many of the things offered, half of them she had never even heard of. Coming fresh to such propaganda from a real and serious threat to her inmost self, it seemed to her simply a series of gay, nonsensical notions. However, the animated pictures with their absurd catch phrases and catchy little tunes were replaced after a few minutes by a stern-faced man sitting behind a table who was disturbed and angry about something in a strident and poorly modulated voice. The way he talked—she did not discover what the subject was—but his manner reminded her of Vincent in his blackest moods, so she turned the switch and he was swept off in a dwindling star of light into silence.

If only Mark were here, she thought, and even the crackle of a newly lit fire could not disperse her isolation within the house and the house itself enclosed in its ring of trees and veiled in impenetrable, streaming dark. Others went away but she stayed here. Mark went away, Vincent frequently went

310

away, before their time her father had left the house, and before them for hundreds of years other unknown men had left this solitary enclosure for foreign lands. Long voyages stretched away, discoveries of strange places, knowledge of foreign ways and tongues, romantic or terrible adventures had come full circle back to this place, incommunicable to those who remained always static in the home. Local history recorded generations of sons from this staid dwelling who sailed away to return changed, or to leave their names written in the waters of all the oceans of the globe, their bones on every shore imaginable. Some were privateers, some even pirates, some Queen's men and King's men, one or two joined the old merchant companies in the Far East, for the establishment of a Cathay Traders' Guild was mentioned in Folliot's chronicle. Several joined the Honourable John Company, at least one of whose servants from here was murdered with abominable tortures by wild hill men in northern India. Later, a sailor by means no longer known, found himself in Amritsar during the Mutiny and was massacred there. The last heir of the family who owned the place before Jenny's father went down in the *Hampshire* in 1916, and it was the death of his bereaved parents that left the house abandoned. Jenny's reverie fastened on the thought of this tragic young figure, for he, too, was an only child, like herself, and she attached him to her own fate in her mind because, like Mark, who had seeded his being in her heart, he went to sea when the terrible adventure of this century called him with its cruel and wonderful power.

It was fitting, mysteriously right, that the house belonged now to people who came from a distant land to take up an allegiance in this place the fervour of which those past wanderers would have understood. It seemed to Jenny that the house needed an active, conscious love at this sad and confused moment of its history when the taking-for-granted, almost contemptuous affection of stay-at-homes was not enough to prevent disloyalties like Vincent's. Of the three who came to this refuge in the scattering explosion of war, two were now dead at the hands of their enemies and only Jenny was left; she did not question that her parents both died in the service of their new fealty, for the allegiance that Vincent had denied. For whom or why Vincent committed his treason hardly interested his widow; it was the fact of disloyalty that mattered. It was clear that it was undertaken for interests opposed to those of his own people, and the extreme secrecy of the entire process proved to her candid view that it must be wrong, even if a case could be made for those other interests. In less fortunate countries loyalties can really be divided and it is possible to be condemned a traitor and remain honourable. But not here, where anything that needs reform can indeed be altered; that made the rejection of natural allegiance unreasonable, an act of deliberate hatred and the sign of a deep and base corruption of the mind.

Jenny had not spoken aloud in the way she now felt since the death of her father. She learned during her school days to keep quiet about such sentiments, which would have been found ridiculous by all her friends. This reticence did not change her deep belief, founded in the contrast between Britain, which she thought of as England, and the Balkan confusion from which they came. The years of a long colloquy with Maculan fixed forever an ancient chronicle of recurring warfare, unrest and tyrannous, arbitrary government in Rumania, where centres of civility and culture maintained themselves with constant strain unsafely in an alien disorder. Jenny knew and consciously valued her adopted country because she was aware in blood and nerves and memory of the lack of that order, of those duties and customs that seem sometimes to natives to be outworn and unnecessary. To anyone of Jenny's heritage the betrayal of England must be the denial of civilization itself. It was as simple as that for Jenny.

Her own dim memories of the university town in Transylvania were rather of a pervasive atmosphere than of single events; of clear events the only important one was departure. The going away of her mother she did not recall; one day the Limmerts took her out and when they came back to the newly bought house in which restoration made adventurous excitements for the child, her mother was no longer there. Nor was there a moment of realisation that she was gone forever; in answer to her questions the return was postponed again and again. Her father spent every minute he could with his daughter, and before the exploration of the house was anywhere near exhausted, there was school. Only as she gradually grew into the new life did the one circumstance hidden among all the others become clearer, that her mother was lost. The putting off was replaced, without the child noticing it, by an apprehension of grief and remorse in her father that kept her silent for his sake. The unspoken tragedy was in the webbing of their life together, woven into the older lining of unsafeness, indecision and disorder.

Just the same, Jenny thought, fumbling for a thread there, she did remember something that brought the loss of her mother into focus. The accumulation of what she remembered and what she had heard of her original home amounted to the darkness of ignorance and the threat of force. There the rulers and their servants could order any citizen to do as they wished, entirely at their pleasure. If the people, including the foremost citizens, were said to have rights, these were fictional, in imitation of other societies. Property, including professional qualifications, was held in reality only by permission, and for arbitrary imprisonment there was no redress. The city and university where their home was formed a cultivated enclave surrounded by a state of barbarism, the mass of the people being too unlettered and too sunk in miserable poverty even to conceive of education or to imagine what "rights" might be. The small educated class, tolerated by the rulers because they were useful, was almost entirely of foreign extraction like Maculan himself, and it was cut off from the abject brutality of the illiterate majority by a gulf unbridged by even the most perfunctory system of general education. They were not of different classes but were different kinds of people, speaking literally and symbolically different languages and fixed in immovable castes. All they had in common was that they were all ultimately at the mercy of the rulers. In such a society the only hope of change was escape, and this was possible only to the rich and privileged or to the gypsies.

Only once in Jenny's memory did the atmosphere of naked force native to Rumania reach as far as Maculan's escape, and she was no longer sure of the date at which this happened. It must have been during their first year in this house, for after

313

that time no messenger, no matter how well disguised, could have reached England, whether from the "government" of Rumania or from the Germans, who actually dominated the country. So the incident she mistily recalled must have taken place, at the very latest, just before the fall of France, and she supposed it was during the spring of 1940. This deduction she made because of an impression of extreme surprise in her father at the arrival of the visitors. She was, naturally, familiar with the German language from infancy and she knew they did not speak German, nor was it Hungarian, for her mother being of that strange clan, she spoke Magyar until it was buried and forgotten at school. It may have been Rumanian, which her father thought of as a dialect. Certainly it was not French. It could have been, it now occurred to her for the first time, Russian. She did not know, she only knew she had not understood a word of what was said.

Three men, seeming to her very tall, came straight in, of that she was sure, for she had been long enough in England to find it extraordinary that men should walk into a house not theirs without waiting for at least a perfunctory invitation or asking permission or perhaps taking permission for granted, as close friends do. No, these three entered this very room in perfect silence.

When they spoke it was with no pause of consideration for what was to be said: one of them began to speak and Maculan answered without hesitation but with the surprise that belonged to her memory of the visit, a surprise, almost astonishment, that they were there. It now became clear to Jenny that her father knew these men; they were not strangers, for he did not ask questions, and no names were exchanged in introduction. They could have been from his former university except that they did not speak in the tone of respect, not even reluctant respect, that anyone coming from Cluj must have used to Maculan, who was already a famous man in that part of the world. Rather, they were brisk, businesslike, she thought. Just as her father did not challenge their unceremonious entry, which evidently was to be expected of them, so the three men in their manner took some circumstances for granted; they did not start their conversation from "scratch."

314

In those days there was a writing table of Maculan's in this room and he sat at it. The three men, all much taller than he was, stood: one leaned against the panelling, one after a time sat on the arm of a chair. But they were not informal. Above all, they were not friendly and neither was her father.

This lack of an amenable quiet, although nobody raised his voice, pervaded the scene; in some sense, which the child could apprehend, these men were outside the urbanity of her father's cultivated acceptance of other people. It was in this that the old memory of some intrusion or threat of force into a domestic community, totally at odds with anything of the kind, came back to Jenny as the only occasion on which her father's account of his former home connected, and collided, with his new home and hers. These men were not only foreigners, but brought with them a quite different concept of human intercourse from the climate—sharply tasted by the still foreign child as different and agreeable—of England. If they had entered with every surface civility possible or if they had never spoken a word, they would still have brought with them some inward brutality that was not hostility but a profound *indifference*. The feeling in the air of a consciousness in the visitors of some means of coercion was so strong that the child began to cry, leaning against her father's desk chair, so that he put his arm round her to draw her to him. The hard armrest prodded painfully against her thin little ribs, but she was glad to be held. He did not otherwise take any notice of her, deliberately holding her separate from what was going on. The gesture of embracing her was that of one who assures a child that in a moment he will have attention to spare for her, if she will just be patient. All the time they went on talking, the three men and Maculan.

After some time her father got up, still holding his daughter, and moved away from the desk, becoming noticeably shorter and of slighter build than the intruders in the child's foreshortened view. He waited until there was a pause and then spoke for the first time in English, his use of the language being a part of his answer.

"You may be right in your assessment, but even if I agreed with you that this country will lose the war, I should still stay here. I know, if you will forgive me pointing it out, better than you do that the situation is threatening in several ways and that it is possible we shall go down. But I have chosen my path and nothing—certainly no argument you have used—will change that. I stay here."

At once all three men began to talk together and much more loudly. Her father waited them out although he was no longer listening. He was, the child could see, considering something else. Presently he said quietly that there was not much point in continuing the argument; he suggested that they should go. And at last, reluctantly but baffled by Maculan's coolness and simplicity, they did go, leaving with Jenny the impression of a failed reconnaisance, an unexpected setback. She knew now that the three men must have known that ultimately they could not overbear Maculan, not in this place.

Maculan, taking the child with him, followed as far as the front door and watched the three get into their car and drive away. As they disappeared, he spoke again, still in his pedantic English, which always emphasized the use of his carefully acquired idioms.

"Either they do not know what has become of Meriana or she is not in their power. If they knew for sure she were dead they would risk lying and would have promised me a reunion. But they neither know nor do they know whether I have news." He closed and locked the door and drew her away with him. "Stupid," he said to himself, shaking his head. "To come all this way without making sure about that."

That was the last time Jenny heard her mother's name. But that night and for many nights after, she knew he walked about the house for hours, unable to rest. She would hear his steps, like a sentry, on the old creaking boards of his small fortress.

After that, too, the house doors remained locked even in the daytime, and burglar alarms were included in the new electric wiring. But there was never any repetition of the visit nor did her father ever explain to Jenny what the visitors were discussing. The outcome of course, she understood, and that statement became a central point in Jenny's understanding of her father. So, too, without her knowing it at the time so clearly, did the atmosphere the three men brought with them.

316

That was a threat, Jenny judged it now, not perhaps specifically against her father but a general menace of barbarians against a civilized world. The messengers went quietly and as far as Jenny knew, they never returned. No doubt Maculan took measures against them of which Jenny knew nothing. But the outer dark approached with them. And to that gloom of ignorance, obscurantism, tyranny and corruption Vincent had allied himself. Which group or faction of tyrants Vincent was bought by did not matter in the least. He preferred their world to Maculan's, to hers, to England.

These thoughts were interrupted at last by a loud wailing from Polly, protesting at the delay in her supper. The cat was pacing up and down the hall and followed Jenny eagerly into the kitchen, with her tail up and waving, but emitting sharp cries of remonstrance. The empty kitchen reminded Jenny of another duty: the Sandfords and Mr. Folliot were coming tomorrow and this entailed, as always in a place so far from a town, the preparation of a meal. Even with Mrs. Godolphin's aid, Jenny felt ruefully that her reputation for hospitality was about to take a sharp fall.

There was some fish for Polly left from her own main meal. It was not disgusting, but mashing it with a fork Jenny felt again that shift of balance inside her and this time it was accompanied by a distinct sensation of nausea. As she opened the refrigerator door again and took out a bottle of milk, she thought of a possible reason but dismissed it at once. She poured milk into a clean bowl and put away the bottle. She picked up the two dishes of food—Polly still would hardly leave the kittens, so she must be fed in the drawing room —and carried them across the hall, all the time holding that thought away from her as impossible. I wouldn't feel anything so soon, she thought. It couldn't be. Then, in a kind of panicky joke, I should have to switch the time. The cat now purred with satisfaction and, leaving the lights on, Jenny went back into the kitchen, where the local newspaper lay on the table. It would somehow be improper to consult the *Times* on such an intimate matter; the weekly county chronicle was more domestic, more approachable. From the newspaper's date she counted carefully back and found herself unsurprised at the

317

result. She felt, as soon as it was proved by numbers, that she had known in any case. Suddenly she recalled Mrs. Foster's remarks about Norma Godolphin and began to laugh to herself, rather shocked to find that she was filled with a flood of excitement and joy.

CHAPTER XXIV

"CAN YOU not just tell me, in so many words?" urged Jenny. "You could look upon it all as just terribly, terribly embarrassing, really."

"Embarrassing? It certainly is that! If that were all!"

"I know. That's just what I mean. Ignore the rest. If I can bear to listen, you can bear to say it."

"I'm not at all sure that you can bear it."

"That man Vail should have told her."

Animosity did not suit Eileen's seductive voice, which Jenny, for some forgotten reason, thought of as "chocolatey."

"He was forbidden to." Teddy answered his wife with uncharacteristic abruptness.

"Extraordinary! Why, I should like to know? Isn't that his job? It's all his doing, after all."

"They don't tell me everything, either. I just don't know why."

"I daresay it is a general rule in such investigations," said Mr. Folliot carefully. "Come, Sandford, let us get it over."

"It's so desperately, miserably, mean!" Teddy stopped again, but nothing happened to save him. "All right. Vincent was selling everything he knew, every bloody thing, to a foreign power. Right from the start. All the time. We haven't yet computed what he cost the company but it must run, all in all, to six figures over the years." He looked quickly at Jenny, hoping perhaps that some cry or gesture would save him from going on, but she stared blankly into the dancing flames of logs burning in the white marble fireplace with the shell crowning it. "It was treason, too."

"Treason," echoed Jenny.

"As you know, much of our stuff is for defence. Vincent did

not deal with the NATO side, but he knew the contracts, what the others lacked, what we wanted from them. These things all mesh together. Just because he was selling civilian software—I can't help using some jargon—to people who might be potential enemies, he had to know where the military began and ended in their uses. Put it like this: Vincent sold an innocuous bit of measuring equipment used in mining, harbour-building, perhaps even large-scale forestry. If he gave the buyer all the illicit military info with it, the buyer could put his own people to work readapting the gadget back to its military use. He's saved years of work, his best men freed for other projects. As senior sales director Vincent was included often in discussions, negotiations not immediately his concern. He knew enough to know, when he was not told some detail, more or less how to connect it with what he did know. The very point of his not being informed could be valuable. Especially since much of our work is development. I mean, few inventions arrive out of the blue. They are worked on from their predecessors, related to past designs, or by cooperation with foreign models, improved by patents negotiated by one of the service departments from another designer in a different company. We, for instance, are still producing your father's inventions in almost their original forms, but we also make what you might call the grandchildren of Maculan's stuff. And the chief of the foreign sales department was necessarily included in much of the demonstration, testing, discussion of new adaptions. Not only did he need to be informed, there was absolutely no reason to hide anything from him, except some service stuff on the secret list. It was all *his* as much as ours. And, an important detail, Vincent's training was technical, not theoretical. He used that—we know that now, too late. He used to say he had to see things working, watch them being made, to go through the process, in order to understand them. It used to be a joke; he'd say that I understood by calculating formulas on paper but he was too stupid for that. Of course we both knew I'd lost any mathematical skill I ever had, I've been an administrator for years; that was the joke."

"I see. Yes, I see. You were grist to the mill. Whatever grist may be."

"In ten years he's done a lot of damage. Vail says they would have got him for certain, in time. But God knows when. In Vail's line, too, of course, details fit gradually together, and he says Vincent has provided answers to several things they were working on."

"Of course he says that now," said Eileen bitterly. "But if he does know, why does he keep on pestering?"

Teddy sighed heavily, not an histrionic sigh intended to stop his wife but almost an inward groan.

"It's my opinion the so-called Security Executive is incompetent. I don't believe half what they say, allege, about Vincent. They are putting things on to him because he's dead. How do we know that Vail can really attach Vincent like a label to things he's supposed to have found out? He's probably covering up a whole list of outstanding questions now there's a scapegoat!"

"That, needless to say, is quite out of the question," said Folliot with a worn precision that betrayed impatience with what was clearly not a first hearing of this view. "His keeping on is surely proof of his search being genuine."

"How d'you mean? I don't understand."

"Why does he go on looking if he has what he wants? A cover for his own loose ends?"

"Because he needs hard evidence." There was so much venom in this assertion that Jenny took in through startled nerves that Eileen's anger was fear. That Eileen should have any cause to dread Mark's questions was absurd and Jenny dismissed the impression the more easily since it conflicted with her much stronger feelings of envy and astonishment at the familiarity with which her guests spoke of Mark. They came from seeing him, could often be in the same room with him, discussed his actions as if he were just someone, anyone, they knew. Jenny possessed only his letter, she could feel it now, stiffly folded paper in her pocket, a few words, short, abrupt, almost stern with refusal to take love for granted. When the post came that morning Harry Blane was already at the door, asking if she needed anything from the town, and she scribbled so hastily a reply for him to take with him that she could not even remember what she wrote. But I can write to him again, now that I know his address in London, she assured herself; the thought was of a dizzying sweetness.

But that sudden stab of an impression that Eileen was afraid sharpened her sense of what was going on about her. Treason: the word was big with foreboding. As long as her own thoughts about Vincent remained solely hers they might be true and real for her, but, Vincent being gone, that was an end of them and of him. Described, confirmed by the words Teddy used, they became alive in a quite different sense. A private perfidy that almost destroyed her, Jenny, took on its public infamy that belonged to ancient concepts of outraged majesty, Shakesperian thunder, the awe-inspiring loom of a judge pronouncing icy condemnation to banish felons from human society. The Tower reared its dark mass as seen by a child of ten, and great doors bound with iron swung closed with a hollow boom for a lifetime. Treason was a crime more damnable than murder, the uttermost shame loaded with a thousand years of commination, its symbol the tall executioner in his black, slitted hood leaning on a great ax.

"It's no use, Eileen, we have to face it. Vincent was lying, deceiving us all from the first moment. There's no way of getting away from it."

Teddy's voice sounded ragged with anxiety, its rounded, jolly claim to be a decent fellow scraped thin by worry. Even the nursery quality of the diminuitive became suspect; it would be better to use the correct Edgar and admit the relationship to renaissance tragedy.

"I still can't . . ."

"But my dear Eileen, it is not you we are discussing," said Mr. Folliot in his driest voice. "At the moment it is our unhappy duty to inform Jenny of the position we are in."

"We still have to explain to you how all this was discovered," Teddy was quick to cover the rebuke. "I made some notes, to keep things in order. You don't mind? It must all seem to you very unfeeling. But there is just no way of putting such things gently, you understand?"

"Best get it over, as Mr. Folliot says. I have to know. And I want to know."

Teddy gave her a grateful and wondering look, and launched with stammers and pauses into a speech that was, apparently, more than half-memorised.

"It was like this. Immediately after the accident that killed Vincent, you remember that Mr. Folliot came here to clear up your—and Vincent's—affairs? The first thing he found was that there was practically no money in the bank and a number of outstanding debts. Not household things, but, for instance, the second car was not paid for."

"Second? Oh, Mona's car. That explains the letter from the insurance company!"

"There were a lot of other things—do you want me to go into details?"

"No. No, don't do that."

"There was an air-credit card issued on the company's authority and paid by us. But otherwise Vincent's travelling expenses, which were naturally heavy, seemed hardly to exist in the records. He carried other credit cards not backed by us, and he paid them cash every six months. That is very unusual, but it does happen; it wouldn't of itself have made anyone suspicious. Only the outstanding bill, when Mr. Folliot checked, turned out to have been paid over the counter as usual the very day after the accident. As you know, the car was a total wreck. Obviously, someone took the risk, the lesser risk, of paying the bill in the hope that the evidence—the credit card Vincent had with him—would be destroyed. Only it wasn't. At first Folliot assumed that the lack of money was accounted for by an extravagance that certainly wasn't visible in the way this place was run, and he thought he could guess what that was."

"Mona," supplied Jenny.

"Precisely. In fact, the records of a foreign bank account were found in her flat, into which she paid regular sums. Whether she knew the source of Vincent's generosity, we shall never know. But these payments were not nearly enough to explain the shortage. It's clear that Vincent was salting money away himself. We don't know where, but obviously abroad; it would have been found in this country. Until he discovered the payment of the main credit-card bill, which Vincent himself cannot have paid, Folliot suspected simply that Vincent had been fiddling his accounts with us. That would have been bad enough, but there was more. There were papers in the cupboard by Vincent's desk. Lists of components, specifications and the like. They were locked up, of course, but even if they had been found in his possession he could have explained them. Perhaps with difficulty, but he could have done. Only he was no longer there to explain. And I think you will agree with us that what might look risky to an outsider was not really dangerous. Vincent was a very orderly man, he kept his drawers locked and you were the only person who could have gone to his desk and understood enough to be puzzled by these papers—if you had a key, that is. We were sure, of course, that you would not do that, and so would Vincent have been. In the circumstances, we were sure of that. Hm. No need to go into *that* further.

"So, we have the account paid after Vincent's death and we have some business papers, not in themselves too suspicious. Clear so far? Now come two small things. In this wall cupboard in the panelling of Vincent's room, there was a little cassette. One of a kind without a key, that opens by a number sequence. After trying everything possible the cash box was broken open. The only thing in it was a slip of paper with a list of numbers on it. I may as well say at once that it has still not been deciphered, but the security police believe that it must be some message in the pipeline at the time Vincent left on his last journey. Again, it looks risky but much less risky than anything kept in his office, and probably the box was used only when some message awaited an answer, and was then destroyed. This was all very puzzling, naturally, and distressing; Mr. Folliot will tell you himself how he sat and thought it over. Then a way of testing occurred to him that would not reflect on Vincent if he should prove to be wrong."

"You mean, if I should prove to be wrong," put in Folliot.

"What? Oh, yes, I see. Folliot telephoned me. He gave me the list of numbers in groups of seven digits, and he read out some of the documents. I then went to check. The numbers meant nothing and still mean nothing to us, to the chief engineers, to the accountants. The lists of specifications we found without much trouble. But they turned out to be things that had nothing at all to do with any contract Vincent was then concerned with. And most of them were service matters from the secret list.

"There was no course open to us but to report Folliot's

324

findings to the proper authority. And that we did. Folliot went to London, and a few days later, as you know, Vail came here to start his investigations."

"A deception that nothing less serious than a major crime could excuse. It has been much on my mind ever since. I hope, my dear Jenny, that you can bring yourself to believe that I wished only to save you unhappiness. If I had told you my suspicions and they then proved groundless you would have suffered bitter anxiety as well as your private grief. So I reasoned."

Mr. Folliot was looking at her and clearly awaiting a reply to his confession. At last Jenny found one.

"I'm glad you have gone back to calling me by my Christian name," she said.

"You never saw this cassette with the code opened, Jenny?" asked Teddy.

"No, never. But as you hint—suggested—I was not likely to."

"It wasn't new. About five years old, the manufacturer says. We reckon that Vincent began keeping any such memoranda in the house here, instead of at the office, after there was a security scare. That was five or six years ago. A typist in Vincent's office got mixed up with an executive from another company, and he in turn got into trouble in Poland. That must have been a shock to Vincent, a warning of how easily things can go wrong.

"It is fairly obvious," continued Folliot, "that apart from such matters as figures, things that nobody could carry in his head, there was never any evidence in this country. And whatever Vincent was forced to keep a record of here in the house he certainly disposed of as soon as it was out of date. Otherwise, Vincent must have done everything on his journeys abroad. He never met anyone in this country, never communicated, probably had only one means of contact for emergencies. At least, so the security people now think. There may not even have been even one contact until about three years ago."

"I thought you said five years ago?"

"No," said Mr. Folliot, "it is confusing certainly. But the bank records show quite clearly—the manager was most oblig-

325

ing and waived the formalities, since I have known him for many years—that the change in Vincent's financial arrangements must have begun just over three years ago. At that time the joint account was closed, replaced by a single-signature account in Vincent's sole control with limited drawing rights for household expenses to Miss Laver. At the same time Vincent ceased to use this account for anything except the running expenses for Grove House."

"Three years ago."

"I have been unable to find any indication of a cause for the change."

"Perhaps his, er, his confederates wished it?" suggested Teddy.

"Unlikely. It meant their direct intervention. So very incriminating if it came out. As, of course, it did."

"We don't know that Vincent's credit cards were always paid direct by his fellow conspirators. They may—and I think myself it's more likely—have given him cash to pay the accounts when he met them abroad."

"You are right! We only know that the final payment was made by someone other than Vincent. But that still does not explain why he ever changed his banking arrangements from a perfectly ordinary current account to a method that must have aroused curiosity if anyone at Tantham and Maculan became aware of it, if only because he informed no one."

"I know why he changed," said Jenny.

"You know!" They all stared as if Jenny's participation in their reconstruction of Vincent's life were somehow out of character. Her passivity was so much taken for granted that it occurred to none of them that she might be a source of practical information about a man she had lived with for ten years. In the kindest possible way, they simply overlooked her. Vincent's carefully, slowly modelled picture of his wife had so deeply taken root in their view of her that it did not appear, even to Mr. Folliot, as a possible part of his disguise. But no sooner did Jenny think of protesting or explaining than another thought, of a cunning that surprised her, supplanted a mild rebellion. The less reality she possessed for friends and neighbours, the more would the already living child be taken

326

for granted as part of herself; it would be swathed in her own veil of uncertain identity.

"Have you found something?" Folliot turned to stare about the meticulously arranged drawing room as if some discovery must be visible. They were in this room because, being so little used, it did not yet share the rapid slackening of domestic order, and here there was little prospect of any noticeable change. As if recognizing this, Folliot looked at the door to the hall, toward the stairs and the upstairs room where his own unwilling exploration took place. "Did I miss something important up there?" he murmured almost to himself.

"Vail said nothing . . ."

"He was frightened."

"But of what? Nothing had changed!"

"It was me."

"You!" The explosive sound was so incredulous as to sound derisive.

"No, not *of* me." Jenny stopped. Possible words swam away into a dark sensation of oppression that was engulfed in the remembrance of the past. A cloud of unknowing, the phrase presented itself, and she felt the suffocation of fear that prevented her from expressing herself, as it always had done.

"He was afraid," she wailed and wanted to go on, finish sensibly with some indication of Maculan's death, that threatening slip of the tongue three years and more ago. But as she sought for words, the reality of Vincent's fear throttled her, as if it still existed after Vincent's physical death, and she was pierced with a pang of anguished pity for him as for herself. The menace he must have always carried about with him seemed to lurch against her like a big and untamed animal, and she cried out and blundered against the painted Venetian console, gripping its jutting rim with one urgent hand. There was a dry, small crack under her fingers and a sliver of the old wood, flaked with gilt, broke off.

She stared at this slip of crumbling wood, forcing the nightmare away.

"I can't," she gasped.

"Can't?"

"Talk about it."

She could hear the half-panicky exasperation of their voices, but the effort of trying to speak was too much.

"You need a drink," said Teddy, and she could hear him clearly now.

"There's nothing in here."

"I'll go and get the tray. I know where everything is."

There was the chinking of bottles and glasses as Teddy crossed the hall. He bumped the white door open with his shoulder, reappeared, looked about him impatiently and found a low table where he put down the heavy tray with a puff of exaggerated relief. Eileen assembled glasses, but it was Teddy who brought her a drink. She did not like the taste of whisky but found it quickly reviving.

Somewhere in the house a clock chimed the hour, wrongly, and Folliot took out his half hunter from a waistcoat pocket with a neat, practised move of the hand.

"You are in no state to . . ."

"Oh! Please, Mr. Folliot. I'm all right. That can wait until I . . . perhaps I can write it down. But do go on. Coming all this way!"

"I fear you cannot understand the documents I gave you unless I explain at least a little, in outline," he continued. "But unless you are sure I will not distress you, it would be better to postpone further business."

"It's only personal things that upset me," she said humbly. "Please go on."

Mr. Folliot examined her face quietly; she seemed, and indeed was, quite calm again. In fact, he noticed how much better she looked than she did only a few weeks before, in spite of the slight attack of nerves that was only too natural in the circumstances, and, considering Jenny's temperament, not a matter for surprise.

"I will certainly keep away from personal matters," he said, smiling slightly. "I, too, find business easier to discuss. I want to try to explain the results of this shocking affair which you will find set out in the internal report I have given you. By itself, you may not understand it."

He was seated beside the bookcase desk, the sloping cover of which was let out and on which his papers were laid. He ordered these exactly in line with the inlaid border on the shining wood to give himself time to consider his words, just as he would have done in the board room or his own office.

"You will appreciate that Maculan's reorganization of what was formerly a family concern involved what is called making the company public. However, Tantham and Maculan shares are held, apart from ourselves, by other companies concerned with our work and by two merchant banks, one of which is controlled to a certain extent by government funds. All the holdings are covered by what in effect are agreements not to allow the stock to be dispersed. About ten days ago one of the commercially held blocks was put on the market without warning."

"Disgraceful breach of a confidential agreement," said Teddy.

"Just so. But it has happened. I know Morgan-Bebbington well. A senior advisor died recently, upon whom he greatly relied for sound counsel. And they have been having a great deal of labour trouble. He tends to nervousness in any case. It was panic rather than calculation. What happened essentially is what is misnamed rumour. We may suppose that in spite of the utmost discretion by everyone concerned, an officer of the Special Branch is seen with someone, or going in and out of somewhere. Or possibly an official of the Security Executive leaves London for some weeks and it becomes known where he has gone. That is enough; things are overheard, combined, people talk. It is pointless to condemn the process; that *is* commerce. The ignorant say 'someone is bearing the market,' because the ignorant who love such half-understood phrases must have a focus for blame when things go wrong. That is quite false, for the complex of open secrets is, in essence, the market, and the rumours that move confidence up and down are not wild gossip but, most unfortunately in our case, hard fact. Moreover it is a well-known state of affairs that companies such as ours are frequently fully extended in research costs, sometimes for long periods, and this extension sometimes coincides for months or even years with contract negotiations not yet completed or not yet financed. It is not unknown that one of the Service Departments recently informed us that it was dropping its tentative interest in a piece of research that is about to come to fruition. This has happened

329

before, but it comes now at a conjunction with these other matters which is more than unfortunate. A very large investment has lost its obvious potential customer before it could prudently be shown to any other possible user. Do you follow me? Do you get my general drift?"

"Yes. Yes, I think so. I wonder." Jenny's tone was abstracted. "I wonder if someone in that Defence Department could be a friend of Professor Polter's?"

"Polter? The television historian? What on earth has he to do with this?"

"Nothing, I suppose," Jenny answered Eileen's irritable question. "I'm sorry I interrupted. Do go on, Mr. Folliot."

Folliot bent his head, accepting the apology while expressing doubt as to Jenny's capacity for seriousness.

"As matters stand," he said resignedly, almost ceasing the effort to make himself clear, "Tantham and Maculan, big though we are, is poised at an arrow point converging between the confidence of our associates and the extension of our resources."

"Does that mean . . . are you trying to tell me that the company may fail?"

Both surprise that she had after all understood him and habitual discretion kept Mr. Folliot silent for a space. But at last he decided.

"Yes," he said.

"You do understand that this conversation is entirely confidential?" said Teddy hastily.

"It's all the fault of that blundering . . ."

"Do let's be fair," said Jenny, rising quickly from her chair. "We can at least put the blame where it belongs. The destroyer was Vincent."

Eileen reared quickly up, sank back and gave out a slight sound that hung in the air as a moan.

"Clearly I am warning you of what may conceivably happen. Not of anything imminent, or by any means certain. There is a long way to go and much to be tried before anything so appalling could actually occur."

"There are several possible solutions." Teddy gave the impression of chattering. "Even if the situation worsens. And even if, what is more dangerous than anything, our difficulties become public property."

"By 'public property' you mean 'publicity,'" Folliot instructed Jenny while addressing Sandford. "The kind of knowledge I have been referring to is of another order. Press publicity would, it hardly needs emphasizing, be a catastrophe. But a quite unlikely one; discretion is in the interests of all parties, including that of the reputable financial journalists."

"The point is," said Teddy carefully, "that personal discretion is needed from us all. Probably only a disclosure with some *personal* flavour could make a general news story."

"Such as my stone?" asked Jenny. All three of her guests frowned at this second apparently meaningless interjection, and their brows expressed anew all their past fears as to Jenny's stability.

"No, I'm not crazy," she assured them hardily. "I mean the ancient fertility stone that Mark and I discovered after the storm brought down one of the beeches. Surely you haven't forgotten it?"

"But how could that. . . ?"

"I will tell you," said this new Jenny. "One of my neighbours, a retired Colonel Bartle, is the Chairman of the County Historical Society. He came to see the stone. And he brought a reporter of the local paper with him."

"I should think it unlikely for such a local affair to be connected with the company," pronounced Mr. Folliot.

"But wait a moment," objected Teddy. "This local man may be the Press Association reporter here. I had better go and see him."

"Wait. Wait. This visit was when?"

"Sunday before last."

"Then it has almost certainly aroused no general interest."

"But if somebody sees it who knows about the rumours going around? Connects it with a name, either Maculan or Cheyney?"

"That sounds awfully farfetched, Teddy," said Eileen.

"Not at all. You know nothing about how the press works. That's exactly how things do happen."

331

"I do not understand you." An anxiety was to be heard behind the severity of Mr. Folliot's voice.

"Look, there is a story buzzing about. Nobody is supposed to mention it for reasons of public policy as well as libel. But every journalist in Fleet Street worth his pay is looking for a way out of the gentleman's agreement not to use it. Those agreements are always between *editors*, and some of *them* don't really like their own silence. Once broken, the line can't be held."

"We must bow to your experience, naturally. You have far more dealings with the press than I do."

"I don't say it will happen. Only that we all have to be very careful. And care includes not offending anyone who asks questions, while telling him nothing." Teddy looked at his wife as he said this. "We have to bear in mind the attitudes of the general public. A great many people do not equate industrial undertakings with the national welfare. Especially in defence matters, because this is a time of pacifism and many people who emotionally reject militarism do not differentiate between Algeria and our own defense of these islands. And while we're on this subject, there is another danger. There is the chance of some pacifist member of Parliament putting a loaded question in the House."

"That is a possibility always in my mind."

"It's incredible that the powers that be could let a company like Maculan simply go bankrupt!" cried Eileen. "Can't we use our influence to force the security people to call off their bloodhounds? After all, nobody can be tried!"

"That would be the most perilous course to take," Folliot replied. "Not only because it is the duty of men like Vail to find out just what happened and how it could happen. But, as well, because much public money is, and has been, involved. The authorities have a right and a duty to know what became of it."

"But I have nothing to do with the taxpayers' money! Why does he keep questioning me?"

"Not only you, my dear." Folliot's voice was weary with the repetition.

"Because they've got to know," said Teddy patiently. "He's tracking back into the past."

332

"Tracking back into the past!" Eileen almost wept. "It sounds so sinister!"

"There's no other way of finding out how Vincent came to Maculan."

"But we know how. That wretched man Jackson introduced him."

Jenny saw Folliot glance at Teddy and slightly shake his greying head. Teddy lifted his solid shoulders helplessly and went to the tray with the bottles.

"You don't mind, Jenny?"

"Of course," she said. "Be barman, give us all a drink." She moved about switching on lamps against the gathering evening which loomed now in heavy mists of dark velvet where all day it had been silvery white.

"Do you always get this fog after a downpour?" Eileen looked out and shivered. "It's uncanny."

"Usually," said Jenny. "It will be gone by morning, but I'm afraid you will have to drive slowly down the hill. It's rather treacherous and patchy sometimes."

She edged past the wheeled tray loaded with homely tea things left there by Mrs. Godolphin before her departure. "Nobody ate a proper tea," she mourned, and laid a hand against the brown kitchen pot, incongruous in the mannered surroundings. It was still slightly warm.

"It's the time of year," she said.

"What is?"

"This mist after rain. The first signs of spring. It will probably rain again tomorrow.

"There is one thing." Jenny turned now to Mr. Folliot. "Perhaps the main thing, for me at least, that we haven't talked of."

"You mean for whom Vincent was—doing all this?" He intended to say "for whom Vincent was betraying us all," but feared to sound histrionic.

"Oh, no. That is fairly obvious. And it hardly matters—to me, you know."

They did not know and they showed that with shocked, almost suspicious disapproval in their looks.

"You will find much detail in the documents I brought for

you." Folliot looked about him. "Your set does not appear to be here."

"I left them in the other room."

"There are an analysis of the financial position, but copies, too, of the reports as far as they have been divulged to us, from the security police."

"I'll get them," said Teddy. "I'd like to keep them under my eye until they are under lock and key."

"I may read them this evening."

"Ah, yes. Well, of course, there is nobody here who would steal them. . . ." He stopped, struck by the tremendous inappropriateness of that assurance.

"Any more," finished Jenny quietly. The fire needed more logs and she dragged some out of the log box, two days ago vacated by Polly. She crouched down in front of the fireplace, sniffing the aromatic ghost of apples as she brushed the dust off her hands. "They haven't been properly dried out." She faced them again. "The thing I need to know is why Vincent did this."

"Why!" In spite of Folliot's control, there was relief in the exclamation.

"Don't you feel you have to know why?" she insisted, misinterpreting his expression.

"I do indeed," he sighed. "It is something I fear we may never discover. Only if Vincent had survived the crash and we could have asked him would an answer have been possible. And, God forgive us, we can hardly wish for that."

Eileen made once again that strange, small moaning sound and Jenny shuddered visibly, putting up a protective hand before her face.

"D'you think it could have been envy?" hazarded Teddy slowly. "I mean, he may have felt that we were born to —something—that *he* must fight for?"

"You two were born to security, you and Eileen. I was not. Maculan was catapulted out of it. Jenny, surely, was repeatedly exposed to fearful uncertainty. Indeed, to my bitter remorse, she still is."

"Yes, I know you were yourself a 'scholarship boy,' my dear chap. And it is our policy, has been since Maculan joined the

334

company, to reward ambition and hard work rather than inheritance." Teddy was visibly floundering in elusive imponderables. "And I know the old man judged me more strictly than others just because I seemed to be getting an assured job from my father. It's one of the things I've always been pretty proud of, as a matter of fact. But Vincent may not have felt all that as real. He could have looked upon it as hypocrisy. What I'm trying to say is, he may always have felt envy from inside his mind at not having been born and brought up in favourable circumstances, so that he was never able to get outside this obsession and recognize that he'd gone beyond it, that he could discard it. That his feeling of inferiority didn't fit any more with his real position in the company, in the world. Irrational. Just the way he *was*, and he never questioned its validity."

"But he was proud of his achievement," said Eileen, half to herself. "He enjoyed it, almost boasted of it when he first came. I remember."

"But there is something in what Teddy says," agreed Jenny quickly. "In some way Vincent didn't believe in the reality of what he'd achieved. In some deep part of his mind he seemed to think it was a trick, a kind of magician's spell that worked without him understanding how. It might fail, so he constantly had to test it out. . . ."

"We can no longer assess the springs of character. I prefer myself to stick to a more pragmatic explanation. Vincent probably made a contact before poor Jackson suggested to Julius that he might come to us, when his future was open and he might well feel in need of, let us say, a patron. Then, when his job was arranged, either he did not trust his luck to hold or he did not think far enough in advance to drop his alternative friends at once. By the time his civilian life was settled, it was too late. He was too deeply compromised to risk exposure by refusing to go on."

"Yes, you are probably right." Teddy was glad to retreat from his excursions into fantasy. He began to rise and the others moved with him.

"It's dreadful to leave you alone like this," said Eileen vaguely.

335

They found the hall in gloom at five o'clock, outer fog fading into inner dark. Wall lamps came alight to push at the muffled evening with soft, pale enclosures of light.

"I don't know how you can live alone like this, especially since the Fosters went."

"I'm used to it."

"But what do you find to do all by yourself?"

"I work," said Jenny.

Work, she thought, when the door was closed and locked. All those men and their families; the Apprentices' Scholarships, the Music Society. Many of them own their own houses, built them. How can they ever get such jobs again, in this part of the country?

She wandered back into the warm and lighted room; the cigar smoke made her go to the nearest window to raise the lower sash and let in the soft, cold damp that smelled of grass, dank moss, a faint spicy tree smell, a pervasive smell from cows. She drew it right down. I knew before they told me, she thought, and that assurance of her own common sense was a comfort.

"Of course, she knew," said Teddy above the humming of the car. "I thought that was clear, didn't you, Folliot?"

"It was my impression that she's rather thick with Vail," said Eileen.

"It would not be remarkable if Jenny knew; she has much time for reflection. I agree that she clearly was not surprised."

"What I was afraid of was reproaches, and I don't mind admitting it."

None of them added to this theme.

"But she looked, somehow, changed," said Eileen slowly, her quite real if patronising liking and sympathy for Jenny overcoming the irritable concerns of the last few days for the moment.

"It would be a remarkable person who was not changed by such events."

Eileen allowed them to suppose that this was the kind of change she noticed in Jenny. But the events of the last few weeks were calculated to make Jenny, if possible, more nervously reserved, more unsure of herself than before; a complete collapse of her nervous system would not have been surprising. But Eileen had the impression of a still muffled and tentative but strong and perhaps growing current of vibrant energy in place of, or underneath, Jenny's passivity. And this she found very strange indeed. The very manner of Jenny saying simply that she was working was strange. Only a few weeks before she would have—she did—deny any professionalism in her sculpture; she disguised her own seriousness as well as her talent by allowing the contemptuous term "hobby" to be used for what was, and Eileen was consciously aware of this by now, the purpose of living to Jenny. The protective secrecy was so entirely dropped that not even an assertion of change remained; she was working at her trade and that was all.

"Don't you agree, darling?"

"Sorry. I wasn't listening."

"Teddy was obligingly disagreeing with me," explained Folliot from behind Eileen's head. "I was saying that I blamed myself now, tardily, for having allowed Cheyney to adopt Jenny and her inheritance so quickly, without any scrutiny."

"If you had interfered," replied Eileen, "it would have meant a delay of only a month or so at most. Vincent would have married Jenny anyway."

"You think so? I feel now I ought to have insisted on a wait of some time. Perhaps as long as several years while the child went to university."

"It's not like you to be illogical. Why should you have done any such thing? It never occurred to any of us, and Vincent would have got round her if it had. It didn't even occur to her father to object to the friendship or flirtation or whatever you'd call it."

"It is true he was paying her some attention the previous summer," pointed out Teddy.

"But that was a first little schoolgirl romance. Even so, Julius watched them with what was no more than a half-jealous, half-amused tolerance that summer. But if there'd been any sign of Cheyney declaring himself, of becoming serious, Julius would have looked at a proposed suitor for his girl with a different eye."

"Well, as far as I recall there was no sign at all of more than the only young bachelor dancing a bit with the available girl who just happened to be the daughter of his employer; what else would one expect? The first time I noticed any marked attention was, I seem to connect it in my memory, with Christmas. And Maculan said nothing then that I remember."

"I don't believe I noticed much myself, even then. I do vaguely recall something during the summer holidays previous, because I compared the picnics and tennis flirting with my own girl who is, of course, just about the same age and she was—so I seem to have it from my wife at the time—in the same stage with Cheyney. Well, we are probably all building up unrealities that happened at other times or didn't happen at all!"

"You were quite surprised, I'm sure of that, when Vincent went straight off to see Jenny the day we got the news. That's quite clear in my mind still."

"Oh, by that time," said Eileen, "it was definitely an affair."

"No doubt the shock of Maculan's death obscured other impressions for all of us," Teddy said. "I can't claim to remember exactly what happened for the next few days, even about business matters, although there must have been a good deal of uproar."

"That is certainly the case as far as my memory reaches," agreed Folliot.

CHAPTER XXV

"YOU ARE surprised to see me again so soon," said Professor Polter on a rising note of inquiry. "But not too surprised, I hope. You know, you were quite haunting me. I was not at all astonished to get your note! It seemed very much an answer to the way I was thinking of you all the time I was in Shropshire. So I just came back here from Bridgnorth instead of going to Oxford, which is where I ought to be. I do hope you don't mind?"

"Of course not." Jenny felt helpless once again, faced with this candour that was not candid. "Only astonished that my little call was so effective. I rather gathered that you were going to dine in Shropshire so I didn't know that you would still be, if not near, at any rate on this side of the country."

"I expect I put it rather elastically. In fact I was intending to stay a few days. Long enough, anyway, for your letter to be sent on from Oxford. So here I am!"

From the uncertain outline of this explanation Jenny perceived, with the increasing acuteness of understanding that was her graduation from a long course of education, the unlikelihood of Polter's statement being exactly true. Instead of being abashed by this idea, it reminded Jenny with a fresh and steady urgency of her purpose in wishing to talk to her visitor. They were, whether or not Polter knew it or desired it, in the midst of their subject, and that was where they were going to stay.

"It's only fair to tell you at once," she said with a mild, almost pleasureable malice, "that I know."

"Know?" He was interested and amused. "Know what? Do tell!"

"I know what you were talking about when you were here before. About my husband's job. And about you."

"Me? Vincent's job? But I had nothing to do with Vincent's job!"

"Yes. You know how he came here first, what he was doing. And I know now, too."

"But of course you know what Vincent was doing. What has that to do with me—how he came here first? When I first met Vincent he was already working for the Maculan Company." His voice humoured her, but he was at the same time denying something not yet said.

"I worked it out for myself," she said steadily. "But now I have facts and figures as well. Your golf-playing business types, the hearties you talked of, they were here with long explanations, reports, analyses. They didn't like to talk openly about my father's death, naturally. That is only in the reports. But the rest, oh, we really had it all out. Why Vincent came here, why he married me. That he was a spy. A traitor."

"I just don't believe it!" Polter stared aghast, too astounded to be outraged. It was too absurdly indecent to be taken seriously. "How could anybody say such dreadful things to you?"

"You mean only *business* people could?" She shook her head slightly, smiling. She was humouring him now. "They are not so different from unbusinesslike people, only perhaps a little more conventional. In fact, I think you might rather like Mr. Folliot; he's what would at one time have been called a man of honour. Stiff, you know, very careful to tell the exact truth. And quite radical. He's put a special paper into his reports, outlining a proposal to exempt all the house loans of the staff from the credit side if the company should have to go bankrupt. I thought that rather touching. I was worrying about that sort of thing myself, but you see how important it is to understand such dreary details. Folliot knows what can be *done*."

"You're teasing me, as if it were all really true," Polter clutched at the back of a chair, "but though I can't see why you should, I don't believe you. It's one of these horror stories we read in the Sundays. Science fiction fantasy. Maculan cannot really be in any danger of insolvency! What you said about Vincent is the wild figment of an active fantasy!" He leaned sideways as if knocked off balance by the wildness of it. "And as for what you hinted about your father, words just do absolutely fail. Even if it's some kind of macabre joke, you really ought not to think such things, let alone say them!"

"You are quite right about that. They warned me not to talk about it. But naturally it's quite all right to talk to you because you know it all already."

"I do not know anything. And if you want me to believe this farrago, you will have to explain. You sound so confused, and I don't wonder, that I can't at all grasp what I am supposed to have done. Or, if it comes to that, what poor Vincent is supposed to have done."

He looked quite sternly at her, but as if trying not to laugh; rather, she imagined, as he might look at a favoured student who was constantly late with essays.

"And you know," he added, "if I'm involved, you really might at least tell me how and in what."

"I do wish you wouldn't!" she said seriously. "What I said in my note to you is quite true. I must understand, I must know, and you can explain to me. I must know why—*why* Vincent did it. You can trust me when I tell you that 'they' won't do anything to you. They say your career is over and you are ill. It would cause too great a loss of public confidence if someone like you, someone so admired and respected, so well known, of such prestige, were to be put on trial. And, I rather think too, there isn't enough evidence, hard evidence, as they say."

"Ah," he said quite easily, "your young man, I forget his name for the moment, he does believe now in my stricken state? Oh, yes, yes, I understand *now* why he was here. At the time of my first visit, I admit I did not see through him. Confused by whisky and a succession of shocks, I must have been rather slow that day. But I have since found out who he is. And he, no doubt, has made inquiries about the state of my health. What a civilised lot we are, to be sure!"

Polter moved from the support of his chair and walked with his somewhat rigid gait about the room, touching things here and there with gentle, twiglike fingers, moving the bust of Maculan in relation to the other objects on the table, disarranged by the hurried activities of Mrs. Godolphin. He twitched a curtain into a more graceful fold and stayed with his hand on it to stare out of the window at the dripping grass, the weeping trees, on which could now be seen the finest smudge of green haze in spite of the low cloud bulging almost down to their crowns, which flattened all colour into simply what contrasted with the slatey, gleaming grey. He sighed deeply and turned back to Jenny.

"But you I'm a little surprised at. He, Vail, he is only doing his rather dreadful job, but you, you little sly boots!"

"I didn't know! He told me nothing, except that I must work it out for myself. I did that. Yes." She sat down, weighted by the powerful thought of Mark bearing the inverted stigma of those least entitled to judge him. "I worked it out for myself, after your visit."

"But if you didn't tell him, let him know, how was he here to greet me, as it were?"

"He wasn't here to greet *you*," she said surprised. "He was waiting for someone—unknown—to get in touch with me."

At this he stared, and although his eyes opened and his lips, too, so that he presented a study of a man gaping, Jenny felt sure that he was really very surprised; his look of astonishment was a part of overacting that was long since second nature, but the reaction itself was not invented.

"You see," she explained, "when Vincent was killed all kinds of details were seen by outsiders, by Mr. Folliot, for one, for which there was no reasonable explanation. I suppose your friends who sent you here didn't think of that?"

"I'm quite sure they did," he replied slowly, thinking this out. "And I ought to have done, too." He sat down carefully, in a chair opposite Jenny's so that he could examine her face. "You say it was this Folliot who discovered some—what? Some discrepancy, documents that ought not to have been in Vincent's office? Not you?"

"Not in his office. There was no evidence there. Here, in the house. Mr. Folliot came to help clear up papers. You know, insurance things, a will perhaps. And things like patent rights that Vincent always handled, documents of my father's. Well, mine really. Only I didn't think of them as mine."

"Are you telling me that you knew nothing until Vincent's death? Nothing?"

"Nothing."

"Oh, come! You discovered nothing during his lifetime that indicated a different loyalty in Vincent's life? Nor did he ever hint at anything of the sort?"

"Nothing," she said again, quietly and seriously, understanding that this was crucial.

"Then you really didn't know what I was talking about the first time I came to see you?"

Jenny shook her head. Then she frowned and bit her underlip, raising a hand slightly in a small clutching gesture. "It wasn't, by then, quite so definite as absolutely not knowing. I knew by then that Vincent had deceived me about his mistress, his secretary. And I knew, too, that he had hid this affair with a most elaborate disguise. Much too complicated for it to have been anything but a life-and-death matter to him. Vincent was not a man for whom human beings were important enough, neither me nor Mona, nor anybody, for him to kill my suspicions with a deception that changed our whole lives. It was clear, no, I mean I could see dimly, that there must have been a more powerful motive for his big, thought-out structure." She turned to him, quickly sketching with her hand. "I had it in my mind by then, this structure, like one of those fantastically detailed paintings of imaginary architecture. There's an artist, not very well known, he called himself Nomé, who painted the very thing in the seventeenth century: tall buildings all exposed like entrails, exactly like places that could exist yet so crazy and overextended, so rickety, that at any moment they might collapse of their own complicated construction. Yes, but I couldn't think past that faint vision. Not until after you came here."

"But why was this woman so important to him? Did she know something?"

"We don't know whether she knew anything, we shall never know. For me, Mona was only the starting point. The shock of discovering Vincent's construction made me face its implication. Because nobody in his senses would have undertaken to convince me that I was mentally unstable just to give Mona a fig leaf."

"Mentally unstable," Polter said blankly. "That was Vincent's construction?"

"That was Vincent's plan. Not just a plan, he carried it out very logically for a long time, and until ordinary common sense was applied to it like a lever, it remained standing."

"But of course, it wasn't this woman at all, it was fear of losing his job if you divorced him. Then everything would come out. Is that what you mean?"

"Vincent knew I would never divorce him. I was entirely under his influence. In any case I am a Catholic."

"Of course," said Polter. "I remember now—"

In her eagerness Jenny hurried past this second admission.

"No. His rage at my accusation over Mona was in itself a cover for a deeper secret. He let out once, in a moment of annoyance, a tiny detail that might have showed me he knew something about my father's death. At that time there was not the least foundation for thinking the loss of the aeroplane was anything more than an accident. I doubt if I should have conceived such a thought, even if Vincent had not covered his slip at once with an outburst of anger over *something else*, over his secretary. But I believe now that his reaction, sustained you understand for several years, was much more powerful and unreasoning than the quite practical fear—practical to him in his circumstances, I mean—of my making a connexion from his knowledge of a detail of the flight that caused my father's death to a guilty knowledge about the disaster. My husband was a very calculating man, you know; everything was reasoned, worked out, well organized. But in that one case he felt such a deep superstitious fear that he overreacted. Although, in fact, about a year before his own death he did have to drop his campaign against me. I became so ill that I decided to go to a psychiatrist. He never mentioned my mental state again, neither did he buy me any more sleeping pills or sedatives—depressants or whatever they are called. So I quite rapidly got better. But the fear remained."

"The fear of madness?"

"Yes. I knew you would understand! It really is queer that I can talk to you about it. I just couldn't to anybody else."

"And the impossibility of putting your own sanity to the test kept you passive, or anyway quiescent? Oh, yes, I can feel that. That is quite a workable insight. Yet I would hardly have expected such intuition from Vincent, somehow."

"You think it was suggested to him, a weapon against a threat, by someone else? Mona Laver or someone? It can't have been. He reacted immediately, as if by instinct. Once recalled, I can remember it clearly. Not actual words, of course, but the instant switch to aggressive action."

"No, no. There was no one in this country he was on the kind of terms with to get advice of that kind. And, very unlikely, don't you agree, that the Laver would have been able to keep up a *conscious* act of that kind for long? No, she must have believed his diagnosis, accepted his view. But I mean something a little more than a deeply rooted intelligence. The counterattack must have been, as you say, instinctive. *That* came out of the depths."

"The depths! Then, the deep well of his own fear. Only from there could he have known instantly what to do."

"I think of him as unconscious of his constant danger. Naturally, he must have had moments of intense nervousness, even short periods of actual risk as when that fellow got into trouble in Warsaw. But no ever-present sense of threat."

"It may not have been conscious, but it must have been there. How else could he have known so surely the means of controlling me? Because, you see, that was an extension of a method already in use. He always did control me by fear."

"I didn't know that," said Polter flatly, his dismay at this quiet piece of horror too swift for a surface reaction; at that moment he was not acting.

"What did you suppose, then, was the real relationship between us?" she demanded bitterly. And very quickly, before he could even think of an answer, "Don't lie. We've gone beyond that now."

"The truth is, I didn't consider it. I was not, you understand, in constant touch of *any* kind with Vincent. Our acquaintance was of the early days and ended there."

"But you knew of the marriage plan. And the rest. What went with that plan."

"Yes, I was there when it was first born. But, bear in mind, I didn't know then or at any time that there was no feeling at all on Vincent's side. That became clear to me the first time I came here and met you. Then I could not help knowing. The contrast between what you *are* and what I knew of Vincent was so crass that there can only have been a long, and mortal, conflict. But I didn't know that ten years ago. And I must explain to you something you can hardly be aware of. Often to men who live exposed and dangerous lives, personal relationships are of the most vital and dominating, exclusive importance. They literally cannot live without them, especially their family ties. Often, too, a kind of knowledge grows into such relationships, submerged, unspoken. That is what I meant when I asked you if you did not somehow *know*."

"Yet you say that when we met you realised that the bond between me and Vincent must have been conflict?"

"I hoped for an amnesty on that inward charge at any rate. But I already knew it was a hope against hope."

"What you say about personal ties. That means—because I can feel that what you say is true—that I failed Vincent. He was sincere in an oblique sort of way when he constantly reminded me of his disappointment. If I'd cared for him as the simplest of women could have, I should have known and accepted his life. He often said that."

"But you didn't love him. There *was* no bond. The moment I spoke to you I knew that spiritually you were virginal. No visceral grasp enclosed you. But you're not a narcissist either. No self-adorer made that singing bird."

"He said I was incapable of any such bond."

"You may be, although I doubt it. But your lack of a relationship with Vincent can't prove it. Because it's quite plain now, much as I may squirm, that there was a vacuum on his side. Your lack of feeling was inevitable, you were a child then, and as children do, you replied to the *real* situation, which was an empty space."

Jenny saw that Polter was attempting to comfort her, and by the effort lessen his own sense of responsibility.

"All this only takes me further from understanding why Vincent 'took the course he did,' " she said stubbornly. "And it's that I have to know."

"I don't know the answer," he replied helplessly. "I only know what Vincent told me and that, as always, was a rationalisation. It has to be and it always is, because very few men, and certainly not Vincent, ever know themselves well enough to know why they do things."

And slowly, searching his memory to reconstruct Vincent's story of a decade before, he knew, even as he told it, how far from the original was his account. His precise voice sank lower and lower in the quiet room as he wound dreamily through a tale old enough to have been of *ultima Thule* and when he ceased they sat in silence, so sad, so lost was that pathetic echo of humiliation. At last he sighed and spoke again.

"The bitterness of the young! Poor Vincent asked for every blow fate could offer him. Everything he did invited his own unhappiness until one can almost feel he courted his own death in the end. And all the time he thought he was achieving what he desired. Somewhere, you see, a long way back, just before the time of the Renaissance, we all took a wrong turning—we all want the wrong things for the wrong reasons and try to get them by the wrong means. Vincent, with his cruel childhood, treats you with brutality, cobbles together his agonizing construct of a life that was no life, and all that's left is his travesty of a 'salon' half-remembered from the worn-out remains of an aristocratic tradition once seen, we don't even know where."

"Sandford suggested that Vincent's motive was some deep envy," said Jenny at last. "It seems he may have been right."

"Not *only* envy. If that were so, half the new class of quasi-educated young in this country would adhere to the conspiratorial extreme left instead of joining the ludicrous labour lot."

"That's true," said Jenny, and she thought of Mark as he looked with his vivid dark energy talking to Polter of himself and herself, who might both have lost their way as Vincent did with no less, if no more, reason. This thought showed in her features as a lightening, a glow of secret sweetness visible to Polter and he took it in with a queer little shift of feeling. The neuter artist to whom his sympathy went out turned in a mysterious lifting of vision into a woman.

"Can't you tell me?" She hesitated, fearing in spite of her need, to trespass. "It might explain something to me if you could, why you 'took the course you did.' I mean, I can't keep up the thought that you are in any way an enemy. We are friends, really, in some mysterious way, in spite of . . ." She stopped, unable to express her thought. Her use of the word "mysterious" echoed from his own mind with a sense of un-hindered communication and it startled him in its implication of an insight in Jenny, a moment of what he thought of in himself as second sight, jumping from her to him like a spark, or perhaps from him to her. And immediately, uncannily, Jenny carried the wordless correspondence further by getting up and crossing to the dark gape of the fireplace to push more logs into the glow of the fire. A flicker of sharp crackles of light shot up as scraps of bark dust caught instantly, flying up among the flames.

"I told you before. Sheer naughtiness. And, of course, the motive that brought me back here. Curiosity. I've always been possessed of a vivid curiosity."

"That doesn't satisfy me."

"Nor me," he sighed. "Nor me. But if I talked for an hour without stopping I should get no nearer. The quacks would tell you it is the memory of childhood injuries, and they may be right. Of course, I loathed my father and still more my mother, their dreadful falseness sickened me right down into my soul from before I can remember. But that is a standard explanation and explains nothing, as your friend Vail pointed out.

"I'm not trying to be vulgarly flippant. It simply comes out like that. One talks like a book all one's life about anything and everything. But when it comes to reality the words turn to pinchbeck. If I say that the only human being I loved until I was in my late teens was my nurse, it's no more than the truth. She used to take me to see her family in Finsbury Park and we made toast for tea at the kitchen range. That tasted much better than at home. I adored that kitchen, all dark and smelly and hot. When I was about seven they sent her away and I went to school. I can still feel that wound, sore inside me. I remember the sensation when they told me that I must smash everything and I gloated over a fantasy of my parents lying in their blood—for some reason in evening dress. 'Lying in their blood' expressed exactly what I wanted. I wonder where I picked up that phrase? Later I did love other people and that was torment—occasionally for a short time, ecstatic torment. Most of them didn't know. Those who did were nearly all venal. At this distance that's what love amounted to. But how it

348

all came about, who knows? All the things that happened to me happened to millions of others who turned out quite differently. Perhaps it isn't childhood, perhaps it is just chance. I happened to meet a certain man at a point in my life when I could be persuaded that I could help change the world—for the better, naturally. I most enthusiastically wanted to change the world; perhaps I confused that illusion with the idea that it would then change me. That was over forty years ago and at that moment the world certainly needed changing. Forty years, and it wasn't until two years ago that I finally confessed to myself, could no longer hide in the deeps of my heart, that the cause I had spent my life in, and spent my wits excusing—always covertly, by inference, never openly—was not only a failure, it was wrong. It took me all that long time to get back to that simple meaning. The wrong was not teething troubles, mistakes made from eagerness, distortions, all the other sympathetic lies. It came from unchangeable traits of human nature so universal that those who lack them are called saints. Envy, induced ignorance, self-righteousness, self-pity, a gratuitous cruelty that is never met with in animals but only in man, these universal faults are encouraged, even enforced, by the faith I have spent my life furthering. Such disgusting characteristics are valued as virtues, and any modifications that creep in here and there are left over from the past and treated shamefacedly as weaknesses.

"I knew, of course, I did know, for many years. But once I had taken up a position, the self-righteousness so deeply embedded in all of us refused to admit a mistake. The more clearly one is wrong the wider and higher one builds the defence against this knowledge and the more passionately one seeks to convince others."

"And two years ago? That must have been Hungary."

"Yes, it was Hungary. Can I talk about it, I wonder? I never have. For months afterwards I could not even think of it without tears."

There was silence for some time but at last he began to talk, quietly, in a strained voice very different from his histrionic tones.

"Some students collected money for medicines which they took in their car. They got in quite easily over the open border. But then things looked black and I was afraid, because they were known to be of my circle and I knew I should be blamed. It was the sort of exposing thing I had spent many years avoiding. I flew over, hired a car and went to the town, where there was a big hospital. I knew they were there. I thought it would be easy for me to get them out in the confusion, even if the troops occupied the place, and that proved to be the case. The doctors and nurses were mostly young, and by the time the tanks came, only the young remained. There was heavy fighting in that town during the original uprising; a police training school in the town did not go over to the rebels as most of the police did. So the hospital was full of wounded, rebels *and* police. When the staff heard the tanks were in the town they formed a delegation and took up a position across the gates to prevent their patients being arrested, as they knew was being done in Budapest. Do you know that happened? You could never imagine it.

"The thick black hulks of the tanks came up the country road. There was hoar frost everywhere, thin snow, a dark grey sky, bitter cold. Very flat country, you could see for miles. The tanks were huge, the biggest there are. I'd never seen tanks before. They didn't stop, never shouted challenges, they came steadily and quite quickly on, rumbling and lurching, with a loud rattling of chains; as I thought, but that was the caterpillar tracks. The young people stood still for a while, watching them, in their white coats and uniforms, both doctors and nurses. When they saw that the tanks would not stop, a shudder and a murmur went through them and the whole crowd watching, and they began to back away up the wide entrance with gardens each side, to the hospital steps. The shame and fear in the faces of those young people was so terrible that I dreamed of it for months after. Only one fair-haired boy, a junior doctor, stood his ground, shaking his fist and raving insults at them which, of course, could not be heard. The first tank rolled over him and went on forward without a pause, with the entire squadron behind, until they could go no farther because of the steps. Then they stopped and when the rumbling and rattling stopped there was absolute, dead silence."

Jenny put up a hand to her face and the tears in her eyes spilled down her cheeks without her noticing.

"Understand me," he said at last. "It doesn't matter whose tanks they were. And it doesn't matter who the young people were. It was simply so."

"And you?" she finally asked, as he did not continue.

"Me? I pushed my three students into their Hillman and we fled, like criminals, before the troops could encircle the town." A nerve under his eye twitched and he pushed up the side of his spectacles. "When we got back, I did not recant. I said nothing."

"You must be very unhappy," she said.

"Excellent comment!" He pushed up the side of his glasses again. "As you see, in the end one says nothing and it's all an exercise in self-pity. What I really do is ask you to be sorry for my faults, to bully me up with sympathy and sentimentality."

"I really am sorry for you, truly."

"That's no use. You would have to be revengeful to give me what I need. That would only be just—why won't you? It would be a refuge for me from the outside world where I can never find the courage to tell the truth, and you could revenge yourself by tormenting me with my dreary third-rate sins."

"But why would I do that?" she asked reasonably. "I would be in bondage with you, then."

"Yes, you are wise. And tomorrow I shall be able to make a dinner table laugh over my attempts at private confession. It is one of my best performances. The subject is never mentioned and it is always—but always—assumed that I mean some intrigue over an appointment or a naughty episode, such as the seduction of a beautiful, slender boy. And how I wish it were."

Jenny shook her head, unwillingly laughing.

"You know quite well what you ought to do. I'm not going to pander to your little act."

Polter shuddered, for a moment entirely back in his role.

"My dear, I could never stand the ridicule, never. That would be the real punishment."

"I rather think you might enjoy it," she said slyly.

"Ah, you don't know how many enemies I have!"

She said after a little while, "It doesn't tell me anything

about Vincent. There's no connexion there to anything that could so deeply have influenced him."

"Perhaps not directly. But the connexion is there. Consider: I felt myself excluded from the community, it might be from remote childhood or later. Vincent did not need to be neurotic to feel that. He *was* excluded, by the remnants of our foul class system. Oh, I know it is dead now, but not in his childhood and, even now, it still heavily influences millions of people from its grave. Much more important than sex to human beings is the sense of community. Sex is an animal instinct; community is human, the deepest human instinct. The clan instinct is the clue to the human soul as it *is* and not as a theory. To be alone, outlawed from the clan, is death to humans, literal physical death except to a tiny and temporary civilised minority. Spiritual death in any case. Men will do anything to remain in the clan. From the moment Vincent felt himself—he didn't know it, naturally, it is too deeply rooted in the collective unconscious for superficial awareness—from the very moment that Vincent was accepted as a valuable member of a closely bound clan, he was enclosed body and soul by that clan. Conspiracy gave him companions, brothers. He *was* because he belonged. He would even have killed you; I'm sure of that. He would have done anything rather than lose that group identity. If you had taken your plan to seek medical help to its logical conclusion, you would have 'committed suicide.' Whatever his remorse, he would have done that."

They stared at each other and Jenny knew that what Polter said was true. She gave a deep shudder, not of retrospective fear but of a formless, awestruck certainty that swam up from some unplumbed depth, that Polter's view was the centre and the answer to her question about Vincent. She did not feel that she understood or perhaps ever would, but there—dark, deeply hidden—lay the truth.

"But I have no community in the sense you speak of," she said slowly.

"But you have. You have the group of England and you have, too, the republic of artists. You know from your father that there are people—and you will find your way to them, too—who are like you and who would and will understand you."

So moved was Jenny by this thought that her eyes filled again with tears and she shook her head to disperse them.

"Listen," he said eagerly and leaned toward her closely. "If you think about it long enough, not with your intellect but *consider*, you will begin to understand it because one cannot really say it, however carefully one tries to be simple and true. But in time you will begin to know the infinite need to belong absolutely to other humans, not *one* person but wider and bigger than our little local and recent beliefs. It's the only explanation that covers Vincent and others like him, and it answers the unanswerable problem of those extraordinary confessions of the old Bolsheviks in the great purge. First, they felt themselves rejected, outlawed from the clan, and a terrible loneliness and disgrace seized their souls; then they were given the chance to be taken back. They would confess any nonsense to gain that reconciliation. If the group needed ridiculous lies about having tried to kill Lenin or something, then deeply and essentially, the group was right and in the confession, in giving the group the last gift of accepting the role that was needed for its unity, the outcast was taken back into the community. At a depth that no words can reach, they died for the Party or the Church; they belonged, and future men would understand what they had done."

He got awkwardly to his feet and moved uneasily to and fro.

"The ease with which I slide into talking openly with you is more than a little unnerving. Never before, never once in all these years, have I talked of such matters outside. The mental condition is often referred to as controlled schizophrenia, but that is only a crude approximation. It's more like the taboos acquired in childhood. By the time a boy first goes to school he is not likely to mention excretion by accident; it just does not slip out. Only in jokes may the forbidden be approached verbally, removal to a fictional plane and the obligatory laughter is the crossing of fingers that disarms the sanction. It's the same process in conspiracy. The subject may be approached only under an elaborate camouflage of incantations that defuses the threat of punishment. Such approaches have a kind of excitement, like the feeling of 'dares' at school. There's no doubt this is the reason for much of the mumbo jumbo that surrounds the conspiratorial life. Consider rationally all those tricks of hiding papers in trees, passwords, false names and the rest of it; they are atavistic magic rituals to avert the wrath that follows touching the taboo."

"And you have the feeling of breaking the taboo?"

"In a deliberate, almost ceremonial fashion. One has known for many years, clearly, that the approach processes were irrational. Although they can induce sensible caution in activities that may be dangerous in a perfectly ordinary way—as one might say, in a police way—in their complications they often increase the practical risks rather than avoid them. Think how ludicrously conspicuous some of them are! Yet the ban is very strong and, once discarded, I rather doubt if it can be assumed again seamlessly. I almost feel as if my indiscretions to you may be known if I should meet one of the friends in the next few days!"

"Then your talking to me, your feeling that I ought to punish you or bully you, that can't really help you?"

"Not with the friends, by no means. Rather the contrary: if they suspected my weakness and calculated that I could be a danger to them, they would be very cross indeed, as annoyed as the naughtiest little boy could desire! On the other hand, if they thought that a scandal over me would be useful, they might even encourage me to babble further and more publicly as a final service to the cause, now that my practical value is at an end."

"With your retirement?"

"Exactly. A further public brouhaha might well suit their book. Just consider! Every student ever recommended by me to an official position becomes a security risk. Every piece of advice I have ever given takes on a poisoned second aspect. Really, I wonder it has not been thought of, but fortunately such a subtle ploy is beyond their wits unless I suggest it myself. And in any case, they'll be very well pleased with the *éclat* they will get."

"They will get?" cried Jenny.

"Oh, certainly. That can hardly be avoided. The bag of flour poised on the top of Lord Tantham's library door requires only the merest touch of an excuse to fall and envelop the noble lord and his colleagues in a cloud of public derision."

"What makes you so sure the storm will break in London?"

"But where else would it be?"

"So far none of the events since—well, since—have taken place in London?"

"Oh, but my dear, they have, they have! Your Vail is not the only flatfoot involved. The gathering rumours about Tantham and Maculan, the inquiries made this last week about me, such things are causing subterranean rumbles in pub and club, as a casual acquaintance of mine assures me on the telephone."

"You speak as if it were already an open secret. That is not quite how I understood it from Mr. Folliot and Teddy Sandford. They seemed to think. . . ."

"Not an *open secret*. *They* don't come out."

"Have you been questioned yourself?"

"Not yet. But friends of mine have been asked various details about me. Times and places, you know? Obviously things that were in the files with no identity attached, which are now being tried on for size."

"This is horrible!" Jenny clasped her hands.

"No, no," he assured her. "Not as bad as that. There will be a small puff of scandal. The government will intervene. Tantham and Maculan will regain their balance, in both senses. Well, we hope they will. But this house is in no danger. You are safe."

"I don't think I am safe," she said slowly. "I am dependent on the company."

"What do you mean, dependent?" He was suddenly sharp and concise, a serious alarm in voice and eyes. "Your father must have left a good deal of money. You are, not rich perhaps, but not poor either."

"I think it's all tied up in Tantham and Maculan," she wavered. "That is, I know it is."

"It can't be true!" he shouted. Unused to the pitch of violence, his voice cracked, comically. He jumped to his feet and shrank into himself, wincing with pain. "I understood your fortune was untouchable! It isn't true, you are trying to frighten me. Tell me you are only punishing me!"

"But I'm not. You've been misinformed, if you thought . . ." His reason for believing her financially secure was so obvious that for a moment neither of them could put it into words. At last Jenny stammered into speech, her voice so low and shaky that she could hardly be understood.

"You were assured by your 'friends' that what you were doing for them as a last service would not damage me personally. That is what you mean."

"Yes. I made it a condition. It was the only time in forty years that I put any limit on how far I would go for the cause. The cause. And they gave me my little comforter. But, of course, it was a lie."

"They may have been mistaken," she begged, distressed beyond bearing by the haggard old doll his whole person was changed into.

"They were not mistaken. They've known for years from Vincent every detail of your affairs, and the company's too." He thought it over. "And, from their point of view, they are, of course, quite right. They pursue their aims logically. I am now expendable. And that is proved, if it needs proof, by the very fact that I accepted their word at the exact moment when I could no longer bargain for it. Senile. Time to go."

"Please don't go, not for a little, not until you've . . ." Jenny began to weep, drearily, resignedly, for Polter was in fact suiting the action to the word. He shook his head, speechlessly, and she understood that he found his presence there insupportable.

"But you did try," she wailed at his back. That made him turn from the door with his hand already on the lintel. He looked at her and came back to where she stood. A queer little smile appeared on his lips, crooked and loving. He put his thin arms round her, unpracticed and clumsy like an adolescent boy, but stiff with sixty-odd years, and for a second leaned his head with the sound of a great sigh, against Jenny's.

"How glad I am that this is almost over," he said, and gave her a kiss that landed in her hair.

PART THREE

CHAPTER XXVI

HER THOUGHTS dwelled on flight, not from the house but towards people; she felt her distance in space from the town as a barrier rather than a gap that she must urgently, at once, storm. She thought of the studio, but for the moment work could not help. What she had just witnessed could only damage, if it did not altogether prevent, any concentration. Then for a bewildered moment she asked herself if it was wise to leave the house quite empty. Who knew, after such revelations, what people who could involve themselves in such depths of impiety might not do? And those unknowns, whom Polter referred to with such abysmal misuse of words as "the friends." They might not have relied on Polter alone, or their needs might not be confined to discovering what she, Jenny, was about. They might wish to search for something left behind by Vincent and not discovered by Folliot, Mark, herself. Or they might have some revenge in mind for their disappointment, their loss? But surely not; they must know by now and for some weeks past that Vincent's secrets were in other hands. Any action against herself or her home would so clearly be proved in advance to be their doing that they would be careful to stay as far from her as possible.

No, there was no present danger of another foray into her territory. And if there were, she must still test the sanity of herself and the small world she inhabited by at once seeing and hearing other people who went about their ordered and orderly affairs as if conspiracy, perfidy, wickedness on the scale described by Polter were indeed, as he cynically averred just before he gave himself the lie, imaginative inventions of the Sunday newspapers.

Her project was very small, she was humble in her claim

upon normality; she did not envisage being included in the life of the town, only to be allowed to look on, to make sure it was there.

But it was a long way to walk and the little carrier used by Foster was beyond her skill to drive. Then she thought of her bicycle, untouched for years. She hastily pulled on an old blue raincoat, indestructibly surviving from school, and a waterproof hat with a floppy brim and ran across to the stable. There was the machine, pushed against the wall by a lawnmower and the big plant spray stained all over with pale green insecticide. She hauled it out anxiously, and kicked at the tyres. To her surprise they seemed to be sound and she pumped them breathlessly; the basket on the handlebars was ragged but that did not matter and she set off immediately. It was no longer raining hard, and the slight wind promised an end to the long downpour by evening. The air was fresh, loaded with wet scents, and she rode, winding uncertainly, uneasy at the speed, down the hill road. Both in color and weight the air seemed to lift towards lightness by the mere fact of movement, of doing something.

The outskirts of the little town were delightful. A few scattered smallish houses stood among trees and bushes, filmed with dim green and here and there with visible leaves. Then came bungalows with white and coloured paintwork, neat, square gardens, the first one with a yellow plastic fountain among the spears of budding daffodils, the next with a stone lamb gazing placidly towards windows with frilled pink curtains. To the left stretched a semicircle of terraced brick houses built by the County Council, each with its flower garden before it like an apron, and behind, stripes of prepared ridges for vegetables. They showed washing-lines with surprising washing on them flapping wetly, and extravagantly large and crooked television aerials. A red milk cart stood still and there was a group of children in little sou'westers and rubber boots calling and laughing, holding their bicycles and with school satchels slung across their backs. Beyond those houses were water meadows with pollarded willows; Jenny could bring back their almond smell by looking at them, and the sky was filled with torn clouds, drifting eastward from the ocean.

Nearer into the town were little shops with newspaper stands outside and advertisements for sweets and cigarettes. Everything was washed with the clean scrubbed cleanness of nearness to the sea. The renovated Georgian house owned by the Estate Agent was set back from the road, the former garden now a macadamised parking place gleaming blue-grey, almost black where the clerk emerged from his Morris, pointing with his pencil in the direction from which Jenny came. At his side stood a stout old man in a russet tweed suit of plus fours, arguing about something. The stout man stamped off, swinging his arms, followed by a black-and-white spaniel, and the clerk shook raindrops from his shoulders and ducked inside the open office door with its pretty fanlight. A young woman in a brilliant shiny blue raincoat dropped a coloured magazine and bent crossly to pick it up, flicking water off it with a frown.

On a hillock were some larger houses of staid dignity among grown trees, their bar gates with old white paint standing open. One, surrounded by dripping laurels, carried a tall, wide board saying "Antiques" in Gothic script and underneath, in the corner, "Member of the Antique Dealers' Association." Did they meet, the members, and talk about Rockingham china or George the Third silver? Or about the dealer in the next town who skillfully "restored" things and sold them as original? Jenny was sure there was such a man, but, of course, not in this town. The Vicarage, with yawning dark windows, late Victorian; Samson and Waite, Seedsmen and Fodder Merchants. The tall spire of St. Mary's, unfortunately rebuilt in the aftermath of Ruskin with mistaken enthusiasm. On a vivid green rise stood the dim grey of stonework where the rival priest lived, her priest. Next in startling contrast to his house of Gothic revival, his small church, aggressively modern. That was a useful proposal of community; I shall go to Mass next Sunday, thought Jenny with surprise. At the traffic lights she stood, one foot touching the ground. "Frank Wellings, Family Butcher and Grazier, Prime English Lamb A Speciality." Did he really still graze his own lambs? "And he shall graze his flocks," with an expanding calm of music. They had never dealt at that butcher, whether or not he grazed his own cattle. Across a space there reared the Market Cross with a bicycle stand beside it. Jenny dismounted, reeling somewhat from lack of practice. She saw now that the frame for the basket was bent and the basket had to be wrenched free; the bicycle, unused, had been pushed hard up against the stable wall for years. Looking round the almost empty square she recalled a moment of childhood when a question from her as to where, then, *was* the market made some forgotten grown-up laugh at her ignorance. The town market had been held on The Green down by the riverbank for centuries and this small uneven "square" was nowadays a car park with, at the moment, few cars. Across to the right was the Cross Keys Hotel, against which she had warned Mark when he first came. A pity the food was so wretched and there was no heating; it was a dear old house and looked almost elegant from the outside. She signed the petition some years ago that unsuccessfully tried to prevent the houses next to it being sold to a chain-store selling brightly coloured underclothes that turned out to be a godsend to the female population, with its low prices and high standards; but it remained an eyesore architecturally. Why cannot they build their fronts to look like the rest of the town, Jenny wondered, since all these small country towns are so alike they could still be uniform and yet not look like a deliberate affront. She turned her back on the affront and faced the public library, which was just as bad, she thought, only being older and a Tudor imitation in local stone was tolerated or, rather, not really seen. And next to it, a joy to the eye, the fishmonger with his old-fashioned sloping marble slab open to the street where a middle-aged figure stood with a tall boy, heads bent towards each other in murmured con-versation.

"Hullo, Jenny, how are you, haven't seen you for ages, isn't the town sweet in the afternoon when nobody's about? One should always come at this time. You know my youngest boy? We were talking about your stone. Such a coincidence!"

The youngest boy was an enormous youth who towered over Jenny's head, and stammered. She was afraid of Lady Mainter, known to have disliked and disapproved of Vincent—why? A question never before posed.

"Good afternoon, Lady Mainter." Voice sounding shaky, how stupid to be nervous. "When did you get back from

Rome?" Her eldest son is at the Embassy in Rome, yes, but what is his rank, and how many children? It no longer mattered, because the youngest was slowly getting out a strangled request about the stone. "I hope your son and his family are well? No, I meant the son in Rome. But I should love you to come and look at it. You'd better come soon, the archaeologists want to remove it for whatever they do. Tests, I think. No, I don't know, with chemicals, perhaps? You could consult Colonel Bartle, he'll be down in a minute, I saw him just now outside the Estate Agent's and he's walking this way. I'll ask him when."

"When, Mrs. Cheyney?"

"When? Oh, you mean when will they take it away? That's what we have to ask Colonel Bartle." What on earth was this boy's name? Surely she must know it, and she hardly recognized Colonel Bartle just now, but here he was with his stamping gait, a russet block of colour. A chorus of good afternoons.

"Lady Mainter was asking when you're thinking of taking my stone away. I had a letter from the President of the Society about the Museum, but I don't know whether it ought to be moved."

"Don't you think it might be better left up on the hill?"

"You'd have an awful lot of sightseers once the learned journals get on to it. You won't like that, I should think? Better for *you* in the museum?"

"I don't know that I agree. It ought to stay where it belongs, don't you feel that, Jenny?" Lady Mainter's "Jenny" came out with a challenging intonation. Jenny did feel that, but the reason for her hesitation was that she wanted to find out what Mark thought about it. They were all talking at once, as usual.

"Why don't you come up? Oh, any time, I'm always there. Naturally, bring your visitor, too."

"Tomorrow, certainly, remember that, Togs, don't forget. Lovely idea. Oh, dear, there's Rollo waving like mad, we've got the dogs in the car, Mumbo has to go to the vet, that's what we're doing in the town. I must tear myself away or they'll scratch the inside of the car to pieces once they see us. Total indiscipline. Don't let them out, Rollo, I'm coming. Oh, sorry. Didn't mean to bellow in your ear."

"I say—just thought of something."

"What is it, Togs, dear? Oh, chess. Yes, of course. Do you play chess by any chance, I remember your father did? You do? Heaven. My father-in-law, you know. You've saved my life."

"We're all hopeless. He gnashes his teeth at me."

"Don't exaggerate, Togs, you'll put Jenny off. We'll arrange tomorrow, when we come up. Oh, Lord, those dogs, who'd have dogs? Haven't seen the darling house for ages, simply years, always have been green, quite green, about that house."

Insane barkings, slam of doors, large, silent, grey slipping-away car.

"Gorgeous motor, what? Speaking of which, how did you get down into town? The car was . . . I'm so terribly sorry. Unbelievably tactless of me. My wife always says . . . Oh, *bicycle*? But you'll have to learn to drive, you'll be so cut off without . . . You did say you don't drive? No, I don't believe there is a proper driving school about here, but I'll ask old Paynter. He teaches people, now that he's retired. Nothing like learning to drive from the police, get it right then, can't go wrong, eh? I'll have a word with him and let you know directly. You sure you don't mind if I bring the secretary, then, he's a perfectly decent chap, not like a reporter or anything. You'll be interested, I'm sure, he can really talk about these things. Well, then, until tomorrow." He was still talking half to himself as he raised his tweed hat and left the shadow of the thought that they were all determined—across a barrier making up their minds to it—to be kind and neighbourly. What stories were already being discussed? Did they feel bad conscience? Curiosity? Simply embarrassment that Vincent had not been popular? All those things, and kindness too. And the impossibility of saying, of injecting into the streaming conversation, her objection to a newspaper reporter, even one specialising in archaeology. All very well for Teddy to say be careful, but how could one say at the very moment of renewing neighbourly relations that a stranger was unwelcome? It was that very thing that always put everyone off in the past.

The fishmonger still wore the traditional "boater" and an apron of lateral blue-and-white stripes over his clean white coat. Like a doctor in Professor Polter's shocking story.

Jenny did not know that her face changed when she

364

thought of that story, but it did and noticeably. She only saw the reflexion of her changed expression in the fishmonger's broad smile that became reserved as he suggested soles.

"I'm alone at the moment. So it would be only one sole. And something for Polly, with all those kittens, she needs lots to eat."

He was a stranger to her, she realised, and she asked after the former fishmonger, whom she recalled as a short, grey man. That was his father he said, now retired, and he found himself quite a stranger after working away for some years before he took over the business. Quite a foreigner he was, but it doesn't always do, families working together, there has to be one boss. For some reason this remark at once seemed tactless to the man, and his face changed as he spoke and he twitched his eyebrows with concern. Conscious of making an effort, his smile fixed itself and he talked as if suggesting a short stroll to a difficult invalid, of sending orders up to the house. He did not want to press his wares on her, but there was no need for her to come down to the town every time she needed a fowl; they sent up to the Blanes twice a week to collect poultry and eggs. All you need to Ma'am, is to pick up the phone.

It was clear he knew that the Blanes had taken over her chickens while she was alone, so he knew the Fosters were away. Of course, everyone would know that. The butcher clearly did because he now telephoned for orders, as if that useful custom had not been broken off years before by Vincent. Astonishing that she had not noticed that until now.

"I thought Foster would have said something to you," she said, untruthfully, since it only now occurred to her. "I should be glad if you would send up. Which days do you go up to the Blanes?"

That she did not know this routine disturbed the shopkeeper afresh. What on earth did she do all the time, up there alone and knowing nothing and nobody? Funny lot they were and no mistake. For Jenny, however, from the inside of her own isolation, it was delightful to be making domestic arrangements with this pleasant man.

The shop was beautiful, with delicate colours of fish and bright green parsley laid out, speckled plaice and battleship-coloured soles lying in patterns, blue-green herrings and barred mackerel and above them, on the shining steel rail, ducks hanging in their glorious plumage. The egg baskets, woven in semicircles of nutty brown osier, matched their fragile burdens in colour, as if the eggs, ranging from palest ivory to dark brown, were working up to the colour of their container. Some of those were from her hens, the man said, seeing her glance over the display, and it would be only fair if she got a rebate on the price while she was obliged to buy. A thick fold of white wrapping paper hung on the end hook of the overhead rail by one corner, so that it draped itself in a diamond shape with a rounded fold and was not quite white but an almost pink creamy softness. As the man bent over the wide slab, stretching out his arm, he made an arabesque of movement, changing all the shades in the subdued mat light. The trouble with having stuff sent up, thought Jenny, was that she would not see the shop but she did not say this; she was learning.

The young man in the bookshop was a newcomer and less friendly. Jenny was pointed out to him, as she walked towards the shop, as the widow of that man killed in the car crash; an unamiable, almost libidinous inquisitiveness could be seen and felt in the man's manner when Jenny spoke to him. He felt it due to himself to show his equality, as a great reader himself, with Jenny, who had not thought of him as unequal and therefore found his aggressiveness disconcerting. Assured loudly that he knew just the kind of book she required, she was almost intimidated into buying what he showed her on the display table. There stood a photograph of a fierce woman with a cloud of dark hair surrounded by piles of a book described as a scalding exposure of racial and class antagonism in the South Africa of today. The novel was called *Man, Them Kaffirs* and the coloured jacket showed three tall men in laced knee boots drawn in perspective from below, bending over a recumbent black girl with cattle branding irons in their fists against a background of bleak yellow rocks. To make the point unmistakably clear, the black girl was naked.

"But I am afraid I don't know anything about Africa," Jenny excused herself. "I was really looking for the paperbacks, but they seem to have been moved."

366

"I have completely reorganised the department," the young man informed her contemptuously. "The cheap editions are now all in the room over there."

"Thank you, how practical," said Jenny faintly and moved quickly away from his sadism and the ugly book jacket to the shelter of the despised corner room. Behind her the assistant made an audible comment about provincials and their bourgeois taste. Another replied in a warning undertone and they put their heads together. When Jenny came out again, carrying her purchases, she could see they were discussing her; something about the way they looked away from her struck her with a shock of near panic. For the first time she wondered if it could be known here in the town that the police were interested in Grove House. In fact, this was not known yet, but a cautiously phrased complaint by Mrs. Foster before she left had been freely translated into "official receiver" from "officials" by the alchemy of gossip, and it was already being mentioned as a fact that the Cheyneys were bankrupt and the widow was about to be sold up.

Ignorant of the direction gossip was in fact taking, Jenny yet understood the dangerous difference between the kindly incomprehension of the fishmonger, whose wish to show her consideration was by no means entirely prompted by his own shopkeeping interest in a customer, and the lewd greed in the manner of the younger man. Given the slightest chance, *that one*—she expressed her apprehension of him as alien and hostile in the local idiom—would strip her naked. He was a striking example of the need to keep secret the parentage of her child. She could formulate to herself how he would describe those days and nights with Mark by reference to what she had heard in the past from Vincent on the love affairs of others; always of others. This aspect of her own conduct seen through the eyes of malice was very unpleasant, but Jenny faced it, not only because she had been educated by the nuns at school to face the existence of sin, however little it appeared as applying to herself. It was something she would have to deal with in the coming months; already, where the child was concerned, cowardice could no longer exist. Supposing the time factor could not be successfully hidden, then what?

Jenny paused to consider this, gazing blankly at the fluted

base of a Victorian teapot offered for sale in the silversmith's window next door to the bookshop. She would have to go away to a nursing home at least a month before the birth was due, she saw, some way from home. London perhaps. It was years since her last visit to the capital; that overwhelming crowd would certainly offer complete concealment. Another complication was that Mark, on his return, might see that she was pregnant and want to claim the child at once as his own. So far, it was hers alone, but she was obliged to admit that Mark might see the matter in a different light. Certainly he had drawn a picture of determined bachelordom, but if she felt the child as a living being that was also a part of herself, so might he. Her abstracted eyes wandering over the assortment of silver objects rested on an ecclesiastical candlestick, and reminded Jenny of the thought of going to Mass on the coming Sunday.

She could not rejoin the community of the Church and continue to think of Mark only as a lover. This thought presented itself as a great, wide and impassable obstacle to her barely formulated conception of her future. There was no way round *that*. If the child was to have an unassailable home for body and soul, its mother must either marry its father or live alone as a widow. The widow of Vincent Cheyney, who would be for everyone but herself the father of the child.

The rejection of this thought was so sharp that Jenny started physically and under her breath she said, "No!" with an effect to herself of such violence that she turned her head to make sure no one was near enough to have heard. She shook herself free of that appalling prospect and walked quickly across the street towards the bank. She was watched by the bookseller's young man, who wondered to his companion how she had the face to show herself here. Overdraft, he'd lay a fiver. He only just knew what an overdraft was, and up to now had never been inside the pale, cool building just like every other branch of that bank, all over the country.

Here Jenny could at once identify the flavour of her reception. Here she was back in the miasma of the past, where the elderly cashier greeted her with covert pity and a combination of shame and scorn that came from his detailed intimacy with the Cheyney bank account. He knew, none better, how scandalously Jenny had been treated financially, but he knew equally the folly and weakness of Jenny's allowing it to happen. The cashier was very well aware that even in her extreme youth his own wife would never have allowed her affairs to be so mishandled, and quite rightly so. He recalled, as if it were yesterday, her bullying him into asking the famous and intimidating Julius Maculan for advice about her small inheritance, and even accosting the famous man herself. She asked what she should do, with the simplicity of common sense, and Maculan, with the same simplicity, told her. On his excellent counsel they bought a piece of land that lay just where two years later the government needed to extend the testing shop for Maculan's crucial contribution to what was then called the war effort. He could hear his important client now, answering his apologies for his wife's pestering such a busy man about trifles. Maculan smiled with those piercing and kind eyes and replied in his queer English.

"Your wife is a wise woman. She will now have a stake in the country." He loved such phrases and used them with emphasis and pleasure so that they took on anew their real meaning. And he went on to explain his scheme for issuing stock in the company to employees and work people against their war-ensured overtime pay.

"You will see," he said, nodding his large head, "in a few years the men who say now that this little scheme of mine is a *racket*, they will be complaining that their fellow workers have stolen the *march* on them!"

His prophecy came true. The cashier knew how true, for the men who invested in what was now one of the largest undertakings of its kind in the country owned their own houses and sent their sons to the university. Those who mistrusted the idea still lived in "council houses" and their children left school at fifteen. Yet Maculan's own daughter had allowed herself to be cheated by that condescending, careful husband of hers and his hard-eyed secretary. The cashier never mentioned a word of all this outside his own living room to his wife, but it was there in his manner under the neutral politeness.

Jenny found herself once more slipping into the flinching, apologetic tone of her former life, as if the money she was withdrawing were not her own and the bank were doing her a favour.

The upward ride was quite steep below Gullion and Jenny was obliged to walk part of the way, but it was no longer raining and, except for the tug of the heavy basket, she enjoyed the exercise. The ordeal of a first visit to the bank was successfully over, and she was quite proud now about that few minutes, so much dreaded beforehand. She should, she felt, manage very well without the Fosters for a few weeks.

The effect of seeing clearly her real and serious problems was to reduce household matters to triviality. Even the fear and aversion aroused by Professor Polter's confessions in all their menacing ugliness and strangeness were dimmed as if they belonged to some time in the past. Her confused feeling of intimate sympathy for Polter's sad lostness, which lacerated her by bringing her too close to his guilt, almost sharing it, became somehow less unbearable, less incomprehensible, in the recognition of her own complex and conflicting desires and needs.

Desire was Mark, need was the Church; the child was both. They were all equally present and urgent, belonging to each other but conflicting. What would not combine harmoniously was the thought of Mark and the thought of marriage. For Jenny the experience of marriage was that of a prison where she was condemned without knowing why she was forced to suffer. Mark had freed her; she could not transfer that liberation, the deepest joy she was aware of ever knowing, a marvellous discovery of undreamed-of pleasures, to anything that could be related to life as she had known it with Vincent. Marriage was all shadow, restraint, caution, strain, deepening into panic fear of the loss of herself. The memory overwhelmed her darkly and she pushed it away; she could not and would not think about it. It must wait. All in good time Mark would come back, a way would open up. That he would return was a fixed point somewhere in the future that shimmered like summer colours. Jenny neither questioned that nor did she allow herself to examine it.

From that day on, as Easter and spring approached, Jenny began without any more enterprise than was needed to supply her own wants, to be drawn into a more natural relationship with the life around her. Tradesmen came to the house for the first time in years, the retired police sergeant came every day to teach her to drive Foster's little van, she cycled over to Mainter and played chess with the aged Admiral Mainter, and was included in the small excitements of her archaeological "find."

CHAPTER XXVII

EVEN THE problem of pregnancy, which Jenny, old-fashioned as she was, expressed to herself as swindling the time, seemed to solve itself for the moment. For one morning a poor, mangled baby rabbit lay on the back doorstep. Mrs. Godolphin was sure Polly was the culprit, Jenny equally certain that a fox had killed it and for some reason abandoned its prey. Which of them was right hardly mattered, for in the middle of the argument Jenny was sick and for a woman with five children of her own, this was enough. It happened to be the day the cinema programme in the town was changed, so that Norma took the news with her in the evening and, since there were no Fosters to offer an alternative explanation, the respectable one was taken for granted and Jenny advanced from a tragic young widow to the even more pitiable figure of a tragic young widowed mother. Like many people who reach adult understanding late, Jenny learned fast, once the process began and, without saying a word, she allowed herself to be fitted into this convenient role. There remained a little matter of six weeks or so to be accounted for, but that problem was in the future and could be dealt with when it was imminent.

During Mrs. Foster's reign Mrs. Godolphin saw little of her employer's private life, but she might still have "wondered" if it were not that the gossip about bankruptcy failed for the lack of bailiffs and notices of auction sales or of Grove House being put up for sale. This failure made an explanation of all the rumours necessary; it was supplied by the presence of the "young man from London," who was now supposed to have been putting Jenny's affairs into order, only just in time to save her from penury. In fact, the very disguise used by Mr.

Folliot and Mark Vail to cover his presence. Somehow a concern with mysterious things like stocks and shares and patent rights made Vail inhuman to the local people, and the truth of Jenny's baby did not occur to anyone, any more than the real reason for his stay in the district did. That was too far outside their experience for even the most active imagination to hit upon it. Only one man in the locality knew the paternity of the child, and the priest was not likely to divulge it.

So the useful function of gossip worked itself out and all might have been well, in spite of one or two people noticing that the outward showing of Tantham and Maculan reflected what must be a certain slump in their standing. What was already a serious worry to Mr. Folliot and his colleagues was, in Jenny's immediate neighbourhood, considered to be a temporary setback due to a sudden death. Twenty-five miles away in the company offices there were set brows, and far away in London rumours flew about like pigeons in Trafalgar Square of "overextension" and "capital strain," and note was taken of huge investments in future projects which for some reason the government department concerned was showing reluctance to continue with. For there, Vail and his colleagues, although unknown to the general public, were readily identifiable to a number of people in the City, in Whitehall and in Fleet Street; it was, as Mr. Folliot and Teddy Sandford had feared, an unavoidable process.

These dimly outlined clouds did not yet seem real to Jenny. She was much occupied by work, in which a burst of creative and physical energy showed itself that seemed quite independent of her state of mind. She felt at peace, with the dazed lassitude that naturally follows a deep shock; lonely as she was, Jenny was still glad of the quiet allowed her for recovery. She did not want to think; above all she shrank from exposing herself in any relationship in the smallest degree demanding. In a way incomprehensible to the utilitarian modern mind, Jenny's reacceptance of the comfort from her religion was a relief that drew a line through Vincent's death and the events that followed it. The outward aspects of the drama were somehow closed, rounded off, by the accounts of it, on the one hand from established society in the person of Mr. Folliot, on

373

the other by the messenger from those shadowy outlawed figures who lurked behind the so unsuitable, the so perfectly disguising camouflage of Polter. The grumbling and flickers of lightning that might mean a coming storm over the monumentally solid foundations of Tantham and Maculan were not real to her, for she lacked any knowledge either to interpret the signs or to imagine a world without the support of her father's achievements.

Besides, Mark was pursuing his researches in the no man's land between international business and that unmarked area referred to as "security," with a determined curiosity that Jenny understood, rightly, as enjoyment. She envisaged Mark's expeditions, to Canada, to the ancient seat of learning recently vacated by Professor Polter, to various far-ranging and scattered undertakings of industry, commerce and research as skirmishes in a silent war where the antagonists never declared themselves nor were to be seen in the open. He would emerge again into the world of here and now when his task was completed; in the meantime his absence was a promise for Jenny that the outcome would be a complete vindication not only of his own actions but of her soundness. It was very important that Mark's reconnaissances should remain hidden; Jenny did not want to know more than that they were being carried out, for nothing that resulted from Vincent Cheyney's actions was to be allowed to touch the future child, not even through the umbilical lifeline by means of its mother's knowledge.

Vincent Cheyney was not only dead and gone; he was shut out. His once horizon-filling presence had been replaced by a great expanse of light and air to which Jenny did not give the name of relief. The seal on that shutting out of the past was now sanctioned by the Church. That this reckoning was accompanied by stern reproofs for Jenny only made it the more consoling in its reassertion of authority.

She felt herself as waiting, alone but not abandoned; she knew absolutely that no explicit sign from her was needed to bring Mark back when he was freed from his involvement with the dead man. Their letters, which never mentioned the matters dominating their lives, held the roads and bridges open for that return and were the channels for emotions that might have overwhelmed Jenny if they had come too near during the next few weeks. Instinctively she held off feeling while body and spirit recovered and rebuilt. The amiable and undemanding intercourse with neighbours was as much as she could manage.

Three, four, five weeks slipped by. In the gentle climate of that southwesterly country the seasons moved smoothly without abrupt changes. The damps and blowing winds of winter in a district in which frost was rare and snowfall an event of moment by which periods of years were measured, gave way imperceptibly to early summer.

The tall sentinels that surrounded the house were, as always, the tally of the year. Every day tiny, thin cones of shiny brown thickened and split until the moment when the just-showing leafage was yellow passed in a day into a million points of palest, gleaming green. On an afternoon when the sun shone warmly after a shower the trees were thickly haloed in a shimmer of glittering colour quite unrelated to their winter stiffness. Every year there was this moment when half-open foilage was there but too touchingly tender and young to belong to the aged trunks or the still visible high branches.

The sheltered lilac, always the first to venture, was already faded, the first of the tulips set by Foster breaking out of obstinate tight buds. Jenny, accompanied as always by Polly, was crouched down to examine the snaky rolls of leaves energetically spreading on the new roses, and deciding to consult the nurseryman about when to dung them. She rose with a distinct annoyance at the scattering of stones and the harsh purr of a motor engine. To her astonishment Jenny saw Eileen Sandford's station wagon, usually full of the boys' sports gear but today empty but for its owner. Except for the day of Vincent's death Jenny could not recall such an arrival; like everyone connected with Vincent, the Sandfords always let her know when they were coming.

Faced by this abrupt reminder of her husband, Jenny felt at once the impulse to flee, and then to hide the fact that she was in the garden for no better reason than just to stare at the growing flowers. But even before she could throw off her old cowardice she was made aware that there was no need to do so. Eileen was entirely engrossed in herself. She was also, and obviously, very much upset. Even the swing of her long legs out of the driving seat was clumsy, uncertain, as if her normal, confident control of muscle and nerves was somewhere interrupted. Her tweed suit and woollen shirt with the scarf in the neck, her country shoes, her well-brushed head that clearly had not missed its weekly treatment by a good hairdresser, the firm and competent hands emerging from pigskin gloves were all exactly as usual and yet quite changed. A cruel air of masquerade somehow showed through the outward woman, turning her clothes and other accoutrements into necessities for a successful presentation of herself. She was not a handsome and energetic countrywoman, full of the concerns of a considerable household, sons, social activity and local administration. She was suddenly another creature entirely, dressed up as the Hon. Eileen Sandford, J.P. Within a few weeks Eileen had aged years, her face was set hard with nervous anticipation, she was both angry and frightened. Even the bold brown eyes were changed, they flickered and shrank, denying her smiling apologies. Something was happening to Eileen quite outside her experience.

"Can't think how you manage without the Fosters." She looked about her as if asking herself what she was doing here. "Especially out-of-doors."

"I don't manage, not really," said Jenny. "But I rather dread anyone new."

"Of course, they won't come back. Another difficulty brought on us all by that wretched man!"

"You mean. . . ?"

"Vail, naturally. Frightful creature. He's back again from Canada, you know. Rooting about, pestering. I suppose he hasn't been here? No, seems to be finished with you. You're lucky." Eileen stared up and about. "Bluebells. Much earlier here. You're very sheltered, in spite of the hill. It's . . . ." Her voice weakened and dragged and she contemplated her gloves, one off and one still on. "I just had to get away from home for an hour or so, so I thought I'd come and see how you were."

"What a good idea! I'm glad you didn't arrive half an hour ago, I was having a driving lesson."

"Oh, you're learning?" Eileen sounded surprised.

"Well, I have to, really. I seem to be coming along quite fast. Colonel Bartle knows the testing man and he says they will give me a licence quite quickly if I promise to park the car in the town and only drive very slowly for the first few months."

"But have you bought a new car, then?"

"No, we're using the little van that Foster used; it does well enough for a start."

"But you can't go about in that thing!"

"It does look a bit odd parked in front of Mainter," admitted Jenny. "But nobody bothers about such things here in the wilds, you know."

"You *don't* take Foster's carrier to the Mainters!"

"Of course, almost every day. Mr. Paynter comes to pick me up and drives over with me. That's my lesson, d'you see. Then he goes home, he lives just by Mainter. Then either Togs or the Admiral comes back in the car and takes back Paynter's Morris. We've got it all worked out."

"But why? Why d'you go over to Mainter every day?"

"Oh, you don't know, of course. To play chess with the Admiral. They all say he's an absolute old devil, but he's always very sweet to me. Even when I checkmate him, he only just growls in his throat. Not that I manage that very often."

"He must be about eighty," said Eileen resentfully. "You seem to be quite social!"

"I am. I'm going to be the guest of the County Historical Society tomorrow. That's why I didn't go to play chess today. I have to finish writing how we found the stone."

"We?"

"You remember! Mark and I found it the day after the storm, when you and Teddy were held up on the hill by a fallen tree."

"Vail! But you won't mention *him* in your speech! God, Jenny, do be careful!"

"Well, everyone knows he was here, you know. Shall we go in and make tea?"

"Yes, but—I suppose they still believe he was here from Folliot's office?"

"I expect so, if they think about it at all."

"The way you speak of him! As if he were just a man we knew, as if you quite liked him!"

"I did like him."

"Yes, but I mean, now. You can't still think of Vail as a friend now. I know you got on rather well with him at first. I remember Teddy saying he'd quite made himself at home here. But after all this disastrous—surely you . . ."

"Eileen, you sound quite out of breath. Are you feeling all right?"

"Of course I'm not all right! I'm driven out of my mind by this horrible questioning, this ghastly man Vail!"

"But is he interrogating you? You personally, I mean?"

"And now you sound surprised! I thought the entire world knew! Certainly *he* doesn't try to disguise it, to be discreet! I'd always heard how secretive these security people are, but there's not much secrecy to be seen in Vail!"

"In the, sort of, closed circle? In the company, you mean? I expect he knows that we all want to get at the truth. Tracking back into the past, wasn't it Teddy said that?"

"But why?" Eileen wailed, and turned her head this way and that in a gesture Jenny found very frightening. She recognised the bewildered search for a way out. "Vincent is gone. Nothing can come of the investigation. And every day it goes on increases the danger of publicity."

"They have to know the extent of the damage. When you think what Vincent cost us all, surely we have to know?"

"That's what Teddy keeps saying! But I . . . That's why I came over today. I was sure he was coming back again. He goes over and over the same things, years back, details nobody could remember now. Oh! Let's talk about something more pleasant. Tell me about the Mainters."

"There isn't much to tell. They've been awfully lucky with the house, you know it's got this agricultural research group; that saves them and the agronomists are rather nice. The place is so big they wouldn't need to see each other but they do, in fact. Togs is rather gone on one of the girls."

"I shouldn't have thought Lady Mainter would care much for that sort of people. Aren't they terribly clever and experimental?"

"They are, but, my dear, the Mainters are all socialists! Except the Admiral, of course." Jenny looked round at Eileen. They were now strolling, Jenny in front with Polly, up the path to the kitchen door. Yes, Eileen looked calm again now, or calmer. That lost, intense look was fading from her eyes. "They are eagerly awaiting great changes. They say that. It's all rather fanciful. What they are really doing is preparing to board the bandwagon of the future as it comes over the horizon."

"Oh, dear, Jenny, when you said that, I had the strangest feeling. As if from somewhere the past came back."

"It did, I expect. It's what Father used to say. Strange, isn't it, if he were still alive I should probably call him Julius by now. Togs addresses his mother as Penelope—usually Penny-piece—when they're at home. It must be nice to have a family."

"Family!" Eileen moaned. Then swiftly retreating from her thought. "Did he say that, that about bandwagons, your father? Can you really remember?"

"I'm not sure that I do. Things just swim up, now and then. I suppose we all quote the things we heard in childhood, without quite knowing it."

The guest sank down on a kitchen chair by the big table and gazed dimly at the grainy surface of the deal, as if seeing her own childhood when such objects were blessed with the faintly illicit enjoyment of "below stairs" in the homes of the wealthy upper middle class. Eileen was acutely aware of the deep but outwardly almost invisible differences of custom that divided her own early surroundings from those of an aristocratic family such as the Mainters, where the relationships to servants were intimate and often lifelong. It had always been one of the slightly absurd sources of her assumption of superiority to Jenny that she did know such things, and it caused now a strange sensation of discovery, a shift of understanding, to feel that Jenny did in fact acknowledge those distinctions but from outside them and without feeling their validity for herself. Eileen was certainly not conscious of returning to her own childhood in order not to admit the torturing thought of her sons, but pursued a little trail of related interest as if for its own sake.

"You must have always felt that Vincent was not quite what he gave himself out to be," she said slowly. "He often made small mistakes in the early days."

"Yes. But his being new to all sorts of things was only, for me, a reason for sympathy. I do still believe, it's not only taken from my father, that it's what people achieve that matters. And so, the further they have to come, the greater the achievement. That was one of the things about Vincent . . . you see, I admired him for trying. That's what makes me still a foreigner, perhaps, that I didn't feel and certainly didn't share, the English—what is it—disdain for people who have to learn the finenesses of living or just conventions. One can't say the refinements nowadays, but that is what I mean. I did so much learning myself as a girl, I knew what it was like, that disdain. It was only later, after the drawing room was redecorated and other things like not knowing *why* my father was a wonderful human being and why this house is beautiful. Not knowing for himself without it having to be explained. That I saw gradually that there was some—coarseness—in him. But I didn't admit it, you know, not at all; I accepted his views. For years I was sure he *must* be right about all the things I knew were wrong, so I had to believe that I was all wrong."

"Yes. But I mean, if you did know inside, why didn't you feel the *other* thing that was at odds with you and us and everyone? There must have been a million discrepancies in quite ordinary things."

"I suppose there were, yes, there were. But I accepted that they were part of his job, travelling so much and doing things I didn't know about in places I didn't know with people I didn't know. And in our own lives, our private lives, there was always the explanation of his affairs."

"Affairs."

"It was agreed they were to be my fault, right from the start."

"Yes. And we all agreed, too. Looking back now, the word that keeps coming into my mind, I don't know why, is brutal. There was somewhere something brutal in Vincent."

"He wanted, hidden in himself, to destroy people. Yes, that is true."

"He wanted to damage me. I curse Vail, but I know it was Vincent. I'm not such a fool as that! He wanted to maim things, people, anything he couldn't understand. And, all these years later, he's done that. Yes, he's managed it."

All this time Jenny was watching the electric kettle, pouring milk for Polly and the now wandering kittens, who homed back to the source of food, a process that was beginning to be transferred to Jenny from their mother, who already was showing signs of indifference. She now poured the sparklingly boiling water over the tea, which gave off a delicate fragrance so utterly domestic and comforting to both women that they drew it in like incense. They were speaking very quietly, so that the afternoon peace of the kitchen surrounded them and the small sounds of a kitten lapping milk and a leaf flipping outside the open window were quite loud.

"You're worrying too much about it. Look." Jenny put down the tray between them and sat down across the whitish table from Eileen. "Why don't you tell Mark whatever it is. Then you would be—free."

"Tell? How can I? It would all come out, it would be in those dreadful reports. Think what would happen if the boys ever knew! What would they think of me! God, that tortures me! And there's nothing to tell. I don't know what he wants."

"But you don't have to tell him that."

"That?" She put down her cup so clumsily that it rattled untidily against spoon and saucer.

"Eileen, I've known for years."

Eileen caught a harsh gulp of air and began to cry.

"That's just it, don't you see? That's just it." She raised her voice through her tears until she was almost shouting. "It's all connected. That's just the trouble. As if he knew he would get me with it, all these years afterwards. I can feel him enjoying it."

"Rubbish," said Jenny sharply, automatically taking over Eileen's role of practical good sense. "You're letting it all get out of hand. Don't talk like that, it frightens me. What did happen? What is it Mark asks you about?"

"I can't remember. I don't know."

From the sullen, sideways look Jenny gathered once more the apprehension of how she herself had suffered only a short time ago, filled with a distressed anxiety near to alienation that suspected everyone. A heartrending pity and understanding filled her for this fresh victim forced to adopt the symptoms of a paranoia that was really Vincent's. Jenny felt clearly what Eileen meant when she cried out that Vincent was "getting" her; it was the spread of a baleful infection.

"You can remember. Listen, Eileen, it was just the same for me. I had to bring back terrible things, things I could never speak of. I thought once one night when I couldn't sleep that I would say those things to you to stop you ever mentioning Vincent again. But it would be impossible, and I don't need to do it anyway. What I mean is, I know what you're going through."

She ceased speaking. In the intricacy of the thought she was lost for words.

"You have to say it, get it off your chest, spit it out," she burst out. "It's the secrecy, don't you see, that gives Vincent his power! But not Vincent himself, some awful dark mastery that he lived under, and Polter and no doubt many other people; it's the hunger for conspiracy, for a secret power over others that makes them really into victims. It's a disease and it can only be cured by dragging it out into the open."

"Polter?" cried Eileen, catching at any diversion. "The television historian? What has he to do with all this? You spoke of him the last time I saw you."

"It doesn't matter what, any more than it matters what they all conspire *for*. It's conspiracy itself that fascinates them and drags others into itself. You, me, all of us. It sounds stupid nowadays, but it's a moral infection."

"All very fine." Eileen tried to laugh and choked on the effort. "But that doesn't solve the practical question. Supposing I do tell him, what if he arrests me?"

"Arrests you!" Jenny gazed unbelievingly across the table. A globe of chill silence seemed to enclose her head in which the words echoed, battering like a soundless explosion. "Arrest!" She must say something to deny the possibility, but she could not think what.

"You see? Your moral infection is not so easy to cure. That report was a numbered copy, it seems. *I* didn't even know what that meant then. And Vail says there were fingerprints on it. They knew even then that somebody leaked it, over ten years ago that was. Vail thinks it may have been the first time—the first thing Vincent did."

"But they may not be . . . Why should they be your prints? Have they asked you to have your fingerprints taken?"

"Not yet. But they will. I know that. Vail wants me to offer. He's waiting for that."

"But why should . . . ?" Jenny dropped her head with a sickening sensation of black weakness. She knew only too well that any prints would not be Vincent's. How many hundred times had she seen his hands, held out upright with a photograph or some paper held between them, touching only the edges. "Tell me," she whispered.

"Your father was brought a copy of a report, from the Joint Chiefs of Staff. Only he and Teddy were allowed to read it. It was picked up the very next day. It was so secret that Teddy wouldn't even lock it in his safe overnight. He brought it home in his briefcase. Vincent was there, he came in for a drink, he was there a lot at that time. Then Teddy had to go out again for half an hour. I can't remember exactly now, but Vin gave him some message and he went away and left the case in his study table drawer. I didn't know it was there or what it was. But Vin did. He must have overheard something."

Eileen stopped, trying to control hysteria. "It was Teddy who remembered bringing the damned thing home. I'd forgotten all about it, years ago. Teddy told Vail and then Vail started on me. He knew at once what had happened. Once Teddy remembered."

Jenny could reconstruct the scene in Eileen's pretty morning room as if she had been there and not at school. Vincent would sit there with his hostess on the sofa with its voluptuous round depth of softness, laughing and flirting with her. He would tease her about Teddy, slyly suggesting a self-importance about little secrets in the husband to increase the amorous pleasure of deceiving him. It would be turned into an erotic joke between them, a love play. Possibly that was the first time Eileen and Vincent made love, there in her own home with the then quite small children upstairs in the nursery; that would account for Eileen's remembrance of the occasion, for it was clear that she still did know every detail. It had occupied a hidden corner of her conscience for years, soundly and rightly because of the children. Either before or afterwards Vincent suggested, of course for fun, that they should steal a look at this famous report Teddy was so pompous about and, blinded by sensual pleasure of anticipation or fulfillment, it would seem amusing to Eileen too.

"You could say that you did handle the papers, perhaps," she offered in a strangled stammer. "You could say you might have put them back in the case for Teddy. When he was called out. Or before dinner, after he read the report, when you were both leaving the room?"

"You see, you're recommending lying now! Do you think Vail would believe me?"

It was true, and Jenny was not shocked by her own suggestion. It seemed to her, as well as to the mother, that the most important thing was now, now that such an outrage had taken place, to make sure that Eileen's sons could never know of it.

"He wouldn't believe you, but if you suggest it, he might accept that way out. I think, you know, he must know what happened. I can imagine it myself, so Mark with all his experience must absolutely *know*."

"It's so shameful," Eileen moaned, weeping afresh. "I can't think now how I could ever have . . . What is that?"

That was the front doorbell ringing almost over their heads on the old bell board.

"Oh, heavens, I forgot! It must be Colonel Bartle with the secretary of the Society to collect my account—you know, about the stone. The secretary is going to have it typed out. In his office. Oh! Eileen, he's on the local newspaper. Wait, stay here. I'll get rid of them, say I've got a visitor, some excuse."

"You can't go to the door like that. You're as white as a sheet. You look like your own ghost. Oh, God, what are we going to do!"

"We mustn't panic. Nothing has happened. It was only —what we were talking about. If I don't go, then they will really think it odd."

"I must get away. I'll go out this way."

"Your car, they will have seen it parked."

At the door, Eileen turned, blundering, literally frightened out of her wits, and not by the small social difficulty but by the sheer horror of her own commonplace, forgivable sin come back a decade later to entrap her. The two women stared at each other in a moment of total understanding. They could read the thought that jumped from the one to the other as if another voice spoke it aloud: Imagine Vincent living like this all the time! And at the terror of that communication, panic gripped Eileen. A senseless atavistic demand possessed her to escape and she ran, dropping her gloves and bumping against the door jamb with a cry of pain. It did not matter if the two unknown men saw her—they were the threat, the outside world, and she must get away, only get away.

Jenny called after her, expecting no answer, and then swung around, bumping in her turn against the corner of the solid, large table. She must distract the attention of the two men at the door. If they noticed that Eileen's departure was a panic flight they must inevitably connect the reason with their own arrival. The change from matters of fundamental import—for what Eileen and Jenny had been discussing was the spiritual welfare of Eileen's children—to convention was so enormous that it took every scrap of physical energy Jenny could muster and, as she crossed the hall to the door, she felt a menacing clutch in the region of the solar plexus as the tension of muscles and motor nerves tightened on her aorta, reducing sharply the flow of blood to the head. She shoved the cloud of dizziness away from her as if it were a material presence, only holding on to the massive portal for support as she pulled it open to the perfectly ordinary men who waited.

Fortunately she was expected to be pale and shaky and hardly needed to act more than to allow her weakness to be seen. In the usual greetings and apologies, the sight of Eileen blundering across the garden to the station wagon went unseen, and even the roaring reverberation of the motor was hardly heard as the door fell shut. The local reporter and honorary secretary of the Historical Society only half turned to see, and politely hoped they were not interrupting Jenny.

"No, no. Mrs. Sandford was just going. We were just chatting, you know, and didn't notice the time and she has an appointment."

She herself, facing the door as it closed, could see the wild swoop made by the long car as Eileen turned it too hastily, and she heard the scattering of gravel, but her companions, expecting nothing unusual, noticed nothing. Colonel Bartle was taking charge of their interest.

"Before we discuss your address to the Society, I must give you some wonderful news. The interest in our stone—I do feel it as ours, although of course it is yours, I know—is even greater than we hoped. Yes, indeed. You may know that Professor Polter mentioned it in his last television lecture? Such a wonderful series I find, do you not agree? And now the 'British Heritage' people are thinking of showing the stone in their next program. Isn't it splendid? They have been on to us by telephone and want us to engage your permission. Naturally I made that a condition, because they would like to show the whole surroundings as well as the stone itself, before we get it down to the museum. I do hope you feel that you can manage such an exciting visit. They would show you the greatest consideration, I am sure. I mentioned your recent bereavement and they promised to respect your privacy. I insisted on that."

"Television!" cried Jenny faintly, but in his innocent excitement Colonel Bartle misinterpreted the note of dismay as shyness and began to rally her with bluff promises of taking everything off her shoulders, they would do it all, she should not be troubled in the least; and as to the meeting tomorrow, the secretary would read her speech if she did not feel up to it, and that would really be an almost private occasion. She could trust the secretary here not to report anything personal in his write-up and there would be only one other journalist present. And he was a specialist on archaeology. Jenny had already been so very kind, she would recall allowing the Colonel's friend to come some weeks ago. This Mr. Jenkinson was from the most respectable of all newspapers in the capital and had even read a paper once before the Royal Society. Jenny could be assured that his interest was solely in the ancient Britons. Colonel Bartle mentioned that newspaper with deep respect. His own name had not appeared in its august columns since the last occasion of his being mentioned in the list of military appointments many years before, and he clearly felt that such a mention was an accolade rather than a scandal. All other newspapers were, it was taken for granted, scandalous, but this was quite different.

But not for Jenny, who perceived at a stroke the great difficulty of those who wish to avoid public interest in their affairs. It was anything but easy to follow Mr. Folliot's instructions, for the very act of objecting would attract the suspicion that there was something to hide. Jenny floundered, hampered at every word by her ingrained dislike of telling untruths. She felt, too, that nothing she could now say would change the course of events, for it was clear that the remorse expressed by Professor Polter had been a matter of semantics or, at the most, of personal feeling, which did not affect his actions. He had spoken of the stone before millions and must have mentioned its whereabouts and its ownership.

"Yes, Professor Polter did come to see me," she heard herself saying. "But I don't think I understood that he was interested in the stone. He said it was outside his own period and subject."

"You didn't see the programme then? Oh, you should, really. Most interesting, his great sweeping view of our history, you know, so expressive. As to your stone, it was mentioned as an example of the enormous span of the story of these islands, just in passing almost. But, of course, a wonderful thing for us here, to be included by such an eminent historian. His talks do show, I do think, the potentiality of television for good. So educational, it must be a revelation for young people. Don't want to talk like an old fogey, but really, young people seem to have no respect for the past and its glories. I'm sure Professor Polter does a great deal to change that attitude, because he is one of the most popular television lecturers."

"His intention, you know, is to bring history home to the people," said the secretary rather shyly. "I think that is a really noble idea. I'm sure you agree, Mrs. Cheyney, that our past belongs to all of us. Sometimes it is rather claimed for one group, one class, but Professor Polter has quite changed that view with his broad inclusiveness."

A wild desire to burst out laughing, although the whole subject was no laughing matter, forced Jenny to bestir herself. The offer of drinks caused a flurry of disclaimers and acceptances and she managed to transfer the conversation to her own notes for the meeting on the morrow without having made any promises on the dangerous ground of interviews with herself.

By the time she was alone again Jenny's anxiety about Eileen had been allayed by admiration for Eileen's competence. Still, it would be prudent to telephone and warn Teddy that his wife was in a highly nervous state. No, that would be a conversation beyond her powers; she could never conduct it so that Teddy would understand her without her having to state her concern openly. And granted the reason for Eileen's distress, that would be unthinkable. She decided instead to talk to Mr. Folliot, with whom her relations were both less intimate and more adaptable to euphemism in this delicate matter.

But she could not get the number, which seemed to be constantly engaged. She tried Mr. Folliot's home, with the same result. She began again, and with the long-drawn burr of no connection as it repeated itself over and over again arose a worried sensation of her being far, far away and cut off; this reverted, as the useless efforts continued, to a renewed pressure and anxiety in the middle region where the balance of the body lies, so that she felt dizzy again with a dismaying hint of her own weakness. And now that she could not reach Mr. Folliot it seemed an urgent necessity to do so, not only so that he could drop a word to Teddy but to warn him that the threat of publicity was becoming a reality.

When she did at last put down the telephone Jenny remained sitting where she was in a black oak chair of the *art nouveau* style that was used normally only for dropping gloves and parcels on, for its fantastically carved back, entwined with snakes and lilies, made it a most uncomfortable seat. She could feel now the lumps and angles of the decoration against her shoulders as she leaned back, depressed by her failure and aware, in a fashion she had never been up to now, that she was entirely isolated. She told herself that this came only from the inability to make the telephone serve her, but knew quite clearly that it was not so; there was something very much wrong. She would go and write to Mark, that at least she could do.

388

No sooner was she on her feet than the telephone, with the cantankerousness of inanimate objects, began to ring.

"Mrs. Cheyney? Jenny? I've been trying to get you for half an hour!"

"Oh, Mr. Folliot, I've been trying to reach you. I wanted to tell you, Eileen was here this afternoon."

"I deduced as much! There has been an accident. No. No, nothing serious, that is, no one hurt. But serious enough in other ways."

"Tell me what happened."

"She mounted the kerb on a corner. Unfortunately in the town. Smashed up a parked bicycle, dented a police phone box and broke its glass. Then, one thing after another, she lost her nerve and—so very unlike her—began an altercation with the police. They assumed she must be under the influence of drink and took her to the station."

"It can't be true!" cried Jenny, and again the wild desire to laugh overcame her so strongly that she did burst out laughing and almost choked suppressing the sound.

"Oh, worse than that," he said grimly. "Teddy is on the way over to arrange bail. She screamed at the constable, so they say, and even shook her fist at him. A crowd gathered; she was hysterical by that time. Of course it will be in the papers, at least the county paper, if not the London press. It is precisely what we most feared."

"But surely not the London papers? If nobody was hurt?"

"My dear girl! Justice of the Peace arrested on drunken driving charge? Lord Tantham's daughter assaults police officer?"

"Oh, God. But Eileen wasn't drunk. We didn't even have a sherry. We drank tea."

"Yes, but tell that to the outraged police now! They are furious, in no mood to overlook a minor driving misdemeanour. And not even minor. Material damage and driving to the danger of the public. The car mounted the pavement."

"This is simply terrible," said Jenny helplessly. "Is there anything I can do?"

"Yes, there is. Keep quiet. The police may telephone you to confirm Eileen's story that she was with you and drank nothing. But speak to nobody else. Nobody, you understand?

Especially not to any strangers. Somebody may come tomorrow, reporters, but do not even speak to them."

"Strangers! Reporters! But Mr. Folliot . . ."

"Ah! My other telephone is ringing. It must be Teddy, at least I hope so. I must go. I will call again later."

Before she could stop him, Mr. Folliot was gone.

"The whole thing has descended to farce," said Jenny aloud. "Black farce." And since it was as yet unknown to her that farce for the participants is anything but funny, this thought reassured her. Indeed, although she felt both shock and sympathy for Eileen's mishap there was as well a certain mild little satisfaction in the spectacle of a so exemplary figure transformed into Till Eulenspiegel.

In this restored mood it did not seem impossible to persuade Mark, without betraying Eileen's confidence, that he could combine duty with kindness as far as she was concerned. With hardly a pause for reflection Jenny settled down to write her only letter to Mark that concerned itself with his work. With an innocent disingenuousness—she was by now aware that Mark saw through her with the greatest ease, and that that was one of her small weapons—she suggested an agreed little deception that would enable Eileen to "confess" her folly without including the details. She even explained to Mark why the devious course was necessary, but she did not mention directly any of the facts told her by Eileen, she only implied them and took them as known. She felt pleased by her arguments; Mark could be distantly seen as shaking his head and laughing to himself at her having become such a clever little thing.

CHAPTER XXVIII

THE MAN introduced by Colonel Bartle as Jenkinson was tall and looked taller than he was from his excessive thinness. His face was haggard and grey, the knobbed bones of brow, cheeks and jaw lent him the look of one surviving a natural catastrophe, perhaps a shipwreck. That it was a disaster of nature from which he was left over starving was conveyed by his air of stoic helplessness, only increased by his clothing, which might well have been some time in sea water. He spoke in a gentle, exhausted voice, low and cultured, and the only feature about him that did not indicate death fairly soon from malnutrition was a pair of lively, comical eyes and his attenuated hands, which were never still. By some magical contrast, however, he made Colonel Bartle, renowned for his youthfulness, look at least his age.

"I'm afraid the television people are not coming, after all, Mrs. Cheyney," apologised the Colonel, including Jenny in his disappointment. "At least I've not heard again. They said there was a hitch, some objection from another department. At least so I gathered, but really, you know, they seem to talk almost another language, and it is quite difficult to catch their meaning at times. We poor country folk, Mr. Jenkinson!"

They were walking from the house to the grove as he spoke and Jenny saw the archaeological journalist slide a passing glance at the old man and then slowly transfer his attention to herself. But he said nothing, indeed he said very little at all except for asking an occasional question in the stream of Colonel Bartle's explanations. He took a number of photographs, fumbling a midget camera out of a drooping side pocket. Then he produced from a flat portfolio tucked under his arm a block of drawing paper and a charcoal pencil and began to make a slight sketch of that part of the grove where the stone was discovered.

"This is for myself," he explained to Jenny. "I'm awfully bad of course, but I enjoy doing it. I have quite a collection." His veiled eyes smiled shyly at her for a second before reverting to his block. The remark gave Jenny an impression that he expected her to know something of drawing, but she took this to be a reference to her father's creative nature.

"You're amazingly quick," she commented, watching his bony fingers with their black-rimmed nails. "You should do the house as well, really?"

"Ye-es. It does very much belong," he agreed.

"I mean," she hesitated. "Don't please feel that you . . ." She did not know how to convey that she was not occupied by other things without falling into one or other of the extremes of condescension or familiarity.

"You're kind," he murmured formally. "Perhaps I might take advantage and come another time; or come back, even?" This last seemed to have just occurred to him.

"We're going back to the museum, you see," interposed Colonel Bartle, "to compare notes, you know."

By the time they left, half an hour later, Jenny had almost forgotten Mr. Folliot's fears. Mr. Jenkinson was more like herself than anything connected with "publicity." She could quite imagine herself taking him into her studio or on one of the chess visits to Mainter. Just the same, without examining why it should be, she was not surprised when the aged Morris appeared an hour later and the long, thin figure unrolled itself from behind the wheel.

"I managed," he murmured, "I am rather ashamed to say, to shed Colonel Bartle. I felt I must have a word with you. Such a *nice* man, but . . ."

"The light is rather gone, today, for sketching," said Jenny as she led him towards the door. "But do have a cup of tea. I was just going to make it."

"The sketching can wait." He waved it languidly away. "I'd love tea." He seemed to go off into a daze, so Jenny went to the kitchen and found him dithering in just the same place when she came back.

"This is really a frightful imposition," he began, trying to exert himself. "But I felt I really could not . . ."

"Not?"

"Not warn you. You seem to know so little what has been happening. . . ? In the press, you see, this is all the great topic of the moment. And, you know, I was a real Fleet Street chap before I came into a bit of money and could do what I wanted, more or less. And of course, I'm around in our office where one hears things."

"Oh, dear, I do hope you're not going to interview me? I did so like you."

"Lor' no. Not me." He was as horrified as his frail health allowed. "But the others. . . ! They'll be popping up any moment. I do think you should get some friends to rally round. Preferably someone who has a little experience—with the press, you know? I mean, call up reserves, as it were?"

"You mean, people from London? You are not drinking your tea, Mr. Jenkinson."

"Ah. These biscuits are good, aren't they?" He looked wistfully about him, refraining from taking the last biscuit.

"Oh, Mrs. Godolphin made a fruit cake. I'd forgotten." Jenny was already on the way to the kitchen, where he followed her.

"That looks substantial," he approved faintly. "But listen, there isn't much time. They will be battering at the drawbridge any minute. You *must* take my warning seriously. Couldn't you telephone somebody from the company?"

"But it's half across the county, that would be much too late if what you say is true. But . . . ," only now struck by some slight hint of urgency, "I don't at all understand."

"No. That's just what is so worrying. Can I have some more tea? And then you go and call your people. Perhaps they are already on their way over here."

"But why should they be? Do tell me what you are talking about."

"Television crews, the lot."

"But you heard Colonel Bartle say they weren't coming!"

"That lot isn't. Because the others are. They must be very slack, your chaps, they might have alerted you!"

393

"Mr. Folliot did say something, but he thought they wouldn't be interested in me. He expected reporters in his office. There have been enquiries, he said so. But he seemed to think, not here."

"He seemed to think! Of course, here. Where else?"

"Perhaps I will telephone. You're making me quite nervous."

"Splendid girl." He set down his teacup and stood up, taking her upper arm for a moment in a shaky hold. "Do come on! What is it *now*?"

"I was wondering if I should lock the door?"

"That would be fatal. You will have to face the music. It's a new law of psychodynamics. Television gets everywhere, no stopping them. Oh, it's 1968, all right." They arrived at the hall door without appearing to move while he spoke. "This hall looks immensely bigger than it is. Proportions, I suppose. Pity somebody took up the old flagstones and laid timber."

"The floor is laid over the stones. My father meant to have it removed. But it would cost the earth, now."

To Jenny's surprise, when she reached the offices, she was told that Mr. Folliot and Mr. Sandford were on their way to Grove Hill. She was also told that a television team had left just before the departure of the two directors.

"You see? I was right, wasn't I?" Jenkinson complained gently. "You seem—you must forgive me, but this is hardly the moment for convention—so completely ignorant that I'm amazed to see that you have a television set here. You might never have heard of the box at all. Though it does seem to be brand new. It looks quite *snazzy* in this lovely room. Don't you use it?"

"Not much. I don't seem able to make it work properly, so I don't turn it on much. It sort of jumps."

"It sort of jumps," he mourned. "Then you don't know the sort of thing you're in for at all? Still less how it happened?"

"Happened?"

"Listen, carefully. The programme about your stone was proposed by someone who'd heard a vague rumour—London is full of them—and thought *all that* would just make the prehistory lark more interesting to the public. But one of the Barley's narks got wind of it at a technical conference and snapped up the idea for *his* master, since it offered a way *in*, d'you see?"

"I don't even understand what you say, let alone what you mean!"

"Try. Try. The Barley lot heard it all weeks and weeks ago from Polter and others of his kind. . . ."

"Polter!"

"Of course, Polter. He's been peddling the tale for nearly two months. Polter goes everywhere, is in with every set, everybody. He's been chattering like a magpie. That's always his method, talking away without seeming to say anything. That's how he puts over his version of anything that concerns him. And this story concerns him very much, it seems. But nobody has touched it so far because it would annoy the security men. But now, you see? This woman yesterday who got herself arrested for drunken driving. . . ."

"Eileen was not drunk!" cried Jenny, outraged. "She was . . ." then recollecting that she ought not to talk about this . . . "upset," she finished weakly.

"Precisely. Upset by Mark Vail. And it is Vail that Polter's chums are out to get. Vail is very unpopular indeed with all the trendy, liberal types; and, you know, we're all that type in London, nowadays. Vail is too good at his job. He has to be discredited. Various people have been watching your little drama for ages, watching to see if they could get a toehold. You may imagine them with beady eyes looking through the other end of a kaleidoscope, and your undrunken girlfriend has shaken it nicely up. They have a lovely angle now of this nice, innocent provincial lady who has been driven to distraction by police harassment in a case *that has been kept from the public*. And the public has a right to know. But to know in the way Polter wants it to know. I use Polter as a symbol, almost, you understand."

From some thread in this wandering and slowly unwound discourse, Jenny did in fact begin to catch a glimmer, not exactly of what was happening, but of the entangling fashion, helped by Mr. Jenkinson's languid, often broken, course of explanation, in which it was all being made to happen.

"Oh dear, oh dear." Jenny sat down, feeling helpless and rather silly.

395

"You mustn't misunderstand." She gave him a look at this of such a depth of not understanding that Jenkinson gave a jittering crow of laughter. "No, I really *mean* the public has a right to know. A lot of taxpayers' money has gone into some of the Maculan developments and unless the story as it goes the rounds is all totally wrong, which can hardly be the case, some of it has been misused. And in defence spending, d'you see? Defence! *The* most controversial and unpopular way of spending money in our pacifist society. And I don't feel you should hope, either, that the circulating stories are all wrong, or that the reports that will now appear will be all wrong. Journalists often get facts right, nearly always, in fact. They just don't get all the facts—how could they?—and they do astonishingly often draw the wrong conclusions from them. You grasp, don't you, that facts are facts, but conclusions are a matter of fashion? Down here, in this heavenly calm and far from the madding and all that, one doesn't I daresay, go in enough for fads and fancies for you quite to get hold of how much fashion dominates."

"That sounds as if you don't agree with this pacifism? This fashion?"

"Who me? Lor' no. I'm a man of blood. In my ghastly experience, if one doesn't stand up for one's tiny self, to the wall, to the wall!"

"A man of blood," murmured Jenny, bemused.

Mr. Jenkinson was clearly now enjoying his own gloom.

"News, you know, is an odd and a fascinating business. Everybody without exception loves gossip: news, that is. And espionage, treason, plot, are the most intriguing form of gossip, as good as a sports scandal and nowadays better than film stars' copulations. The only time people discover they don't like the news is when it's about themselves."

"But I've been told that I mustn't say anything!"

"That won't save you, you won't get away with *that*. And, you see, the telly, it's the sacred cow of the moment. Barleyman will get away with things, you will see, that no newspaper would dare to do to you. Oh, oh, the things the Barley has done! He is pathologue, a jackanapes of vanity and envy curdled into self-righteousness. And you, you represent a beautiful mosaic of everything he most envies and hates. I don't mean you personally, nobody cares about you. I mean, you own this marvellous house, you get your money from—partly at any rate—weapons of war, your father was a foreigner. Your late husband committed treason, as we hear, but for reasons that Barleyman will make a salmagundi of. And it has all been kept quiet. Polter, now, *he* says that it was all done for love of peace and it's the war men who try to keep it under wraps. Peace, peace. The word is written on Barleyman's banner in letters of napalm!"

Jenny stared at him transfixed by the drifting eloquence while he drank tea by now quite cold.

"You don't quite believe me, do you? Well, you will see. May I?" And he reached for another thick slice of the moist, heavy cake. "Ah. Do I hear the sound of wheels?" He held up the cake as a sign for quiet and they listened.

They reached the window, Jenkinson still eating his cake, as the crunching of a rather heavy vehicle over the stones ceased. Outside was a large closed truck with three huge initials on its side. As soon as it stopped the doors of the cab and at the back opened and five men slipped out. They carried various pieces of equipment and set them down on the silvery little stones of the drive, diving at once back into their storehouse for more dark coloured square boxes with dials and indicators, more big gleaming lamp reflectors, more coils of snaky black cords, massive cameras, long steel tripods. One man called something from the back of the van which could not be heard, but the answer of a short, stocky man who was nearer and turned towards the house was quite clear.

"It's a real Gothic. Light's not bad, and plenty of cloud. We'll get some classy footage, but get your asses off the ground there, there's no time to waste."

"We've got about fifteen minutes," called another voice. They were sorting out their large objects, carrying them away, running out cables. In a few minutes there was nobody to be seen except one man in a black zipped jacket who lounged by the hood of the truck smoking a cigarette and who was evidently the driver. Nobody rang the doorbell, nobody entered the house.

"They're really going to make a job of it. I wish your friends would appear."

"You make it sound as if there were going to be a battle."

Jenkinson did not reply to this but lounged from one window to the other trying to see what the technicians were doing, but they were now invisible. Jenny watched him, disturbed by his sinister prophecies, but not able to take them seriously, for both his choice of words and his manner made everything he said unreal. She was intrigued as well as disturbed, almost excited, not by what was going forward but by some flavour in Jenkinson that reminded her strongly of Mark, in spite of the divergence between the two men of every outward characteristic.

Mark was black-haired, controlled of movement, neat in habit, self-contained, disciplined. Jenkinson, fairish in coloring, was loose-muscled, expansive of gesture, untidy nearly to sordidness in clothing and person; his slow and vague way of speaking produced an effect nearer to Polter's than to Mark's. Yet he conveyed a relationship to the latter that connected in turn to the Professor in the opposite direction. Jenny did not apprehend this likeness as a superficial one, although it seemed to be conveyed by outward mannerisms, including the pitch of voice and choice of words. The surface resemblance was something Jenny lacked the knowledge to assess, the metropolitan fashion of the time, a *dégagé* but faintly scornful questioning that implied an admission of everything being in a condition of imminent dissolution impossible to prevent.

It was a major example of those "fashions" to which Jenkinson referred, and since topical modes always refer to the past and not to the present, this one which, even in 1958, was penetrating down into the half-baked and unthinking layers of society as a childish nihilism, was the aftermath of the Second World War. It was the gradual emergence of the unassimilated condition of defeat, attached as such unadmitted disasters invariably are to quite other imponderable objects. To Jenny it was bewildering because she made its acquaintance within such a short space of time in three such disparate personalities as Mark Vail, who was committed to the preservation of the polity; Professor Polter, who was committed to its radical alteration, and Jenkinson, who implied a refusal to take any part and simply stood in an attitude of looking on. The effect of this atmosphere in Jenkinson for

Jenny was to bring Mark forward in her consciousness—in the common phrase, literally to remind her of him.

Much nearer the frontal area of thought to her was another repetition that came over as cloudily menacing; this was the mention of foreignness. One of the few things Jenny had tried to hide from Julius Maculan was her knowledge of xenophobia in their adopted country. She learned to be wary of it at school, where one or two girls sometimes tried to increase their own worth by reducing Jenny's with the emphasised use of the pronoun "we." "We" pronounce certain words differently and especially foreign words for which Jenny used the correct—that is, foreign—sound; "we" do not do this or that; or "we" do such things differently here. Her father was protected from such affronts by the very great practical value of his intellect, which ensured him the respect and friendship of those who might well have treated him as an enemy alien were he not Julius Maculan and the inventor of devices they needed. His daughter, when away from his side, did not enjoy this shelter of prestige and self-interest. She well knew how the English could behave to strangers.

She knew, too, with her bitterly acquired and still new self-experience, how subtly and cleverly Vincent had used this weapon in his devious assault on her inner strength.

Now two of the intruders were visible again. They approached the house across the grass, so absorbed in their own concerns that they did not notice the new rose beds and walked directly across the raked earth, trailing their serpentine cords, by now decorated with various twigs and grasses. They both wore polo sweaters under suede jackets, with tight black trousers; one jumper was white and the other black. The man in the white one listened through bulky black earphones and fiddled with intense concentration at the controls of a large and evidently heavy gadget box in his left hand which pulled him over sideways. He turned about in intimate conformity with the gestures of the second man whose dark lank curls showed a tonsure on the crown of his head when he bent it. They were followed by an assistant who lifted the coils of wiring as they moved; it was all oddly graceful, planned, and very practiced. Then the three similarly dressed figures stood together consulting for a few moments before they moved towards the house entrance while a fourth man came out into the view of the two watchers, from the doorway, which was out of sight. They all strode to the van and then after some bending and lifting walked back towards the building with such definiteness and briskness that the effect of a chorus was achieved. What they were doing was mysterious to Jenny, but they all now carried different bulky pieces of equipment which were all black or very dark grey, reminding her of a phrase often heard in her girlhood when something so secret that even its inventor did not name it was referred to as the black box.

"Ah," sighed Jenkinson on a downward expiration, "now we shall see action."

A second arrival, this time a low sports car, now appeared in the driveway and came to a halt behind the truck. From it stepped two more men. From the way the others all turned towards it, it was clear that the focus of the chorus was now on the scene. For a brief space everyone but the truck driver disappeared from view and the driver joined in the activity for the first time by beginning to carry the lighting accessories after the rest of the team. Jenny waited for the doorbell to ring, but this did not happen because the house door was not locked.

Instead, a sharp rap announced the entry of the group into the room where Jenny and Jenkinson waited.

"Yes, here we are," said one of the two new arrivals, and led the way for the rest. Since Jenny said nothing—she did not know the conventions for this new form of social intercourse—the man who had spoken raised his eyebrows, which were very black to match a close, thick cap of hair brushed forward over his brow.

"You were expecting us?" he confirmed. "We wired ahead." This was true only in the literal sense, a telegram having been sent off too'late to warn the household.

Jenny made a vague gesture with one hand and moved forward irresolutely.

"You must be . . ." She found she had forgotten the name Jenkinson used but offered her hand to the spokesman. "How do you do."

The entire group, now all inside the room, became quite still, all eyes on Jenny.

"Christ," said a voice blankly. "Doesn't know us."

Two of the detachment peeled off and went one to each side of the room where they began to examine the lower part of the panelling swiftly, bending double to do so and moving aside any piece of furniture that stood in their way. One of this pair was the man who had spoken to Jenny, and his movement left the second passenger of the sports car standing alone. This man now stretched out an arm and pulled the cord switch of a standing lamp by the long sofa that formed an obstacle between the door and the tall stone fireplace. As the illumination showed up his features he tipped up his chin sideways to Jenny, who stared back at him obediently. She was quite ready to conform, as soon as she knew what was expected of her, with some stereotype of behaviour that her ingrained modesty suggested was known to everyone but herself. So, rather than expose her ignorance, she waited until guidance was given as to what she should do or say.

The man who switched on the light shifted from his pose and frowned.

"I am Barleyman," he said with displeasure. "Round the Clock."

"Round the. . . ?" asked Jenny.

"Round the Clock," emphasised a man who had not so far spoken.

"Never heard of Barleyman?" asked one of the panel searchers. "Must be joking." In his quest he was now beside the small round table on which stood various small objects including the bust of Jenny's father. He pushed the table away from the wall by an elbow against its central leg, for he was crouched over. But the old floor there was just a trifle uneven so that the table tipped and the bronze head rocked and then rolled over with a thump to the edge of the table, from which it fell hollowly to the floor.

"Ignorant cunt," observed his companion at this clumsiness. He was now feeling under the edge of the window seat. "Ah. Here we have one at any rate."

"You may find what you are looking for more easily if you

401

follow the wiring of the lamps already plugged in," pointed out Jenkinson. "Without breaking half the valuables in the room. And may I mention that there is a woman present, who also happens to own this place and she is not a waitress from some barrack room?"

"Ah, Jenkinson," said Barleyman easily. "I hardly saw you. Are you becoming a militarist as well as a fascist?"

He himself did not swear; that became noticeable because all the supporting members of the team constantly repeated adjectives or adverbs attributing to the nouns and verbs they used sexual, excretory or blasphemous qualities. Some of their expressions were quite new to Jenny and she would dearly have liked to know what they meant. No, Barleyman did not speak in vulgarisms or even use slang. He was altogether an unnoticeable man in presence: of average height and figure, neat unmemorable features, neutral voice. His clothes were inconspicuous; lacking the modishness of his colleagues, he lacked as well their physical harmony. Looking at his face Jenny found nothing that could be taken hold of in sculpture; a portrait would be meaningless. Yet she could not connect his appearance either with the conventions of Mr. Folliot or of Colonel Bartle. As for a comparison with his distant colleague Jenkinson, they might have come from different planets there was so little likeness.

"You have a television set," Barleyman of Round the Clock returned to Jenny. "Do you not follow current events?"

"Round the Clock is a programme of comment in the evening on the day's news," explained someone kindly.

Jenkinson explained. "The set was new a few weeks ago and seems not to work properly, or so I gather."

"If you don't see television," Barleyman wanted to know from Jenny, "how can you follow what goes on in the world, how can you know what society thinks and feels?"

"Well, I expect I don't know," agreed Jenny. "Except for the papers, that is."

"Newspapers," said the black-haired man, and removed the bulb of the lamp Barleyman had lighted, replacing it with a much stronger one of his own. "This is just to improve the domestic lighting," he explained. "We run the main floods in from the van. And I've put in a transformer so there won't be any shorts."

Sure enough, two of them were going in and out reeling cable cords while the driver brought the big film lamps. They made several trips for the lights and disposed everything with extraordinary speed, lifting long coils and loops of wiring over and round things while two others rolled the big cameras to and fro to assess their needs. Jenny did not like to interfere with this obviously difficult business, but she wished someone would pick up the bronze from the floor, not because it could be damaged but because she did not like to see her father's head lying there on its side as if he had been carelessly decapitated.

Barleyman was talking into an almost invisible microphone and getting answers from the man with the sound apparatus, neither of them taking any notice of the other conversations, largely of obscenities, being exchanged by the technicians. The lighting arrangements being now complete, the room was instantaneously flooded with a blaze of savage yellow-white heat. Now Barleyman was talking more loudly in a way that reminded Jenny of those works of literature fashionable a generation before, that reproduced the inner musings of their characters in what was known as stream of consciousness. Many of his remarks were addressed to himself or to his famulus with the recording box, but some to the others. These were instructions in a language of their own which the group could disentangle from the stream of consciousness without difficulty. They seemed to understand each other less by words than by some form of extrasensory perception, attuning movements and sounds with great skill.

Gradually Barleyman was saying things to and about herself—though without in fact speaking to her—and Jenny began to pick up references to things said to him before, in the company offices, in the town and even in the hamlet of Gullion and at the Blanes' farm. There were passages recognizable as descriptions of the countryside, then of the hill, the grove and the house itself. The beech grove figured as a somehow gloomy indication of the remoteness of her life, and the discovery of the archaic stone became symbolic of a state of

403

existence so out of touch with the modern world that it could hardly be called living. At one moment Jenny was startled to hear that Barleyman was speaking of Vincent's mother, but the reference passed so swiftly she was not sure it really happened. There was no reason why the public should not be just as interested in Vincent Cheyney's mother as in his wife, she pointed out to herself, if there was indeed a wide interest in Vincent Cheyney at all; still, it seemed unreal to introduce a figure into Grove House which in real life Vincent had always determinedly kept away from the place. But Jenny gradually became aware that the monologue was building up a picture of herself. And her remoteness was not loneliness but a chosen isolation, an exclusiveness—the word was used of her neighbours in a way that sounded to Jenny somehow like the advertising for large London shops—that declined to include itself in the life of some community with which Barleyman stood in intimate relation.

Barleyman now put his microphone into a pocket and issued some rapid directions, while the man who had travelled with him produced a little brush and a large powder puff with which he removed all the shine from Barleyman's face and tidied up his already tidy person, adjusting his hair with care and twitching at his tie and collar. He then turned to Jenny, indicating a wish to do as much for her, but she backed away from him so quickly that he desisted.

During this process Barleyman was talking to the others in what is known as standard English; when he spoke into the microphone his voice and accent changed slightly, sounding a little rough and with a vaguely "regional" accent which, however, was not easy to place. At one moment there seemed to be an almost Yorkshire vowel sound, then again something like Suffolk and occasionally he blurred an "r." At some time during this preparation two new figures entered the now crowded space, but only gradually through blinding light did Jenny make out that these were Teddy Sandford and Mr. Folliot standing by the door. Once it looked as if Mr. Folliot was attempting to interrupt what was going forward, but a combination of the unfamiliar and bulky equipment creating traps in every direction and the hypnotic effect of Barleyman's total self-absorption reduced him to compliance.

"I think we're almost ready," announced Barleyman at last. "Let's just check names et cetera."

Jenny's name was easy, but there was some difficulty with Maculan, which Barleyman pronounced Macúlan. It took quite some persuasion from Maculan's daughter, with the help of Mr. Folliot, before he would say Máculan. In the midst of all the unfamiliarities so suddenly filling her living room, Jenny was puzzled by this because the name was not unknown and was always pronounced correctly in public. But she saw from his face that Mr. Barleyman was not pleased at her insistence; in fact he became quite irritable and it dawned on Jenny that he was saying the word wrongly on purpose. The mistake made him more like the unseen members of his audience.

There was now, by common accord, complete silence. The men holding the loops of black wire tiptoed on padded soles and nothing was heard but the uneven whizzing and crackling of the lights and the quiet hum of the cameras. Barleyman stood easily, resting his weight on one foot, an old-fashioned "pork pie" hat put into his hand by his acolyte. He was shorter than the other men, his clothes dark and conventional with none of their outré elegance. His hair was cut short and brushed straight, his tie dark and narrow, the white shirt collar could have been that of any city clerk, his features with a pleased little smile now showing for the audience were neither handsome nor plain but perfectly ordinary. Barleyman lifted his left hand. Then he let it drop and tilted up his chin in the gesture Jenny had already seen, while his right hand raised the hat in the gesture of one who greets an acquaintance in the park on an evening too warm for headgear. He smiled a little more broadly and began to speak.

"Good evening, everyone. As you know, today's programme is entirely on one subject, a strange and tangled story of which until today you were allowed to know nothing. You will hear about Vincent Cheyney, the rich director of the multimillion company Tantham and Maculan, usually called the Maculan Company. This company is a distinguished part of what General Eisenhower once called the military-industrial complex and makes many of the advanced weapons that we have to produce to keep up with friends and others in

NATO, across the Atlantic and in other places. They make more friendly things as well, you will be glad to know, including some of the equipment that sends this programme into your homes. Now Vincent Cheyney died very suddenly a few months ago in a road accident, and after his death extensive enquiries were started into the business affairs of the company. I am not allowed to tell you just what those enquiries were or the names of the people who carried them out because they are civil servants who, in the great tradition of this country, may never be made responsible for their orders or their actions—only politicians are responsible. At the moment the Minister in charge is saying nothing.

"What we do know is that the questioning was so intensive in some directions that at least one person questioned, a lady connected closely with the Maculan Company, has now had to go into a nursing home, where she is under sedation and is not allowed to see anyone, on the instructions of her husband and the doctors. And all this would not have been known had she not been so distressed and unnerved by the inquisition she was subjected to that she drove her car into a tree and was arrested as being incapable of driving. It must be a most urgent matter to make it necessary to bully women, you may think; yes, to bully women, I said. That was what I thought, but the only answer I can get from the authorities is that it is all a routine affair; there is no other comment. But I could ask Vincent Cheyney's friends, and they did answer my questions. They begged me to quote them anonymously, and when one thinks of the patient in the nursing home one can understand why they are nervous. These friends of Vincent Cheyney told me that he worried about his work and that he cared only for peace, the peace of our country, the peace of Europe and the peace of the world. Yet the Maculan Company has many connexions with large and secret defense contracts in the United States and in West Germany among others. Neither the American nor the German government has any comment to make.

"Now you have already seen and heard the Managing Director of the Maculan Company, who is the husband of the lady I told you about. We talked to him, again as you will see, in his palatial office. He, too, had very little information for us, although he must know something about his own company's business. But we, at the powerhouse of Round the Clock, are not so easily discouraged, as you all know. We are always concerned that the public should be able to form a balanced opinion of what is its own business, public affairs. So today we left our studios to travel far away into a little known nook of our country, a district of big estates and historic houses, a leisurely world that none of *us* are likely to attain. And we are there now, in the home of Vincent Cheyney. It is a far cry from our daily tasks and yours. This is the house of a man of mystery, who dealt in war but longed for peace.

"It is an ancient house and this beautiful apartment is the living room, which is lined with priceless panelling, though that may seem to some of you to be a little dark and formal for ordinary tastes. The whole place was restored at the beginning of the last war by its then new owner. That was Julius Maculan, the inventor, who came from a distant country to contribute his genius to our war effort. Vincent Cheyney's wife was Maculan's daughter, and Cheyney was not a poor man, as you can all see. But his possessions did not succeed in making him happy, if we can believe his friends.

"Well, before I came here, I asked the spokesman for the Special Security Services, which has been making all these enquiries—oh, yes, they have a spokesman who is allowed to talk to the press and television—and this spokesman denied what was told me by those who knew Cheyney well. He said that Vincent Cheyney was selling the military secrets of our country to some group he referred to as our enemies. That a man with such a house, such a way of life, should do that may seem strange, but that is what was said and that is all I was told. That was an official statement. Cheyney's friends are not official spokesmen, of course, but they say something quite different, that Cheyney cared for peace. And they have some evidence on their side, for Cheyney knew what war is, my friends. As many of you did, he played some part in the defeat of the greatest military conspiracy in the history of the world, the Nazi Germans. So, there is a conflict of evidence here and we hope his widow can help us clear it up.

"Mrs. Cheyney, your father was the famous inventor, Julius Maculan, wasn't he? Can you tell us how he came to our country?"

At this moment Jenny understood clearly for the first time that this invasion, like so many larger ones, needed the public seal of the victim's approval; she was to be paraded and thus formally seen to endorse her own humiliation. Not only the confrontation but the question itself was unexpected, and she hesitated in astonishment, blinking uneasily into the Cyclops camera now trained upon her face. She raised a hand to shield her face from the lights focused on her, for their almost blinding blaze partly prevented her from seeing the man addressing her. He made a sharp chopping movement with one hand, conveying to her that she was not to shade her face, and she obeyed. She must not hold things up, she felt, and spoke then, hastily, stammering a little with nervousness but feeling absolutely obliged to do what was expected of her.

"He came for the first time in the early thirties, but not to stay then. . . ."

"He had not made up his mind whether or not he wanted to stay?"

"I was going to say . . . But no, there was no question then of his staying. You see . . ."

"Not until later? When the dark threat of war threw its shadow over his own country?"

"The threat of war was always—I beg your pardon?"

Whatever Barleyman had said, or she thought he said, was not repeated. Jenny waited a moment, her eyes flickering to and fro for a lead, peering into the lights. Barleyman made another gesture that she should continue. This was not seen, since both cameras were trained on Jenny. She licked her lips and frowned, trying to concentrate.

"It wasn't like that at all," she began. What was she going to say? She did not know. But she knew this sounded quite wrong and she must say something for her father's sake.

"My father loved this country," she said too loudly. "He used to say he was more English than the English because he chose to—"

"British, we usually say," said Barleyman indulgently.

"No, English, *he* said. You see, he never went to Scotland

"—or . . . or Wales and he knew that people here are very fussy, very particular about that, but abroad, you see, nobody ever says Britain, they always say—"

"Yes, but we are not talking about abroad just now," Barleyman's voice was kind and encouraging. "So, British, let's say."

"But you are getting it all wrong about coming here. I mean, it was quite different."

"We are trying to understand. How do you mean, different?"

"What you said about this house. As if . . . And he didn't come here because he was afraid of the war."

"But of course not. Did I say that? I'm sorry if I did."

"But." She gulped and started again. "But when he bought this house it was derelict; it had to be partly rebuilt or we couldn't have lived. . . . It was the only suitable—I mean, it was near the testing shop. Where he had to be, d'you see?" She ran down, stuttering and almost gasped, "Nobody wanted the house then, it was just when the war started."

"That was when he came to stay? Bringing you? And your mother, too?"

"Yes but my mother went back and—"

"Your mother went back to Rumania? Alone? After the war began?"

"Well, it was just before, a few weeks—"

"You said the war had just started?"

"That was when he bought this house, but . . ."

One camera swung round towards the door, including the room in the scene, and caught Teddy Sandford's face in its sweep. He did not know it although Barleyman seemed to divine the move by that extrasensory perception and moved his eyes to take in Teddy, leading the attention of anyone watching, including Jenny. Teddy, watching her and not the camera, did not try to change his expression. It was strained and anxious and as the conversation reached unintelligible confusion, he screwed up his features in the comic anguish of one watching a loaded tray of china about to crash.

"Is something wrong, Mr. Sandford?"

Addressed, Teddy tried to clear his face of all meaning. He grimaced widely, gave a snort intended to be a laugh of

409

disavowal and waved his plump, rather pampered hands.

"Well," said Barleyman with polite reluctance, "let us leave the past, then. Your terrible loss must have been a great shock to you, Mrs. Cheyney. We all feel for you and I'm sure you have the sympathy of us all." This in the respectful tone of one offering condolences, and with a glance into the camera to include the unseen watchers in his remark. Jenny was still trying to concentrate on her father, and for a moment it seemed to her that he referred to the death of ten years before. Then she shook her head with a puzzled twitch of the eyebrows and stumbled again into speech.

"Oh. You mean Vincent? Yes. Yes, of course."

"You shared his political interests, I expect?"

"Politics? Vincent never talked politics. He was not in the least interested—as far as—as far as I know."

"But his pacifism? And the authorities seemed to think...?"

"The authorities? No, that's quite wrong. Vincent didn't even vote. I don't think I ever remember him discussing anything political. Not even, you know, the way people talk at parties or—no, never, now I come to think of it."

"Then you think the official view may be wrong?" He sounded puzzled himself now.

"Well, if they say so. I mean, I don't know what the official view is. But I suppose. . . ."

Again he left the theme, and the conversation became easier. Jenny was pleased to tell Barleyman about her home, its age, the various periods at which it was built and rebuilt. Then later, he asked whether an officer of the Special Security Service before mentioned had visited her as well as others connected with the Maculan Company.

"Oh, yes," she agreed, surprised that he did not know. "Mr. Vail stayed here for a time."

"He stayed here? He questioned you, as he did Mrs. Sandford?"

"Questioned? Yes, yes he did." But she sounded doubtful and her voice changed without her knowing it.

"I believe Mrs. Sandford came to see you before she had this unfortunate accident. You are close friends, aren't you?"

"Oh, yes, poor Eileen. I mean Mrs. Sandford. She came over. It was when she drove away that it happened, after that,

I mean." The memory of that afternoon disconcerted Jenny and she looked even more frightened, although her nerves and her stomach were quite calm at the moment, she was relieved to feel. "But the accident wasn't serious, nobody was really hurt."

"She must have been very much upset, though, to drive into a tree?"

"Yes, I didn't realize she was so—so distraught. It wasn't a tree—"

"It was not anything that happened here that upset her?"

"Here? Oh, no, what could . . . ? She was telling me about the questioning. She didn't understand that Mr. Vail has to find—I mean, it was worrying for her and she got distressed."

"It had been going on for some time? The questioning?"

"Yes, she said so. I would have suggested her not driving if I had realised. But I didn't think, you see she—Mrs. Sandford—is such a good driver. She does everything well, you know. She's wonderfully competent."

"Then she must have been, as you said, quite distraught, beside herself, to make such a mistake driving?"

"She must have been. But, you know she was upsetting herself about it more than. . . . It was the repetition, I think."

"You don't know, Mrs. Sandford did not confide in you, what her trouble was?"

"Oh, no. I don't really know much about it all, the whole thing. I haven't been told much. . . ." This came out with a falseness that caused someone in the room to release a small groan of helpless misery into what was for a moment rather a pause of quiet.

"Not even though this officer, this security officer, was staying here?"

"No. He, naturally, did not tell me. And you said yourself, we are so far off the beaten track here. We don't know what is going on in the world, I suppose."

"And not from your husband, either? He did not discuss his work with you?"

"Vincent? With me? Goodness no, he never. . . ." It was impossible to find any way out of that sentence and a mulish, badgered look came over Jenny's face.

Mr. Barleyman turned from Jenny at last and began to ask

411

questions of Mr. Folliot, trying, it seemed, to draw him into a general conversation. But Mr. Folliot was so stiff and formal as to appear hostile, which indeed he was, and would answer only with monosyllables, which amused Mr. Barleyman and he smiled into his cameras with a friendly, rather confiding smile. At last, the whole team understood, without anything being said or done, that the interview was ended and they scattered, carrying lamps and cameras, to make more film of the house.

Later while the van was being repacked with all the unfamiliar gear, Jenny bethought herself of the proprieties as she understood them, and suggested a drink. Mr. Barleyman accepted for the whole team except for the driver, who was not allowed to take alcohol while working, and they all came in and stood about chatting easily for ten minutes or so. The occasion was now almost a party and it was noticeable that everyone present was concerned to be pleasant and told amusing stories about a recent programme in which they interviewed an eminent Churchman who held strong views on almost everything except, as it seemed to the benighted Jenny, the doctrines of Christianity.

Then at one of those invisible signals from Barleyman the team, all of whom had ceased to swear while being sociable, made their farewells and thanked Jenny. Barleyman himself came last and paid her compliments with his kind smile, which included her in what they had all been doing.

"Without cooperation we cannot do our job of keeping the public informed. Without information there can be no genuine public opinion and I'm sure you agree that as life gets more and more complicated, public opinion gets more and more important. Now there is just one thing I want you to be clear about. What we have been doing here this afternoon is making a recording on what is called videotape. This is necessary because there are other sections of this record of current events, and the whole thing needs to be put together in the studio to make a coherent story. Besides, you yourself are not used to broadcasting, good though you were—you were excellent—but naturally to make things clear to the viewers it all has to be tidied up—edited. The finished programme will be on the air tomorrow at our usual time and you will be able to see it because I had Bruno—that's the clever man over there—adjust your set for you. All you have to do now is to switch it on, you know how to do that, don't you? There. You see? Well, now we shall leave you in peace again, Mrs. Cheyney. I just want you to know that you have earned the gratitude of the British public by your wonderful cooperation. Thanks again for all your hospitality and kindness. Goodbye, until we meet again tomorrow on the screen."

Mr. Barleyman bowed after this long speech and, waving his hat as he went through the door, rejoined his assistants, and the sound of engines was shortly to be heard.

"He was really nice, at the end," said Jenny, feeling for some reason relieved that she was able to like Mr. Barleyman. "But I can't think how they will get any sort of reasonable story about Vincent out of the nonsense I talked. I expect they will have to throw it all away, don't you?" she appealed to Mr. Jenkinson.

"An amusing idea," mourned Jenkinson, "but I rather fancy you will not be so amused when you see the programme."

"But they can't alter what is on their tape, can they? I'm sure it will be quite useless."

"He won't actually alter a single word. Or rather, they won't, the technical boys, the cutters and editors. And, I must say, they won't need to."

"You think they'll use that rubbish?" asked Teddy. "Sorry, Jenny."

"I'm sure they won't," argued Jenny, now quite happily. "I don't think I've seen any of these Round the Clock programmes, but there are some other interview programmes and they are always quite different from such chatter. I mean people seem to talk so much more tidily than I do."

"Of course they will use it," said Mr. Folliot.

"They are hugging themselves, or Barleyman is. You cut your own throat, not to mention Vail's, with a generous completeness that I haven't seen equalled since I stopped attending trials at the Old Bailey." Mr. Jenkinson swirled his drink round in his glass and watched it with profound gloom. "But you'll see all that for yourself, tomorrow."

"You are about to undergo a crash course in public relations," Teddy assured her. "Jenkinson here is right. I didn't get the point myself, before."

413

"There have already been murmurs about a Royal Commission," said Mr. Folliot. "I heard from Lord Tantham. After every editor in Fleet Street has followed Barleyman's line for a week, Tantham will no longer be able to resist the pressure."

"I shouldn't be surprised if the murmurs are joined by others demanding a disciplinary enquiry into Vail's methods," Jenkinson hazarded. "I must go. And, like our friend Barleyman, I must thank you for your hospitality, Mrs. Cheyney. And for the opportunity of watching the great man at work; it was a liberal education."

"Of course, the general current of public opinion is much in his favour at this time. But it is informative to watch him, as you say. An atmosphere is produced, one does not quite see how, in which it is almost impossible to intervene." Mr. Folliot shook his grey head at his own impotence. "I was much impressed by my own feeling of helplessness."

"He takes his own power for granted, you see, that is his secret."

"But why doesn't the public see through him?" demanded Teddy. "Doesn't anyone see that it's all completely one-sided?"

"People are not all stupid. But no other possible argument is even hinted at."

"Not even a hint towards any other view is offered!"

"Just so," agreed Jenkinson. "Barleyman puts his thought, as the only possible opinion, into each segment of the public separately in the viewer's own head, in the privacy of his own sitting room."

"And naturally the viewer finds himself intelligently agreeing, as he thinks spontaneously, with the famous commentator." Mr. Folliot shook his head again, resigned to the worst.

"Still, one shudders to think what may happen if this country finds itself in danger again," persisted Teddy. "It's defeatist indoctrination, nothing less. The man is practically a traitor!"

"If he were he would be easier to deal with." Jenkinson was now half out of the door, and turned to reply. "He's just incredibly vain, sure he's right. And his certainty infects the audience. *That's* the trouble."

He was once more disappearing and again turned back.

"It's none of my business, you will say. But I am really so struck all of a heap by your—ah—well, perhaps better not carry on in that strain. But you made some mistakes, d'you see, that make me feel you won't cope much better with others."

"Others?" cried Jenny, startled.

"Of course, others. That's what I mean, you're just not up to this sort of thing. Look—" He ticked off points by pulling limply at one long finger after another. "First you didn't recognize the great man when he appeared. Mistake one. Then you corrected his pronunciation, and you let it be seen that you understood his wishing to mispronounce a foreign name so that it sounded Scots, understood that he was being folksy. Mistake two. And, more difficult to express this, but you showed the whole time, in spite of your nervousness, which made it worse since even your shyness couldn't hide it, a comical sort of air of not taking the whole thing seriously. Barleyman absolutely isn't used to that, you know. So mistake three. I don't feel that a warning from me will help much, but I can't not say it. You are going to be inundated with reporters and photographers and you must try to be careful with them. Only, of course, you don't know how." Jenkinson gazed sadly into Jenny's worried face, and then turned to her two companions. "She shouldn't be left alone, you know, really. It's going to be a massacre."

"And there aren't even any gates to be closed," added Teddy. "No way of keeping the world out."

CHAPTER XXIX

SINCE NOTHING happened on the following day, Jenny was glad she had resisted the not very wholehearted efforts of Teddy Sandford and Mr. Folliot to quarter one or the other of them in the house as bodyguard. They were fully occupied elsewhere, she sensibly told them, and they were obliged to agree that this was only too true. She was able to spend the entire afternoon, without a single interruption, in her studio, and returned to the house to find Polly and the kittens sitting solemnly awaiting her. On the excuse of its being one of those cool dim days of late spring when evenings can strike chill, Jenny lit the side-room fire and was so much amused by the springs and tumblings of the little creatures that she almost forgot to switch on the television set at the prescribed hour.

The famous fanfare and the whirling spirals of the introduction already filled the screen; the loops, which reminded Jenny of the reels of black cable, resolved themselves into the resounding announcement of "Round the Clock."

When she heard the now familiar voice and saw the figure, at first standing in the studio, hat in hand, it came home to her for the first time how very different people are in the flesh from their photographs.

The studio set gave place to a narrow lane, winding upwards between high banks, a slanting shot of Grove Hill from the distance, then the Blanes' farmyard. From close underneath, the grove, rooted in breathtaking beauty, displayed its still grandeur, and Jenny leaned forward, entranced by the strange outside glimpse of her familiar sentinels. A little pang of jealousy that the proud secrecy of the trees should be so exposed to the eyes of indifferent millions mingled itself with her sharp sense of their withdrawn dignity. The damaged chestnut tree dominated for a long moment the foreground, with its gaping slash of black cinder, so that any view of a garden was obscured and then, sliding over the broken tree, the house loomed, dark and quiet, looking as if it might well be unoccupied and, in its own sufficiency, unlikely to welcome newcomers. As if seeing it for the first time Jenny noticed the uneven positioning of windows and chimney groups, the unplanned slopes of roof, which together lent the place a curious look of slyness, like an old man's face where the features are bent and distorted by the experiences of a long life. This was so far from anything presented by the house in its reality that it came over with a shock as a crass lie, and yet it was unquestionably the same house she had lived in since her childhood and perhaps, it now unnervingly appeared, had never really seen.

All this time Barleyman was speaking the introduction recorded the day before, and now he appeared on the screen in a picture that darkened significantly, a panelled apartment of high and sombre proportions. With powerful effect the camera's eye swooped up in steep slants at umbrous wood; the deep carving of ceiling moulding lowered overhead as if knightly pennants might almost still be hanging up there in the dusty shades of centuries. This aspect of noble surroundings from another age was underlined by Barleyman's voice and tone, which now took on colour and meaning as posing an immense and untraversable distance between the place he was in and himself, and still more, when he gave his confiding smile of reassurance, between this place and the watching dwellers in cosy living rooms.

Startlingly, the picture lightened into a small and untidy bungalow sitting room where a large dog lay on the hearth rug before a modern tiled grate, and a stout woman in a coverall answered a question with the information that she was Mrs. Cheyney, Senior. Jenny quite caught her breath at this fictionalised presentation of what were facts, no question of that, but dramatised with an effrontery that was no compliment to the onlookers on whom the trick was practiced. Surely a gasp of resentment must go up from the throat of the simplest among the audience at such shameless deception.

Almost before Jenny could collect her wits to concentrate

on what the stout woman, stroking alternately the dog's back and her own curled grey hair, was saying about her son's childhood and his volunteering for the army, the screen was again showing that dark and alienating magnificence of the side room. It was and was not this room, the only real grandeur of which was its survival from a time when panelling was a normal wall covering for the homes of solid yeomen. Unsatisfied by the point already forced home, the camera repeated its conjuring up of Jenny's surroundings with a cleverness that was almost witchcraft. There was a swoop at the much higher walls of the hall and an expanse of oak floor running in parallel lines that showed on the screen as larger than the whole area of the house in actuality, all covered in a wheeling flick of the mechanical eye. This slid then to details of carving, revealed a window quoin of bevelled stone, a shot from the floor at the wide fireplace that made it cavernous behind Barleyman's modest figure. Jenny relived with a physical realness near pain the presence of Mark leaning against the fireplace.

Even stranger, when the cameras at last approached the owner of all this magnificence, it was no more Jenny they reproduced than the house was the house. But, frighteningly, it might really be Jenny as she was and not as she saw herself? Here was a thin, dark creature who might have been quite old, of indecisive movement, flickering glance, shaky hands. She looked almost shifty, at once haughtily reserved and defensive; she appeared to be backing away from the light, and this was so, but in the picture it looked like cringing. Foreignness having been established by her opening answers about her father, the English voice now took on the dubiety of a deception, and the slight figure was indefinably but undeniably alien. Here was an interloper occupying a treasure of island history; her pride in her home became gloating. The question entered Jenny's own mind, as she watched what she could only with an effort recognise, and listened to words she knew for her own, as to how she came to be here and what she was doing here.

The picture changed again. Here was Harry Blane with Mrs. Blane in her white apron standing in the doorway of the farmhouse, looking up at the grove above them on the hill and echoing her own statements of the great age of the place, the generations of Blanes settled on the land, the recollection of the coming of its new owner. Nothing was said that suggested animosity in the Blanes towards the Maculans, but the editing had removed as too long a rambling account by Mrs. Blane about her affection for Maculan and his generous investment in her own house. What was retained, without any explanation, were the phrases telling of the arrival of an unknown coming from they knew not where, at the beginning of the war. And when the cameras swerved once more upwards, upwards where the great trees reared their cathedral sternness, their immense antiquity, it would have taken a rare spirit of independence not to accept the implication.

From the country homeliness of Mrs. Blane the picture moved back to the flimsy modern bungalow where the stout woman, now holding a mixing bowl and egg whisk, talked in a fretful Midlands complaint. She had not seen her son for years. Vin got a commission, was an officer, rose in the world. She understood he'd married a foreigner, very rich, she dared say; her father was famous but the mother did not know why. Vin was always a clever boy, took after his father in that way, terrible shock his death had been but no, her husband didn't want her to go to the funeral. And there was the money, mourning clothes and railway fares cost a lot nowadays. When had she last seen Vin? When was it, sometime in the war. No, he never came to see her since his marriage. Didn't get on with his stepfather, you know how it is. Yes, here was a picture of him at school, that was him in the middle row, she couldn't quite recall the occasion of the photo, some football match. Oh, Scouts uniform they were wearing, so it was. No, he never took any interest in politics as a boy that she knew of; she supposed Vin would be a Conservative, they all are, aren't they; he was a Director of this company, after all. She couldn't quite get the name of the company, it was on the tip of her tongue but Vin was always ambitious and wanted to get on. He took a lot of exams in the army. Well you've been very kind, thanks very much, it was lovely; the neighbours would have something to talk about.

Before Jenny could formulate clearly her feeling that this exposure of the unsuspecting woman was an insult to human

419

dignity, Grove House was back on the screen, astonishingly now in the drawing room, which did look such a caricature of what Vincent's mother might expect of a rich company director who would be a Conservative, that Jenny laughed aloud. Barleyman was talking of peace and armaments, NATO and a man of mystery. How did he get into the drawing room? The background became unclear; there was the travesty of Jenny again, dismissing Eileen Sandford with what sounded like flippancy, admitting her own questioning and the presence of a police officer in her house. She lifted a thin hand on the screen and pushed her hair away, arresting the movement nervously and frowning in the very personification of one who realises too late that she has said something incriminating. If anyone missed the point, Teddy showed his expression of absurd anxiety as he listened to Jenny talking.

Now a roar of traffic indicated a big city, massive buildings and a doorway that metropolitans would recognise but which meant nothing to Jenny. The voice of another commentator discoursed fluently on military security and then, without taking a breath as it were, of public investment in the testing of some apparatus developed by Tantham and Maculan, the nature and purpose of which it was forbidden to mention. Now the meaning of the setting became clear. From the doorway issued several men out of darkness into sunlight. With a sharp jolt of her nerves Jenny saw that one of them was Mark. An older man, wearing a black hat, said crisply that he had already told the television network that there was no comment. Mark turned hastily away from the camera and walked off down the crowded street with his sloping gait, his shoulders hunched as if he could feel the public eye on him.

In a luxurious office, yet another man with distinguished grey temples and a stern, cold look said something about the national interest and safety; Vincent Cheyney, he averred, was the meanest kind of traitor. Barleyman took him up on that. No trial could be held and nobody was entitled to judge Cheyney. "I was asked for my opinion," said the elderly man angrily, "and that is my opinion." He could make no further comment, the matter was highly confidential and he was bound by the Official Secrets Act. Only afterwards did Jenny recall that this was Lord Tantham. Without pause or announcement the scene was shown of another office, no longer the fine dignity of George IV furniture but the look of tomorrow, that so quickly is yesterday. Jenny recognised the company offices, but the majority would assume the two rooms were both in London; there was no indication of removal from the street scene, with its thunderous tall buses and a glance at Whitehall familiar all over the world.

Jenny perceived from this at first puzzling sequence that much of what was false in the programme was not deliberately untruthful but the outcome of the moving camera technique. The men making the film knew that the Chairman's office and that of the Managing Director were separated by a considerable journey into the west country, which they must have made at least once themselves, and they may well have assumed either that the audience would see the change to landscape from townscape or that –in the interest of speed—it did not matter. In fact, in this instance, the untruth was not important; it altered nothing of moment to the story being told. But Jenny found this untruth shocking, at first because the story was in fact her own life and she could not help knowing that it was distorted into fantasy; and gradually, with increasing anxiety, as she began to perceive the great weight and scope of Barleyman's attack. Jenkinson may have been right in his view that the object of Barleyman's hostility was Mark Vail, but in his onslaught the reputation and stability of a great industrial undertaking was being systematically undermined, upon the existence of which, at its simplest level, the livelihoods of several thousand families depended.

The adroit fashion in which the interview now proceeding on the screen was managed underlined this thought. Here was Teddy Sandford, hiding as always his competence and conscience under a pose of jolly stupidity. He was stocky, bluff, abrupt, complacent. Bound to ward off Barleyman's questions for reasons that were never presented, he was seen not to be answering at all. He repeated several times that he did not know the reply to a query, he was not aware of some detail, once that he was not empowered to disclose boardroom figures. The exposure of a pompous fool parrying Barleyman's reasonable requests for enlightenment was complete when Teddy, confused by a sudden change of subject, stopped in the middle of a sentence, stared and then said loudly that his wife was under sedation and could not receive visitors. Jenny did not know it, but the next sequence was cut out of the film; Teddy pointed out that Eileen's distress was to be laid, with much else, at Cheyney's door and not at that of the authorities, who were only trying to discover the extent of the damage done by the dead man. What remained to be seen might almost have meant that Eileen Sandford was being drugged to prevent her talking to Barleyman. Jenny expected Mr. Folliot to appear and adjust the balance of evidence, but he did not; in fact he very unwisely had refused to do so. Barleyman said so in a laconic sentence.

She hardly took in the end of the programme; the fanfare sounded again, an announcer spoke and then the screen was filled by a swaying mob of juveniles shouting and waving to a young man in jeans who descended from an aeroplane holding a guitar which he began to play as soon as he reached his admirers. The noise of a wailing voice, almost drowning the howls of the young people, filled the room with a battering disharmony that seemed to shake the television set. Jenny recovered her wits enough to grasp that this was another programme and switched it off.

Her bewilderment was so great that she sat for some time not even trying to order her impressions. Just as the scene of this room in which she now sat was that room shown on the screen, so were the other scenes "real" and the words heard spoken, by herself and others. Yet it was a phantasmagoria, a confidence trick, a miracle of technique in which no camera or microphone, still less any guiding intelligence, ever appeared to insist on their influence; the thing looked and sounded as if it had just happened without manipulation, just as it was. If the scenes shown had been fiction, they could hardly have distorted more what they depicted; but what they showed existed, and existed in the exact form and bulk and sound presented. That figure, somewhat resembling herself but certainly not herself, was what she had now become for millions. Mark, shown as retreating, really had walked away from the camera, he must have done. The jowly round comic evading candid questions about the taxpayers' money was now implanted forever as unfit for responsibility, the wicked uncle in a pantomime of the class war.

She sat still, aware of hunger but unable to pull herself together enough to get herself something to eat. More than anything, a sensation of unprotected nakedness frightened her. From a privacy she was aware of as far too complete, she was suddenly totally exposed to what could only be a hostile crowd. The stings of a million eyes touched her with what must be distrust and contempt; for her the alienation produced by the film was so great that she could leave her own internal concept of everything that had happened since Vincent's death and see it from the almost opposite direction proposed by Barleyman. She felt no indignation, the blow was too powerful for that; what she felt was fear. An inherited, a very old instinct, told her that she was alone here in this house, without fences, without gates, without help and faced by a huge concourse of strangers under the persuasion of a spellbinder who could have no other effect on them but to turn them, for Jenny Cheyney, into a mob.

The telephone began to ring and she knew what it was. The first three calls were from newspapers. Then began the scurrilous badgering. After half a dozen incoherent tirades from private persons who could simply pick up their instruments and dial her number from far and wide as long as they had access to the county telephone directory, Jenny left the receiver off its rest and thus cut herself off from help as well as obloquy. For the first time since Vincent's death Jenny herself locked the doors of her house.

In the dawn, filled with the soft effulgence of sun-shot mist, the first photographers arrived, followed an hour or so later by the reporters. The entire range of that day's newspapers brought up from the town showed that Mr. Folliot's forecast was correct: almost without exception Barleyman's interpretation was accepted and copied without question. Only one journal mentioned Vincent Cheyney by name with disapproval; in all the others he was dismissed as misled at worst and in most of the accounts he figured as an idealistic pacifist trapped into the traffic with arms by unnamed forces. Julius Maculan was an inventor of terrifying weapons of destruc-

423

tion; in one account his name was connected with notorious arms dealers of the past, in several as a mysterious and implicitly sinister figure of unknown antecedents looming out of the murky shadows of the Balkans, in not one as a contributor to British prowess in the Second World War.

The local evening paper, the same one consulted weeks before by Jenny as to the date of her pregnancy, brought news of a demonstration encamped outside the gates of Tantham and Maculan in protest against the manufacture of aggressive armaments. Later in the evening the television news showed pictures of this force, a gypsy encampment with tents and caravans.

Naturally, the living were of more interest than the dead. In the ensuing days the Sandfords, the Folliots, Jenny and anyone from the offices or the works of the company who liked the sound of his own voice, were quoted and photographed over and over again. In contrast to the confounding unreality of what appeared in print, the journalists themselves were rather pleasant in their complete absorption in their strange trade.

After the first day or so Jenny found them excellent company and learned through them not to take their products too seriously. As Mr. Jenkinson had told her, the facts they did get hold of were almost always correct; those left out of their accounts were ignored, either because some attitudes were already taken for granted and therefore not mentioned, or because other things were not known about. When Jenny or the older and more experienced among the reporters produced fresh "angles" or "stories," these were seized upon with glad cries of surprise and written up with an eagerness just as great as the original distortions had caused. They were in the main as loyal to each other and as ready to help each other as they were companionable, trading their wares amongst themselves like children swapping marbles.

That the photographers caused much damage in the grove and the garden and frightened the cattle belonging to the Blanes was a more serious matter than Jenny's immediate and total loss of privacy. After the first three days of the siege, Harry Blane rigged sheep barriers across the road on the hill at the point where the Maculan property ended and the path became public.

Compared with the general public, the press, with all its inconvenience and intrusion, was bearable and at times amusing. But when sackloads of letters began to arrive, fairly evenly divided between begging letters and obscene abuse, the misery of exposure to a multitude of prying eyes changed to sickening disgust. She was awash in a slopping pool of libidinous filth. It was Mr. Jenkinson, reappearing to inspect, as he said, the scene of the crime and to show Jenny his own article about the now forgotten stone, who explained that she must request the post office in town to redirect everything addressed to Grove House to the main offices of Tantham and Maculan. To call in the police, he patiently lectured her, would only increase her troubles, since they would wish to prosecute those letter writers unwary enough to enclose a clue to their identity. He turned over a few of the missives with a languid hand.

"It is at moments like this that one understands how the world is like it is," he mourned. "This is what the people one knows are *really* like." He turned over a drawing unspeakably bad in both senses, so as not to have to see it.

His own contribution to the story was of an erudition that came from another world. Jenny could hardly have understood it, even if peace were granted her to read it carefully. As things were, she was interrupted after a minute or so by the arrival of a long bus full of sightseers led by an enterprising tourist agent with a megaphone.

"Has this happened before?" asked Jenkinson.

"This is the first busload," answered Jenny. "But cars drive up all the time and people stand for hours, staring."

"But you must get the police to bar the road," wailed Jenkinson, roused from his weariness by such helplessness.

"I'm afraid to. They might come through the grove and then they would do a lot of damage."

"Fencing?" he cried faintly.

"I can't afford it," she answered simply. "In any case, there has never been any wall, any barrier here, not since the place was built. It's always been open."

425

"It would spoil the peaceful ambience, it's true," he said. "Alas! The modern world." But he trailed his long person outside and wrote down the name and address of the owner of the vehicle, with some ostentatious walking to and fro, which did intimidate some of the curious group that showed signs of approaching the house itself. They retired to the shelter of their bus and after some discussion and bluster, the driver turned, rolling one thick wheel over the grass verge and crushing a rose bush in the inadequate space.

"You will have to go to the police," he insisted on his return to the side room. "At least they can erect notices above Gullion—you know, 'No Thoroughfare' and 'Private Road.'"

"I talked to the people at the farm," offered a reporter. "Thought they might set up a sort of watch, with their men. But they are hard at work all the hours God sends. It's a pretty hopeless position, up here."

He was sitting with Jenny, having a cup of tea and cheering her up, as he put it, with his account of how much the tenor of the newspaper reports had changed for the better in the last day or so. He was a stocky, middle-aged man who had seen much of the world, and he went now to the window, where Jenkinson followed him.

"The 'No-More-War' people are in the act, I suppose you've heard," he said softly. "They are extremists, as you know. I shouldn't be surprised if there weren't trouble."

Jenkinson sagged at the shoulders. "Shameful business. The place will be laid waste. And what has she ever done to anybody?"

"Married this shyster Cheyney," the answer was laconic.

"Are you staying on? Over the weekend, I mean?"

"No, I've been called back. Tomorrow morning. But the 'No-More-War' boys won't start a big do at the weekend when there's nobody to cover them. That's laid on for Monday, with the telly teams alerted, as usual."

"Officially, no. But their hangers-on? Some of them are a pretty undisciplined bunch and if they come on in advance of the organisers they may get out of hand."

"Yes, I know that. But what to do? I'm only here to file the stock exchange angle. We have a lot of foreign customers who are watching what happens to Tantham and Maculan—and I mean, watching closely."

426

"Yes. I wondered at seeing you here. It would normally be covered by a local man?"

"Probably. At any rate, not by me. But it's an international story."

"But can't you suggest that you should be replaced, just in case?"

"I did. They are not interested, not till Monday."

Jenny's arrival with fresh tea prevented further discussion.

"I'm sorry I was so long. But the cleaner has gone for today."

"You should have said," protested Jenkinson, trying incompetently to take the tray from her.

CHAPTER XXX

THE UNEXPECTED silence of Saturday morning was not the pleasure it might have been. What in retrospect was a week-long conversation seemed preferable now to the silence. For solitude and quiet were newly loaded with a lowering hostility, peopled by an unseen crowd, not of familiar neighbors but of sick and ugly strangers whose minds spewed out the filth of those hundreds of letters. And these intruders were not entirely the creation of Jenny's imagination: there were people about quite different from the busy press reporters and their ubiquitous photographers. Three young men in black leather jackets reconnoitered the Blanes' fence outside the grove on the orchard side until Harry Blane warned them off. And another man, in unseasonable sheepskin, watched Jenny for several minutes through the drawing-room windows, thinking himself invisible as he stood quite still beside one of the great beeches. She went into the unused room to open the windows, for it felt airless in there, but she changed her mind when she saw the watcher, although some new intransigence of pride in Jenny stopped her from closing the shutters.

Yet, feeling herself watched, she was forced to watch them, and after a time saw two of the men in black coats—or were they two others?—quickly cross the driveway and lose themselves in the trees. One was carrying an apparatus connected in Jenny's mind with the police at the yearly horse trials at Mainter; a portable two-way radio. And she was right; the man spoke into the "walkie-talkie" device and could be seen listening to the reply. But they were not police, she was sure of that. They looked something like the youngsters waiting for the town cinema to open its doors, and something like the engineering students she had met from time to time when they made training trips from the university to the Maculan testing shop in the town. They gave off, too, an air of undertaking something, a look of self-conscious seriousness and planning, almost like amateur actors at remembered school festivals. She waited for them to approach her as all the journalists did, to ring the doorbell, to wave an arm and ask her to come out to them. They did not do that, they kept as far as they could out of sight, and after watching for a while Jenny ceased trying to believe that they were newspaper or radio people. They neither looked like press representatives, lacking the casual, concentrated professionalism of the now familiar clan, nor did they behave like them; there was nothing of the comradely, gregarious newspaper manner about them if only because they looked undefinably self-important. Only because the last week had led Jenny to expect strangers to be reporters could she ever have thought they were. They were not simple sightseers, either; there was a breath of conspiracy about the way they tried to keep away from the house but still kept looking towards it.

Going into the kitchen where the modern cupboards and machines built into the old spaces did nothing to banish a hollow ring of shoes on stone flags now that the back of the house was almost always deserted, Jenny thought she heard a voice calling outside. She looked but there was no one there, or no one visible from the window. Her hand on the back door to open it, Jenny found herself holding her breath. I am imagining things she told herself, and the rebuke, instinct with threat from a time that now seemed quite remote, made her grip the doorknob convulsively. It rattled loosely in its fitting. Not much of a lock, she must get it replaced. She admitted now that she was frightened. She must be logical, control herself. To do that she must have the feeling of safety. Not now but later, before dusk, she would close the shutters. The thing to do at the moment was to make sure the outbuildings were locked so that nobody could go inside the stable or the toolshed and stay there without being seen.

The outside doors were in fact locked, to the disused dairy, the chicken house, Foster's toolshed, where once that packet of books lay hidden behind flower pots on a rickety shelf. Jenny even forced herself, driving unwilling feet to make sure of the latch on a tumble-down little shack beyond the orchard, where nothing was kept but a bundle of garden stakes. There being no lock she clamped a rusted padlock on it with the rueful conviction that it would never come unlocked again without force.

There was no longer anyone to be seen either going through the kitchen garden and orchard or crossing back to the cobbled court to inspect the stables and the studio. The door used by Mark stood ajar. In the old stable she was instantly aware that she was not alone. Foster's small van stood there as usual, her bicycle, the lawnmower, ladders, the spray and the coiled black rubberhose used in dry seasons for watering the grass. Nothing stirred as she stood there waiting for the sound to repeat itself. Then muffled but quite loudly someone spoke above her head and footsteps crossed the studio floor. She was no longer in the least afraid and went quickly but softly up the open steps of the stairway and pushed the rough door gently so that it swung back.

There were two boys in there, no older than Norma's brothers, but these were not country-bred youngsters who turned as the door creaked, for they showed neither fear nor even embarrassment at their discovered trespass. They simply stared at Jenny.

"What are you doing in my studio?"

"Just looking around. Are you . . . ?"

"You must leave at once."

"There you are, Simon. The authentic voice of the bourgeoise. Private property."

"This will all belong to the people soon," the second youth told her seriously.

"It takes the police eight minutes to get up here from the town. You have plenty of time to disappear."

"You don't understand," explained Simon. "We don't mind being arrested. All publicity is good."

"I don't mind your being arrested either," agreed Jenny, calling the bluff. "And don't imagine that I shall refuse to charge you." She found herself enjoying the unusual sensation of being in command of the situation.

"I think she means it," said Simon.

"With breaking and entering."

430

"Common trespass is the most you could hope for."

"That door was locked," said Jenny. She produced its iron key from the pocket of her jacket.

"Prove it."

"And how do you know we came in that way? There's a second door."

"Which is permanently locked. It's dangerous. I can tell you exactly the last time it was used." That was on the Saturday afternoon a lifetime ago, when Mark and Jenny left the studio by that door so that the Fosters would not see them go to her bedroom.

"Well, you can't telephone the cops as long as you stand here yakking."

"What makes you think I have not already called them?"

"You didn't know we were in here."

"There are at least six men hanging about here. I saw them, including you two, I suppose."

"Just taking a country walk. Even property owners can't stop that."

"Just as you wish. But you'll miss your demonstration if you get picked up now, before it starts."

"She has a point there, Simon."

Jenny stood aside from the door to allow them to pass through.

"I am sure you know exactly where the boundaries of my property run. Keep outside them. And tell your friends. And you'd better watch out for the men at the farm, too. They are much more bad tempered than I am. There is a bull there, too."

"A bull?" For the first time there was a sign of nervousness. "It ought to be forbidden!"

This made Jenny laugh and her amusement produced a slowly sullen resentment.

"All of us about here know where he is, you see."

"Is it out? Loose?" asked the younger boy, whose name was not Simon.

"Oh, yes," Jenny lied coolly.

"We'd better warn the chaps." Simon was out of the door now, glad of a face-saving excuse. As the second youth crossed the stable he aimed a kick at the lawnmower, which shifted a

431

few inches with a loud clang as the grass-catcher fell off to the stone floor.

"Don't forget the laws of property!" called Jenny as she ran down the steps after them.

"Effing bourgeois cow," observed Simon over his shoulder.

"Bourgeois yourself," replied Jenny, and turned her back on them to lock the stable door. She pocketed both keys and watched them covertly as they lounged across the grass, past the blasted chestnut, and walked into the grove. Then she went inside "Mark's" door. Although the encounter had stimulated her into imitating the urchin manners of the two louts, she found now that she was shaking and felt fear again. As soon as the door was locked, like every other door to the house now, it produced the unpleasant sensation of imprisonment. This was not entirely subjective; Jenny could not leave the house without running the gauntlet of an animosity that might actually come in if its carriers once knew there was nobody there. Unfortunately, in their old-fashioned concern to save Jenny anxiety, the two journalists had spoken yesterday in undertones to each other instead of warning her.

She went now to the side room, where she could watch the drive, in the hope that one or the other of her new acquaintances would appear. She even thought of telephoning Mainter and asking Togs and the Admiral to come over, but a fear of making a ridiculous fuss or, worse still, of involving other people in some uncertainly visualised "scene," prevented her doing that. Her still incomplete education was not yet at the stage of knowing that both the old and the young man would have been delighted to assist at such unusual excitements.

There were no reporters' cars in the drive, but there was a new group of strangers. There were five or six of them, but they moved about constantly, discussing something, so that it was not easy to count them. From the deep window embrasure, one knee on the green cushion of the seat, Jenny watched them, herself out of sight. These were not schoolboys like the youngsters in the studio. These were grown men, one of them carrying the two-way radio slung over his shoulder. They were not now trying to hide their presence; it was as if they took their right to be there for granted. In the hall the telephone began its loud, burring ring, but Jenny made no move to answer the summons. Only when it stopped did the silence strike her with the idea of calling the police, but like the threat to the two boys it was an abstract notion and she did not mean to translate it into action. The boys, with others like them, were visible standing irresolutely together just inside the shelter of the beeches. They too watched the group in the drive, waiting for something.

Jenny did not have the least connexion to what was going on out there. Like almost everything that had happened since Vincent's death, it was occurring without her participation and was being done to her or about her as if she, as a person, hardly existed as one whose wishes might be consulted or who might be included in events.

With one tremendous exception everything happened of itself, the results of past actions by others carried themselves forward into the present in fresh actions as to which Jenny had no choice except to remain there, watching. From the moment of Maculan's death Jenny's world was usurped by a whole cast of actors, and she imagined them now as circling about with their heads together like the group of men in the drive at this moment, some faceless and nameless and some remembered but changed so that their features were now unrecognisable from their former looks, by all the actions they had taken without reference to her. All those things done unknown to her had transformed or, rather, revealed, the actors who carried them out into people Jenny had, in the reallest sense, never known. They had formed a closed group in her vicinity but not including her, just like the circle out there, with their discussion of some project, plan, undertaking she was not told about. Some came from the distant past and far places, some were only recently present and she could still hear them making decisions, taking part sometimes with care, like Teddy Sandford and Mr. Folliot, or like Polter, and sometimes with disastrous momentary unwisdom. But they all, including the crash that existed in Jenny's mind as a noise like thunder that killed Vincent, resembled each other in one particular: they took her inactivity for granted.

There was only one moment at which she acted, and that action was seeded in her whole being. That was the future.

That she had willed and done, herself. But even now the lifelong habit of passivity held her; she came to look out of the window for someone known who would tell her what to do. Was that what she was doing on that now so remote early evening when she stood here at this very spot trying to take in the announcement of Vincent's death? Did she look then, thinking of her father and of the great presense of the trees, for a figure of male authority? Having read of such impulses she took them, as most people do, not only for true but for inevitable, a fact of nature.

Now, faced by an even less welcome intrusion than those of the past days, one so much less welcome that it took on the menace of an invasion, did the crucial thought enter Jenny's mind. She could take a hand herself. Whatever folly she committed could hardly be more catastrophic than the results of passivity were showing themselves to be.

At the moment she acted the fear disappeared. With it went the laming obscurity as to what was going forward outside. The purpose of the intruders did not matter, and what they might want had nothing to do with Jenny.

She went at once without considering what to say or do, and as she approached the men standing together in the driveway she could see that her decision was sound. Each lifted and turned his head at the same moment in a movement so expressive of astonishment that she could have laughed aloud.

"Good morning," she said as she came up to the group. "Did you wish to see me?"

A confused murmur of indecision arose, then there was silence until, after a noticeable pause the man with the radio transmitter acknowledged her presence by inclining his head. Seen close to he was a schoolmasterly looking man of about fifty with spectacles in thick horn rims; he was at the moment filling an old briar pipe with a good deal of deliberation. It may have been this performance that brought back visiting masters at school or it may have been his shaggy tweed jacket and dark-green flannel shirt with its hand-knitted woollen tie. Or perhaps it was the way he finished what he was doing before answering Jenny.

"Good morning," he said at last, lifting his pipe and clamping it between his teeth. "A nice day."

This remark was evidently considered masterly by his companions, for they smiled appreciatively, glancing at each other.

Instead of obeying her first impulse to answer politely, Jenny raised interrogative eyebrows and remained where she was, simply looking at him.

"Perhaps you can enlighten us," said the man at last with a facetious air. "It seems not to be clear where exactly the boundaries of Grove House lie." He shook a box of matches, selected one and struck it, watching its little spurt of flame, which promptly flickered in the slight breeze and went out. Dropping the dead match on the granite chips upon which they all stood, the man took another match, this time successfully applying it to his pipe. The light bent inward as he drew noisily on the mouthpiece, puckering up his mouth and then releasing both the tension of his lips and a small cloud of strong-smelling smoke. Jenny looked at the fallen match and then bent down, picked it up and stood holding it.

"Why?" she asked.

In his surprise he took the pipe from his teeth for a moment to fix her with his gaze. "Why?" he queried, and put the pipe back to pull on it again.

Once again instinct warned Jenny not to reply and once again he waited and then spoke.

"It is a matter of the law," he informed her kindly. Yes, he certainly was a schoolmaster. His companions all approved this by an audible murmur, some of them shuffling their feet, some smiling again, but Jenny remained silent.

"We are concerned here with a nice point pertaining to the regulations governing the right to demonstrate in support of a cause or conviction in public places."

"Ah, then I can help you," said Jenny mildly, as if she did not know she was interrupting. "The nearest public place is the village. Gullion, you know. And the road up to there. From Mrs. Godolphin's house the road is a private way. The land on either side, and indeed the whole of Grove Hill, is private property."

"Indeed?" The pipe now needed another match and the whole process was gone through again while they all waited.

"You can, I take it, substantiate that statement?"

435

"I don't need to," said Jenny. "It is you who need to do that."

"I beg your pardon?"

"Oh, do stop being silly. Even if you didn't know the road was private and leads nowhere but here, it must be perfectly obvious to the dopiest village idiot that where you are standing is the path to my house."

"You are telling me frankly that I—we—are silly?" He was weightily amused.

"I could hardly be franker," she said. The man, holding his pipe as a marker by its bowl and pointing the stem first at one and then another of his silent companions, looked round about him at the trees and the sky. His patient acceptance of obloquy evidently went beyond words.

"I should like to have your name and address," continued Jenny. "You haven't a card on you, I suppose?"

"In point of actual fact, I have a card. But I should require to know first for what purpose you require it."

"So that I know whom to charge with any damage that your people do here," said Jenny. "I shall not prosecute you if you all leave at once, but naturally anything broken will have to be repaired. And two of your followers have already forced the lock of my studio. There may be other breakages I haven't seen yet." She pointed with a dramatic gesture to the rosebush crushed the day before by the tourist bus. "Look at that!"

They all looked. There was the sound of an engine and the crushing of stones.

"That will be the police," said Jenny, her sense of absurdity getting the better of her prudence so that she risked a damaging anticlimax to the impression now created. Carefully, she did not look at the approaching motor, but out of the corner of her eye saw to her delight that it was the black and shining Austin that might well be a police car.

"My name is Hinbest," pronounced the pipe smoker, "and you do not need a card for my address. I am well known to the police forces of this country as the Secretary of the No-More-War Guild. They know how to reach me. This is not the first occasion on which I have been threatened by the power of reaction."

"Ah, Hinbest, hullo there!" A voice so known, so intimately familiar that Jenny's head swam with the instant transfer to reality from farce, although it spoke in a tone never used to herself. "Reduced to pestering strange women, you naughty man? They'll get you for rape, yet, if you don't take care!"

"Mr. Hinbest was just going," Jenny answered as calmly as she would any ordinary mortal, half over her shoulder, laughing lightheaded with surprise. "How are you, Mark?"

"I'd be a sight better if this travelling circus would clear off back to the smoke," he said, now beside her. "Why don't you wait for the cameras on Monday, dear boy? I'm sure they'll all be here, ready to get you on every screen in the country."

"We have changed our policy to one of noncooperation with the media, as you must very well know. A surprise to see you here. Have you been transferred to crowd control? Bit of a comedown, I should say."

"Not a bit of it. Very fine body of men, splendid fellows, but I have not been transferred. I just remember you with pleasure from that gratifying little conversation we had the last time General de Gaulle was visiting here."

"You have a long memory, Mr.—Vail, isn't it?"

"You know perfectly well who I am," said Mark, still in the falsely breezy tone, "just as well as you know you're on private ground here. You'll find your troops with the busses down the road. The police stopped them from coming any farther, the old spoilsports. Bad-tempered lot, these country police."

"I take it I am to be deprived of my freedom of movement?" said Mr. Hinbest, with resigned dignity, taking one step after another in the direction of the group that preceded him towards the gateless entrance guarded solely by the aged stone posts.

"Certainly not," chided Mark, shocked at this. "The sergeant is not even coming up to warn you. He said Mrs. Cheyney could take care of you."

Even at a distance, now of several paces, Jenny could see that Mr. Hinbest's expression changed markedly at this insult, as it had not done at the suggestion of his being a rapist. But she did not watch him further, for Mark was moving slowly away, taking no more notice of the disappearing men as he stepped over the bordering flower bed and strolled towards another point of the grove, crossing by the blackened chestnut tree. As he moved he made a tiny gesture with his chin, and Jenny jumped the bare earth and followed him.

"I shouldn't have said that," he said to her in the very quiet voice which did not carry. "That annoyed him. We'd better go right round the grove to make sure all his yobs are gone—for the time being."

"You think they will come back?" she murmured, maintaining a public manner as Mark did.

"Almost certainly. That is why I came myself. Couldn't get you on the telephone. The police have been trying from the town, too. See, through there, a couple more." He changed direction and as they walked, very slowly, hands in pockets and heads bent as if discussing crops or some other country interest, the waiting figures dispersed before them. "I got back to the works last night, just in time to hear that the demo there meant to come over here in force this morning."

"In force?" she said, dismayed.

"I'm afraid so. They've been camped outside Tantham and Maculan for days and they're angry and frustrated. The temptation to change the direction of attack was too much for them when they heard Hinbest was going to be here. He's the leader of the other faction, you see."

"Oh. They split up amongst themselves?" she asked dimly.

"Recently. The larger group maintains contact with the press and broadcasting, and Hinbest disagrees. He seems to feel they shouldn't sully the purity of their convictions by allying themselves with the lackeys of the bourgeoisie." He glanced sideways at her, a quick flash of intimacy. "Don't laugh. It's no joke. You have to realise that this mob believes that it believes. In *fact* they are just looking for a focus for their anger—or perhaps, restlessness of some other kind. They believe, however."

"There is no way of keeping them out, if they do come up here."

"No. We shall have to barricade ourselves in the house, I fear." Again he shot her that intimate, anticipating glance. "I hope you have some food supplies."

"For the weekend, anyway."

They were round the orchard now and although there seemed to be nobody left about, they continued their tour.

"You dealt splendidly with that lunatic Hinbest," he said presently. "I meant it when I said that. But it wasn't wise of me. The others are quite another matter, though. The police will read them the usual lecture in Gullion, but I rather think they won't be stopped."

"Is it true they don't mind being arrested?"

"Old Hinbest said that, did he? It's true sometimes. Depends how much they expect to get out of it in the way of convincing people that the police and the law are some kind of fascist plot. But in this case, I rather fancy they intend to risk it. The other lot, that is."

"Then I really did put a spoke in Mr. Hinbest's wheel?"

"You certainly did. But he won't even speak to the leaders of the crowd on its way here. Just like Hinbest's type, to let you tell him just what would interfere with his plans. Or perhaps he was feeling uncertain in any case, and really welcomed the obstacle. Difficult to say."

"They all seem to have gone."

"Yes. I think we could go in now."

Looking round the paneling of the hall, Mark said, "It's odd, isn't it? I've been dreaming about this place."

The armour of his public manner changed towards the more familiar aspect of Mark indolently lounging, but the accompanying attitude of the world's being there for his entertainment was by no means part of this relaxation. His alertness took simply another form, that of one waiting for some event he is unable to prevent.

"Yes," he murmured with satisfaction, nodding his reaffirmation of his so harmonious surroundings. "Even better than one recalls it. Just the same, I have a bone to pick with *you*."

"With me?" Vividly astonished, she stared. "You mean because you came without me asking you to—as you said, remember, when you left?"

"Oh, that! No. You didn't let me know about the child."

"You know!"

"Know? One of millions who do. You really shouldn't be let out alone. Imagine giving an interview to the Woman's Page Editor of the Sunday *World*, and *then* asking if the entire population doesn't know every detail of your private life. Including a posthumous baby for the tragic little widow."

She quite gaped now, in dismay, a hand to her face. "No!"

"But yes. Don't you even read what they write about you?"

439

"I forgot her. There have been so many. Yes, now I—she was awfully amusing!"

He groaned aloud.

"It's unfair to blame you. Even a much more wily bird than you would have been caught in this maelstrom of publicity. But I must say, it gave me a jolt."

"But I'm sure I never mentioned—how could she know?"

"My darling girl, what do you think they pay her the highest salary in Fleet Street for? She saw, of course!"

"But there's nothing yet to see!"

"To her razor eye there obviously was."

"But would she dare to print that, without checking?"

"Of course she checked. With Mrs. Godolphin, with Norma. Though I'm surprised not to hear that she followed you into the bathroom and took a sample! She's perfectly capable of it."

He was staring up at the tall window and at the sight, his private anger retreated from his mind.

"These windows. We'd better get the shutters closed."

"That window has no shutters, it's too high."

"But the others? We're in enough trouble without getting half the windows broken."

"Broken?" she cried out. "You think . . . ?"

"Afraid so. Let's not take the chance, anyway."

"I was going to close them this evening," she admitted.

He was opening the drawing-room door.

"Thank goodness, the shutters are all outside," he said. "You did think of it, then?"

"It wasn't that, I didn't think about violence. It was just the feeling of people being about, unknown, strangers. I locked up all the outside doors. There were some boys in the studio. And I was all alone here."

"Oh, God." He gazed in front of him, focusing on some inward perception of the outrage in which they were trapped. Jenny was throwing up the sash of the nearest window and now stepped over the low sill to unhook the heavy wooden shutters fastened back against the outer stone wall.

"These windows aren't really supposed to have shutters," she said, half to herself. "They were only mounted on them because the frames aren't weatherproof."

"Bit of luck, that, at any rate." He came to help and put up a

440

hand to try the lock. "There must be a key thing for these?"

"Now where did Foster keep it? He always did the shutters."

"It must be the big handle screw that hangs on the wall by the kitchen door from the hall. I'll get it."

"I haven't closed them since the Fosters went," she said as he returned. "Even when it does rain hard, it usually comes from the west so we need them only if the wind is in the east."

"I gather it's all my fault the Fosters left. So you got your way, after all."

"I no longer wanted them to go by that time."

"I suppose not." He busied himself with the locking implement, frowning in unnecessary concentration "I'm sorry about the Fosters. And a lot of other things."

"It wasn't your fault."

"But it seems to be. And other things *were* my fault "

"No more than mine."

"I'm older than you. More experienced. I should have thought of it."

"Perhaps you meant it to happen? Without knowing you did? I'm quite sure I did."

"Deliberately?"

"Oh, no. Just—you know how one does things."

He shook his head dubiously at this aspect of knowing.

"You are very experienced, aren't you? I noticed that when you were talking to Mr. Hinbest. That was a quite different you. I didn't like it at all."

"It's a matter of convention," he explained. "One way of getting things said while saying something else. It saves face."

"Like Barleyman. Only he wasn't out to save anyone's face."

"I say!" He laughed uneasily. "I hope you don't mean I'm like Barleyman."

"There you are, you see. You're doing it again."

He turned to face her, hefting the big locking handle in one hand as if weighing it.

"You talk about doing things, knowing and yet not knowing, what you're doing. I, you see, am more openly conscious of what I'm doing here. I want to go to bed with you. Here and now. Go to bed and stay there and not face that lot out there, nor face the other things that led up to this. But I have to face them."

"What? Face what?"

"I've asked for a disciplinary enquiry into my conduct of this case. Until then, I am suspended from duty at my own request. In a week or so it's quite possible that I shan't have a job. Not likely, but possible."

"But what has that to do with—anything?"

"What has it to do. . . ! Don't you understand what I'm saying?"

"Yes. You're saying you won't marry me. But . . ."

"Not won't. Can't. Or not now. I asked for the enquiry weeks ago, after Barleyman's amateur theatricals. My offer has now been accepted. That makes me look like a fortune hunter if I now . . . d'you see?"

"Fortune hunter!" Jenny laughed with both shock and relief. "I don't think there's any fortune left to hunt."

A low, ragged murmur from outside swelled enough for them to hear it, and they both raised their heads, holding their breath to listen intently.

"Did you hear something?"

"You heard it too? On the other side of the house. Quick with the last shutter! We must get the others done, on the front, especially upstairs."

"They are all casements, we can close them from inside."

It was almost dark in the long room now, its posed artifice barely visible. Only through cracks and joins in the old wood came slivers and slants of fragmented light. As they emerged together into the hall the confused mutter of noise became louder, the sound of a gathering number of voices.

At the foot of the stairs they looked up at the big window that had so impressed Professor Polter.

"Upstairs first," said Mark urgently. "If they get rough they'll throw things upwards. They always do."

He was at the square of the turn, four steps up, when a splintering crash stopped him. Aghast, they took in jagged glass, a scarred crossbar, strips of leading bending inward, a loud thump and a hollow rumble. A biggish stone crashed through an upper pane and rolled almost to Jenny's feet. They both froze rigidly, staring at it in unbelief.

Then Jenny, feeling that fierce clutch in the middle of her body, gave a little strangled cry and spread out her hands, groping for the oak chair with its intricate carving. It was fortunately close behind her and when her fingers found it she backed, swaying, and lowered herself into it, bending her head towards her knees.

"Did it hit you?" Mark shouted, and leaped down the steps between Jenny and the tall window. "Are you hurt, Jenny?"

"It's all right," she whispered confusedly, searching upwards for his hand. "I just felt faint. It's your son, he doesn't care for so much excitement."

The banality of this restored them and for a second it seemed possible to stay there, eyes closed, held together in an urgent grip. The uproar outside subsided somewhat as the crowd took in the decisive act that committed it to further violence.

"Oh, God, why didn't you tell me?" he demanded, his voice rough with rage and humiliation. "It's mine, after all!"

"Forgive me," she whispered, only half taking in what was happening.

"I don't mean that!" he disclaimed furiously against the shouting, which again grew louder. "I meant, I could have got you away from here if I'd known."

An amplified voice yelled orders, in the distance whistles shrilled.

"I can't even protect you from this canaille outside!"

"Let's go up and close the shutters," she begged. "I'm all right now."

"Yes, you'd better stay with me. But don't go anywhere near a window, for God's sake."

"We couldn't marry just yet, in any case," she stammered, pausing halfway up the stairs to explain, but he forced her on, away from the venerable spread of menacing glass. "For the child's sake. It would only create another scandal, don't you see that?"

He gave constant hurried looks at the window, ranging now above them to their right, and shoved Jenny with a gasp of relief into the door of her bedroom.

"Sit down," he ordered, "here, away from the windows."

He left her to open the casement and reach outside for the fastened shutters. Instantly, as the barrier was opened, the confusion of cross shouts came into the room and the words of conflicting slogans could be picked up from the roar, in which

443

names could also be distinguished. One voice howled "Cheyney" and something about "peace."

"But the child's name!" Mark shouted across the room and slammed the iron bar into its socket, damping down the racket again. "My son can't be born Cheyney!"

"He won't be. I shall go back to my father's name."

"Maculan! Of course. Why didn't I think of that!"

"It would hardly have come well from you," she said shakily, trying to laugh.

The uproar was now such that they could hardly hear themselves speak, but the simplicity of Jenny's idea echoed inside the outer chaos as if they were enclosed together in a ringed space of sureness and calm. A vibrant charge of excitement filled them, in which danger, anger, triumph and joy fused into a huge elation.

The sounds from the garden changed, they were now dominated by a battering of mechanical shouting and the repeated shrill sounds of police whistles.

"They've brought up reinforcements," Mark guessed, moving hastily to the next window. "It's the police at last, in force."

A distorted voice through a megaphone instructed Mrs. Cheyney not to approach the windows, not to be afraid, in giant, hollow shouts of her name, over and over again. The name battered from the midst of an unintelligible uproar, echoing off the stone walls and back again from the surrounding ring of sentinel trees. The unfenced, unprotected peace of four hundred years challenged the mob that violated it and, as the police amplifier ceased bellowing, they could hear the crowd chanting its ritual song.